P9-CCK-529

Nevada Barr studied acting at the University of California, and spent several years working in the art and theatre worlds. At thirty-six, she had a complete career change and became a park ranger. Since then Nevada has worked on Isle Royale in Lake Superior, at Guadalupe Mountains in Texas, Mesa Verde in Colorado and is now a ranger at Natchez Trace Parkway in Mississippi.

Track of the Cat introduced park ranger sleuth Anna Pigeon and won the Agatha and Anthony Awards for the Best First Mystery Novel of the Year. She tackled her second case in *A Superior Death*, and won tremendous critical acclaim:

'Outstanding evocations of creatures and climate, plus an ability to describe a physical hazard . . . that makes you catch your breath. Distinctly different from standard crime fare. Informed, intelligent, altogether excellent' *Literary Review*

'A well-constructed plot' *The Sunday Times*

'One of the pleasures of Nevada Barr's books is their splendid settings . . . [She] skilfully portrays the characters who inhabit them . . . It's all a refreshing change' *Sunday Telegraph*

'Brilliant nature writing with a beautifully crafted mystery as a bonus' Sara Paretsky

Also by Nevada Barr

Track of the Cat
A Superior Death

Mountain of Bones

Nevada Barr

HEADLINE

Copyright © 1995 Nevada Barr

The right of Nevada Barr to be identified as the Author of
the Work has been asserted by her in accordance with the
Copyright, Designs and Patents Act 1988.

First published in Great Britain in 1995
by HEADLINE BOOK PUBLISHING

First published in paperback in 1995
by HEADLINE BOOK PUBLISHING

10 9 8 7 6 5 4 3 2 1

All rights reserved. No part of this publication may be
reproduced, stored in a retrieval system, or transmitted,
in any form or by any means without the prior written
permission of the publisher, nor be otherwise circulated
in any form of binding or cover other than that in which
it is published and without a similar condition being
imposed on the subsequent purchaser.

All characters in this publication are fictitious
and any resemblance to real persons, living or dead,
is purely coincidental.

ISBN 0 7472 4895 8

Printed and bound in Great Britain by
Cox & Wyman Ltd, Reading, Berks

HEADLINE BOOK PUBLISHING
A division of Hodder Headline PLC
338 Euston Road
London NW1 3BH

For Deb and Ed without whom . . .
well, frankly, I shudder to think

Chapter One

No graveyards; that bothered Anna. People died. Unless you ate them, burned them, or mailed them to a friend, the bodies had to go somewhere. In any event, there would at least be bones. A civilization that lived and died for five hundred years should leave a mountain of bones.

No graveyards and then no people. Inhabitants cooking, weaving, farming one day, then, the next, gone. Pots still on cold ashes, doormats rotting in doorways, tools laying beside half-finished jobs.

So: an invading army swooped down and massacred everybody. Then where were the bashed-in skulls? Chipped bone fragments? Teeth sown like corn?

A plague: the American version of the Black Death, an antiquated form of Captain Tripps, killing two out of every three people. The survivors abandoning a desolated community, carting thousands and thousands of dead bodies with them? Not bloody likely. Not in a society without benefit of the wheel.

Once people got factored into an equation all bets were off; still, there ought to be corpses. Anna couldn't think of any civilization that couldn't be counted on to leave corpses and garbage for the next generation.

A hand smacked down on the Formica and Anna started in her chair.

'Where were you?' A stocky woman with salt and pepper hair, looking as if it had been hastily hacked off with pinking shears, poked her.

'Any where but here, Al,' Anna whispered back. She dragged a hand down her face to clear it of dreams and looked surreptitiously at her watch. The staff meeting had been dragging on for two hours. The coffee was gone and there never had been any doughnuts.

Alberta Stinson, head of interpretation for Chapin Mesa, said: 'Stay awake. The Boys are on a rampage.' Al always referred to Mesa Verde's administration rather disdainfully as 'The Boys'. 'I may need you.' Stinson was a stocky woman, fifteen pounds over what the glossy magazines recommended. Leading tours, giving programs, wandering the myriad ruins on the mesas, the weather had creased her face from forehead to chin, and the skin around her eyes was crinkled from squinting against the sun's glare. Near as Anna could tell, the woman had but two passions in life: discovering why the Old Ones had vanished and seeing to it that any despoilers of their relics did likewise.

Anna pulled Stinson's yellow pad towards her. Beneath Al's sketches of nooses, guillotines and other means of mayhem, she scribbled: 'No help here. I'm a lowly GS-7. No teeth.'

Al snorted.

Thirty minutes had elapsed since Anna had mentally checked out and still the debate raged. Money had come down from Congress, scads of the stuff, allocated for the digging up and replacing of the antiquated waterline serving the homes and public buildings of Mesa Verde National Park. Since May heavy machinery and heated arguments had roared over the ancient land. Meetings had been called and called off on a weekly basis.

The resultant acrimony clogged the high desert air like dust from the ditcher. As always in small towns, toxins trickled down. When the powers that be waged war, the peasants took sides. Even the seasonals gathered in tight groups, biting assorted backs and sipping righteous indignation with beer chasers.

New to the mesa, Anna'd not been drafted into either army, but the constant dissension wore at her nerves and aggravated her hermit tendencies.

Around a table of metal and Formica – the kind usually reserved for the serving of bad chicken at awards banquets – sat the leading players: a lean and hungry-looking Administrative Officer with a head for figures and an eye for progress; the Chief Ranger, a wary whip of a man determined to drag the park out of the dark ages of plumbing and into the more impressive visitation statistics additional water would allow; Ted Greeley, the contractor hired to pull off this feat in a timely manner; and Al Stinson: historian, archaeologist, and defender of the dead. Or at least the sanctity of science's claim on the dead.

When the Anasazi had vanished from the mesa, their twelfth-century secrets had vanished with them. Stinson was determined to stop twentieth-century machinery from destroying any clue before it was studied. Since the entire landscape of Chapin Mesa was a treasure trove of artifacts, the digging of so much as a post hole gave the archaeologist nightmares. The contractor had been brought on board to trench seventeen miles of land six feet deep.

Theodore Roosevelt Greeley of Greeley Construction had a job to do and was being paid handsomely to do it. Though Greeley had a veneer of bonhomie, he struck Anna as a hard-core capitalist. She suspected that to his modern manifest destiny mentality, the only good Indian was a profitable Indian.

Fingers ever-tensed on the purse strings, the Chief Ranger and the Administrative Officer leaned toward Greeley's camp.

Anna and Hills Dutton, the District Ranger, were the only non-combatants present. Dutton's impressive form was slouched in a folding chair near the end of the table. He'd removed the ammunition from the magazine of his Sig-Sauer nine millimeter and appeared to be inventorying it bullet by bullet.

'Anna?'

As was his wont, the Chief Ranger was mumbling and it took her a second to recognize her name.

'What?'

'Any input?' The Chief was just shifting the heat from himself. None of this august body gave two hoots about what she thought. She and Hills were only there because the secretary refused to go for coffee.

'Well, if all non-essential personnel were required to

live out of the park the problem would be alleviated considerably.' Non-essential included not only seasonal interpreters, but also archaeologists, department heads, the Administrative Officer, the Chief Ranger and the Superintendent himself. Anna's suggestion was met with annoyed silence. Satisfied she'd offended everyone at the table and it would be a good long time before they again bothered her for her 'input', Anna retreated back into her own world.

When visitors left for the day and evening light replaced noon's scientific glare, she escaped the hubbub.

It soothed her to be where the people weren't. After working backcountry in wilderness parks – Gaudalupe Mountains in Texas and Isle Royale in Lake Superior – Mesa Verde, with its quarter million plus visitors each year, struck her as urban. During the day, when the ruins were open to the public, she couldn't walk far enough to escape the hum of traffic and the sullen growl of buses idling as they disgorged tour groups.

After closing time, on the pretext of a patrol, she would slip down into the new quiet of Cliff Palace, one of the largest of the Anasazi villages ever discovered. Climbing as high as was allowed, she would sit with her back to the still warm stone of the ancient walls, around her rooms and turrets and towers, sunken chambers connected by tunnels, plazas with stone depressions for grinding.

The pueblo hung above a world that fell away for a hundred miles, mesas, buttes and green valleys fading to the blue of the distant mountain ranges that drifted into the blue of the sky. The air was crisp and thin. Without moisture to laden it with perfumes, it carried only the sharp scent baked from piñon and ponderosa.

From her perch high in the ruin she would gaze down Cliff Canyon. Dwellings appeared singly, first one, then two, then half a dozen, like the hidden pictures in a child's puzzle game.

Tiny jewel cities tucked in natural alcoves beneath the mesa stood sentinel over the twisting valleys. Nearly all faced west or southwest, catching the heat of the winters' sun, providing shade through the summers. The towns were built with fine craftsmanship, the work of practiced masons evident in the hand-chipped and fitted stones. Walls were whitewashed and painted, and decorations of stars and hand prints enlivened the sandstone. Doorways were made in the shape of keyholes. Ladders, constructed of juniper and hide, reached rooms built on shelves forty and fifty feet above the slate of the alcove's floor.

These were not tents for folding and slipping away silently into the night. These were edifices, art, architecture. Homes built to last the centuries. If the builders had been driven out, surely the marauders would have taken up residence, enjoyed their spoils?

If the Old Ones had not died and they'd not left of their own volition and they'd not been driven out . . .

Then what? Anna thought.

Food for thought.

Plots for von Daniken.

Anna's radio crackled to life and everyone at the table, including Al, looked at her as if she'd made a rude noise.

'Excuse me,' she murmured.

As she left the room she found herself hoping for something dire: a brawl at the concession dorm, another medical at Cliff Palace, a bus wreck – anything to keep her out of the staff meeting.

'Seven hundred, three-one-two,' she answered the call.

'Could you come by the CRO?' the dispatcher asked. Frieda, the Chief Ranger's secretary and the park dispatcher, was always even-toned and professional. From her voice one could never tell whether a bloody nose or grand-theft auto awaited at the Chief Ranger's Office.

'I'm on my way. And thank you.'

'KFC seven-hundred, fourteen-eighteen.'

The Chief Ranger's Office was built from blocks of native stone and beamed in logs darkened by time. Like the museum and the upper-echelon permanent employees' houses, the CRO was an historic structure built in the nineteen-thirties by the Civilian Conservation Corps when 'another day, another dollar' was the literal truth.

Anna banged through the screen door and leaned on the glass-topped counter. In true bureaucratic fashion, the inside of the graceful little building had been cobbled into cramped 'work areas' and further vandalized by the addition of indoor-outdoor carpeting and cheap metal desks.

Frieda Dierkz looked up from her computer. In her thirties, with short reddish-brown hair cut in an earlength wedge, more hips than shoulders and more brains than just about anybody else in the Visitor Protection and Fire Management Division, Frieda was the heart of the office. Or, more correctly, as the computer-generated sign on the bulletin board above her desk announced, Queen of the Office. Anna guessed there'd been a time, maybe not yet quite passed, when Frieda had hoped to be Queen of a more intimate realm. But a plain face and, more damaging to matrimonial prospects, an air of absolute competence, had made her a career woman.

Though Frieda might have seen that as a bad thing, Anna didn't. It was always the breadwinner, she'd noticed, who had the adventures. Support staff – whether at work or in the kitchen – seemed ever relegated to keeping the tedious home fires burning.

'So . . .' Anna said for openers.

'Patsy called. Tom's in the park.' As ever, Frieda was economical with words.

Patsy Silva was the Superintendent's secretary; Tom the estranged husband. Ex-husband. 'What this time? Bad guitar music at three a.m.?'

'Suicide notes and chocolates. The chocolates were put through her mail slot. The dog opened them. Half melted on May's bank statement. The dog threw up the other half on a four-hundred-dollar Indian rug.' Frieda laughed. In his capacity as two parts joke, one part pathos, Tom Silva had been a thorn in law enforcement's side since Patsy had been hired the previous winter. Had they lived outside the park they would have been the problem of the Colorado police. Inside park boundaries the task fell to the rangers.

Anna hated domestic disputes. The good guys and the bad guys kept switching roles; an outsider didn't stand a chance. 'Where's Stacy?' Anna hoped to drag another ranger along for moral support.

'Occupado. Another medical at Cliff Palace. Elderly lady.'

'Damn. What does Patsy want us to do about it?'

'Just go talk to her, I guess. She wasn't too specific. "Do something but don't say I said." '

Anna nodded. 'On my way.' Halfway out the door she stopped and turned back. 'Frieda, can I come visit Piedmont tonight?'

'Anytime,' the dispatcher returned, already back at her computer. 'If I'm not there, let yourself in. Door's never locked.'

The tower house was the most picturesque, if not the most convenient, of the historical homes. Named for the round tower that housed the master bedroom, the staircase and a small round living-room, it sat on a gentle hill just west of the museum behind the more conventional homes. For one person it would have been perfect. For a woman with two teenage daughters it had proved a nightmare of bathroom scheduling and closet space allotment.

Rumor had it, because of the girls, Patsy would be moved as soon as a two-bedroom became available leaving the tower house up for grabs. Due to the housing shortage when Anna had entered on duty eight weeks before, the District Ranger had parked her in the women's dormitory till more suitable quarters could be found, so it was with a more than slightly proprietary eye that she allowed herself to be ushered in.

Patsy Silva was compact, with the voluptuous curves

of a woman who has borne children. Her hair was close-cropped and honey-blond, her eyes made impossibly blue by tinted contact lenses. Teeth as straight as an orthodontist's slide rule were shown off by hot pink lipstick drawn on slightly fuller than her natural lip line.

Patsy smiled and waved distractedly toward the living room with its mess of clothes and magazines littering every flat surface. 'Missy and Mindy are over at Frieda's watching the VCR,' she said as if the temptation of video explained a hasty and untidy departure. 'She's got quite a movie collection and lets the girls watch almost anytime. It helps.'

Anna nodded. Bucolic park living was fine for adults and children but could weigh heavily on adolescents with a long summer on their hands.

'Sit down. Sit.' Patsy shooed Anna toward the kitchen. 'Coffee or anything?' With the offer, as with most of Patsy's communications, came a tight bright smile. More a habit of placating, Anna suspected, than a genuine show of happiness.

'Coffee'd be fine.'

The kitchen, the only square room in the house, was small but efficiently made, with blond wood cabinets and a· restaurant-style booth under one of the two windows. Anna slid into the booth. Patsy busied herself at the counter. Anna wasn't particularly fond of reheated coffee, but people seemed more comfortable after their hospitality had been accepted. Maybe some ancient instinct about breaking bread together. Or maybe it was just the comfort of having something to keep their hands and eyes occupied.

Patsy put the cups on the table along with a sugar bowl and creamer in the shape of ceramic ducks wearing blue calico bonnets.

'Thanks.' Anna pulled the cup to her and poured pale bluish milk out of the duck's bill. Patsy's smile clicked on then faded slowly, the effort for once proving too great.

'It's Tom,' she said as if admitting a tiresome fact.

'Chocolates.'

'And a note. It's awful. How can you protect yourself from that? The police act like I'm lucky to have such an attentive husband.'

'Ex-husband.'

'Yes. Thank you. He makes me forget. Ex husband. Ex, ex, ex as in exit, finito, gone. Except that he's not.' She put her fingers to her temples, looking as if she would have run them distractedly through her hair had not each wave been expertly coaxed into place.

'What makes him more than a nuisance?' Anna asked. At a guess, she might have added 'other than guilt?' How could a woman not feel guilty for walking out on flowers, candy, and serenades?

'I was afraid you were going to ask that,' Patsy replied with an explosive sigh. She slumped back in the booth. 'I don't know. I mean, he doesn't really do anything. It's just kind of an increasing sense of weird. Know what I mean? As if my not folding like I always did with the flowery courtship business is pushing him near some edge. This last note seemed, well . . . edgy.' Patsy apologized with a particularly bright smile.

Anna would have laid odds that Patsy Silva had apolo-

11

gized a lot in her thirty-seven years; sorries and smiles poured like oil on life's troubled waters. 'Can I see the note?'

'Yes. I kept it. At least I've learned that since the divorce. Anything edgy, I keep. You can't imagine how silly this all sounds, even to me, when I try to tell it to some big burly policeman who thinks his wife would die and go straight to pig heaven if he ever paid her this kind of attention. Here it is.'

While she'd talked, Patsy had rummaged through a doll-sized bureau complete with miniature vanity mirror. Decals of ducks matching the creamer were centered on each tiny drawer. From the bottom drawer, she pinched up a scrap of paper. Holding it by the edge as if she didn't want to smudge incriminating prints, she laid it on the table.

In a childish but legible scrawl, more printing than script, was written: 'What do you want, Pats? I've give you everything. A car, nice close, everything. What do you want? Maybe you want me to do like that guy you told me sent somebody his ear. I'll go him one better. I'm not living without you, Pats. I'm not.'

'And you think it's a suicide note,' Anna said. To her it read more like a threat but she was not privy to the inner workings of Tom Silva's mind. Being the new kid on the block, Anna'd not yet caught up on the gossip.

'I wish it was a suicide note!' Patsy snapped.

Anna liked the anger better than the shiny smiles. At least it rang true.

Patsy, who'd been rereading the note over Anna's shoulder, slid onto the bench beside her. Such proximity made Anna uncomfortable. Before her husband, Zachary, had been killed, when she'd lived in the confines of New York City, Anna'd fought for personal space on elevators and in subway cars. Since joining the Park Service and moving to less constricting climes, the need had increased, rather than the opposite. An acre per person and bull horns for communication struck her as about right for socializing.

She turned as if to give Patsy her full attention and put some space between them.

'I told Frieda it was a suicide note because it seemed easiest – you know, made sense for me to be calling.' Patsy picked up her coffee but just stared into it without drinking. 'It was that ear thing he said – like Van Gogh. Besides the chocolates there was an envelope. One of those little square ones that come with florist's arrangements.'

Anna waited, sipping coffee made gray and tepid by skimmed milk. Patsy didn't go on with her story. 'And the envelope?' Anna prompted.

'I burned it.'

Since silences didn't draw Patsy out the way they did most people – too many years of being a good girl and not speaking till spoken to, Anna guessed – she asked her what was in the envelope.

'A little piece of brown material, soft, like expensive crepe. Tom isn't circumcised. I think it was foreskin.'

Anna winced. It seemed a little 'edgy' to her as well.

For maybe a minute neither spoke. Whether Patsy sensed Anna's discomfort with her proximity or, once her information was told, no longer needed the closeness, she moved to the sink to dump her untouched coffee. When she returned she resumed her place on the bench opposite.

'What do you want me to do?' Anna asked.

Patsy burst into tears.

While Patsy Silva cried, Anna thought.

'I don't suppose Tom has any outstanding wants or warrants against him?' she asked hopefully.

Patsy shook her head. 'I'm sorry.'

Anna didn't know if she was apologizing because she still cried or because her ex-husband wasn't a known felon. 'I'll run him anyway. You never know.' After a moment she said: 'Maybe a court restraining order; keep the guy away from you. I'll look into it; see if you have to prove harassment, what it will take to keep him out of Mesa Verde.'

'It's too late. He's here,' Patsy cried, sounding like the little girl who saw poltergeists. 'He's got a job with the contractor putting in the new pipeline.'

The waterline. It was getting so Anna was tempted to blast the thing herself. Perhaps Mesa Verde's staff had been on the outs for decades – living in isolation where dead people were the main natural resource had to have an impact – but since she'd entered on duty the pipeline had been the lightning rod.

'Are you dating anybody?' Anna asked abruptly.

Patsy looked pained. 'Not exactly,' she said, not meeting Anna's eye.

She was dating somebody. A tidy old fashioned triangle in the making. 'Does Tom know?'

'No! I don't even know for sure.' Patsy smiled a shy smile. Inwardly Anna groaned.

'Talk to him,' Patsy pleaded.

'Sure,' Anna promised.

'Talk to his boss. Mr Ted something. He seems reasonable.'

'Ted Greeley. I can do that.'

'But don't get him fired. With Missy and Mindy both in High school next year we're counting on the child support.'

Anna repressed a sigh. Domestic stuff. 'Gotta go,' she said, glancing at the clock over the sink. 'Quittin' time.'

Patsy laughed for the first time in a while. 'Hills blew his over-time money on an all-terrain vehicle. I'm kind of glad he did – he's so cute at budget meetings when he begs.'

'Take care,' Anna said, setting her Smokey Bear hat squarely on her head and taking a last look around quarters she hoped soon would be hers.

'I'll keep anything else ... personal ... Tom sends and give it to you,' Patsy promised as she held open the door.

'I can't wait.' Summer was off and running.

Chapter Two

No rest for the weary – or was it the wicked? Anna couldn't remember. There was definitely no rest for those fated to share dormitory quarters.

Her briefcase, used for carrying citation notices, maps and brochures, banged against the screen door, jarring her elbow. Simultaneously her ears and nose were assaulted. The first by The Grateful Dead and the second by a kitchen that would daunt even the most hardened health inspector.

Early on in this allegedly temporary housing arrangement Anna realized she had two choices: bite the bullet or play Mom. As she had neither the taste nor the inclination for the latter, she had spent the four and a half weeks since the seasonals entered on duty knee-deep in unwashed dishes and empty beer cans. The mess wasn't as hard to take as the noise. After some sparks had flown she'd been given a room of her own but the walls of the flimsy, pre-fab structure were so thin at times she swore they served better to conduct than deflect sound waves.

Clad in a homemade ankle-length sarong of double-knit, Jamie Burke was draped across one sofa. Jennifer

Short, the other woman with whom she shared the two-bedroom house, was sprawled in a pajama-party attitude. They were intelligent, funny, interesting women. Left ignorant of their domestic habits, Anna would undoubtedly have found them delightful.

As she tried to slip unnoticed to her bedroom the imperious call of: 'Stop there!' arrested her progress.

The order came from Jamie, one of the army of seasonal interpreters hired each summer to lead tours of the cliff dwellings and, for a short time – or so Hills repeatedly promised – Anna's housemate at Far View.

Dutifully, Anna waited, briefcase in hand.

In her late twenties, Jamie had the look of someone who has been athletic all her life. Muscular hips and legs gave her a stocky silhouette that was accentuated by the flat-brimmed hat and cloddy shoes of the NPS uniform she wore on duty.

In contrast to her juggernaut physique, her face was a perfect oval, the skin flawless, setting off pale blue eyes and a sensuous mouth. Jamie's hair, fine and smooth and blue-black, fell to her knees in a single braid thickened by red yarn woven through and bound around, Apache style, at the tail.

Jamie boasted that she inherited the black tresses from a half-blood Cherokee mother but Anna strongly suspected that she dyed it. In a women's dorm there were few secrets. All of Jamie's body hair was not of the same raven hue.

'What's up?' Anna asked, trying to keep the weariness from her voice.

'Stacy had to walk an old lady out of Cliff this morning. Where were you?'

Anna ignored the accusatory tone. 'What was the problem?'

'Some kind of pulmonary thing. Wasn't breathing right. There was that old guy last week.'

'Yup.' Again Anna waited.

'They're pissed. I'm not surprised either.'

Now Anna was lost. The previous week's carry-out had gone well. The man's wife had even sent a glowing thank-you letter. 'The man's family is pissed?'

'No-o.' Jamie drew out the syllable slightly as if Anna was too obtuse for words. 'The Old Ones. The Anasazi. They should close this park to everybody but native peoples. It's not Frontierland, it's a sacred place. We shouldn't be here.'

Jamie Burke leapt from one drama to the next. In the few short weeks Anna had known her she'd been through exposure to AIDs, engaged to a nameless state senator in Florida, and involved in an affair with a married man so discreet it had to be imaginary. The pipeline was a bandwagon made for jumping on.

'Ah. Chindi.' Anna used the Navajo word for spirit or – she was never quite sure – evil spirit. 'Could be. Listen, I've got to slip into something less deadly.' She grimaced at her gun and escaped down the hall.

Once divested of the dead weight of her gun and the air-tight shoes required by NPS class 'A' uniform standards, Anna felt less hostile. By the time she'd poured herself a generous dollop of Mirrason Pinot Blanc, she was civilized enough to join the party in the front room.

The television was on with the volume turned down and Jamie was verbally abusing Vanna White as she turned the letters on 'Wheel of Fortune'. It was a nightly ritual that seldom failed to amuse.

'Arms like toothpicks! Look at that,' Jamie was exclaiming. 'I don't think she's pretty. Do you think she's pretty? Who in God's name thinks she's pretty? Little Miss Toothpick Arms. Little Miss White Bread.'

Anna curled her feet under her on the knubbled fabric of an armchair. The boxy room was furnished in Early Dentist's Office but it was serviceable. Anna, barefoot, in pink sweatpants and an oversized man's shirt, girls – or women that looked like girls from a vantage point of forty – scattered about with Budweisers, Anna had a sense of being an uncomfortable traveller in time. Even the cheap southwestern print of Jamie's sarong put her in mind of the India-print bedspreads she'd found so many uses for in her college days.

A woman out of time, Anna identified with the Anasazi. In a gush of self-pity she felt her world as dead as theirs. She missed Christina and Alison, the woman and her daughter, with whom she'd shared a house in Houghton, Michigan, when she worked on Isle Royale.

Chris was a rock: gentle and soft and stronger than Anna ever hoped to be. Alison, at six, was like a kitten with brains – irresistible and a little scary.

Anna'd left hearth and home on the pretense Mesa Verde was a promotion as well as a return to her beloved southwest. In reality she'd cleared out because she knew Chris was in love but wouldn't move in with her sweetheart if it meant abandoning Anna. So Anna'd abandoned her.

I'm a fucking saint, she thought sourly, watching Vanna turn E's on 'Wheel of Fortune.'

The job wasn't too bad. Though at times Anna felt more like a nurse than a ranger.

Mesa Verde was an old and staid National Park. As early as 1906 it was clear that the ancient cliff dwellings, though already largely looted of artifacts, were a part of America's heritage that must be preserved.

Visitors to Mesa Verde went out of their way to get there and had the money to do so. Consequently, the clientele tended to be older, with gold cards and expensive RVs. Retired folks with bad hearts and tired lungs from San Diego, Florida, and the south coast of Texas up at altitude for the first time in thirty years. If drug dogs were called in Anna suspected they'd sniff out more nitroglycerin tablets than anything else.

There'd been two fatalities – both elderly visitors with cardio-pulmonary problems – and eleven ambulance runs, five of them out of Cliff Palace. And it was only early June.

Swallowing the last of her wine, Anna leaned back and let the alcohol uncoil her mental springs.

Jennifer wandered back to the TV with a fresh beer.

Short was a round-faced woman with good hair, bad skin and too much make-up. Fresh out of Tennessee State's one-semester course, she was the new law enforcement seasonal in her first National Park job. Jennifer was a Memphis belle in what Anna had thought was a bygone tradition: all magnolia blossoms, little-ol'-me's-led-a-sheltered-life, and eek-a-mouse. Proven tactics, guaranteed to turn the boys to putty.

Anna hadn't yet decided whether she was more irritated or intrigued with the femme fatale routine. On the one hand it would be interesting to watch. On the other, given the job, it could get a person killed.

'Jamie, I saw that poor little thing you were talking about,' Jennifer was saying. Or, to be more accurate: 'Ah saw thet pore lil' thang yew were tawkin' abaht.'

'She had the cutest face, but her little body! I just couldn't live like that. High school is going to be pure hell. It'd be a mercy to drown people like that at birth. I don't want to sound mean, I mean for their own sakes. I wouldn't want to live like that. I just wouldn't.'

A natural silence fell and they all stared at Vanna. Jennifer had been talking about Stacy and Rose Meyers' daughter, Bella. A sadness threatened Anna and she was glad when loud knocking interrupted her thoughts. She made no move to uncoil herself. Jennifer sprang up, 'I'll get it' out of her mouth almost before the knocking ceased. The first week on the mesa she had announced one of her prime motives for choosing law enforcement: a way to meet straight men.

A moment later two seasonal firefighters from the helitack crew followed Jennifer back in. Because of the wealth of ruins and artifacts on the mesa all wildfires were put out in their infancy by a crew of wildland firefighters flown in by helicopter. Dozers and other heavy equipment customarily used to cut fireline would be so destructive to the cultural aspects of the park fire was never allowed to spread if it could be helped. When nothing was burning, helitack performed the high and low angle rescues often needed to evacuate sick and injured people from the less accessible ruins.

Jimmy Russell and Paul Summers had the youth and

build of most seasonal firefighters and the living room fairly crackled with sexual energy. Russell's heavily-muscled arms and back were shown off in a tight T-shirt emblazoned with a flying insect wearing a yellow shirt of fire-resistant Nomex. A budding good ol' boy from Kentucky, Jimmy chewed his words like tobacco. Summers was a striking blond with a born-again surfer haircut and finely chiseled features. Somehow managing to look sophisticated in worn Levis and a baggy, wrinkled, oxford shirt, he carried the libations: a six pack of Coors Lite dangled from each hand.

'Hiya, Anna.' Paul smiled at her and she was annoyed to find herself flattered.

Popping a Coors, Russell settled cross-legged on the carpet. Jamie pulled herself around on the couch and began kneading the muscles of his neck and shoulders.

Let the mating rituals begin, Anna thought sourly. Unfolding her legs, she levered herself up: time to go visit Piedmont.

On the way through the kitchen she grabbed up what was left of the Mirrason Blanc.

Frieda Dierkz had a house in what was called the Utility Loop. It was near the Maintenance yard about a mile from the Headquarters/Museum Loop. The houses were small, white, one- and two-bedroom homes with the charm and inconveniences of 1940's construction. These homes were for lower-level permanents, the GS-4s and -5s and -7s. Higher-ups claimed the beautiful historic homes in the Headquarters Loop. The fire dorm, where helitack was housed, was also on the loop, as were a couple of aging trailers rented out to seasonal interpreters each summer.

Frieda lived in 34. Most of the front yards were over-grown with weeds and native grasses. Her marigold border and tended lawn looked out of place in piñon-juniper country.

A sad-eyed black lab was resting on some newly dug-up and soon to be dead marigolds. He thumped his tail half-heartedly as Anna came up the walk.

'Hi, Taco.' She stopped to pat him on the head. The dog yawned widely to show his appreciation. 'Where's Piedmont?' Anna demanded, cradling the animal's jowly face between her hands. 'Don't tell me you've eaten him?'

'Alive and well.' Frieda had come to the door and stood behind the screen. A large yellow tiger cat, so limp it looked dead, was draped across her arm. With her free hand she pushed open the door and let Anna in.

Anna traded the wine bottle for the cat, buried her face in the soft fur of his neck and breathed deeply. 'Ahh. Thanks. I needed that.'

'For me?' Frieda eyed the already opened bottle of wine.

'Park Service social motto: Bring something to share.'

As Frieda went into the kitchen to get glasses, Anna sat down on a couch identical to the one in the Far View Dormitory and spread the cat across her knees.

Seasonals in the Park Service were not allowed the solace of pets. As long as Anna was stuck in the seasonal housing dorm, her cat had to board with a permanent employee fortunate enough to get 'real' housing.

Frieda returned with two K-Mart wine glasses and poured them each a healthy slug.

'If you're in the middle of something, Piedmont and I can go out in the yard,' Anna offered. 'I just needed a medicinal cat this evening.'

'Don't know what I'd do without Taco,' Frieda said by way of agreement. She propped her feet up on the scarred coffee table and took a long drink.

'But Taco is only a *dawg*,' Anna confided to the cat in a stage whisper.

The dispatcher laughed. It was a rare sound and surprisingly pleasant, close to what Anna and her sister, Molly, had called 'The Princess Laugh' when they were children. A sound that put one in mind of tinkling bells. She and Molly had even spent time practicing it but had never graduated from girlish 'tee hee hees.' Bells were for princesses. And, evidently, the Mesa Verde dispatcher.

'When I see you with that cat I can hardly believe you're the same hard-ass who tickets little old ladies for parking their wheelchairs in the Handicapped spaces without a permit,' Frieda said.

Frieda was just making conversation but still Anna was stung. 'I don't,' she insisted but felt compelled to add: 'How am I to know they're handicapped? For all I know it could be Joe Namath parked there.'

'Namath's handicapped,' Frieda returned. 'Bad knees.'

'Gotta have a permit.'

Again the dispatcher laughed her silvery laugh and they drank in silence. Tired of being adored, Piedmont leapt off Anna's lap. Moments later they heard feline

25

lappings from the direction of the bathroom bowl.

'What do you know about Tom Silva?' Anna asked, her mind inevitably returning to NPS chores.

Frieda thought for a moment. 'Patsy was divorced when the Superintendent hired her – last fall, November, I think. She brought the girls up to live with her when school ended in May, so Tom hasn't been around much socially – not where you'd get to know the guy. I've seen him up here. He's good looking. Younger than Patsy, is my guess, but not by much – maybe thirty-five or so. Maybe just looks young. He's got that kind of perfect olive skin that's practically indestructible.'

'Does he come up to visit the girls?'

'More than Patsy would like. She thinks it's just a ruse. I guess his lack of interest in his kids was part of the reason she left him. From hints she's dropped, I gather Tom's thirty-five going on seventeen. She once said she couldn't handle being a single parent to three teenagers. Luckily he's been doing roofing or framing or something for an outfit in Grand Junction. The two-hour commute keeps him down to a dull roar.'

'The contractor putting in the new waterline just hired him,' Anna said.

'Oops.'

'Yeah. Oops.' Piedmont came back and settled down on the couch just out of Anna's reach. She contented herself with holding the tip of his tail. Occasionally he twitched it to show his displeasure.

'Sulking,' Frieda noted and Anna nodded. They sat for a while without speaking. It wasn't a comfortable silence, at least not for Anna. She hadn't known Frieda long enough for that.

'Do you think Silva's dangerous?' Anna asked.

'Maybe. No – I don't think so. He seems like a guy more into gestures.' Cutting off one's foreskin was a hell of a gesture, Anna thought, but she didn't interrupt. In park society a person's private life seldom was, but as far as she knew Silva's penis had not yet made it into the public domain.

'The one time I met him he did strike me as a bit of an opportunist, though.'

'Like a magpie? Won't kill it but doesn't mind eating it if someone else does?'

'Exactly like that. You hit it. He even looks kind of like a magpie, dresses too well, talks too loud, struts.'

Silence fell again. It was a little easier this time but after a minute or so the strain began to get to Anna. 'I better go,' she said, giving Piedmont's tail a last gentle tug. 'I want to call my sister tonight and it's already nine-twenty New York time. Thanks for the visit.'

'Thanks for the wine,' Frieda replied as she followed Anna to the door.

On the four mile drive back to the dorm Anna found herself once again lonely for Christina and her daughter, missing Molly, missing silences that didn't chafe.

Fending off self-pity, she forced herself to concentrate on the delicate scent of juniper blowing in the Rambler's window, the piles of cumulonimbus the setting sun was painting in glorious shades of peach, the glistening peaks of the La Plata mountains, still wearing a veil of winter snow.

From many places the view was unchanged from when the ancients had inhabited the mesa. A time Anna liked to believe was simpler. Along Chapin Mesa Road were villages, skeletons now, but still imbued with an unmistakable human spirit. If she squinted, let her mind play, Anna could almost see women with bundles on their backs watching thunderheads build as she did, wondering if the rains would come in time for the corn.

The considerable benefit of this environmental therapy was blasted away the moment the Rambler pulled into the dorm parking lot. The nucleus of people she had left had spontaneously combusted into a flaming beer party.

Something that, to rock-and-roll trained ears, sounded like 33⅓ Muzak played at 78 was audible through the open windows. Half a dozen cars were parked in the lot and at least that many bodies were standing around in the living room. Theatrically, Anna rested her head against the steering wheel and groaned.

With ill-concealed bad grace, she slammed the car into reverse and drove back down the Chapin Mesa Road.

A mile shy of the Museum Loop she turned onto a spur road, parked and let herself into the Resource Management building. It was small and square, built of the same pink stone blocks as the Chief Ranger's Office. The single room was filled to capacity by two desks, filing cabinets, dead lizards, bones, rocks and what had to be at least fourteen years worth of accumulated paperwork.

For those lucky enough to have keys – the people who really needed them and law enforcement – Resource Management had the after-hours attraction of a private phone.

Anna cleared off a chair and, still standing, punched in the twenty-five numbers of her sister's home phone and her AT&T calling card. She suspected if she could clear her brain of all memorized numbers there would be space enough created for housing all of Shakespeare and some of Johnson.

As Molly's smoke-roughened voice growled a characteristic 'Dr. Pigeon,' Anna dumped herself in the swivel chair.

'I'm too old for this,' she said in lieu of a greeting.

'Damn old,' Molly agreed.

'Too damned old. If it wasn't politically incorrect, I'd get my eyes done.'

'On an NPS salary you could only afford to do one.'

'Some psychiatrist you are. Whatever happened to "you're as young as you feel" and "age is just a state of mind"?'

Molly laughed, a chuckle that sounded evil to the uninitiated. 'That's what young psychiatrists tell their middle-aged clients. I'm pushing fifty. Take it from me: damn, yes, it's a bitch. Gird up the sagging loins and get on with it. Come to New York. I'll buy you a day at Elizabeth Arden's. "Behind the Red Door": not quite an erotic fantasy but one that sells just as well. Youth! Men want to buy back the dreams they once had of themselves. Us old bats like the dreams of our middling years, it's our faces we want to buy back.

'So, one foot in the grave, the other on a banana peel. How's the rest of your life?'

Anna laughed. Her face could fall, her hands gnarl, her hair acquire another streak of gray. The camaraderie of women on the wrong side of *Mademoiselle*'s hit list was a joy she'd never been taught to expect.

'Dorm living is a drag. I'm leaning hard on the district ranger.'

'Hills Dutton.'

'I was trying to avoid the name.'

'Got to be an alias.'

'Nope. Too imaginative. Forced to think up an alias, I expect Hills would ponder a good long time, read all the Standard Operating Procedures, then settle on John Doe.'

'Is he going to get you a house?'

'I don't know. To give the devil his due, he's up against it. They're redoing a waterline laid down a zillion years ago. A whole passel of archaeologists have been brought on board to analyze every foot of the digging. No housing left, everybody's hair in a knot, heavy equipment roaring around.'

The waterline put Anna in mind of the afternoon's drama and she was glad to unfold the story of Patsy's Tom and the piece of foreskin.

After she'd finished there was a silence broken by a sighing sound. Molly was lighting up. Camel straights: Anna had heard them sucked into her sister's lungs for twenty years. Molly was an MD, she knew what the cigarettes were doing. She was a psychiatrist, she knew why she smoked them. And Anna was in law enforcement, she knew drugs had a logic of their own. So she said nothing.

'Sounds like the man's in trouble,' Molly said finally and Anna imagined thick smoke coming out with the words. 'A construction worker?'

'That's what I gathered.'

'Not a likely candidate for voluntary therapy. Any alcohol problems, drugs, things of that sort?'

'Probably,' Anna replied, then thought better of her prejudice and added: 'I don't know, really. I've heard he goes on a drunk now and then.'

'People who cut themselves – hurt themselves – usually have a problem with self-esteem. A healthier attitude is "damned if I'm going to hurt any more over you." He may be harmless. I'm talking physically here; emotionally he could be devastating to anybody who gets tangled up with him. But now and again it goes beyond self injury. In extreme cases I've seen the murder/suicide pattern. Shoot the wife then shoot yourself. That's rare but not so rare it doesn't crop up in the case history books and on the front page of the *Post* fairly regularly.

'I'd tell her to watch him, Anna. Watch him and watch herself. Whoops. Got to go,' Molly finished in the abrupt manner Anna'd grown accustomed to over the years. 'I've got an article due tomorrow for the *Times* on co-dependency. An are-you-or-aren't-you kind of thing. Of course it turns out everybody is. Keep me posted.' She rang off leaving Anna still holding the phone to her ear.

Shoot the wife then shoot yourself. Anna hung up the phone. Before she wrote Mr Silva off as a magpie she'd do a little digging. It hadn't escaped her notice that over a third of the women who came to hospital emergency rooms for treatment had been damaged by husbands or boyfriends.

Full darkness had come and she drove slowly back up to Far View. Cottontail bunnies, scarcely bigger than kittens, tried to find their way into the next world under her tires, but she successfully avoided them.

At the dorm, the parking lot was still full, the noise still blaring and the bodies still in evidence. Anna slumped down in the Rambler's seat, wondering not for the first time if she should have taken the promotion that, along with Chris' defection, had tempted her back to the southwest, whether the seductive sense of smug selflessness and the warm dry climate had been worth the tradeoffs.

Chapter Three

Before she'd properly gotten to sleep, Anna's alarm was buzzing like a hornet. She swatted it into silence and lay for a minute staring at the accoustical tile ceiling above her single bed. The beer party had clanged on well past midnight.

Now that she had to get up the house was finally quiet. Rolling up on one elbow, she looked out into the new day. A breeze blew cold on her naked skin. At eighty-two hundred feet, summer never got a firm foothold. Chapin Mesa, a thousand feet lower than Far View, was often as much as ten degrees warmer.

A family of chipmunks had taken up residence under a scrap of black plastic Maintenance left behind when they finished the rear deck. With much flipping of tails, chattering, and scurrying, they were maintaining their cute Disneyesque image. Anna'd been so inculcated with Chip & Dale that she'd felt betrayed when she'd first seen a chipmunk breakfasting on a luckless brother squashed in the road. Roadkill provided food for a lot of animals. Anna sometimes speculated as to whether or not scavengers looked upon highways as a sort of endless buffet catered by Chrysler.

Squeaks, flusters, and the chipmunks vanished under the plastic. A lone red-tail hawk spun careful circles over the service berry bushes.

A toilet flushed. The dorm was stirring earlier than anticipated. Leaving the chipmunks to their fate, Anna pulled on her robe. This morning she intended not only to get a shower, but a hot one.

Jennifer shuffled past in the hall. Her eyes were puffy and her cheeks dragged down. ''Morning,' Anna said.

'Unhh.'

As Anna lifted the coffee pot down from her kitchen cupboard she heard the thump of a wished-she-were-dead weight falling back into bed.

'Three-one-two in service.' Anna made the call around her second cup of coffee. Once the initial insult of regaining consciousness was over, she enjoyed early shifts. Since neither the cliff dwellings nor the museum opened for visitors until nine, the park was quiet.

In the clear morning air a comforting illusion of isolation crept over Anna. Law enforcement at Mesa Verde required metermaid-cum-nursing skills that taxed her energies in a way the hard physical work in the back-country never had. Peoples' needs were immediate and complex, their wants changing with the hours. Anna suspected mankind descended not from the ape but from the mosquito. In swarms they could bleed one dry.

With morning's peace came the animals: those just coming on diurnal duty, those going off nocturnal shift, and the crepuscular crew with a split shift framing the day. Two does and a fawn still in spots grazed between the white-flowering service berry bushes; from a fallen log an Abert squirrel showed off its perfect bushy tail.

At Far View Lodge, a black bear lumbered down from the direction of the cafeteria where it had undoubtedly been raiding garbage cans. Anna hit her siren and the bear bolted across the two-lane road into the underbrush below the Visitors Center.

This year several 'problem' bears had been knocking over trash cans. The bureaucratic machinery was beginning to grind at its usual snail's pace, but Anna doubted a solution would be found, agreed upon, funded and implemented before these particular bears died of old age. Or were shot in the name of visitor protection.

She gave one more blast on the siren for good measure, then headed down toward Chapin Mesa, opening gates to ruins that Stacy Meyers had closed on night shift seven hours before. Coyote Village was first. Just a mile south of Far View, it was one of the highest pueblos on Mesa Verde, and Anna's favorite. Though it lacked the drama of the cliff dwellings with their aeries and towers, she loved the maze of intimate rooms and the patterns the ruined walls made against the dun of the earth. Perhaps since it was less alien she could better identify with the people who had once dwelt there, and so wonder at what prosaic magic had caused them to vanish.

Archaeologists hated the word 'vanished', with its implication they'd not done their homework. Visitors loved it. In it was carried the mystery they felt walking through the ancient towns, peering in windows dark for seven centuries.

Theories of where the Anasazi had gone proliferated: war, drought, famine, loss of topsoil, overpopulation. No one concept carried the burden of proof. Theories changed with the political weather.

More than once it crossed Anna's mind that the best thing about the Anasazi was that they were gone. Their ruined homes forged chalices into which a jaded modern people could pour their fantasies. Never in dreams were there noisy neighbors in the dwelling next door, the reek of raw sewage, chilblains or rotting teeth. In memory, especially one so magnificently vague as the lives of the Old Ones, the sun always shined and children didn't talk back.

In a tiny room, not more than five feet square, a cottontail nibbled at grasses prying up through the smooth flooring. Not wishing to disturb the new resident, Anna left quietly.

At Cedar Tree Tower ruin she watched the sun clear the treetops and pour its liquid gold into the centuries-old kivas. These circular underground rooms, roofless now, were centers for worship or clan gatherings or places of work: the interpretation changed over the years as fads came and went and the science of archeology grew more exact – or thought it had.

For Anna it was the symmetry and sophisticated simplicity of function that spoke to her of the Old Ones. Air-shafts to ventilate fire pits, complex masonry, fitted stones hand-crafted by a people who had no metal for tools.

In Europe King Arthur was dreaming his round table. Peasants lived in huts, the black plague waited just around the century's turning and war and starvation were a way of life. Here where Colorado, Utah, New Mexico and Arizona would one day meet, a people had farmed, traded, worshipped and worked in peace and prosperity for six hundred years.

Park interpreters stressed the terrible hardships the Anasazi must have faced, the daily battle to wring a livelihood from an ungiving land. To Anna the kivas, the tunnels, the towers, the plaster and paint and pottery, suggested a people with an eye for beauty and at least enough wealth and leisure to pursue it.

The sun higher and the shadow play over, Anna continued to the last gate on her rounds, the one located at the four-way intersection near the museum. It blocked off the loop roads leading to the mesa top ruins, Cliff Palace and Balcony House. As she had every Tuesday for the last six weeks, she made a mental note to tell Stacy not to twist the chain into a figure eight before latching the padlock on his late shift. Placing the butt of the lock up as it did made the key easier to insert, but the chain was pulled so tight it took a wrestling match to get the lock arm pulled free of the links.

As she was securing the gate, Meyers called into service. Due to a paucity of vehicles, he would patrol with her.

Stacy and his family lived in a one-bedroom bungalow several houses down from Frieda's. With his daughter, Bella, it had to be cramped, but he was lucky to get it. A temporary appointment didn't carry much more in the way of perks than a seasonal.

Anna pulled up in the shade of an apple tree that

grew near the wall shoring up an elevated yard. A picnic table sat under the branches. Two plastic milk bottles with the sides cut away lay tipped over near it. Presumably at some point Mrs Meyers had intended to hang them for bird feeders. The bottles had been in the same place since Anna entered on duty. The lawn was ill-kept and, for a home where a child dwelt, surprisingly untrammelled. No one used this yard as a playground.

Anna had only seen Bella Meyers a couple of times when Drew Kinder, the helitack crew's foreman, had taken her out in the firetruck. Bella was sort of a mascot of Drew's. She looked to be six or seven years old. From the waist up she had developed normally. There was no distortion of her facial features or upper body, so when she scrambled out of the Drew's truck and revealed the stunted lower limbs, it had taken Anna off guard. Bella suffered from dwarfism.

Stacy and his wife, Rose, never brought her to any of the endless potlucks Mesa Verde was so fond of. There were two schools of thought in the park about this obvious cloistering. One was that the Meyers were ashamed of Bella's deformity. The other was that the child suffered from delicate health.

Though the latter was the more charitable of the two rumors, it struck a deep chord of sympathy in Anna. Stacy wasn't a permanent employee. He was on what was called a temporary one-to-four year appointment: no medical, no dental, no retirement. A GS-5's eighteen thousand-plus a year wouldn't go far to purchase comforts or speciality needs for a delicate child with a physical disability.

The sound of the screen door banging announced Stacy. A tall slender man, six-foot-two or -three, he had dark hair and eyes, and a neatly trimmed beard. On his narrow hips the gun belt looked out of place and the long sensitive fingers clasping his briefcase more suited to a surgeon or pianist than an officer of the law.

Rose Meyers followed him out.

Mrs Meyers kept to herself. Jamie and Jennifer were convinced she felt government employees beneath her socially. Anna'd never spoken to the woman. She'd called Stacy at home on business once or twice but always got the phone machine with Rose's over-sweet message: 'Hi! I'm so *glad* you called!'

Mrs Meyers didn't look glad this morning. Her heavy face was twisted into a mask of contempt. Short dark hair was molded in sleepy spikes. Rose carried quite a bit of excess weight. The pounds didn't form voluptuous curves or wide generous expanses as on more fortunate women, but sagged in lumps like sodden cotton batting in a ruined quilt.

"Bye, darling,' Stacy said and Anna smiled. No one but Cary Grant could call somebody 'darling' and not sound stilted. Stacy leaned down to kiss his wife but Rose stiffened as if the kiss had a foul taste. Anna looked away to give Stacy the illusion of privacy.

Moments later he threw his briefcase and hat into the rear seat and slid in beside her.

"Morning,' she said. Stacy didn't respond. Anna was unoffended. She clicked on the radio for company.

'Where to this morning?' he asked after a while. Wherever his preoccupation had taken him, he was back with her now, the light in his brown eyes lost its inward shadows. His were compelling eyes, as liquid as a doe's, and framed with long lashes that showed black against clear skin. He put Anna in mind of the young dandies from the turn of the century who'd purposely exposed themselves to tuberculosis to attain the pale burning look lent by a fire within.

'We're going out to Wetherill Mesa,' she told him. 'Patsy's husband Tom's been hired on by the pipeline contractors. He'll be surveying line near mile two. We need to talk with him.'

'Has he been bothering Patsy again?'

'More or less. Sending her candy and notes that sound threatening or suicidal depending on how you look at it. This time he sent her a bit of something that Patsy thinks was foreskin.'

'Holy moly,' Stacy said and: 'God I hate law enforcement.'

Stacy had chosen law enforcement not as an avocation, but as a way in. With crime pouring out of the cities onto the nation's highways, more law enforcers than naturalists were hired in the National Parks, more citations given than nature walks.

'You're a born tree hugger,' Anna remarked amiably. 'I could do without the domestic stuff. One way or another the ranger always comes out with a sore thumb. Matrimony is a dangerous game to referee.'

'Were you ever married?'

'Widowed.' She could say it now without feeling a hollowness in her chest.

'Lucky.'

Anna laughed. 'Troubles at home?'

Realizing what he had said, Stacy apologized. And blushed. Anna had never seen a forty-five-year-old man blush before. It charmed her.

'Not Rose. Rose's good to me. I just wish I could do more for her. She's used to better. You should have seen her in high school. God was she beautiful! She didn't even know I was alive. I was just this pencil-necked geek who played trombone in the marching band. She even modeled for *Glamour Magazine* once.'

Anna knew that. Stacy had dropped it into their first conversation. Evidently he dropped it into most conversations about his wife. One evening after she'd sharpened her tongue on Vanna, Jamie had ranted on about it. '*Glamour*! Give me a break! Maybe for the *Glamour* Don'ts! And a quarter of a century and sixty pounds ago.'

Stacy noticed the smile. 'She did you know.'

'She's a good-looking woman,' Anna agreed politely. 'So what did a pencil-necked geek have to do to get a fashion model's heart and keep it?'

Stacy laughed. 'Are you kidding? In high school Rose wouldn't give me the time of day. No, we met again about three years ago. I was out on the west coast visiting old friends and there she was.'

'Love at first sight?'

'Let's say interest at first sight. I was going through a divorce. Rose saved my life,' Stacy added simply. 'I'll always owe her for that.'

'Your ex the one that made widowerhood seem so desirable?'

'She wasn't a bad woman. There were just too many people she had to meet – without her clothes,' Stacy paraphrased Leonard Cohen.

'Ah.' Anna wasn't going to touch that remark with the proverbial ten-foot pole.

Past the Far View Cafeteria, she turned left onto the Wetherill Mesa road. It wound down the mesa's edge for twelve miles. Along the way there were overlooks, most on the west side. The views changed with the hours of the day and with the weather. Sleeping Utĕ Mountain nearby kept watch over the town of Cortez in the valley. The solitary white mysticism of Lone Cone pierced the horizon to the northwest. The Bears' Ears peeked coyly from behind a distant mountain range. To the south glimpses of Ship Rock in New Mexico tantalized. The craggy volcano neck bore a startling resemblance to a ship in full sail gliding through a sea of haze created by the power plant near Farmington. Farmington, Cortez and Shiprock were home to most of the non-tourist related industries in the four corners area; smelting the silver for the jewelry trade, the machinery for the farmers.

Wetherill was just one of the five mesas, spread out like the fingers of an open hand, that made up the park. Each had its dwellings, cities and towns. Like Rome, Pompei, Atlantis, all that remained were ruins and speculation.

'Rose would never leave me,' Stacy said quietly.

Since the silence between them had been so long, and he seemed to be speaking only to himself, Anna pretended she hadn't heard. She pulled the patrol car off onto the overlook where Greeley's company pickup was parked and switched off the ignition. 'You want to do the talking or shall I?' she asked.

'You do it, Silva's supposed to be quite the ladies' man. Maybe we'll get lucky and he'll underestimate you.'

Anna laughed. 'I like you, Meyers.'

Following the pink plastic tape marking the section of line already surveyed, they started down into the ravine. Mesa Verde's oakbrush grew to the size of small trees – some reaching twenty feet or more – but retained the many branches of a lesser shrub. In places the bushes were virtually impenetrable and provided habitat for quail, rabbits, and other creatures who lived longer if they went unnoticed.

The survey crew had cut a swath through the brush with loppers and chainsaws. Suckers, severed just above ground level, stuck up sharp as pungi sticks. Intent on where she put her feet, Anna nearly ran into a man working his way up the hill.

'Whoa there, honey!' He spoke with a slight lisp and he put his arms around her as if she was going to fall. 'I do love hugging women packing heat.'

Anna extricated herself from his grasp. The man was Ted Greeley. He was not much taller than Anna, maybe five-foot-eight. In his early fifties, he had startlingly blue eyes and snow white hair that hugged his round head in tight curls. He'd kept himself in good shape. Anna couldn't but notice the muscular arms when he'd grabbed her. Beginnings of a pot belly attested to the fact that physical fitness was an on-going struggle.

'Checking up on me, eh?' He reached down and pulled

up a blade of grass to chew on.

'Good morning, Ted,' Stacy said.

'Ted,' Anna echoed the greeting. 'We need to talk with Tom Silva. Is he working this stretch of line?'

'You girl rangers really make a difference.' Greeley winked at Anna. 'In the construction business all I ever see are men's ugly pusses. Say, how's that wife of yours, Stacy? Still eating your cooking?'

Stacy just smiled.

'And how's my little Bella?'

'Bella's fine,' Stacy's tone was icy and Anna sensed a sudden hostility. 'Dispatch said Tom Silva was working this section. Do you know where we can find him?' Stacy dragged the conversation back to business.

Greeley's smile broadened. 'Tom in some kind of trouble? Let me know if any of my boys get out of line. You know what they say: you get in bed with somebody, it pays to stay friendly.'

'No trouble,' Stacy said stiffly. 'We just need to talk with him.'

'Help yourself.' Greeley gestured down the hill. 'He's holding the dumb end of the tape for an overpaid surveyor, so don't keep him too long. Anna.' He tipped an imaginary hat as he brushed by her.

The surveyor was at the bottom of the ravine setting up his tripod. 'Silva?' Anna asked as they approached.

'Keep walking,' the man replied without taking his eyes from his instruments. Ahead, down a fresh-cut line, a second man sat on a boulder smoking a cigarette.

'Tom Silva?' Anna asked when they were close enough to be heard.

'You're looking at him.' Silva blew smoke out in a thin stream and looked Anna up and down. The half smile on his lips suggested she should feel complimented.

She didn't.

'I'm Anna Pigeon. This is Stacy Meyers. Can you take a break for a minute? We'd like to talk to you.'

'Taking five, Bobby,' Silva shouted past them. 'Somebody set the law dogs on me.' He smiled up at Anna. 'Pull up a rock and sit down.'

Anna crouched, rocking back on her heels, her forearms resting on her knees. Stacy remained standing, seeming tall as a willow from her new vantage point.

For a moment Silva studied them and Anna him. The morning's heat was beginning to collect in the canyon, held close by the oakbrush thickets. Shirtless, rivulets of sweat traced trails through the dust on Silva's smooth chest. Stick-straight black hair stuck out from beneath a battered, straw cowboy hat. With his unlined olive skin and dark eyes, he was pretty rather than handsome.

Meeting Anna's eyes, he crushed out his cigarette and pointedly tucked the butt into the rolled cuff of his jeans. 'No litter here,' he said. 'This is a National Fucking Park.'

A challenge: Anna chose to ignore it.

'Patsy asked us to talk with you, Tom,' she said evenly.

'What's old Pats up to now?' He shook another Marlboro from the pack that rested beside him on the rock, then made a show of offering one to Anna and Stacy.

Anna declined. Stacy just shook his head.

'Suit yourself. Mind if I do?' The question was rhetorical and neither bothered to reply. Silva didn't light the cigarette but played it between his fingers. The gesture was so classically phallic that Anna felt tired.

'Patsy's concerned that some of the presents you've been giving her might have more than one meaning,' she began. 'This latest – attention – has her fairly upset.'

'So she screamed for the rangers? God, Pats loves a good scene.'

'Your ex-wife—'

'My wife,' Tom interrupted.

'—would be more comfortable if you stayed away from her.'

'Hey, a man's got a right to work. She's always hollering I don't pay enough goddamn child support, now she's trying to lose me my job. Christ!'

'Patsy's not trying to get you fired, Tom. She mentioned specifically that she didn't want that to happen. She just wants you to stay away from her.'

'What grounds, man? She's got my kids for Christ's sake.' Tom quit playing with the cigarette and lit it, striking a wooden match with an expert – and probably much rehearsed – flick of his thumbnail. 'There ain't no way she can keep me from going over there. I've never done a damn thing, not one damn thing she can hold up in a court of law to say I can't. Hell, I never even hit her.'

'I believe you, Tom,' Anna said soothingly. 'But there's a thing called harassment. Patsy has pretty strong feelings about some of your gifts.'

Tom shook his head. Smoke poured from his nostrils. His eyes were fixed on a point beyond Anna's left shoulder. Behind her she could hear Stacy shifting his weight.

'She's got a scrap of skin in an envelope, Tom. She said it was foreskin. That's a pretty loaded thing to send somebody.' Anna was uncomfortably aware of the unintentional humor. She heard Stacy clearing his throat, a small cough that could have been thwarted laughter.

Fortunately Tom seemed not to pick up on it. For a moment he sat smoking and Anna waited, letting the silence soak in, work for her.

'Christ! It was a joke,' he finally burst out.

Stacy spoke for the first time. 'A joke? It must've hurt like crazy. Where's the funny part?'

Tom looked up at him, his mouth twisted with irritation. 'I didn't take a fucking knife to myself if that's what you mean. The doc did it. Pats had been after me for years. I thought she'd like it.'

'You got circumcised in your thirties?' Stacy asked. Anna bit back a laugh at the 'oh ouch!' she could hear under the words.

'That's right.' Tom smiled, his teeth were square and white. 'Barnum and Bailey got a new tent.'

Inwardly, Anna sighed. 'Here's where we stand, Tom. You, Patsy, me – we've all got to live together on this mesa top. At least for a while. I'd suggest that you steer clear of Patsy. If you've got visiting rights to your kids, you two work that out. I'll ask Patsy to file whatever agreement you reach at the Chief Ranger's Office. You stick to that and you won't have to deal with us, okay?'

'Fuck!' Tom flicked his cigarette butt into the brush. Anna didn't even follow it with her eyes. 'Why don't you rangers do your job instead of hassling people that work for a living? You get a fucking free ride from the government and can't even keep the fucking roads safe. Monday night a big goddamn truck nearly ran me off the road. Where the hell were you then? Christ!'

'We'll look into that.' Pushing herself to her feet, Anna heard both ankles crack in protest.

'Will that be all, *ranger*?'

'Almost,' Anna returned. 'Just find that cigarette you tossed and put it out and we'll be out of your hair. Fire danger's bad this year. Manning Class 4 yesterday.'

'Find it yourself,' Silva muttered.

'I got it.' Stacy had crushed the life from the butt and now tucked the filter into his pocket.

'Good enough for me,' Anna said. 'Take it easy, Tom.'

'Yeah.'

When they'd passed the surveyor and were climbing out of the ravine, Stacy said: 'Foreskin is a loaded gift,' and the laughter Anna had swallowed came bubbling out.

'The way he was playing with the cigarette . . .' Anna's laughter took over and she had to stop climbing just to breathe. 'You'd think he was auditioning for the role of Johnny Wad in "Debbie Does Dallas." '

'You mean that didn't toss your confetti? I kind of thought I might give it a shot. Run it up the flag pole, see if the cat licks it up.'

Stacy stopped beside her. Pressed close by the brambles, Anna was aware of the smell of him: freshly laundered cotton and soap. Heat radiated from her and it wasn't only from the sun and the climb. Anna stifled her basic instincts and shook herself like a dog ridding its fur of water drops.

Abruptly, she turned and pushed up the side of the ravine. In places it was so steep she pulled herself along using the low branches. Her laughter had evaporated.

'You drive,' she said as they reached the patrol car. 'These seats break my back.'

'You're too short. This is a man's machine. A car for Johnny Wad.' Stacy slipped behind the wheel and slid the seat back as far as it would go.

'Thanks for picking up that cigarette butt. What was I going to do? Shoot the guy? Never try to out-macho a construction worker.'

'Believe it or not, picking up litter is why I went into this business. I don't work for the Park Service. I work for the parks.'

Anna settled back into the seat. 'The NPS could use a few more fern feelers. I, for one, hope you get on permanent.'

'So do I,' Stacy said. 'So do I.'

His tone was so grim, so determined, Anna dropped the subject. Everybody had to contend with their own demons. Some of hers were such old familiars she considered naming them and renting them closet space.

Leaning her head back against the vinyl headrest, she closed her eyes. Zachary was dead eight years come August. She could no longer consistently call his face to mind. Without his memory clear and present, her fortieth might turn out to be a damn lonely year.

Chapter Four

Housemates out, television off, Anna had been sleeping with glorious abandon. Deep sleep, R.E.M. sleep, sleep without nightmares. Of late a good night's sleep had become such a rarity her fantasies about it bordered on the erotic.

Hence the cursing reluctance with which she relinquished it to answer the phone.

'Anna, Frieda. Sorry about this.'

Anna turned on her bedside light and snatched up the alarm clock: two-o-two a.m.

'Nobody else to home,' Frieda said. All law enforcement on MEVE shared an emergency party line called the '69 line because of the last two digits of the number. Every call rang in quarters on Chapin and at Far view. Anna'd been the unlucky ranger who picked up first.

'What's up – other than me?' Anna was already threading her legs into yesterday's underpants.

'Got a report of lights in the maintenance yard. Somebody needs to check it out.'

'I'm headed that direction.' Maintenance was scarcely a hundred yards from the housing loop on Chapin. Stacy would have been the logical one to respond but he never answered the '69. Scuttlebutt was he unplugged it nights. Some said for Bella, others said Rose did the unplugging.

Loss of sleep was a tradeoff for money. Every call, short or long, earned two hours overtime. As she buckled on her duty belt, Anna totaled it up. Two hours at time and a half was close to thirty bucks. She'd've paid nearly that for an uninterrupted night's sleep.

From the patrol car, she called in service. Frieda responded – not because she had to, she wasn't officially on duty. There would be no overtime or base pay for her. Frieda monitored because she took her job more seriously than her employers did. She didn't like rangers out without at least rudimentary back-up.

The air was cool and fresh. Anna rolled down the Ford's windows and let the darkness blow in around her. On her first late shifts she'd had a new experience – or if not new, one she hadn't felt for a long time, not since leaving New York City. Anna'd found herself afraid of the dark.

Walking trail in Texas, skirting islands around Isle Royale, she'd worn the night like a star-studded cloak. But Mesa Verde was all about dead people. In the mind – or the collective unconscious – there was a feeling they'd not all left in the twelve hundreds. Or if they had, perhaps whatever it was that drove them out had taken up residence in the abandoned cities. Everywhere there were reminders of another time, another world.

Given the propensity of Jamie and some of the other interpreters to capitalize on New Age voodoo, Anna never admitted her fear but she patrolled with an ear open for voices long gone, footsteps not clothed in mortal flesh.

A half moon threw bars of silver across the road, enough to see by, and as she turned onto the spur leading to maintenance, she clicked off her headlights. The maintenance yard, a paved area with a gas pump in the center, was surrounded by two-story buildings: offices, garages, a carpenters' shop, storage barns. Built in the 1940s, the buildings were of dark wood with small many-paned windows. One remnant remained from the '30s: the fire cache, where helitack stored the gear needed to fight wildland fire. It was of stone with juniper beams supporting a flat roof. Behind the cache a twelve foot cyclone fence topped with barbed wire enclosed the construction company's equipment behind padlocked gates.

In the inky shadow of a storage barn, the car rolled to a stop. Anna called on scene and received Frieda's reassuring reply. Setting the brake, she listened. Pre-dawn silence, fragile and absolute, settled around her. The pop of her tires as they cooled, the clicking of insects flying against the intruder lights pattered like dry rain.

Trickling out of the quiet, it came to her why Mesa Verde nights pricked some nerve deep in her psyche. Like New York City, the mesa was comprised of peopled dark, dark that collected in the corners of buildings and under eaves, choked alleys and narrow streets. A darkness permeated with the baggage of humanity. Dreams and desires haunted the mesa the way they haunted the rooms in old houses. Traces of unfinished lives caught in the ether.

Anna felt her skin begin to creep. 'Why don't you just

rent a video of "Hill House" and be done with it?' she mocked herself.

Another minute whispered by. Apparently nothing was going to manifest itself in her windshield. She loosed the six-cell flashlight from its charger beneath the dash.

Metal clanked on metal as she opened the car door and she froze. It wasn't the familiar click of door mechanisms, it was what she'd been waiting for: something not right, a sound where silence ought to be.

Noise gave her direction. Leaving the car door open rather than risk a racket, she moved quietly toward the fenced construction yard. Between her car and the fence were three board-and-batten shacks used to store hand tools and pesticides. In the colorless light the short road looked like a scene from Old Tucson's back lot.

Anna followed the line of buildings till she ran out of shadow. Two junipers framed a picnic table where the hazardous fuel removal crew cleaned their saws. She slipped into the protective darkness. Closer now, she could see the gates to the yard. A chain hung loose, its padlock broken or unlocked.

Within the confines of the cyclone fence, heavy equipment clustered like prehistoric creatures at a watering hole. Bones of metal linked with hydraulic cable in place of tendons thrust into the night: the skeletal neck of a crane, the scorpion's claw of a back-hoe, the rounded back of a water truck – one she'd never seen in use though dust from construction was a constant irritation. Easily a million dollars worth of machinery brought in to do the work needed for the waterline.

Again came the clank, softer this time and followed

by a faint scraping sound. Moving quickly, Anna crossed the tarmac and slipped through the gates. Moonlight caught her, then she was again in shadow, her back against a wheel half again as tall as she.

When heart and breath quit clamoring in her ears, she listened. Concentration revealed sounds always present but seldom noted: the minute scratch of insect feet crossing sand, a whispered avian discussion high in the trees. Nothing unnatural, nothing human. Odd, Anna thought, that 'man-made' and 'natural' should be considered antithetical.

Time crawled by, the slight adrenaline rush brought on by the act of sneaking faded and she began feeling a bit silly crouched in the darkness chasing what was undoubtedly a wild goose – or at worst a chipmunk who'd decided to build her nest in one of Greeley's engines.

Probably the last guy out had forgotten to lock the gate. Monday nights Stacy had late shift. He should have checked it but something may have distracted him.

Realizing she'd been taking shallow nervous breaths, Anna filled her lungs. Muscles she hadn't known she was clenching relaxed and she felt her shoulders drop. Expelling a sigh to blow away the last of the chindi-borne cobwebs, she switched on her flashlight and stepped out of the shadows.

Weaving through the parked machines, she played the light over each piece of equipment. Nothing stirred, scuttled or slithered. A backhoe at the end of the enclosure finished the group. Anna shined the light over the yellow paint, up an awkward angle and into the mud-crusted bucket. Nothing.

The goose could consider itself chased. Anna was going back to bed. Turning to leave, her beam crawled along the oversized tires and across the toe of a boot, a cowboy boot, scuffed and brown like a hundred thousand others in the southwest.

'Like a dog chasing cars,' she thought. 'Now what?' Indecision passed with a spurt of fear. She stepped into the shadows and moved the flashlight out from her body lest it become a target.

'Come on out and talk to me,' she said. 'No sense hiding at this point.'

There was only one way out of the yard that didn't involve scaling the fence and Anna waited for the intruder to show himself or bolt for the gate.

The toe twitched. 'Come on out,' Anna said reasonably. 'You're not in too much trouble yet.'

Slowly, with a feeble skritching sound, the toe pulled back into darkness. A peculiar shushing followed and Anna realized whoever it was was pulling off the boots.

Little hairs on the back of her neck began to prickle. 'Enough's enough, come out of there.' She walked toward the back-hoe's rear tire, unsnapping the keeper on her .357 as she went.

The intruder was quick. On silent sock feet, he'd retreated into the jungle of blades, tires and engines. Anna had no intention of following. Backing slowly out of the alley between the parked monoliths, she ducked clear of the moonlight and took her King radio from her belt.

Frieda, bless her, was still monitoring. 'We've got an intruder in the construction yard,' Anna said clearly. 'Get me some backup.'

The radio called stirred the stockinged feet. Distinct rustling from a careless move riveted Anna's attention on a ditcher parked one space nearer the open gate. Staying well back in the shadow, she waited. Silence grated on her nerves and she listened as much for the approach of help as she did for the movements of the person she tracked.

Scuffling: the tiny sound made her flinch as if a cannon had gone off near her ear. Behind her now, beyond the back-hoe; loathe to leave the dark for the glaring moonlight, Anna knelt and turned her light between the wheels. A flick of gray; a tail disappearing through the fence. She turned the flashlight off. Time to move. The rodent had tricked her into giving away her position.

Easing to her feet, she tried for quiet but knees and ankles popped like firecrackers in the stillness.

A foot scrape on concrete and a singing of air: a black line with a hook windmilled out from the rear of the ditcher. Moonbeams were sliced, air whistled through the iron. Someone was swinging a heavy chain with an eight-inch tow hook attached to the end.

'Shit!' Anna dropped to her belly and rolled under the back-hoe as the weighted chain cut through the air striking the tire where she'd been standing. Iron links whipped around the hard rubber and struck the back of her neck, the links cracking against her temple. Shock registered but not pain.

Wriggling on elbows and knees, Anna worked her way deeper under the belly of the machine.

Footsteps, soft and running, followed the cacophony of chain falling. Whoever it was ran for the gate. Courage returned and Anna scrambled into the open. She was on her feet in time to hear the gate clang shut. Sprinting the twisted path across the pavement, she caught a glimpse of a figure flitting through the shadows of the utility buildings beyond.

When she reached the gate she stopped. The chain had been strung back through and the lock snapped shut.

'Damn it!' Greeley had his own locks and the rangers had not been given access keys. With a jump she reached halfway up the fence and hung there. A double line of barbed wire slanted away from the fence top. She could probably thread her way through with only a modicum of damage but not in time to catch whoever had locked her in.

Smothering an obscenity, she dropped back to earth and unsheathed her radio. Not even Frieda heard her call this time. Leaning against the wire, she caught her breath and let the nervous energy drain away. Fatigue welled up in its place and her legs began to shake. Where the chain had lashed ached and her head felt full of hot sand.

She crossed the asphalt and rested her back against the tread of a D-14 cat. Her insides shook and her breath was uneven. What scared her wasn't so much the attack but her lack of readiness to meet it. Like a rookie – or a complacent old timer – she'd wandered happily into the middle of a crime in progress. And nearly been killed for her stupidity. She'd gotten sloppy, let down her guard.

Mesa Verde was a quiet park. She'd let herself be lulled into a false sense of security. It was less the park's age and dignity than the dead-end road that kept crime at a low ebb. Situated on a mesa in the remote southwestern corner of Colorado, approachable only by twenty miles of winding two-lane mountain road, it didn't get the through traffic of a park on a major highway. No accidental tourists on their way from Soledad to Sing-Sing.

Mesa Verde's dangers had struck Anna more akin to the pitfalls of Peyton Place. Societies, like other living organisms, sometimes fell ill.

Scrapes from the chain throbbed and she brought her mind back to the machinery yard. What had the intruder been after? The stuff was too obvious to fence, too big to steal. Something important enough to risk imprisonment. Even if murder hadn't been in the plan, assault on a Federal Officer was a felony offense.

The fog in her head was clearing and only a dull ache behind her eyes remained. Anna pushed herself to her feet. Somewhere beneath the back hoe was her flashlight. Before morning's business stomped over the whole place, she would use it to see if Mr Brown Boots had left anything behind.

Cigarette butts were scattered beneath the ditcher. Sherlock Holmes might have made hay with such an abundance of clues but Anna didn't bother. Half the construction workers smoked and, near as she could tell, all of the maintenance men. Marlboro, Camel Lights, Winston, she noted the brands for the sake of feeling useful but they were too common to draw any conclusions.

In the cab of the caterpillar she found some battered hand tools. Behind the seat of the water truck were a pair of welding gloves and what looked like a gas mask left over from WWII. Unless they were some brand of rare antiques they didn't look worth stealing.

The D-14 cat yielded up the answers. Beneath the iron tread Anna found a baggie with a trace of white powder in it. She didn't taste it. She didn't have to. It was sugar.

Monkey wrenching was the only thing that made any sense. Someone waging guerrilla warfare against the new waterline. There was no telling how much time the intruder had before Anna interrupted, how much damage had been done. As soon as she was let out of her pen she'd have to call Greeley. The contractor would not be pleased.

Monkey wrenching – sabotage – was an ancient form of combat. Anna respected it in its purest form: David Environmentalist against Goliath Industries. Whether or not this was the case with the waterline, she'd not decided.

Rogelio, her lover in Texas, had thrived on such night action. She'd met many of the ecotage experts he ran with. They didn't tend to violence against persons. No swinging of chains, crushing of skulls. Brown Boots had a good deal to lose, it would seem. Or a good deal to gain.

Al Stinson cared enough to throw a wrench in the works, a sabot in the machine, but it seemed absurd to risk a twenty-year career when she had legal avenues at her disposal.

Jamie maybe. She had nothing to lose materially and might still be naive enough to believe she wouldn't be thrown in jail if she were caught.

Somehow Anna couldn't see either Al or Jamie swinging a tow chain but then she'd been wrong about people before. Tom Silva was the consummate drugstore cowboy. He probably had a whole closet full of boots. Assault and vandalism: it wasn't too hard to picture him with a chain. Did he have a grudge against his employer, access to a key?

Again she tried Frieda.

This time there was an answer. 'Sorry. I've been trying to raise somebody for you,' the dispatcher apologized unnecessarily. 'I finally went over to Stacy's. He'll be there shortly.'

'Thanks.' Anna called 316, Stacy's number. 'Wake up maintenance,' she told him. 'Find somebody entrusted with Greeley's master key.'

Minutes ticked by. Anna didn't mind the wait. The night was dry and not too cold. A slight breeze whispered through the pine trees and she wasn't lonely. Closing her eyes she tried to recall everything she could about the intruder. One boot toe, brown, and a retreating form in dark clothing. She couldn't even say for sure if it was male or female, tall or short.

Outfoxed, out-maneuvered and left penned up for everyone to see, Anna was beginning to get testy about the whole affair.

Boots ringing on pavement brought her head around. Stacy, in uniform, defensive gear and flat hat, ran across the maintenance yard following the beam of a flashlight.

'Got the key?' she called.

'Got it.'

Anna pushed herself to her feet and waited impatiently while he fumbled with the lock. 'It doesn't appear to be broken. Whoever it was had a key,' she remarked.

Stacy didn't say anything.

'Did you check it before you went off shift?'

'I honestly can't remember.' Stacy was sullen, it was unlike him. The 'honestly' bothered Anna.

The lock came open and he pulled the chain from the gates. Once freed, Anna demanded: 'Why didn't you answer the six-nine line?'

Stacy turned his back to her and locked the gate. 'The phone plug got knocked out somehow,' he said flatly.

Rose. Anna didn't pursue it.

Stacy declined a ride home but Anna swung through the housing loop anyway. As she'd hoped, Frieda's light was on.

'Dropped by to say thanks,' Anna said when the dispatcher answered the door.

'Likely story. Piedmont thinks you're here to see him.'

It gladdened Anna's heart to see the yellow streak that ran to the screen at the sound of her voice. Scooping him up she kissed him between the ears. 'Coming home sucks without a cat to meet you at the food dish.'

Because all good dispatchers are mind readers, Frieda brought Anna a glass of wine. Out of deference to convention, Anna removed her gun before taking the first draught. Piedmont spread himself down the length of her lap, his orange and white chin draped over her knees.

Anna related the night's tale to the dispatcher. Frieda was genuinely interested and Anna too keyed up to shut up and go home.

'Greeley hasn't made a lot of friends up here,' Frieda said. 'The interps are making quite a stink about the disturbance of the mesa. Al eggs them on – not on purpose, but most of them are of an age when passion's contagious.'

'I'd like to think she'd draw the line at offing a ranger,' Anna grumbled.

Frieda laughed. 'Hard to picture. Maybe it's not ecotage at all. Just pure meanness. Greeley's own guys aren't that crazy about him either. He's a little on the oily side.'

Anna took a long drink of wine and tried to call the construction workers to mind. They all ran together: big men in hardhats. The ache at the base of her skull suggested she pay a little more attention in the future.

'Sorry about the back-up screw-up. I'm glad you're not dead. Would I ever have felt a fool,' Frieda said.

'Did you have trouble prying Stacy out of bed?'

'He was up watching television. I tried everyone else before it dawned on me he might have turned his phone off.'

'Got "accidently" unplugged,' Anna said cattily.

Frieda nodded. This was clearly not a surprise.

It crossed Anna's mind that Stacy would have had time to run from maintenance to the housing loop in the ten minutes it had taken Frieda to come knocking at his door. Meyers had the right temperament for a monkey wrencher – passion and a sense of his own importance in the scheme of things. Had he found the lock open when he made his last rounds and felt an opportunist urge to strike a blow for conservation?

Greeley was insured. Damaged machinery would be replaced. Work would go on. Did Stacy have passion enough to risk felony imprisonment for what was in reality only a gesture?

Anna didn't like to think Stacy would swing an iron hook at her head.

Before she left she presumed on Frieda's hospitality one more time and borrowed her phone. Greeley wasn't answering.

'Must be nice,' Frieda said as she let Anna out.

'Must be.'

'I'll try him again first thing in the morning,' Frieda promised.

When Anna got back to the dorm it was after three and all the lights were blazing. Laughter and the rattle of voices met her at the door. 'You were there, did it happen or not?' Jamie was shouting.

On Mesa Verde, it would seem, no one but Anna had any interest in sleep.

'Jimmy, you saw it—' A thud followed by laughter interrupted.

'Jimmy's had so much he couldn't see past his own nose.' Jennifer Short's Memphis drawl.

'The spirit veil, oooooooh.' Another voice, probably Jimmy Russell's, wailed like the ghosts in the Saturday morning cartoons. Then laughter shouted down by Jamie's: 'Funny, real funny, you guys—'

Anna banged through the kitchen door. Moaning like Casper the Friendly Ghost, Jimmy Russell was traipsing around the living room in a drunken parody of a wraith. His face was flushed and his eyes bright but he was steady on his feet. Anna had known he was a drinker. Noting how well he'd learned to cope, she couldn't but wonder if, at twenty, he was an habitual drunk.

A study in superiority, Jamie was leaning in the entrance to the hall. 'Laugh away,' she was saying. 'They're here. I've seen them before. Are you going to pretend you didn't, Jennifer? You were practically peeing your pants tonight.'

'My, my, Jamie. Such a lady-like phrase,' Jennifer drawled.

Rolling his eyes and fluttering his hands, Jimmy wailed.

'Keep it up. Keep it up,' Jamie said with exaggerated patience.

Sprawled in one of the armchairs, her body limp, Jennifer percolated giggles in support of Jimmy's antics. 'Aw come on, Jamie. He's only teasin' yew.'

'It's not me he needs to worry about.' Jamie had taken on an air of secret knowledge.

'Excuse me,' Anna cut in. 'Could you guys take the party elsewhere? I've got to be up at six.'

'We're sorry, Anna,' Russell said contritely. Head slightly lowered, he looked at her from under thick blond lashes.

Undoubtedly it had been irresistible when he was six.

'Jamie saw the third world or whatever coming through that thing ... a see-poo-poo—' Dissolving into giggles, Jennifer couldn't go on.

'Sipapu. See. Pah. Pooh.' Jamie pronounced the word with the care one might employ when conversing with an imbecilic and not much loved child. 'It's too bad law enforcement doesn't require their rangers to learn about the places they are supposedly protecting.'

The merriment went out of Jennifer's face and a hardness came into it that Anna had never seen before. 'Y'all can piss and moan the rest of the night if you want to. I'm going to bed. 'Night Anna.'

The magnolia blossom apparently had core of good southern steel.

''Night,' Anna returned automatically.

'Jamie really did see something. She's got a weird sense like that – you know, ghosts and shit,' Jimmy Russell said somberly.

The boy was so transparent, if she'd not been tired and cranky, Anna might have found him amusing. Jennifer gone, Russell was trying to re-ingratiate himself with Jamie. Somebody wants to get laid tonight, she thought without charity but with undoubted accuracy.

Russell fell back on the sofa, his feet splayed out in front of him. Brown cowboy boots. Anna had no trouble picturing him with an implement of destruction. Environmental concerns didn't seem to be the Kentucky boy's mainstay but drunken pranks might be. After a six-pack or two Jamie could probably talk him into almost anything.

Anna began to wonder if all the ghostly theatrics were designed as a cover story for more practical measures taken to protect the Anasazi heritage. She decided against mentioning her night's adventure to this crowd.

Jamie interrupted Anna's train of thought. Stalking to one of the two refrigerators in the kitchen, she took out a Tupperware container and kicked the refrigerator door shut. 'Bonegrinder!' As she spat out the word, she jerked open a drawer. In one continuous motion she fished out a serving spoon and popped the plastic lid off the food container.

'If somebody took one of those huge ditchers and started chewing a trench through Forest Lawn you can bet there'd be an outcry. It just wouldn't happen.' Ladling a bite of some pasta concoction into her mouth as if to calm her nerves, Jamie went on. 'You can't go around digging up white people's cemeteries. Oh no. Big sacrilege. They won't get away with it.' Jamie inhaled another serving-spoonful of pasta. 'The whole mesa is sacred ground.'

Though it had been in vogue at one time, there wasn't any archeological evidence to support that theory, but Anna didn't say anything. She dumped her hat and gun on the dinette table and collapsed in one of the straight-backed chairs.

'They're not going to get away with grinding our bones up. Not this time.'

Anna noted the 'our'. She also noted that Jamie's brown roots were just beginning to show at the base of her part. Raising her eyebrows politely, she invited Jamie to continue ranting.

'Solstice is coming,' the interpreter said with finality.

June twenty-first; perhaps that was the proposed date of some planned event. Anna let the idea filter through her mind. Why would Jamie divulge that bit of information in the presence of a law enforcement ranger? Unless, as was often the case in publicity stunts, the law was necessary to provide the drama required to lure out the press. It was illegal for government employees to 'tattle' to the press on touchy issues. But bringing down the wrath of the six o'clock news was almost the only way to affect any real change. Like any other entrenched bureaucracy, the Park Service was filled with people passing the buck and covering the hindmost parts of their anatomy.

'What happens on solstice?' Anna asked.

'It's a sacred day to the Old Ones,' Jamie replied with the air of an insider who only hands out information in pre-approved sound bytes.

'Are they going to hold those Indian dances or something?' Jimmy Russell wanted to know.

'Not likely. "They" have been dead for seven hundred years,' Anna told him.

'They might,' Jamie said cryptically.

'Ah. Chindi.' Anna was suddenly too tired to play along.

'The spirit veil ooooo—' Jimmy's wail ended abruptly at the look on her face.

'Are you driving, Jimmy?'

'Yes, ma'am.' He dangled his car keys.

Anna took them and slipped them into her pocket. If Russell was her chain-swinging eco-terrorist, he was too far gone to do much damage till morning.

'You're drunk. Sleep on the couch. I'll leave your keys on the table when I go to work. Good night.'

A few minutes of murmuring came through the wall as Jamie dragged out bedding for the inebriated helitacker, then the house was blessedly quiet. Anna took two aspirin for her head. For her nerves she recited the only prayer she knew all the way through: 'From ghoulies and ghosties and long leggedy beasties and things that go bump in the night, Lord preserve me.'

Chapter Five

At eight a.m., when Stacy pulled up in the patrol car Jimmy Russell was still curled up on the couch in a yellow fire-issue sleeping bag. He didn't even twitch when Anna walked through. Without so much as a twinge of guilt, she let the door bang shut behind her.

Usually Stacy's aesthetic countenance was a welcome sight, but lack of sleep had left Anna surly. Evidently the night's festivities had left their mark on him as well. In lieu of 'good morning' he said: 'Mind if we stop by my house? Rose's going to Farmington and Bella needs a ride to maintenance. Drew said he'd keep an eye on her till six.'

Anna wanted to ask why Rose didn't take the kid along, but she minded her own business. The radio was tuned to a Navajo station and a language that sounded like Chinese sawed at her nerves. With an abrupt movement, she switched it off.

'Wrong side of the bed?' Stacy asked.

'Tired. My housemates kept me up after our rendez-vous in maintenance. Jamie said she'd seen a veil or some damn thing. Chindi passing from the underworld to this one. They were out at Cliff Palace, drinking and scaring each other is my guess.'

'I checked the book.' Stacy sounded alarmed. 'There were no permits for Cliff Palace last night.'

Any employee going anywhere – or anytime – the public was not allowed had to have a backcountry permit signed by the Chief Ranger. Cliff Palace after hours fell under that restriction.

Anna wondered if Stacy entertained the same suspicions she did about possible monkey wrenching business. 'If that's really where they were then I doubt much harm was done.'

'When I made my sweep at eleven I didn't see any cars,' he said stubbornly.

'Maybe they were on bicycles.' Leaning her head back against the seat, she closed her eyes and let the subject drop.

At the housing loop, she fiddled with the radio while Stacy went in to fetch Bella. A little mental arithmetic told Anna Bella was his step-daughter. She was a first or second grader and he'd met his wife three years ago. Taking on the responsibility, not only of someone else's child, but a child with a disability, spoke of powerful love – or powerful need.

'Hello my little Pine-nut,' she heard Stacy call when he was half-way up the walk. He disappeared into the house to reappear moments later with Bella. The child's face was a testament to her mother's youthful good looks. A rounded heart set off by a crop of carefully tended curls. Brown hair, several shades lighter than Rose's, caught the morning sun and glinted with blond highlights.

Wide-spaced eyes sparkled above a small straight nose. This loveliness made more pathetic the bowed legs, far too short for the proportions of her upper body, and the rolling gait.

Hand-in-hand with Stacy, Bella chattered up at him. For every glitter of hero-worship in her eyes, there was an answering glow of adoration in his. Stacy's slender frame shaped itself into a question mark as he curbed his steps, leaning down to hear her.

What Anna had seen as a burden clearly lightened the load Stacy professed to have carried after his first wife left him.

'You're Anna Pigeon,' the child announced when they reached the car.

'You got me there.' Anna leaned over the seat-back to shove briefcases and hats out of Bella's way. Fleetingly, she wondered if Stacy had been talking about her.

'I read your name tag,' the child explained as she swung herself into the rear seat. 'That's in case you thought I might be psycho or something.'

Stacy laughed. 'Psychic, Pine-nut. Psycho is crazy.'

'I'm not old enough to be crazy,' she said confidently. 'Do you have children, Mrs Pigeon?'

'None to speak of.'

'Oh.' Bella sounded disappointed.

'I have a cat.' Anna tried to exonerate herself.

'Don't you like children?'

'Some of my best friends are children.' Anna was thinking of Alison, her old Michigan housemate's daughter.

The truth must have rung through the words. Bella

brightened immediately. 'That's okay then. If the cat has kittens, can I play with them?'

'Your mom's allergic, Pine-nut,' Stacy reminded gently.

'Not have, Stacy. Play with. I'd wash after.'

'Piedmont's a boy cat,' Anna said. 'So no kittens. But he might like it if you'd come play with him. Sometimes I suspect he misses the little girl we used to live with.'

'Does he try to hide it?' Bella asked and Anna sensed she was already adept at hiding hurt and loneliness.

'Yes. Sometimes he goes out and kills mice. Then I think he feels better.'

'I like mice.'

'So does Piedmont.' Anna was losing ground in this conversation. A smile played on Stacy's lips. She was willing to bet it was at her expense.

The maintenance yard was loud with heavy equipment. Stacy pulled up in front of the fire cache. 'Stay in the car, honey. Too much traffic. I'll find Drew.'

'Are you married?' Bella resumed the interrogation as Stacy disappeared into the cache.

'Used to be,' Anna replied.

'Did he divorce you?'

'He died.' Anna wished Stacy would come back. 'Maybe I'd better go and see what's keeping your dad.'

Her cowardly exit was thwarted. 'No. Stay. Stacy'll be right back. He never forgets. My first dad divorced us because I wasn't born normal,' Bella stated matter-of-factly. 'Momma said.'

Anna didn't know what to say to that. She was saved by Stacy's reappearance, Drew beside him. Drew Kinder was as close to a 'mountain of a man' as Anna'd ever met, made of a core of stone-hard muscle covered with a layer of baby fat a couple of inches deep. Unruly eyebrows and a moth-eaten mustache grew like lichen on his round face.

Next to the helitacker, Stacy's six-foot-two looked average, short even, and accentuated his slenderness. Seeing the two men together, an image of a bass fiddle and bow flashed through her mind.

'Hiya, Drew,' Bella called.

'Hiya, Beautiful.' Drew leaned down, hands on the door frame. His head filled the window. 'I gotta fuel the truck then we hit the road.'

'Hit the road,' Bella repeated as if the phrase had struck a harmonious chord within her.

'I'll help you with the truck,' Anna volunteered. She didn't want to be left alone with Bella again. The child's unrelenting forthrightness was unsettling.

'Can't hack it?' Stacy asked over the roof of the patrol car as she climbed out.

Anna just laughed.

While Drew filled the firetruck with diesel, she leaned against the fender. In his huge hands the nozzle looked like a child's water pistol.

'Bella's quite a girl,' he said.

'Seems smart enough. Too bad she's . . .' Aware she was giving pity where none was asked, Anna left the sentence unfinished.

Drew straightened up. The sun was behind his head. In silhouette he loomed as solid as the proverbial brick out-house. 'Maybe that's what makes her so strong, so smart. She sees right through people. Maybe she got that from being the way she is. Ever think of that?'

'I will now,' Anna promised.

'Her mom wants her to get all these operations on her legs. Pretty painful stuff. Make her more 'normal'. Maybe it's a good idea, maybe it's not. All I know is it's got to hurt. I don't like seeing kids hurt.'

'Nobody does,' Anna said mildly.

Drew shot her a look that startled her with its venom. 'Don't kid yourself,' he said and went back to pumping diesel. 'Her folks ought to leave her alone. I'm a giant. She's a dwarf. We're the variety that adds spice.'

A blue Ford six-pac carrying five men in orange hard-hats pulled up behind them in line for fuel. Ted Greeley was driving.

'Well, if it isn't my own personal ranger,' Greeley greeted Anna. 'How am I doing? Running afoul of the law?'

'Not yet,' she returned.

He looked at his watch. 'It's early.'

'Did Frieda get a hold of you about last night?'

'She did. Damn near too late. You guessed it. The son-of-a-bitch dumped sugar in the gas tank of my ditcher. If anybody'd fired it up I'd've been proud owner of a piece of shit retailing at close to a hundred grand. I'm none too happy one of my boys left the gate unlocked and I'm none too happy one of your boys didn't catch it. I'd hate to think all my tax dollars are paying for are cute uniforms for pretty little rangers.' He winked and Anna managed not to spit in his open eye.

Silva got out of the truck. He had his shirt on this

time – a western cut with pearl buttons – but the tails were out, the cuffs not snapped, and the collar open. He looked just tumbled out of a woman's bed or ready to tumble into one.

''Morning Ranger Pigeon,' he said lazily as he looked Anna up and down. Again she wasn't flattered.

'That ever work for you?' she asked.

He didn't even play coy. 'More often than not. Is it going to work on you?' Silva removed his hard-hat and ran a hand through his shock of black hair. 'Or are rangers' sex drives too low?'

'IQs are too high,' Anna retorted.

Everybody laughed but Silva. Anna guessed she'd struck a nerve. A smile broke slowly on Tom's face but it never reached his eyes. She braced herself. She had the sinking feeling the repartee was about to take an ugly turn.

All he said was: 'Better watch it. I'm getting more and more eligible every day. By August I ought to be Bachelor of the Year. Ain't that right, Ted?'

Greeley didn't return Silva's smile.

'Got to hop it,' Silva said. 'The boss wants to leave early to get in a round of golf. Me, I can't play golf. I'm not over the hill yet.'

'Come on,' Greeley growled. 'I don't pay you to chase—'

Anna was sure he intended to say 'pussy' but he saved himself at the last second.

'—your tail,' he finished.

'See you around,' Silva said to Anna as he put his hard-hat back on.

'By the way, I never did find out anything about that truck that ran you off the road,' Anna told him.

'Was no truck,' Tom said as he turned away. 'I was just jerking your chain.'

He was wearing brown cowboy boots. But then so were Greeley and two of the others. So was Anna for that matter.

Drew finished fueling the truck and Stacy brought Bella to the gas shed. As he lifted her onto the high front seat their radios rasped to life.

'Seven-hundred, this is Beavens at Cliff Palace.'

As one, Drew, Anna and Stacy turned up the volume on their portables. The interpreters in the ruins seldom called in unless there was a problem.

'Lock-out,' Drew offered.

'Let's hope,' Stacy said.

'Shhh.'

'Cliff Palace this is seven-hundred. Go ahead,' Frieda's voice came over the air.

'We've got a little girl here having trouble breathing. She doesn't look too good.'

Anna and Stacy began to run for the patrol car. Anna flipped on the vehicle's lights and siren. 'Nothing like starting the day off right.'

'I do not like medicals,' Stacy said distinctly.

Anna laughed. 'Hey, it's something to do.'

The two-way road to Cliff was narrow and twisting with no shoulders. Despite lights and sirens, tourists plodded ahead, refusing to give right-of-way.

Trapped behind an RV, Anna and Stacy crawled along

at twenty-three miles an hour. Anna grabbed the public address mike and turned the volume up. 'Pull to the right, please. Pull to the right. Pull to the right, please.' She repeated the command until the RV's driver came out of his comatose state and began to slow, squeezing the over-sized vehicle to the side of the road.

'Damn. Just once I'd like to ride shotgun with a shotgun and permission to use it.'

Stacy said nothing. His eyes were fixed on the road as he hunched over the wheel. Above the dark line of beard, his cheek was pale. Tension pulled his shoulders almost to ear level.

Cliff Palace lot was full. They parked in a Handicapped space near where the trail started down to the ruin and Anna called in: 'Seven-hundred, three-one-two, we've arrived on scene.'

Having taken the red trauma pack and an oxygen bottle from the trunk, she led the way down the crowded trail using 'excuse me' the way a frustrated motorist uses the horn.

As soon as they climbed the eight-foot ladder that brought them within the cliff dwelling, they saw the knot of people surrounding the sick child.

On the periphery was Jamie Burke. The moment she noticed Anna and Stacy she marched toward them. They met half way through the alcove and the interpreter started in: 'It's not like you weren't warned for God's sake. Nobody listened. This time it's a child. Solstice—'

'Hold that thought, Jamie,' Anna cut her off. 'I'll get back with you this evening.' Dodging past the other woman she plowed through the tourists at a fast walk.

Mesa Verde's most famous cliff dwelling, Cliff Palace filled an alcove several hundred feet long. The dwelling itself was composed of two-hundred and seventeen rooms, twenty-one kivas and, at the far end a four-story tower, the inside room of which boasted intact plaster with discernible paintings. The entrance to the tower was reachable only by a ladder that led to a narrow path around yet another roofless kiva.

In this congested part of the ruin was a frail-looking child. She strained for air with the rounded chest of those suffering chronic pulmonary disorders. Dark hair fell forward over her face, and stick-thin arms and legs poked out from beneath an oversized T-shirt. The child was propped in a sitting position against a stone wall built seven centuries before she was born. A man – probably her father – sat on the wall, one leg on either side, supporting her. A hand-lettered sign reading 'PLEASE DO NOT SIT OR CLIMB ON THE WALLS' had tumbled to the path at the foot of the wooden ladder.

The girl braced her hands on her knees and leaned forward. Tendons in her neck pulled like ropes with the effort of breathing, yet only squeaks of air were pushed out.

Anna eased through the crowd and put down her gear. 'Hi, I'm Anna,' she introduced herself as she removed a nasal canula from the oxygen kit and fitted it to the cylinder. 'What's your name?' The girl hadn't enough breath to spare for an answer.

'Her name's Stephanie,' the man seated on the wall answered for her. 'Stephanie McFarland. She's got asthma.'

An ominous blue tint colored the skin around Stephanie's lips and in her fingernail beds.

'She was doing fine a bit ago, then she started feeling like she might throw up,' a thin-faced woman in her early thirties told Anna. 'She's been at altitude before and we've never had trouble like this. We're from Denver. It's nearly this high. Steph should be used to it. I'm her mom,' the woman finished in a whisper.

'Well, Stephanie, we're going to get you down to a doctor so you can breathe better, okay?' The girl nodded slightly, all her concentration taken by the effort of drawing and expelling air.

'Meyers, hand me the—' Anna broke off as she looked over at Stacy.

Clutching the red trauma bag to his chest as a frightened woman might clutch her baby, he stood at the edge of the circle of concentration onlookers. The blood had drained from his face and he was pale, Anna was afraid he was going to pass out.

'Meyers!' she said sharply.

The brown eyes turned towards her. They were clouded with fear – or shock.

'Hand me the bag. Then give Frieda a call and see if we can't get helitack down here with a litter. We're going to need the ambulance as well.'

For a moment it seemed as if he didn't understand, then his eyes focussed. Anna watched him for a few seconds more but he began making the calls. She turned down her radio so she could talk with Stephanie and her parents.

Seven minutes and Drew called on scene at Cliff

Palace parking. In that time Stephanie had begun to go down hill. By the time Drew arrived with the stokes, she had lost consciousness.

Keeping up a running commentary to calm the parents and Stephanie if she weren't beyond hearing, Anna had taken the IV kit from the trauma bag and prepped the child's thin arm. 'This is just to get some fluids in her, it may help to break up the congestion. And, too, if she needs medication at the hospital, they can just put it right in.'

She swabbed the skin with alcohol and readied a number sixteen needle. To Drew she said: 'We're not wasting time with this. One try; if I don't get in, we're out of here.'

'Do it,' Drew said.

'Damn,' Anna whispered. 'This kid has no veins.'

'What? Have you got it?' Drew asked.

'No. Load and go. Wait. I'm getting a flashback.'

'Too many drugs in college,' Drew muttered under his breath.

Anna noted the red of blood in the flashback chamber of the IV catheter with satisfaction. She was in. Carefully, she pulled the catheter off the needle, sliding it into the vein. 'Pop the tourniquet.' She taped the catheter in place. 'Go.'

Anna addressed herself to the little girl strapped into the evacuation litter. 'Stephanie we're carrying you out. You're in good hands.' Maybe the child's eyelids twitched in response. Maybe it was just the play of the sun.

Drew had taken his place at the head of the litter. Crouched down, elbows on thighs, he looked solid, like a rock. When he began to rise Anna was put in mind of the unfolding of the stony peak of Bald Mountain in Disney's 'Fantasia'.

Stacy knelt at the foot of the stokes. His lips were pressed in a thin line and his eyes focussed inward, unreadable.

'Ready?' Drew asked.

Meyers didn't respond. 'Stacy!' Drew raised his voice. Meyers looked up like a wounded beast. Slowly he began to lift. 'Atta boy,' said the helitacker.

The Stokes was of orange plastic hard enough to haul up inclines and drag over rough terrain. Encasing the fragile form of the child, it resembled a medieval instrument of torture rather than the secure embrace of modern emergency evacuation equipment, and Anna felt bad for the parents, already frightened half out of their wits.

Four ladders of juniper wood, polished to a dark gloss by the palms of countless tourists, led up twenty five feet through the crack in the cliff's face to the mesa.

Stephanie McFarland would not be roped up this incline but carried back out the entrance trail. The distance was greater but the ascent not so precipitous.

'Coming through,' Drew boomed. Curious onlookers parted reluctantly. Drew going first, the procession began to move down the path fronting the cliff dwellings. Tourists shifted, pressing back against stone walls. Bright-hued clothing, cameras, sunglasses, all combined to create a jarring kaleidoscope of color against the serene peach and buff of the ancient village.

Over the centuries roofs had fallen in, paint chipped

away and fiber mats rotted from the doorways; the clamour of life leached away until the structures had taken on the timeless purity of Greek statuary. But, like the ancient Greeks who had painted their pale marble figures vivid colors, the Anasazi had plastered the warm neutrality of their sandstone exteriors, then decorated them in red and black patterns.

Mesa Verde's Old Ones might have been as much at home with the cacophony of neon and spandex as the moderns.

The pathway clear, Drew picked up the pace. Holding the IV bag above shoulder-level, Anna walked beside the litter. Stephanie's chest movement was barely perceptible and the tissue-thin eyelids blue and delicately veined. Some of the pallor was probably natural but the faint bluish tinge at lips and fingernails was not.

Anna stroked back the dark hair. The child's skin was cool to the touch, clammy.

'Seven-hundred, three-one-four.'

'Seven-hundred,' Anna and Drew's radios bleated as dispatch responded. Anna turned hers down.

'The ambulance has arrived at Cliff Palace. We're at the entrance. Repeat: the entrance.'

'Seven-hundred copies. Did you get that, three-one-two?'

Anna pulled her radio from her duty belt. 'I got it. We'll be up in ten minutes or so. Two helitack are standing by at the stairs. There's a narrow spot there. Send somebody down from the overlook to clear the visitors out of it.'

'Ten-four. I'll send Claude Beavens. KFC seven-hundred, ten-twenty-two,' the dispatcher named one of the seasonal interpreters then, as always, signed off with the call number and the time.

Anna put her radio back on her belt and watched her footing as she trod the uneven pavement. Like all the park's ruins accessible to tourists, Cliff Palace had a paved path leading to it from the parking lot on the mesa top. When the ruins were first opened there'd been primitive trails that ladies in long dresses and picture hats had picked their way down, carefully placing each buttoned-up boot. In the 1930s the Civilian Conservation Corp had come in and earned their depression dollars with the back-breaking chore of carving staircases from native rock and shoring up trails with stone.

Beauty and grace had gone the way of cheap labor. Now the paths were a hodgepodge of asphalt and rock, patched and repatched.

The trail switched back several times then narrowed to hand-hewn steps leading into a crevice between two boulders. After more than half a century the workmanship of the CCC still held fine. Only the lips of the steps had been fortified with scabs of modern concrete.

The stairway, just wide enough to admit people single file, was choked with tourists who'd started down before Claude Beavens had been sent to stop traffic from the mesa top.

'Gonna have to ask you folks to go on back up,' Drew called over the low-grade chatter. The hips of the better endowed scraped a patter of sand from the soft rock as they shifted in the confining space. Faces displayed the sheep-like vacancy of vacationers who've come upon the unexpected.

'Ask the guy behind you to turn around,' the helitack

foreman suggested patiently. He spoke over his shoulder, his thick arms showing no strain at holding Stephanie's little weight.

Attuned to the vital signs of her patient, Anna caught a faint sigh. She laid the palm of her hand on the girl's diaphragm. Through the knit tee shirt, she could feel the bones of the rib cage but not the gentle rise of lungs filling with air.

'What?' Drew pressed.

Anna shook her head, waited. With a sucking sound, like the hiss of a new kitten, the child drew a sudden breath.

'Thanks,' Anna said to no one in particular. To Drew she said: 'We're in a hurry.' Edging past him, she stood at the foot of the stairs.

'Got to move you out. This girl needs medical attention. Up you go. Thanks. Thanks.' Anna spoke pleasantly, but she was prodding rounded backs and pudgy shoulders, herding people up the stairway.

As they began retreating, she turned back to Drew. His head was sunk between his massive shoulders. The little braided pig-tail he affected poked out incongruously as he stared down into the litter.

Adrenaline spurted into Anna's system. 'What? What've you got?'

'Breathing, but way too slow. Assholes,' Anna heard him mutter. 'Bringing a sick little kid way out here.'

Paul Summers, looking as close to a *GQ* model as anyone could in the ill-fitting Nomex, thrust his head over the rock above Anna's head.

'You gonna need ropes?'

'Drew?' Anna passed the question to the helitack foreman. He and his crew were trained in high-angle rescue.

Drew shook his head. 'It'd take too long. Here, Anna, you hold the front.' Stacy's arms had grown slack, his end of the litter close to slipping from his grasp. 'Stacy, pay attention,' Drew snapped as he handed Anna the litter and eased butt-first under the loaded stokes. 'Put the weight on my back.'

Taking the head of the litter, Anna looked down at her patient. Even with the oxygen canister, lashed for security between her knees, turned to fifteen liters per minute on a non-rebreather face mask, the blue tinge around Stephanie's mouth remained.

Crouched down, Drew was in place underneath the stokes. He straightened up and, like a row boat on the crest of a wave, the litter with its fragile burden was lifted into the air.

Anna's arms were fully extended when he stopped. 'Let's do it,' she said.

One step at a time, she backed up the stairs. The orange plastic scraped along the sandstone but, balanced on Drew's back, the Stokes was high enough to clear the narrowest part of the crevice. 'Keep coming,' Anna said. 'We'll make it but just barely.'

'Barely's good enough,' Drew grunted through a kinked esophagus.

Tossed as if on stormy seas, the orange litter wobbled through the crack in the rock. The *GQ* helitacker peered anxiously down, his blond head bobbing in sympathy as he worked his way along the top of the boulders they crept through.

Arms at full reach, Anna was out of eye contact with Stephanie McFarland. As the seconds ticked by, she could feel her anxiety rising.

'Paul,' she called up to the blond. 'What's she look like?'

'Not good.'

'Breathing?'

'Can't tell.'

'Get the bag valve.' Anna kept her voice calm both for her patient and for the audience of tourists she could hear Claude Beavens organizing twenty feet up the trail behind her.

At last Drew's head and shoulders emerged from between the walls of stone. Humped over, he carried the litter onto the landing at the foot of a long metal staircase leading up to a viewing platform cut from the mesa top.

Over her shoulder Anna glimpsed a gauntlet of visitors yet to be run. Instead of stopping them on the spacious platform, the interpreter had arranged them all on one side of the stairs where they stood like a Busby Berkeley musical kick line waiting to go into their eleven o'clock number.

Beavens, all bony elbows and wrists, with a neck so long and skinny his flat brimmed hat took on the aspect of a plate balanced on a broom handle, was waving his arms like an officious dance master. 'People, people,' he shouted. 'Give them room. Emergency evac. Give us rangers room.'

'Down,' Drew said. Slowly he knelt, Anna and Stacy keeping the litter stable.

Watching the big man kneel like a well-trained ele-
phant, Anna could hear her grandmother's divorce-shar-
pened voice: 'Men have their place, I suppose. They can
lift heavy objects.'

Stephanie McFarland came into view. Her face was
gray and her hypoxia had grown more pronounced.
Again Anna laid a hand on the child's diaphragm. Drew
and Stacy repositioned themselves around the stokes.

'Ten,' Anna announced, timing the child's respirations.
'Let's bag her. Paul!'

There was a scuffling sound as the blond slid down
the sandstone to land lightly on his feet a yard from the
stokes. 'Okay!' he called back up the face of the boulder.
An unseen person pushed a green airway kit over the
edge and it fell neatly into his waiting hands. Within
seconds he had the Ambu bag – a soft plastic barrel
about the size of a football with a face mask on one end
and a length of plastic tubing trailing from the other –
out of the satchel. With an economy of movement that
in one so young and so pretty always took Anna by
surprise, he hooked the length of tubing to the green
oxygen cylinder then handed Anna the bag so she could
fit the mask over Stephanie's mouth and nose.

'Take the IV, Paul. Ventilating her at twenty-five
breaths a minute,' she informed them as she began pumping air into the child. 'Go.'

Keeping in step with Anna as best they could, they
carried the stokes up the metal stairs. Drew had taken
the foot and used his height to keep the litter level.

'In and out and in and out and,' Anna chanted under
her breath, keeping time as she forced oxygen into the

failing lungs. Behind her she could feel the gentle battering of camera cases and shoulder bags as she pushed past the line of people along the stair rail. Occasionally she felt something softer than steel mesh beneath her boots and heard a squawk of pain but she was only dimly aware of these things. Her eyes and mind were fixed on the now deep and regular rise of the little girl's chest.

'Looking good,' Drew was saying. 'She's pinking up.'

Anna glanced at Stephanie's face. The deathlike pallor had abated somewhat. 'Paul,' she said quietly. 'Radio for a patrol car escort. We'll be running hot. I want the road clear.'

The firefighter keyed his mike with one hand, keeping the IV drip high with the other, he began a series of radio calls.

The stairs were behind them. 'Clear sailing,' Drew said cheerfully.

Anna secured the stokes to the gurney with webbed belting. Stacy'd gone catatonic and without his help, she banged it ungracefully into the back of the waiting ambulance. Not for the first time, she cursed the antiquated equipment a poverty-stricken Park Service was forced to make do with year after year.

Anna and Stacy rode down in the ambulance. Paul Summers drove, Mrs McFarland rode in the passenger seat. Anna changed Stephanie to humidified oxygen and rechecked the girl's vital signs. Strapped into the seat near the gurney's head, Stacy held the run sheet on his lap, but it didn't look as if he was writing the numbers as she called them out. He'd not said a word since he'd completed his radio requests half an hour before.

Anna patted the little girl's arm. 'You're doing real good, Steph. Hang in there.' The child had not regained consciousness and Anna had no way of knowing if she heard. To Stacy she said: 'Are you okay?'

Stacy just shook his head.

Two emergency room nurses met them in the ambulance bay at Southwest Memorial. Stacy stayed in the ambulance while Anna replaced the inventory they'd used on the run from the hospital's stock room. She then took a couple of minutes to talk with Bill McFarland. Stephanie had had a severe attack once before. Ridiculous as it was, the information comforted Anna, as if the park had been somehow exonerated.

Anna drove the ambulance on the return trip. Paul Summers threw himself on the cot. 'These carry-outs are getting to be a bore,' he complained. 'How many now? One last Tuesday, one the week before that.'

'Maybe it's a conspiracy,' Anna returned. 'Hills gets a healthy chunk of the five-hundred dollars paid for each run for his budget.'

'Hills'd do it, too,' Paul said with a laugh. 'Mr Tightwad. How about you, Stacy, are you getting a cut?'

Stacy's silence remained unbroken. Paul abandoned light conversation with a 'G'night.'

Meyers had panicked, frozen. Anna wasn't so much angry with him as sympathetic. Everybody had a panic button. Heroes just managed to stumble through life without it being pushed. Two hundred feet beneath the icy waters of Lake Superior Anna had met up with her own cowardice.

But she could avoid deep cold water. If Stacy wanted to be a ranger he'd have to get used to handling sick and injured people. In most national parks the only doctors available were there on vacation.

Writing the report on the McFarland medical fell to Anna. In the crowded back of the CRO, where three desks were huddled into a space where only one should have been, she sat in front of an old IBM electric and stared down at the 10–343 threaded around the platen. The form was five thicknesses. Hitting a wrong key meant white-out in quintuplicate.

Putting off the inevitable, she turned to the District Ranger. Hills Dutton was a large square-faced man with thinning sandy hair that curled at his collar. From somewhere in the mare's nest that was his desk top, he'd retrieved a pair of calipers. Shirt-tail in hand, he was measuring the thickness of the excess flesh on his belly.

'Hills, what did you think of the medical today?'

'Nine percent body fat,' he announced with satisfaction and carefully wrote in the numbers on a physical training graph he'd colored with felt-tipped pens. 'Bet you can't top that, Anna. You're a woman more or less, right? Maybe eighteen percent? Women can be up to twenty-eight percent before they're considered fat. Men pork out at seventeen. You got it easy.'

Unzipping his pants, he tucked the shirt in and gave his flat belly an affectionate pat before putting his gun-belt back on. 'Not bad for an old man.'

'Seems like there've been an awful lot of carry-outs at Cliff this summer,' Anna persisted. 'What's usual for June?'

'It happens,' Hills admitted vaguely. 'Lots of senior citizens up here.'

'Today we carried out a third grader.'

'Asthma.' Hills fished a tool catalogue off the top of the pile.

Anna gave up and went back to staring at the 10–343, trying to screw her courage to the sticking place and make that first typo.

'Frieda,' Hills called over the partition to the front desk. 'Call maintenance and see if they've got any old ratchet sets they can spare. I've got to get some for the vehicles.'

'Your credit's no good with maintenance,' Frieda returned. 'So tight he squeaks,' she muttered.

'I heard that,' Hills said. 'Maybe I'll order some. Got any DI-1s?' He named the purchase order form.

'Sure you will,' came the murmur. Then: 'All out.' There was no forthcoming offer to run over to Administration and get them. Frieda's territory as the Chief Ranger's secretary and dispatcher was carefully defined. It didn't include running errands for the lesser rangers.

'I'll get them,' Anna offered, glad of an excuse to postpone writing the report a bit longer. 'I need to talk to Patsy anyway.'

She poked along the twenty feet of path between the buildings, stopping to watch a tarantula make its majestic way across the asphalt. After the tarantulas she'd met in the backcountry of Guadalupe Mountains National Park in Texas, these northern creatures were decidedly non-threatening. Beside their teacup-sized Trans Pecos cousins they seemed almost cute. Still Anna didn't get too close. No one had yet dispelled to her satisfaction the myth that they could jump long distances.

'Don't you just love them?'

Anna looked up from her bug to find Al Stinson, hands on knees, studying the tarantula with a look akin to true love. Off duty, Stinson dressed in classic archaeologist style: Khaki shorts and white oxford shirt. Gray hair poked out around her lined face. Chapped knuckles and clipped nails made her hands as ageless and practical looking as any working man's. 'Just beautiful,' Stinson said of the spider.

'Maybe to a lady tarantula,' Anna hedged.

'This is a female. Lookie.' The interpreter reached down and touched the creature gently on one of its legs. 'See? No hair. I don't know about European girls, but ours don't have leg hair. Only the males.'

'You're kidding.'

'No,' Stinson laid her hand flat on the asphalt and the tarantula tested it gingerly with a hairless foreleg. Something was evidently amiss. The creature backed away and took another route.

'Too bad,' Stinson said. She straightened and rested her hands on prominent pelvic bones. 'It feels neat when they walk on you. Little elfin feet.'

'It'd take four elves to make that many tracks,' Anna returned, not envying Al the experience.

Stinson sniffed the air with a round slightly squashed nose. 'God! I love it.'

Politely, Anna sniffed too. Mixed with the smell of bus exhaust and hot tar was a delicate perfume, warmed off the tiny yellow blooms of a bush near the walk. 'The bitterbrush?'

'I was breathing in the silence. No roaring bone grinder. We may get Greeley shut down yet.' She laughed, a nasal but infectious whinny. 'The Boys will not be pleased.'

Anna realised the interpreter was gloating in her own straightforward way over the pending stoppage of the pipeline. 'Anything been turned up in the dig?' she asked.

'Not much. A fire ring. Some shards – but the whole mesa is covered with pot shards. Some bones were uncovered. May mean a burial. Wouldn't that be great?'

One of the many mysteries of Mesa Verde was that so few Anasazi burial sites were found. Some remains had been uncovered in sealed and abandoned rooms in the dwellings and some in midden heaps below the cliff dwellings, but no burial ground had been discovered and surprisingly few individual sites for a society of near ten thousand souls that had flourished for over five centuries.

Talk of the pipeline put Anna in mind of her housemate. 'Al, Jamie was on duty in Cliff Palace when we had that medical this morning. Lately she's been dropping heavy handed hints that something's going down on the solstice. Is there anything I ought to know?'

Stinson threw back her head like Barbara Stanwyk in 'Maverick Queen' and snorted a laugh. 'The less law enforcement knows, the better I sleep nights.'

Anna laughed with her, partly at the sentiment and partly at a mental image of Al Stinson as Queen of the Cattle Thieves. Amid the merriment she found herself wondering if the maverick queen could swing a chain as well as a lariat.

'If you hear anything that sounds like it could get somebody hurt or fired, let me know and I'll see if I can't fulfill my role as Professional Party Pooper.'

'Better you than The Boys.'

By the time Anna wandered into Administration it was after four p.m. and people were stirring to leave for the day. The receptionist's desk was tidied and, engrossed in a phone conversation, she barely gave Anna a nod.

Anna fetched the procurement forms from the storage room in the basement. On her way back she stopped in the doorway of Patsy Silva's office.

The superintendent's secretary kept her office in a state of impressive order. Plants in macrame hangers, pictures, and a stained-glass image of Kokopelli, the flute player, in the window kept the orderliness from being oppressive.

'Hills could use your decorating service,' Anna said as she leaned against the door frame.

'Hills could use a bulldozer,' Patsy replied with a smile.

'How's it going? I didn't get a list of times and places for paternal visits so I just assumed you and Tom worked it out.'

Patsy turned away briefly, fussed with some papers. Anna tried to read the expression on her face but it was too fleeting.

'We're doing okay,' Patsy said.

'Any more gifts of the weird persuasion?'

'Only this.' Patsy produced an extra bright smile as she held up her left wrist for inspection.

Anna whistled long and low. The watch Patsy wore was – or looked to be – fourteen carat gold with at least a carat's worth of diamonds sparkling around the face.

Even with the union doing its fiscal magic, the watch must have cost Silva a month's wages.

'Tom?'

Patsy nodded and Anna caught the expression again. This time she pegged it: embarrassment. Evidently it wasn't all gifts Patsy took offense to. Only cheap ones.

'Good for you.' Anna glanced at her own Wal-Mart special. She'd managed to kill enough time. In six minutes she was off duty. The 10–343 had been effectively avoided for one day.

She called Stacy on the radio and he brought the patrol car to give her a lift to Far View. He still wore a haunted look and drove through the empty parking lot with the same hunched intensity as when weaving down a narrow road with lights and siren blazing.

'What happened to Bella?' Anna asked to make conversation.

'What do you mean?' Alarmed, Stacy lost his inward look. 'Did something happen to Bella?'

'Drew was on the carry-out. Wasn't he babysitting today? I just wondered where he'd stashed her.'

Visibly, he relaxed. 'Bella stayed at the fire dorm watching cartoons with Jimmy. He called in sick. That's all I need for Bella to catch a dose of something.'

'Don't worry. Unless she comes down with a case of Coors, Bella won't get what Jimmy's got.'

They rode without speaking till Stacy turned off Chapin Mesa Road toward the Far View dormitories. There was something familiar in the drawn face, the tight voice. Putting it together with the medical, Anna realized where she'd seen it before. He carried himself like a man in pain.

'Take off your gun and I'll buy you a beer,' she offered on impulse.

For a moment she was sure he was going to turn her down. 'I'll get you home before six,' she added remembering Bella and Drew's baby-sitting schedule.

'A beer would taste good tonight.'

The lounge at the Far View Lodge was on the second floor and boasted an open-air veranda to the east side. The view, though somewhat curtailed by an expanse of tarred roof studded with air-conditioning ducts, justified the name of Far View. Mesas receded into mists that melded seamlessly into mountain ranges. In the afternoon light, strong at midsummer, the muted blues and grays were given an iridescence that at some times made the mesas appear as unreal as an artist's conception, and, at others, the only reality worth living.

When Anna arrived Stacy was not there. She took a table that backed on a low adobe wall. The plaster radiated heat collected during the day and deflected a cold wind that had sprung up.

Anna's nerves jangled. She couldn't shake an unwelcome First Date feeling. Possibly because she'd taken the time to comb her hair out of its braids and dab perfume between her breasts. A Carta Blanca took the edge off. By the time she was halfway down it, Stacy arrived.

The edge came back.

He looked as awkward as she felt and, wordlessly, she cursed herself for moving their relationship out of the secure arena of work.

Stacy ordered Moosehead and folded himself into one of the wire garden chairs.

'I hardly recognised you with your clothes on,' Anna said.

'Ah. Out of uniform.'

'You clean up nice.'

'Thanks.'

Small talk died. Anna sipped her beer and resisted the urge to glance at her watch. The 'date' had been ill advised. 'I thought the medical went well this morning,' she said to get the conversation into neutral territory.

'God.' Stacy shook his head. Pain was clear in his eyes.

Anna forgot her discomfort. Leaning across the table, she took hold of his arm.

A familiar laugh brought her head up. Ted Greeley had taken a table across the veranda. As he caught her eye, he raised his highball in a salute. Anna smiled automatically then returned to Stacy. 'What is getting to you?'

'Stephanie McFarland died. I called the E.R. before I came.'

Anna felt as if he'd slapped her. 'That's not right,' she said. 'Stephanie was just a kid with asthma. They got the name wrong.'

Stacy shook his head. 'The name wasn't wrong. She died.'

'Fuck.' Anna took a long pull on the beer. It didn't help. 'Third grade. What the hell happened? She didn't have to die.'

'Yes she did.'

Stacy sounded sure of himself, like a man quoting scripture or baseball scores.

'Why?' Anna demanded.

'Figure it out,' Stacy snapped. 'You saw me. I couldn't do a thing, not one damn thing.'

Anna looked at him for a long moment. Self pity in the face of the child's death struck her as blind arrogance. 'Give it a rest. We did what we did. You were useless, not deadly. Don't make yourself so important.'

Stacy stared at his hands. Clearly this was a cross he was determined to bear. Maybe he was Catholic.

'I'm sorry.'

'Yeah. Me too. Sorrier than you know.'

Stacy made circles on the glass table-top with the beer bottle.

Anna finished her beer and ordered another.

'Bella can get bone grafts in her legs,' he said as if this were part of an ongoing conversation instead of a non-sequitur. 'She could dance, fall in love, marry, save the world – whatever she wanted.'

'Does Bella want the operations?' Anna asked, remembering Drew's sour appraisal of the treatment.

'She's scared. But Rose wants them for her. Rose was so beautiful. She once—'

Anna nodded.

'I've probably told you. But she was and it meant a lot to her and she wants that for Bella.'

'What do you want for Bella?'

'I want her to have a chance at the brass ring, whatever that means.' Stacy took a long drink of his beer and let his eyes wander over the panorama that was northern New Mexico. 'It's not cheap.'

Anna's eyes followed his over the soft blue distance. The beers were taking effect. The tension between them was lessening. Words were no longer as necessary.

'Rose's used to better,' Stacy said after a while.

'So you've said. Old Number One was rich?'

'A lawyer. Megabucks.'

'The vultures always eat better than anyone else on the food chain,' Anna said. Meyers barely smiled.

'Rose left him. She says she had a problem with commitment.' Stacy made it sound like a compliment.

Remembering Bella's remark about her dad leaving because of her deformity, Anna said nothing.

Stacy folded his hands around his Moosehead in a prayerful attitude and looked across the table at her. She smiled and he smiled back. Something sparked, ignited the rushes of emotion the medical had left strewn about their psyches. Nature's narcotic: more addicting than crack, harder to find than unadulterated Columbian and, in the long run, more expensive than cocaine. But, God! did it get you there. Anna's breath gusted out at sudden, unbidden memories of love.

'I've got to go.' She stood so abruptly her chair overturned.

'Yes.' Both of them pulled out wallets and tossed bills on the table. The waiter would get one hell of a tip, Anna thought as she walked out of the lounge.

'Can I give you a ride?' Stacy called after her. Anna just waved.

Unwilling to return to the cacophony that was home, she walked down the Wetherill Mesa Road till she was out of sight of the lodge then sat under the protective drapery of a service berry bush. She felt like crying but was too long out of practice.

Chapter Six

Anna groped her way to the kitchen to start her morning coffee. Clad in striped men's pajamas, Jennifer sat at the dining room table eating cereal. Already in uniform, Jamie played with an unlit cigarette.

She held it up as Anna passed. 'Trying to decide whether or not to have breakfast,' she volunteered.

'Better light up,' Jennifer said. 'It's going to be a long day.'

'The longest.' Jamie pulled herself out of the straight backed chair and took her morning drugs out onto the rear deck.

'Long day,' Jennifer repeated.

Since it was obviously expected of her, and early in the morning, Anna actually found Jennifer's refined version of the southern drawl soothing, she asked, 'Why long?'

'Longest day of the year. June twenty-first.'

'Right: solstice. If something doesn't happen, I'm going to be miffed.' Anna spooned coffee into the drip filter.

'Oh, nothin' will. You know Jamie. There's always got to be something. A bunch of the interps got a

101

backcountry permit to go down into Balcony House to watch the moon rise. That's about it.'

'I'd think they'd want to watch the sun rise.' Coffee was dripping through the filter but too slowly. Balancing the cone to one side, Anna managed to pour what was in the pot into her cup without making too much mess. 'That's when all the magic is supposed to happen: spears of light through scientifically placed chinks – that sort of thing.'

Leaning in the doorway, she sipped and watched Jennifer eating cereal.

She and Jennifer had such disparate schedules they seldom had the opportunity to work together. But bit by bit Anna was getting glimpses that this hair-sprayed and lipsticked magnolia blossom had a penchant for heavy drinking, late nights, and speaking up for herself. Anna found herself warming up to the woman.

'Jamie mentioned something about Old Ones and solstice again last week when we were carrying Stephanie McFarland out of Cliff Palace.' Anna threw out the line, not sure what she was fishing for.

'Who knows what Jamie's up to,' Jennifer said impatiently. 'She says she hears indian flute music coming out of the ruins at night; she's always seeing some big thing – ghosts and mountain lions and big horned sheep and cute boys. I never see anything except illegally parked cars.'

Jennifer sounded so disgusted that Anna laughed. 'What about Paul Summers? He's as cute as they come.'

'He's got a girlfriend back home.'

'Back home is back home. Going to let it get in your way?'

'No, but it's sure gettin' in his. I just hate fidelity.'

'Jimmy Russell?'

'He's ten years younger than I am.' Jennifer pronounced 'ten' as 'tin'. She shrugged philosophically. 'If things don't start looking up soon, I'm going to have to start poachin'.'

Anna's coffee was done. She walked back into the kitchen.

'Stacy's kinda cute,' Jennifer mused.

Anna didn't want to get into that.

Running late, she called into service from the shower. At quarter after seven, hair confined in a braid and her teeth brushed, she pulled out of the Far View lot.

Hills was in Durango attending a wildland fire seminar so Anna had the small four-wheel-drive truck. It was newer than the patrol car and had been built by Mitsubishi. Anna attributed the commercial success of Japanese cars to the fact that they were designed and built by a small people, hence they tended to fit American women far better than the wide open spaces Buick and Dodge incorporated into their vehicles. At any rate, the seat didn't hurt her back.

Late June marked the peak of the tourist season and there were cars waiting at the locked gates to Far View Ruin and Cedar Tree Tower. The Four-Way intersection was backed up four cars deep. Anna liked to play hero with the simple act of letting folks go where they wanted to. This morning the kindly ranger routine was turned into a comic interlude while she wrestled with one of Stacy's signature twisted chain locks. Eventually she succeeded and was embarrassed by a round of applause.

Leaving the Four-Way, she drove slowly around the museum loop, stopping to check the picnic grounds for illegal campers. It was blessedly empty and she was spared the unsavory task of rousting out people in their nightgowns.

As she was passing the Administration Building, Patsy Silva flagged her down. The clerical staff wasn't required to wear uniform and Patsy was in a flame-orange blouse and close-fitting gray trousers. Her lipstick echoed the color of her top.

Though immaculately dressed and every hair characteristically in place, Patsy looked somehow disheveled, as if she'd had a bad night or bad news.

'What's up?' Anna asked as she rolled down the pick-up's window.

'Can you believe it, I lost my keys!' Patsy smiled apologetically. 'Would you radio one of the maintenance guys to let me in?'

Anna made the call.

Patsy didn't look relieved. 'Are you all right?' Anna asked.

'I need to talk to you.'

A slight gray-haired man with a dowager's hump came from the direction of the museum. When he saw them, he jangled a ring of keys.

'The superintendent's having a breakfast meeting. I've got to set it up. Can you come over to the house around twelve?' Patsy pleaded.

'Will do.'

Patsy clicked on her smile and started thanking the janitor before she'd closed the distance between them.

Anna managed to kill twenty minutes cruising the ruins road. Cliff Palace was about half way around a six-mile loop. Just before the parking lot the two-lane road became one-way. Beyond the ruin a mile or so, at Soda Point, it crossed onto the Ute Indian Reservation. When the road had first been designed it had been incorrectly surveyed and a quarter-mile stretch crossed the park's boundary onto the reservation. A dirt track, never used anymore, ran for several miles into the pinion/juniper forest owned by the Utes. Brush had been piled across it to deter wandering visitors. A plan to barricade it had been in the works for years but nothing had ever been done.

Where the dirt road started into the woods, on a wide graveled turnout, was a curio shop and a trailer selling Navajo tacos and snowcones. Short of rerouting the existing road, Mesa Verde's superintendent had little recourse but to accept this unauthorized invasion of commercialism. Authorized park concessionaries had jacked food prices so high the little stand did a booming business, especially among the rangers.

Past Soda Point, back on park lands, the one-way road widened to a parking lot at the Balcony House ruin. A mile or so further on, the loop completed, traffic rejoined the two-lane road.

On Isle Royale Anna had patrolled in a boat, in Guadalupe Mountains on horseback. Both were preferable to the automobile. Anna wondered what it was that was so alienating about cars. Somehow, more than any other machine, they seemed to create a world of their own, a mobile pack-rat midden full of personal artifacts that utterly separated man from the natural environment he hurtled through. Maybe, she thought as she crept along in the line of cars trolling for parking spaces at Balcony House, that was why Americans were so enamored of them: power without connection, movement without real direction.

At nine, she returned to Far View, picked up Jennifer and took her to maintenance where the patrol car was parked. As the seasonal dragged her briefcase from behind the seat, she volunteered to pick up Stacy when he came on duty. Anna remembered the poaching threat but forbore comment. If the Catholics were right and the thought was as bad as the deed, she was in no position to cast any stones.

With two rangers on duty and nothing happening, Anna felt lazy. She parked the truck and wandered over to the fire cache to find someone to amuse her. Helitack was gone. Physical training, she recalled. Every morning for P.T. Drew ran his firefighters two miles down the Spruce Canyon trail, then back up the steep pathway to the mesa top.

As she turned to leave, a clattering arrested her attention. Moments later a child's bicycle with pink training wheels came into view around the corner of the cache. It wasn't one of the modern plastic monstrosities, but a classic, old-fashioned, metal bicycle. Extensions had been welded onto the pedals so Bella Meyers could ride.

She rolled to a stop in the shade beside Anna. 'Drew's

not here, Mrs Pigeon. He's supposed to be back by nine but he's always late. He says it takes him longer to shower because there's so much of him. I'm always early.'

'That's good to know. Does your dad know you're here?' Anna was thinking of Stacy's concern about traffic the only other time she'd seen Bella in Maintenance.

'Stacy'd already gone to work. Me and Momma only got back from Albaturkey this morning.'

Stacy didn't come on duty till later and it crossed Anna's mind that the child was lying. But Bella didn't seem the type. Life, for her, had to be full of personal triumphs and grown-up dramas. She had no need to fabricate.

'I thought Stacy was on project shift,' Anna probed gently. Project days were scheduled from nine-thirty till six.

'Sometimes he goes early. He likes to go off by himself and look at birds and things. Sometimes he takes me. I like being by myself with Stacy.'

Anna leaned back against a workbench set up outside the cache.

'That's where they clean their chainsaws,' Bella warned. 'You'll get grease on your behind.'

'Too late now.'

'Glad I'm not your mom.'

'Doesn't your mom approve of greasy behinds?'

'Hates 'em,' Bella returned. 'You know why Stacy always looks so good?'

Anna shook her head.

'Momma dresses him. Stacy'd just put on whatever was laying closest on the floor. Never iron it or anything.

When we got him he was a mess.'

Anna smiled. 'Like a stray dog brought home from the pound?'

'Not that bad,' Bella answered seriously. 'He didn't have fleas or anything. But he was pretty scruffy.'

Anna glanced at her watch more out of habit than anything. There was no place she had to be, nothing she had to do. In parks with backcountry her days had been spent walking, looking for people in – or causing – trouble. In the automobile-oriented front country of Mesa Verde the days were spent waiting for dispatch to send her on an emergency or visitor assist.

'You're too old to have anyone dress you,' Bella said, giving Anna a frank appraisal. 'You do pretty good.'

'Not as good as your mom?'

'No,' the child answered honestly. 'Mom's going to buy her and me all new stuff when she gets thin again and I get my legs fixed.'

Bella seemed disinterested and Anna suspected the new clothes promised a greater delight to Mrs Meyer than to her daughter.

'I got to go,' Bella announced. 'Drew comes walking over now.' Having carefully looked both ways, she rode across the maintenance yard toward the asphalt path that wound down to the housing loop several hundred yards away and invisible behind a fragrant curtain of evergreens.

No one left to play with, Anna decided to head for the Chief Rangers Office to fill out a few forms and pester Frieda. As she crossed the tarmac to where she'd parked, Greeley's six-pac rolled in. The contractor wasn't in evidence and a man she recognized but had never met was driving. Tom Silva rode shotgun. The pick-up pulled in close to her truck. Since there wasn't room for both vehicle doors to open at once, Anna waited while they got out.

Silva was completely dressed; everything buttoned, belted and tucked in. ''Morning,' he said as he slammed the door. He didn't meet her eye and, for once, there was nothing bantering in the way he spoke.

'Good morning, Tom. Have you gotten any closer to Bachelor of the Year?'

His head jerked up as if she poked him with a cattle prod. There was something different about his face as well as his demeanor. He struck Anna as older, less alive.

'I was just messing around,' he said sullenly. 'I didn't mean anything by that. 'Scuse me.' He pushed by her and disappeared into the shop where the soda-pop machine was housed.

Anna speculated as to whether this new subdued Tom had anything to do with Patsy's lunch invitation. The day was definitely getting more interesting.

Anna reached the tower house before Patsy and sat in the sun on a stone wall by the front door fantasizing about how she'd arrange the furniture if she inherited the house. She'd just gotten around to hanging curtains when Patsy hurried up the walk.

'Sorry I'm late,' she panted. 'You could have let your-self in!'

'I've only been here a minute,' Anna assured her. 'I was early.'

'You didn't have to sit out here all that time.'

Anna gave up and let herself be apologized to.

Patsy bustled around the kitchen making bologna sandwiches and small talk. Anna kept up her end of the conversation. Perhaps they were to follow formal rules of dining: no business discussed until brandy and cigars were served.

After every condiment and chip had been taken out of cupboards and put on the table, Patsy sat down. Anna noticed she no longer wore the expensive wrist watch. A Timex with Pluto's face on the dial had taken its place.

Anna bit into her sandwich. Patsy pushed her untouched plate away as if she'd already eaten. 'It's about Tom,' she said.

Anna nodded encouragement.

'He's been so full of himself lately. He was bragging and giving the girls school money. You saw the watch he gave me. I guess he thought he'd bought his way back in. When I said no, he got sore.'

Anna waited but Patsy showed no inclination to finish the story unprompted. 'What happened to the watch?' she asked to get the wheels turning again.

'I threw it in his face. He made a lot of noise about the money having nothing to do with anything, but I noticed he took it with him when he left.'

Anna washed the sandwich down with Diet Pepsi. 'I saw Tom this morning. He didn't seem like his old self.'

'He's not.' Patsy picked up a potato chip and began breaking it into small pieces. 'Or else he's so much more like his old self it's scary. He gave me a gun.'

'Did he say what the gun was for?'

Patsy shook her head. 'I didn't see him. He left it sometime last night. A couple of times I woke up thinking I heard something – the girls are in Gunnison with their grandma. When I'm alone I don't sleep well. I hear things – you know: branches scraping and the wind. I scare myself silly thinking its an escaped murderer or a crazy person.'

'With a hook instead of a hand?'

Patsy laughed. 'You know him?'

'I first heard of him at a pajama party at Mercy High School. When I moved to Manhattan I swear he had a sublet under my bed.'

'Campfire Girls,' Patsy explained her arcane knowledge.

'Anyway . . .' Anna brought the subject back to Tom and his gun.

'Anyway last night I woke up a couple of times but I never came downstairs. I scare myself more if I start peeking in closets and under beds. For once it wasn't all my imagination. This morning there was a gun in the middle of the kitchen table.'

Patsy got up and opened the cupboard door. Bundled onto a high shelf was a blue apron with white eyelet ruffling. She took it down and unwrapped the apron from around the gun.

'It's a derringer,' Anna told her. 'A .22.' The flashy little gun seemed in keeping with Tom Silva. 'Do you know for sure it was Tom who left it?'

'I recognize it. He won it in a stock-car race. And there was a note.'

Somehow Anna wasn't surprised.

Patsy had tucked the note in the pocket of the apron. She unfolded it and handed it to Anna.

' "Pats, see how easy it is to get into this place? Get yourself new locks",' Anna read aloud. 'Definitely edgy.'

'I thought so.'

'I'll look into it,' Anna promised. 'Meanwhile I'd do what he suggests: get new locks. Give maintenance a call, okay?'

Patsy said she would. As Anna was leaving, she stopped her. 'Do you want to take the gun?'

Anna thought about it for a moment, thought of Tom, of the girls. 'Do you know how to use it?' she asked. Patsy nodded. 'Then why don't you keep it for a while.'

Anna went off duty at three-thirty. Ninety minutes before tradition allowed cocktails. She peeled off her uniform and, sitting on her bed, opened the top drawer of the dresser. Expensive lace underwear, a legacy of more intimate times, mingled with cordovan-colored uniform socks, hollow point bullets and half a dozen ragged handkerchiefs.

In the back, lying on its side, was a metal container. With its fitted lid and wire handle, it was much like a paint can sans label.

Jamie Burke professed singular discomfort living in a house tainted by the presence of a firearm. Anna wondered what the interpreter would think if she knew that the remains of Anna's husband rested amid her underwear.

'You were always happiest when you were in my pants, Zach.' Anna smiled as she closed the drawer.

The clock on the dresser read three-forty-seven.

The hell with tradition. Anna went into the kitchen to pour herself a drink. Glass in hand, she wandered out onto the rear deck. Four miles away, on Chapin, it was warm enough for shorts. At Far View, a thousand feet higher, Anna was slightly chilled in long pants and a sweatshirt.

The service berry bushes were in full bloom and the valley between Far View and Wetherill Mesa looked as if it had been decorated for a wedding. Glittering emerald green hummingbirds with ruby-colored throats were busy at the blossoms. Mating, showing off, or just celebrating the day, they flew up thirty or forty feet then dove down in a buzz of wings.

Leaning against the wall of the dormitory, Anna let her legs rest on the sun-warmed planking and closed her eyes.

Tom Silva wasn't the only one who wasn't acting like his old self. Till she'd left Michigan for the southwest, Anna hadn't realized how big a part of her life Christina and Alison had become. The gentle, clear-thinking woman and her spirited daughter had kept her on an even keel. Kept her looking ahead instead of back.

Banging of the kitchen door announced the end of solitude. Jennifer was off shift. Anna took a long drink and held it in her mouth savoring the rich bite of the alcohol and trying to shut out the muffled thumps from within as the seasonal law enforcement ranger noisily divested herself of briefcase and gun belt.

Moments later the sanctity of the rear deck was invaded. Wearing a T-shirt and faded jeans, Jennifer came out to share the last of the afternoon's warmth. She folded down, crossing her legs tailor-fashion, then popped the top of a Bud Lite.

'You devil you!' She shook an admonitory finger at Anna. 'You snatched old Stacy right out from under my nose.'

For a brief instant Anna wondered if Stacy had stated some preference for patrolling with her. She couldn't decide whether she was more flattered or alarmed.

Jennifer laughed. 'Still waters and all that. When I went to pick him up, his wife said he'd already left.'

'Not with me, he didn't,' Anna defended herself.

As if in counterpoint to their conversation, Anna's radio, clearly audible through the open bedroom window, crackled to life.

Three times seven-hundred called Meyer's number. Finally came Frieda's voice saying: 'No contact. Seven-hundred clear. Sixteen-forty-five.'

This was followed by three attempts to reach 'Any Chapin Mesa patrol ranger' and 'No contact.'

'I thought Stacy was on till six,' Jennifer said.

'He is.' Anna waited for an uneasy feeling to pass but it didn't. 'I guess I'd better make a few calls.' She looked longingly at the wine in her glass, righteously considering pouring it over the deck railing. Instead, she took it all in one gulp. Something told her she might need it.

Chapter Seven

Stacy didn't turn up that night. Though Hills Dutton, in his capacity as district ranger and resident scrooge, had grumbled about paying her overtime for working on her lieu days, Anna had been on duty. She was needed to cover Meyers' shifts. And to search.

Investigation indicated that at the end of Stacy's late shift on Monday night, all the ruins gates had been locked and the patrol car he'd been driving was parked in the maintenance yard. Apparently, somewhere on the hundred yards of paved path between maintenance and the housing loop, he had simply disappeared.

Tuesday Hills spoke with Mrs Meyers. Coming home late from Albuquerque, she and her daughter had chosen to spend Monday night in Farmington where they could take in a movie and do some shopping rather than continue the two hours on to the park. Around seven that night – the time Stacy customarily took his meal break when he was on late shift – Rose phoned him from the motel. He had answered and they had spoken for several minutes. Rose said Stacy had seemed calm and cheerful.

AT&T long distance corroborated the call.

Just after eight Monday night, while she was taking her evening walk, Al Stinson said she saw Stacy locking the Cedar Tree Tower Ruin gate. After that Stacy had neither been seen nor spoken to by anyone. At least not anyone willing to come forward.

On arriving back in the park Tuesday morning, Mrs. Meyers found the bed made and the sink free of dishes. As her husband was a man of tidy domestic habits, she couldn't say if this indicated whether or not he had slept at home.

The following day Anna saw Bella on her bike riding back from Maintenance. 9:30 am: Anna guessed she'd been escorting Drew to work after his physical training.

Pulling the car to the side of the narrow lane, Anna called the girl's name. For a moment the green eyes looked at her without recognition. When a spark did dawn it was feeble and suddenly gone as if very little held the child's interest any more.

Bella rode up to the Ford and Anna climbed from behind the wheel. Wordlessly the girl looked up. Anna could read the question as clearly as if it been written in felt marker across the unlined brow. 'No,' she said gently. 'We haven't found Stacy yet.'

Bella didn't change expression but it was as if her soft cheeks froze. Anna ached to see so adult a reaction on a six-year-old's face.

'We're looking real hard everywhere,' Anna told her.

Sadly, Bella shook her head. The curls, as carefully tended as always, glimmered in the sunlight. 'Not everywhere. Not where he's at.'

'No,' Anna conceded. 'Not there.'

'I wish Aunt Hattie would come,' Bella said and propped her chin in her hands, her elbows resting on the handlebar. 'She knows things.'

'How to find things?' Anna asked.

'No. Just things.'

'Like what?' Anna leaned against the fender of the patrol car, enjoying the warmth of the metal through her trousers.

Bella screwed up her face with the effort of thought and Anna was glad to see, for a moment at least, she was distracted from her worry over Stacy.

'Not *knowing* knowing exactly. But Hattie plays with you. Not like she's a grown-up who's playing with a little kid. Like she's *there*. Sometimes we'll be witches. We turned Timmy Johnson into a toad.'

Bella looked pleased. Anna was careful not to look anything.

'Why a toad? So you could kiss him back to handsome princehood?'

'Yuck-oh!' Bella stuck out her tongue as if she was gagging on something foul. 'He said mean things about me.'

Anna could guess what.

'We didn't exactly turn him into a real toad,' Bella said after a moment's thought. 'I mean to other people he still looked like a piggy little boy. But Hattie said he'd turn his ownself into a toad if he kept doing toady things so we just helped a little. I could see the toad parts though, after that. He'd say stuff and I'd squint and laugh at the greeny warts just ready to pop out on his pig face. But that was a long time ago when I was little.'

Anna laughed. 'Do you think the transformation's done by now? Is he all toad?'

'Maybe not,' Bella said kindly. 'He stopped being so toady after a while. He may have saved himself. Aunt Hattie thinks so.'

Bella laid her chin down on the handlebars of her bike and pushed back and forth, rocking herself absently. 'Aunt Hattie's like those big colored balloons, the ones with the little baskets for the people to ride in. She just lifts you up, zoop, zoop, zoop.'

Bella accompanied the words with floating gestures, small white hands like leaves blowing upward.

'We could all use some of that,' Anna said.

'Maybe she'll come. Sometimes she does,' Bella said hopefully. 'I have to go.' She stood up on the pedals of the bike and wobbled past Anna.

'Bye.' Anna felt slightly abandoned. 'I have to go too,' she added childishly.

Bella pedalled faster and never looked back. Worry was back in the hunch of the little shoulders.

That evening Anna spent an hour with Rose going over Stacy's routines and the times of the phone call and her return to the park. Rose mixed vicious snipes at Hills, Ted Greeley, Drew Kinder, the Superintendent and the National Park Service with seemingly heartfelt pleas that no stone be left unturned in the search for her husband.

Bella crept about like a tortured spirit. White-faced and silent, she hid herself behind coloring books that she didn't color in, dolls that she didn't enliven with imagination. Twice the child curled up at her mother's feet the way a dog might, her knees pulled up, her chin on hands fisted like paws. The only time Anna saw her play was when Bella dressed up in Stacy's class 'A' uniform jacket and winter hat. On the child's stunted frame the jacket brushed the floor.

Anna had to look away, aware for the first time how terribly costly Stacy's abdication would be. His wife had an edge; she would cut her way through life regardless. Bella truly loved.

In the end it was the interpreter, Claude Beavens, who found Stacy. Or, more accurately, a family of canyon wrens that had made their home high in the ancient ramparts of Cliff Palace.

Early the Thursday morning after Stacy's disappearance, Beavens was down in the ruins. He climbed into the back reaches of the dwelling in hopes of finding a vantage point from which he might see the wrens' nest. Clambering around the fragile site was forbidden to all but officially permitted archaeologists and NPS brass. But, finding himself with a quarter of an hour till visitors would be allowed down, Beavens had decided to take a few liberties.

Given the nature of his discovery, admitting his transgression seemed the lesser of two evils.

Anna was at Navajo Overlook on the Ruins Road Loop with binoculars pressed to her eyes. Jennifer Short, back to the canyon, stood at her elbow.

'It's not like every damn inch of those trails you keep lookin' at haven't been looked at before,' Jennifer was saying. She leaned against the chest-high cyclone fence. Endless civil suits designed to dig money out of Uncle Sam's 'deep pocket' had forced the government to mar every precipitous view with safety devices. Jennifer's flat-brimmed hat was pushed back to protect her hair-do. It gave her a Rebecca-of-Sunnybrook-Farm look that Anna found annoying.

'If y'all ask me, he just took a powder,' the seasonal drawled, rehashing a theory that had been voiced by a number of people in the park as the search wore on. 'Found himself a woman who hasn't let herself go, kept her figure. Can't blame him. If they ever strayed from the missionary position he'd be squashed flatter'n a bug. Uh-uhg-lee!'

'Reubens wouldn't agree with you,' Anna said mildly. 'I doubt Stacy would either.' Again she traced the fragment of trail visible in the canyon below. Worn bare of vegetation over the centuries by feet and paws and hooves, it showed white, a ribbon in the canyon bottom. Brush and scrub grew to either side, becoming taller toward the cliffs. Finally, at the base, where walls sheered up toward the mesa and the strata of sandstone met a strata of slate, natural seep springs nourished the grander Ponderosa pines.

Anna didn't expect to see the straggling – or fallen – form of Stacy Meyers. It had not escaped her notice, nor Hills', that Meyers had vanished in full defensive gear with his radio. If he wanted to be found or still had strength and voice, he would have called for help. Looking was just something to do. And Anna needed something to do.

Had anyone dared to suggest she was falling in love

with Rose Meyers' husband, Anna would have denied it. When she chose to consider her loss, she could not but see the wraith-like face of Bella and know that the vague emptiness she felt was of no importance. Still, the days of seeking without finding, of work and worry and waiting, had worn her down in a way that was more than professional frustration or budding friendship.

'And that poor little thing!' Jennifer sighed gustily. 'What man'd want to deal with that when it wasn't even his?'

'Bella,' Anna corrected, finding "it" offensive. In saying the child's name something she had sensed from the onset became crystal clear: 'Stacy wouldn't leave Bella. No way. No how.'

'I don't know—' Jennifer began again.

'I do,' Anna said flatly. Maybe Rose, maybe. But never Bella, never his Pine-nut. With that realization came another: Stacy Meyers was dead or close enough it wouldn't matter unless they found him soon.

Anna lowered the binoculars. 'You drive,' she said. 'My back is killing me.'

That was when Claude Beavens made his call.

The transmission was garbled. In the patrol car, Anna fiddled with the radio's volume as Frieda said: 'Unit calling seven-hundred, you are broken.' Scratches and crackles came over the air a second time.

'Head toward Cliff Palace Loop,' Anna told Jennifer. From within the Cliff Palace and Balcony House ruins radio transmissions were frequently too broken to understand.

Frieda repeated Anna's thought over the air: 'Unit

calling seven-hundred you are still unreadable. Try again from higher ground.'

Silence followed. 'Pick up the pace,' Anna said. The patrol car smoothly picked up speed, Jennifer conning the boxy vehicle neatly around the meandering RVs and rental cars.

''Nother carry-out?' she asked.

'Maybe,' Anna said.

'Good. I keep missin' out. Everything seems to happen on Tuesdays when I'm off. I'd be off today if Stacy was here.'

They were heading up the straightaway toward the intersection with Cliff Palace Road when the radio crackled to life again.

'Seven-hundred, can you hear me now?' was bleated out in breathy tones.

'Loud and clear.'

'This is Beavens at Cliff Palace. You better send somebody down here right away.'

There was a short silence. The entire park waited for particulars. 'What's the nature of the incident?' Seven-hundred asked evenly.

'I – uh – I found Stacy Meyers. He's up in one of the back kivas.' Another silence followed, longer than the first. Then in a sudden blurt of sound Beavens said: 'I think he's dead. There were flies.'

'Holy shit!' Jennifer whispered. She flipped on the lights and siren.

Anna thought to switch them off again. No sense going code three to a body recovery. Speed meant nothing to the dead, and the commotion could startle the living into having accidents. In the end she let Jennifer call the shots. Somehow the outward shrieking was in keeping with the small cries trapped in her skull.

And, she told herself, there was a slim chance Beavens was mistaken and Meyers was alive. Slim.

Hills' 4×4 was already there when Anna and Jennifer screamed into the Cliff Palace lot. The District Ranger was fumbling with the lock on the tool box in the bed of the truck.

He handed Anna the green oxygen kit. 'Might as well,' he said, echoing her pessimism. Shouldering the trauma bag, he started down the path at a fast walk. Anna and Jennifer had to run to keep up with his long-legged stride. In an unconscious parody of Scarlet O'Hara, Short was clutching the top of her flat-hat to keep it from flying off.

Tourists drew aside as they passed, curiosity enlivening their stares. Revolver hammering one thigh and the oxygen bottle the other, it crossed Anna's mind that they – or she and Jennifer at any rate – looked like idiots. With his trim bulk and square face, Hills was protected by the inviolate image of John Wayne To The Rescue. Guilt followed; guilt that she could harbor such petty thoughts enroute to what was most likely the death of a fellow ranger.

Armed with cameras, visitors were already fanned out along the low wall that surrounded the overlook platform. Dimly, Anna was aware of the clicking of shutters as photographers tried to capture the ruin below.

At the foot of the long metal staircase leading from the platform, Jamie Burke had just finished unlocking the barred gate, opening Cliff Palace for the day.

'Lock it behind us,' Hills said as he brushed past.

Burke pulled the gate closed so abruptly that Anna had to turn sideways to fit through. As she pressed by, she noticed Jamie's pale eyes narrow as she muttered: 'Claude saw.'

Still holding onto her hat, Jennifer clattered after and Anna was pushed into the stone stairway that formed the first part of the descent to the ruin.

Claude Beavens was waiting for them at the top of the ladder where the alcove began. A green NPS windbreaker was zipped up tightly under his Adam's apple. Bony wrists protruded from sleeves an inch too short. Long knobby fingers danced an uncomfortable jig on his thighs. 'It's about time,' he snapped and his Adam's apple vanished momentarily behind the windbreaker's collar.

Beavens was a skinny, busy man, not well liked by Anna's housemates. He tended to officiousness and factual-sounding declarations that had little basis. Jamie had once grumbled that he seemed incapable of uttering the one true answer to many of the questions about the Anasazi: 'We don't know.'

'Show us what you've got.' Hills could have been asking to see baseball cards or a skinned knee. In the face of his unflappable calm, hysteria was almost impossible.

Beavens settled down perceptibly. His fingers still fidgeted, but now they plucked at the fabric of his trousers instead of simply twitching.

'Yeah. Okay.' He turned and began leading the way down the asphalt path in front of the ruin. At a small wooden sign bearing the number three he leaped up onto a retaining wall that served both to reinforce the ancient structures and to keep tourists from climbing on the ruins.

'Watch where you step,' he said, panic gone and officiousness returned. 'These dwellings are fragile.'

Hills grunted. Behind her, Anna heard Jennifer mutter: 'Crimeny, we're not from Mars.'

With sureness bred of familiarity, the interpreter guided them up the slope above the public pathway. Claude was quick and light on his feet. For all his size and strength, Hills had trouble keeping up with him. To their left the alcove dug deep into the side of the mesa. To the right was Cliff Canyon, filling now with early sunlight. They passed a terrace, then a crumbling wall pierced by a single high window.

Beavens turned into an alleyway formed by two buildings, roofless now but still more than a story tall. To keep her mind from their mission and because the magic of these suddenly deserted and long-empty villages never palled for her, Anna took note of this, her first venture into the closed part of Cliff Palace.

Much of the masonry was intact even after seven-hundred desert winters. The stones still bore the signature of their architects in the many fine chips where harder stones had sculpted them to fit. Rubble, fallen between the walls, harbored dozens of pot shards; pieces of white pottery, some the size of half dollars, marked with black geometric shapes.

The short alley dead-ended at another masonry wall. With a bit of scrambling, Beavens was on top of it. Cat-like he walked along the stonework. Hills followed, then Anna. Last, Jennifer handed up the oxygen kit then climbed. Her boots dislodged a stone. When the sound reached Beavens' ear, he turned as if he'd been stung.

'Careful!' he hissed.

The whisper bothered Anna. People whisper in secret, in church, and around the dead.

The wall Claude led them down widened out into an abbreviated terrace. A sheer, circular wall dropped off to the right forming a kiva, one of the round subterranean rooms favored by the ancient people.

'Not this one,' Beavens said and stopped. 'There.' He pointed. At the end of the flat area where they stood was a low wall, a moon-shaped shadow suggesting another kiva, then a tower of stone with a high window.

Rapunzel, Rapunzel, let down your hair, Anna thought idiotically.

Ever pragmatic, Hills stepped past Beavens then over the parapet. 'Let's get to it.'

Anna didn't move.

Hills looked down into the kiva gaping at his feet then turned back. His square face was devoid of expression. 'Yup. This is it,' he said.

Chapter Eight

An invisible switch was thrown in Anna's head. She ceased being a shocked spectator and again became a ranger. Stepping over the wall, she stood next to Dutton. A miniature hail of gravel dislodged by her boots pattered into the kiva below. The skittery sound thickened the silence, fixed it hard in her ears.

At their feet stone and mortar walls curved away then became one again, forming a circle twenty-five feet in diameter. Approximately four feet down, halfway to the floor, the wall widened abruptly into a bench called a 'banquette' by the archaeologists. Built up from the bench were six stone pilasters. When the kiva was still in use, the pilasters had supported a roof. Like many others, this kiva roof had long since been destroyed by fire. When Cliff Palace had been excavated the debris had been cleared away leaving an open pit.

On the south side of the circle, at banquette level, was a recessed stage-like area that graced most of the Mesa Verde kivas. A hundred theories and ten times that many guesses had been put forth as to its use, but none had ever been validated by archaeoligical data.

Below the recess a rectangular opening large enough for a small child to crawl through led back into the masonry to connect with a ventilator shaft that kept air flowing into the underground room to feed the fire and the occupants. Directly in front of the shaft was a section of wall several feet long and a couple of feet high. This deflector wall was a yard or so from a shallow depression ringed with blackened stone: the fire pit. Forming a south-to-north line with the fire ring and deflector wall was a pottery-lined opening the size of a coffee cup. Taken from the Navajo language, it was called a 'sipapu' and was assumed to be symbolic of the opening through which the ancients had been said to move from the destroyed underworld to this one.

Within the kiva only two things were out of place. A flat-brimmed NPS hat had been placed carefully in the center of the deflector wall and, curled into the fetal position, face tucked against his knees, Stacy Meyers lay on his side within the tight circle of stones around the fire pit. His right arm was stretched over his head partially concealing his face. His fingers were spread. It looked as if he was reaching for – or attempting to ward off – something that had come out of the sipapu.

Protected by the deep alcove, the kiva was perennially in shadow. Even in December the sun did not sink low enough to touch the back wall of Cliff Palace. The temperature remained relatively constant throughout the year. Consequently the deterioration of Stacy's body had progressed in a stately fashion, leaving out none of the classic steps of decomposition.

From where Anna stood, ten feet above and fifteen

feet away from the remains, she could smell the sickly sweet odor of decay. Flesh had made the inexorable change from living tissue to inert matter. From the cuff of Stacy's summer uniform shirt to the tips of patrician fingers the skin was deathly pale and dimpled. Blood, stopped from flowing when the muscle of the heart could no longer function, had settled to its lowest point. A shadow of postmortem lividity showed on the underside of the arm where it stretched toward the sipapu.

Curled on his side, only Stacy's left eye was visible. It was open, the brown iris partly obscured by the upper eyelid, as if Meyers' last glance had been in the direction of the fabled underworld.

A black fly dug at the tear duct, searching for any trace of moisture. Flies clustered around the nares of the nose. In death Stacy's mouth had fallen open, or was frozen in a final cry. His beard and mustache camouflaged the flies and maggots around his lips but the tiny all-encompassing movement was more repellant than obvious incursions.

Two days. Stacy had been missing since Tuesday morning. Two and a half if he had died on Monday night. By now his every orifice would be infested with flies and, therefore, maggots.

The bitter sting of bile backed up in Anna's throat and her vision tunneled. She had been expecting a corpse – expecting Stacy Meyers' corpse. She had steeled herself for it. But in her desert-trained mind, she had seen a desert corpse. A person dead seventy-two hours under the relentless sun of the Trans-Pecos. A body jerked like prime beef, baked red then brown, then black; peeling, sear, dehumanized. Purified by the arid desert winds. The bulk of the human body that was water purloined by the sun. Moisture, blood, the stuff of life, sucked away and a mummy created. A thing so elemental soul and memory had no handhold where grief could cling.

This was immediate demanding death. Death not yet turned back to the earth. This corpse would be hard to make peace with. There was no indication the soul had found its way free.

And it was the death of a friend.

Shaking her head clear of ghosts, Anna schooled her mind. 'Want me to call for the polaroid?' she asked Hills. Her voice had a quaver she didn't like.

'Somebody better.' The District Ranger turned and stared out across the sun-drenched canyon. A wren called its characteristic dying fall of song. 'Yeah. The polaroid, chalk – Ah, Jesus!' he interrupted himself. 'If we chalk the outline of the body on the floor of this kiva we'll have every archaeologist in the southwest jumping down our throats. Hell. Where was I?'

Glad to rest her eyes on the living, Anna glanced up at him. Something had kept her from following his example and turning her back on Stacy. A perverse puritanical lust to punish herself? A desire to bid Meyers goodbye? She made a mental note to ask her sister. 'You were at chalk,' she answered Dutton's question.

Hills ran his tongue along his upper teeth as if clearing them of spinach particles. 'Yeah. Hell. Get chalk, a body bag. Bring down an accident kit from one of the vehicles – its got chalk, tape. You got that, Jennifer?'

As was his habit, Hills had been talking in a low

monotone. Its usual effect was to dissipate panic and reduce trauma. This time he seemed to have outdone himself. Both Jennifer and the interpreter looked as if they had fallen into a trance.

Hills snapped his fingers. 'Jennifer, got that?'

Short came awake with a comic, 'Huh?'

'Here, let me.' Anna pulled a notebook from her hip pocket and hastily scribbled down a list of the items Hills had asked for. Adding a couple of requests of her own, she spoke aloud to clear them with Dutton. 'Get helitack over here for a carry-out. Tell Jamie to keep the ruin closed till we're out of here and get the ambulance up top.'

'Ambulance? Then he's not—' Jennifer began. She'd kept close to Beavens, the crumbling wall blocking her view down into the kiva.

'He is,' Hills said shortly.

'It's the ambulance or we toss him in the back of the 4×4,' Anna said.

'Logistics,' Jennifer said firmly, as if that one word explained away the messy business of transporting the dead. In a way it did.

Anna stepped over the wall and handed Jennifer the list.

'What do you want me to do?' Claude Beavens sounded alarmingly eager and there was an avidity in his face that made Anna uncomfortable.

'Uh ...' Hills looked to Anna but she gave him no help. Making the hard decisions was what he was paid the big bucks for. 'You go with Jennifer, I guess. You can fill out a witness statement. Frieda'll explain.'

Beavens shrugged – a definite pearls-before-swine shrug – then hurried past Jennifer so that he would be the one leading the way out.

'Watch your big feet,' Anna heard him say as he dropped down the wall into the blind alleyway.

'Yew watch yer big mouth,' Jennifer snapped back.

Hills laughed, a high-pitched giggle. Hysteria would have been Anna's guess had she not known the big block of a man always laughed that way.

'Guy gives me the heebie-jeebies.' Dutton shuddered. On so large an individual the gesture seemed out of place.

'Kind of like a Jim Jones wannabe?' Anna asked.

'I guess.' Hills had turned his attention back to the kiva and its contents. 'Shee-it.' His east Texas heritage showed briefly. 'Everybody ever died on me was fresh. Did CPR all the way to the hospital and let 'em die for sure there. What the hell do we do now?'

Anna didn't know. Three times in her career there'd been bodies to deal with, but the crime scenes had been so unstable, they'd needed to be moved. 'Secure the scene, collect evidence, maintain the chain of evidence,' she said parroting a list from her federal law enforcement training.

'Right,' Hills said. 'We'll stay out of the kiva and call the feds. Stay here,' he ordered. 'I got to make some calls.'

He scrambled down the wall into the alley and headed for a place open enough he could radio dispatch. Anna felt abandoned. 'Shee-it,' she echoed.

For a moment she just stared out through the junipers,

watching a scrub jay scolding an invisible companion. Scenes from old movies and books came to mind: wives, mothers, grandmothers, dressed in widow's weeds, sitting in darkened rooms knitting or crying with no company but one another and death personified in the body of the man they'd bathed and dressed and powdered, laying in state on the bier. Unbidden a picture from Dicken's *Great Expectations* took over: the moldering wedding feast, mice and maggots the only partakers.

'Not your bridegroom,' Anna said aloud, narrowed her mind to the task at hand, and turned to face the deceased.

There were a few tracks and scuffs on the stones around the kiva: hers, Hills', probably Claude Beavens' or the stabilization crew's. The surface was too hard to make any inferences. No buttons, threads, dropped wallets, white powder, semen, or anything readily identifiable as a bonafide CLUE was in evidence.

Keeping to the stones topping the kiva wall, she walked around till she stood over the ventilator hole, looking down into the southern recess, then to the deflector wall, then the fire ring with its cold tinder.

No obvious signs of violence were apparent, at least not on the side of the body that was exposed. The soft layers of dust that had accumulated on the floor of the kiva were freshly raked.

It was customary for interpreters to rake out human tracks made in closed areas. Both so the footprints wouldn't entice others to trespass and to retain an illusion of freshness, of the first time, for those who would come next.

One line of footprints crossed the raked dirt. It led from below the banquette on the west side of the kiva to the fire pit.

Stacy reached away from her with one long bony arm that was looking more spectral every moment she was left alone with it. With him, she corrected herself. The flesh was pale, life's blood pooled on the underside of his arm. Near his sleeve, on the upper side, was an old bruise, a reminder that once this flesh could feel.

'Wait,' Anna whispered. Stacy's shoes were off, lying untied very near where his feet were tucked up by his hip pockets as if he'd kicked them off to get more comfortable. Something about the stockinged feet was so vulnerable, so human, Anna felt an unaccustomed pricking behind her eyes.

She forced herself to continue the study. Except for the shoes and the hat on the deflector wall, Stacy was immaculately dressed. If, as Bella said, Rose dressed him, she would find nothing to be ashamed of. His shirt was crisply ironed, his trousers neatly creased, his duty belt firmly buckled on with gun and speedloader visible.

Anna continued her circuit, viewing the scene from every angle. Nothing more of interest turned up. She was relieved when Hills finally hauled himself out of the alleyway and crossed to join her.

'Frieda got the Federal Marshal out of Durango on the line. They'll send somebody up. This won't keep,' he waved a hand toward what had once been a man. 'We got to get what we can, bag it and take it down to the morgue. I've got Drew's boys coming.'

Hills crossed his arms and stared down into the kiva.

'What'd he do? Just walk in, curl up in the fireplace, make hisself comfy and die?'

'Looks that way.'

'Jesus.' The district ranger blew a sigh out through loose lips. 'This is a hell of a note. Solstice. Some of the seasonal interps are going to make hay with this.'

Remembering the strange spark in Jamie's eyes as they passed her by the gate, Anna didn't doubt it one bit.

Chapter Nine

The glass had started getting in the way so she'd left it behind and drank straight from the bottle. Never had the Rambler driven so smoothly. Green eyes of a deer or a coyote flickered in Anna's peripheral vision as the headlights picked them out of the night. A vague and uninteresting idea that she was driving too fast crossed her mind. The proof of it, the squealing of tires as she made the ninety degree turn into the Resource Management area, made her laugh out loud.

When she'd recovered control of the car, she felt between her legs. The wine bottle was still upright, its contents unspilled.

'All present and accounted for, officer,' she said. 'No casualties.' The Rambler rolled to a stop in front of the square stone building. 'Car in gear, brake set,' Anna said. Then: 'Whoops. Key *off*. Too late!' as she took her foot off the clutch, the car hopped and the engine died.

For a time she leaned back against the seat, glad to be still. 'Nights in White Satin' played on the oldies station out of Durango. Through the open window the air blew cool, smelling of juniper and dust. Overhead, without the pollution of the glaring intruder lights that had become epidemic even in remote areas during the last decade, the stars were fixed in an utterly black sky. Small night sounds kept the dark from being lonely. Anna could hear scufflings of some nocturnal creature digging in the pine needles, the sigh of a breeze approaching through the forest's crown, clicking and snapping as tiny twigs or bones were broken.

Only humans, cursed with the knowledge of their own mortality and that of those whom they loved, were truly alone; each trapped in an ivory tower of skull and bone peeking out through the windows of the soul.

The body recovery, as sanitized language would phrase it, had gone on till afternoon. The packaging of the meat that had once called itself Stacy Meyers had taken only a few minutes, but the attendant crime scene recording and preservation had worn on so long even Hills' deep-seated nerve endings had become frayed.

Hills had even less experience than Anna with foul play in the form of park corpses and his plodding meth-odicalness took a definite turn toward the anal retentive. Pictures were taken and retaken from every angle.

'Don't know when somebody's going to pop up out of the woodwork saying how you should of done it,' he explained. 'So by God we're going to do it all. Hell of a note. Where are the feds when you need 'em? We forget something and our tit's in the wringer.'

This and more of the same was muttered in an ongoing monotone as he directed the investigation. After the photographs, stones around the kiva were examined, swept, and the leavings collected in a plastic bag that Anna dutifully marked 'Kiva Dust' with the date and her initials.

'Maintain the chain of evidence,' Hills said.

'It's dirt,' Anna returned.

'You never know . . .'

The kiva floor was photographed, re-raked, all items bagged and marked. Then, finally, Stacy was photographed and zipped into the body bag. His hat and shoes wouldn't fit in the narrow plastic shroud. Anna threw them in the trunk of her car to return to Rose.

The entire 'dog and pony show,' as Hills termed it, had taken several hours. During most of it Stacy lay curled absurdly in the fire pit reaching toward something the living couldn't see, his beard growing ever blacker with flies.

It was odd how the human mind switched off an unpleasant reality. Moose slept seconds at a time, their brain clicking on and off like a binary computer, allowing them to rest yet never be long out of a dangerous world in need of watching. Anna, Jimmy, Drew, Paul, Jennifer, they'd all clicked in and out of the reality of death in the kiva. Jokes were told, people laughed, measurements were taken, even mild flirting between Jennifer and Paul.

Interspersed with this flow of life were chalky looks, strained silences and equally strained conversations as someone saw again Stacy's face, remembered his wife, his child, recalled him as he had been in life, and woke to the realization that this fly-blown corpse was all that remained.

The schizophrenia wore Anna down. She had already

needed a drink in the worst way when Hills dragged her to Meyers' house to give condolences to the widow.

Blessedly he had foisted off the chore of informing Rose onto Frieda. Their visit was mere formality – courtesy, the East Texan said. 'Leave any questions to the feds.'

'The feds' Hills relied on so heavily was a federal investigator the Superintendent had called in. Mesa Verde was under exclusive jurisdiction which placed it off local law enforcement's turf.

The Meyers' house was shut up. Windows closed, blinds drawn like a Victorian house of mourning.

Hills knocked tentatively then stepped back leaving Anna marooned on the welcome mat as Rose opened the door. She was neatly dressed in dark blue polyester pants and a white blouse with a Peter Pan collar. Her short dark hair was combed and she wore pearl earrings, but her face was in disarray; dry eyes rimmed with red, her cheeks drawn and pale.

Anna looked to Hills but he was studying a crack in the sidewalk. 'We just stopped by to tell you how terribly sorry we are, Mrs Meyers,' Anna managed. 'Your husband's body is being taken to Durango.'

Rose waited. When Anna could find no more words, Rose closed the door. In the curtailed view of the living room there'd been no sign of Bella. For that Anna was grateful. The child would have been hard to face. She turned to Hills.

He shrugged. 'That about does it,' he said and: 'You're off the clock.'

'Overtime. You're a real sensitive guy,' Anna groused

as they walked back to the patrol car.

'Gotta be thinking of something,' he said philosophically.

Anna raised the bottle from between her thighs and peered at it, measuring the level against the dull glow of the dashboard lights. One third left. Of how many bottles she wondered. Surely this was only the second. Maybe the third.

She took a mouthful and speculated on any possible New Age numerological significance that one third of the third might have. 'Got to ask Jamie,' she said. 'Wart hog.' This last descriptive was triggered at the memory of her housemate.

Jamie had been hovering at the dormitory door when Hills dropped Anna off. Burke was decked out in the sarong, her hair, free of its braid, fanned into a crimped black curtain that fell past her butt. Kohl – or some modern equivalent – ringed her eyes and she wore a single gold earring beaten into the stylized shape of a lizard. Her face was somber but excitement radiated from her in tangible waves.

'Like a bitch in heat,' Anna told the wine bottle.

'We've got to talk,' Jamie had said grimly.

'Not now.' Anna had tried to squeeze by but Jamie'd laid hold of her briefcase.

'Now.'

Anna dropped her hat and gunbelt on the nearest chair. 'So talk.'

Jamie ignored her rudeness, or was too caught up in

her own drama to notice it. With a sigh, she spread herself on the sofa. 'Stacy and I were very close. Very.'

Anna doubted that, but the declaration in no way surprised her. The dead had more friends than the living. Especially those meeting an untimely end. It was as if knowing a murder victim invested one with some sort of celebrity. Jamie had wanted something to happen on solstice. Murder must've been beyond her wildest dreams.

Murder: Anna hadn't said it to herself so bluntly. Suicide, accident, incident, those were the words Hills had resolutely stuck with all day. In thinking it, Anna believed it to be true. Stacy was too much a conservationist to defile the ruins with his twentieth century corpse.

'We all know dead people, Jamie,' Anna said unkindly. Then: 'Sorry. I'm beat.' She picked up her duty belt and turned to go. Again the interpreter stopped her.

'Claude saw,' she repeated her cryptic phrase of the morning, playing it like a trump card in her bid for attention.

Anna was almost too tired to ante up but she managed a mild show of interest. 'Saw what?'

'The night Stacy was taken. He saw it.'

The spark of interest flickered and died. Anna was too tired to play. 'Get him to write "it" up on his witness report.' She dragged herself to the questionable sanctuary of her room.

The evening continued to unravel from there. Through the thin walls of the Far View dorm, Jamie could be heard holding court. Once – or maybe twice – Anna slunk from her lair to return with reinforcements in the form of alcohol. Finally, needing air, but unable to again run the gauntlet of avid faces greedy for details, she had opened her window, popped off the screen, and climbed out, taking the last undead soldier with her.

She poured wine into her mouth and a bit on her chin. 'Quick,' she said as she closed her eyes and rested her head on the rambler's seat. 'Red or white?' Could've been either. 'Some palate.' She pushed open the car door. For a moment it was impossible to make any headway. Then she remembered to undo her seatbelt and tumbled out.

Molly picked up on the seventh ring. 'What? What is it?' she demanded.

'It's just me.' Anna was mildly offended.

'Where are you? What's going on? Talk to me.' Molly rattled out the words.

'Can't,' Anna replied. 'Can't get a word in edgewise. Just called to chat.'

There was a long silence devoid, for once, of the poisonous note of tobacco smoke sliding into dying lungs. Then Molly spoke very deliberately. 'I don't know what time zone you're in, but here in the civilized world it's three-twenty-seven in the morning. If you're okay, you'd better lie to me. Tell me something dire enough to warrant this rude awakening.'

3:27. Anna pushed the tiny silver button on her watch and squinted at the lighted dial. It was hopeless. The numbers were small and furry. 'That can't be right,' she said.

'Trust me on this one.' A sigh: the cigarette. 'Begin at the beginning, Anna. Before your first drink.'

Anna started to cry, great whooping sobs that hurt her throat. Tears poured down her face, dripped from her jaw. 'Zach's dead,' she barked when she was able. Her sister said nothing, choosing not to try and override the storm of grief.

When finally she quieted, Molly said, 'That's right, Zach's dead. Been dead a long time. Kids born the day he died are old enough to rob liquor stores. What's going on, Anna?'

'Zach?' Anna was confused.

'You said Zach was dead.'

Anna digested that for a moment, taking a little wine and letting it burn under her tongue. 'No I didn't,' she said at last. 'Stacy's dead. Stacy Meyers.'

'Who is Stacy Meyers?'

'Goddammit listen to me!' Anna screamed.

'You're drunk, Anna,' her sister said reasonably. 'I love you – Lord knows why – and I want to help you. But you're beyond me. I'll call you tomorrow.'

The line went dead. Anna laid her head on the desk and wept.

Chapter Ten

Consciousness dawned like a foggy day. Anna opened her eyes. She was face down on a rough brown surface, her cheek wet from drool, and she was terribly cold. Thin gray light filtered from somewhere. Through the static in her head she could hear the fussy chatter of scrub jays.

Without moving, as though to do so might prove dangerous, she took stock of the situation. She was laying on the front seat of the Rambler, her clothes rumpled and damp. Pins and needles prickled through her right arm and leg where they were pinned under her. Graying hair, clumped and sticky-looking on the vinyl, fell around her face.

Slowly she raised her head. Her first instinct had been right: to move was dangerous. Even her eyeballs ached. Her mouth was so dry her tongue rattled between her teeth like the clapper in a bell.

She pushed herself to a sitting position. The sun was not yet up. The Rambler was still parked in front of the Resource Management Office. The car and her hair reeked of stale wine. Anna checked at her wristwatch: 5:35.

She shoved her stinking locks back with both hands. 'What the fuck happened to me?'

The keys were in the ignition. She slid over behind the wheel and tried the starter. There wasn't even a whimper of life. When she'd stumbled out the night before, she had left the ignition on as well as the radio and the lights. 'Lucky for me and God knows who else.' Her head dropped back against the seat and she grunted with the ache of it.

The last thing she remembered was dialing Molly's number in New York. She wondered what she had said.

Tires humming on the pavement brought her back into the present. Soon the park would begin to stir, archaeologists on their way to the lab, the tree kids toting chainsaws into the woods to remove hazardous fuels, helitack jogging by on physical training, maintenance men, trail crew, tourists.

Panic tore the fog of alcohol clouding her mind. This was no way to greet the public. Balancing her head carefully on her shoulders, she retraced her steps to the Resource Management Office. The door was unlocked and open. Inside, on one of the desks, was a bottle with half an inch of red wine in the bottom. Mercifully it was upright and the resource management specialist's nest of papers unbesmirched by her night's debauchery. The bookcase had not fared so well. It was overturned and the books hurled around the room. Memory, like a snap-shot, flashed in Anna's mind: her hands pulling the shelves toward her, books and periodicals cascading down over her feet.

Why she had done it, what she'd been looking for or

trying to prove, remained a mystery.

She dropped to her knees, righted the bookcase, then crawled after its contents and restored them in what she hoped was relative order. Having finger-combed her matted hair and braided it off her face, she tied it with a piece of pink plastic surveyor's tape she'd found in the office.

Putting the best face – and the best lie – on it she could, she walked the mile through the woods to the helitack dorm. Paul Summers drove her back in the fire-truck and jump-started the Rambler.

Driving back to Far View, Anna felt weak-kneed and queasy. A strong sense of God not being in Her heaven and all's wrong with the world pervaded every cell of her body. Not only the hangover shook her, but the hours in blackout. A chunk of time she'd been active, talking, walking, evidently hurling research manuals, was utterly alien to her. A black hole she'd fallen into and, but for a dead battery, might never have crawled out of.

A hot shower steamed the booze from her pores and rinsed it from her hair but not even hot coffee could burn the fumes from her brain. As she pulled on her uniform, she hoped no great feats of kindness, courage or intellect would be required of her for a few days. She longed to call Molly, but embarrassment combined with the need to sort things out on her own stayed her hand.

Purposely avoiding the Museum Loop, the Chief Ranger's Office and most of the visitors, Anna patrolled the traditionally uneventful four and a half miles from Far View Lodge to Park Point, the highest place in the park at 8,571 feet. The twisting road to the mesa cut through the flanks of mountains in two places, Bravo Cut and Delta Cut. Rocks falling from the unstable hillsides littered the roadway and were a constant headache. After rains the rocks were numerous and sizeable enough to present a hazard to motorists. Delta Cut, the higher of the two, presented a slashed hillside to the town of Cortez far below. Held in by a metal railing, the road ran along a ragged drop edged with thickets of oakbrush. Today Anna found nothing but pebbles, none even as big as a woman's fist. Still she parked the car and meticulously began kicking each little rock off the asphalt.

It felt good to be quiet and alone and in the sunlight.

Bit by bit her mind cleared and she thought of Stacy Meyers. Not of Stacy Meyers the man, with his intellectual charm and heartfelt commitment to the land – that would have led her back to those lost hours in the Resource Management building. Anna thought of the 'Meyers Incident', reducing it to a puzzle, a mystery that, unlike mysteries of the heart, might prove solvable.

On the grounds of women's intuition she'd been quick to discount suicide but it was a real possibility and one that would have to be explored. Stephanie McFarland came to mind and Anna remembered Stacy's anguish at panicking. Could he have decided he no longer deserved to live? To a sane mind, it seemed excessive, but Anna knew from experience depression could breathe an insane logic into the most bizarre courses of action.

Anna knew very little of Stacy's inner life, or, as Molly would say, his real life. It was clear that he had financial problems. Short of a generous trust fund, any temporary

GS-5 with grown-up responsibilities would have money problems. Stacy's were exacerbated by Bella's needs and Rose's wants.

Would he fake his own murder to provide for them? Anna took out the yellow notebook she carried in her hip pocket and wrote 'Life Insurance?' on the first clean page. She had worked a couple of suicide investigations in the past and dreaded them. In many ways they were more destructive to those left living than homicide. Always, with unnatural death, came anger. Homicides had a healthy target, a suitable bad guy, a foe worthy of hatred. Suicide carried the same furious baggage but it fed on the bearer. As widowhood was said to be easier than divorce, so murder was easier than suicide. At least no one chose to leave.

The other possibilities were accident, natural causes, murder and, if Jamie had her way, vengeful intervention of spirits. Hills was overwhelmingly in favor of the first idea but even he, faced with the neatly placed hat and doffed shoes, had to admit that: 'If it was an accident it sure was a lulu.'

Anna harbored a secret preference for the Revenge of the Anasazi. Paranormal foul play would be a nice diversion from man's daily inhumanity to man.

Foul Play: Anna smiled at the phrase and flicked a stone off the roadway with the side of her foot. It sounded so English, so Old School, implying subtle distaste for something not quite cricket, not entirely sporting. Homicide had an American feel, a businesslike violence-as-usual ring to it. Anna preferred Foul Play. She said it once aloud. In the gentle silence of a summer's day spoken words grated and she didn't try it again.

The sun was warm on her back and a breeze, blowing across from the snow-covered peaks of the Abajos a hundred miles away in Utah, smelled gloriously of nothing. Up high there was only air in the air and Anna took a moment to fill her lungs to capacity.

If one must think of murder, this was the kind of day to do it: a pure day, one without guile.

Murder then; the motives were usually predictable. Somebody got mad, got greedy, or got even. The pathologically neat arrangement of the scene seemed to rule out a crime of passion. Those killed in sudden heat were customarily found sprawled and bloody in bedrooms, barrooms, on kitchen floors and in parking lots.

Getting even seemed a possibility. By leaving the corpse in such an odd place perhaps the avenger had hoped to pay back not only the dead but, in some way, the living – the widow, a friend, or even the National Park Service. Again Anna pulled out the notebook. 'Enemies?' went under 'Life Insurance.'

Greed was Anna's favorite. Greed seemed to motivate a goodly number of human behaviors, murder among them. But, if greed were the motivating factor, the grandstand play of laying the corpse in the fire ring of a kiva struck her as out of place.

Why wouldn't the body be buried, hidden, disposed of somehow? Only the very naive would think Stacy's remains would go undiscovered in Cliff Palace. Even if the archaeologists or the stabilization crew didn't stumble across it, eventually the odor or the vultures would have given the location away.

Stacy was meant to be found. To prove something? To frighten someone? To stop the search before too many noses were poked into too many places? Beneath 'enemies' Anna scribbled 'Where Else Should We Have Looked?' and 'Greed/Rose' with an arrow drawn back up to 'Life Insurance.'

She'd run out of stones. The stretch of road through the cut was clean. Disappointed to have completed so pleasantly mindless a task, she began to walk back along the highway to where she'd left her patrol car.

A gold Honda Accord was stopped fifty yards or so from her vehicle. The hood was up in the international symbol for motorist in distress. Anna perked up, walked a little faster. Citizen assists were good clean ranger work, the equivalent of firemen rescuing kittens from trees.

A generous behind covered in rich plum fabric was swaying rhythmically to the left of the front fender. Anna approached the far side of the vehicle and looked under the hood. An exceedingly round woman with a froth of chestnut curls shot with gray and held off her face by a yellow plastic banana was chanting 'drat, drat, drat,' and shaking small dimpled fists at an unresponsive engine. Her face was as round as the rest of her and showed no signs of age. Earrings of green and yellow parrots dangled to her shoulders, the birds looking at home against the print of a Hawaiian shirt.

'Trouble?' Anna said by way of greeting.

The woman looked up, bright blue eyes sharp-focussed behind glasses nearly half an inch thick. 'Oh, hello. Do you know anything about these horrid things?'

Her voice was high and had a sing-song quality about

it that was exquisitely comforting. Anna, who usually disliked voices in the upper registers, placed it instantly. In her mind she heard Billy Burke in the *Wizard of Oz* asking Dorothy 'Are you a good witch or a bad witch?' The resemblance didn't end there. This woman was big, two hundred pounds or so, but seemingly as light and translucent as the bubble in which the good witch of the North traveled.

She shook her fists again and Anna half expected her to float with the effort.

'I only know about six things to poke,' Anna apologized. 'If that doesn't work, I call a tow truck.'

'Ooooh.' The woman sounded wickedly delighted. 'Let's poke.'

Anna laughed and took a hard look at her companion. The familiarity wasn't born just of fairy tales. 'You're Aunt Hattie!' she declared. Bella hadn't described her aunt in physical terms but she had painted such a clear picture of her spirit, Anna was certain. Hattie bore a slight resemblance to her sister, Rose, but her features were more refined and looked to have been sculpted by laughter where Rose's were etched by discontent. Rose carried less weight, but she seemed cursed by gravity. The pounds dragged her down. Hattie was buoyant, uplifting.

While Bella's aunt tried the starter, Anna pushed butterfly valves and rattled air filters. Finally, noting a depressing lack of fuel squirting into the carburetor, she gave it up as a lost cause and radioed dispatch to call a tow truck from Cortez.

The Honda disposed of, Anna gave Hattie a lift to the mesa top. Hattie appeared completely at her ease, simply sitting, riding, watching the scenery. Hattie had seemed at ease shaking her fists over a dead engine and Anna was surprised to find herself at an unaccustomed comfort level as well.

'You came because of Stacy?' Anna asked.

'For Bella.'

'Rose call you?'

'Bella,' Hattie said again and laughed. 'This is a bit of a surprise visit, I'm afraid. But I don't think Rose'll mind. She'll have so much on her mind. And I do think she will have a hard time of it without Stacy. He was a good man and Rose isn't used to that.'

'Her first husband?' Anna prodded.

'A pig-face. Rose was besotted.' Hattie shrugged soft graceful shoulders. 'Where's the fun? I liked Stacy. And Bella liked Stacy.'

This last was clearly the most heavily weighted factor in the equation that Anna let it sit without comment for a while. Remembering the conversation she'd had with Bella about her aunt and how she '... lifted people up zoop, zoop, zoop,' Anna said: 'Bella will be glad you've come.'

'Bella's a magical spirit,' Hattie said. 'Till I got to know her I'd pretty much forgotten how the world looks when you're new.'

Not new anymore. After a murder the newness got lost. Even at six – perhaps especially at six. This would rob Bella's world of a lot of magic.

Hattie scrunched down in the passenger seat and leaned her head back. The breeze through the open window ruffled her hair, teasing it into a froth around the banana clip. The parrots danced gaily. Life cloaked Bella's aunt so vibrantly; coupled with the scent of pine and the warmth of the sun, made it infinitely precious. Anna could remember a time, the years after Zach died, when it was a tremendous burden. One she might have shucked if it hadn't been for Molly and a good healthy dose of cowardice.

'Do you think Stacy could have committed suicide?' she asked impulsively.

Hattie straightened up, the languor gone, the blue eyes sharp. 'Rose said he was killed.'

Anna sensed a question behind the statement and waited, hoping the silence would draw it out. On the radio a country western artist began singing 'When I say no I mean maybe.' Anna switched it off.

Conning the car around the last in a series of hairpin curves, she started up the last climb to the mesa top where Far View Lodge looked down over the southwest. An oversized RV plodded ahead at twenty-six miles an hour. Anna was glad of the delay. Once the buildings came in sight, tour-guide questions would distract them both.

'That would be the worst possible thing for Bella,' Hattie said at last. 'The worst kind of abandonment. The most awful rejection. God, I hope not.'

'But maybe . . .?'

'Bella, in a little kid's way, thinks maybe. She never said so much but Rose and Stacy had a shouting match on the phone the night he disappeared. Bella thinks about that. Rose wouldn't've bothered to hide it from her. Rose is a tad self-centered. She believes anything she says or thinks is worthy of publication. God forbid one of her emotions should go unvented.'

The acid touch cut through what Anna had perceived as an almost too-sweet soul and she delighted in it. A few snakes and snails made the sugar and spice more interesting.

'What was the fight about? Did Bella say?'

'She thinks it was about her. A six-year-old's view of the world is limited. My guess is it was about money. Rose always argued about money – even when she had it.'

Rose hadn't mentioned a fight. That didn't surprise Anna. Couples were often embarrassed they quarrelled, never quite believing it was as common as dandruff in most marriages. If the fight had been over money Rose might have had more than one reason for not mentioning it. Insurance companies didn't pay off on suicides.

They crested the hill and the mesa spread south; a green table top. The RV turned on its blinker and lumbered off the road into the Visitors Center parking lot. Talk turned to other things.

By the time they reached the housing loop it was midday and the place was deserted. Anna let the patrol car roll to a stop under the tree in the Meyers' yard then got out to retrieve Hattie's luggage from the trunk.

The screen door banged open and Rose cried 'Hattie!'

As the women embraced in the middle of the walk, Anna dragged the heavy bags from the back of the car. On Hattie's side the hug appeared to be heartfelt, but Rose was kissing air. 'What a surprise,' she said. And: 'I hope you packed a lunch. Stacy left us with nothing to live on. Nothing.'

Anna slammed the trunk a bit harder than necessary.

'Are those yours?' Rose eyed the size of the suitcases.

'All mine,' Hattie said cheerfully.

'You can put them in the front room,' Rose directed Anna.

As her younger sister turned to reenter the house, Hattie put her fists on her ample hips and cocked one eyebrow at Anna in a perfect parody of a disapproving school marm. Anna laughed and hefted the bags. Bella had been right. Zoop, zoop, zoop.

As she dumped the luggage and turned to go, Rose issued a last directive.

'Bella took her sandwich over to eat with that Drew. Tell her her aunt's paying us a visit.'

Anna resisted the urge to pull a forelock and back humbly out the door.

Irritation short-circuited her brain till she'd started the car and driven out of the housing loop. As she was turning right at the stop sign to backtrack around the island of piñons separating the houses from the maintenance yard, the short exchange between the sisters sprang back into her thoughts with sudden clarity.

'Stacy left us with nothing to live on. Nothing.'

No insurance; no insurance, no suicide-dressed-as-murder. At least not for monetary reasons. That was one item Anna could cross off her list.

Bella was just leaving the fire cache. She walked her bike, laboriously pushing it ahead of her as if the machine was as heavy as her heart.

Anna pulled up beside her, letting the Ford creep along at idle, keeping pace with the child. 'I've got some good news for you,' she said.

Bella didn't even look up. There was no more good news to be had in the world.

'Your Aunt Hattie's here,' Anna said quickly.

'Aunt Hattie?' Something, maybe two parts relief and three parts joy, enlivened Bella's face. 'That's okay then.' She pulled herself astride the bike and began pedaling.

'Wait,' Anna called as she cruised up beside the girl again. 'What did your mama and Stacy fight about on the telephone?'

Bella stopped, shot Anna a cold look.

Anna couldn't back down. 'It might be important,' she said.

Whatever Bella weighed in her mind evidently came out in Anna's favour. 'Some man,' she said and rode down the path into the trees.

Suicide was back. Because Rose, like the infamous ex, had 'too many people she just had to meet'? Or murder by the jealous boyfriend? Both solutions were too mundane and melodramatic for Anna's taste. But if people only died for good reasons, a lot of mortuaries would go begging.

Chapter Eleven

Anna had barricaded herself in her room. Etta James singing 'Stop the Wedding' on the boom box served to block the tinny sounds of 'The Wheel of Fortune' coming from the other room. Anna wasn't in the mood for Jamie, even if she was abusing Vanna White. A glass of chardonnay waited on the dresser by the bed. Anna sat cross-legged in the middle of a Mexican blanket bought when she'd worked in Texas. The phone was in her lap.

As the wine worked its way down into the muscles of her neck, she let her head rest against the wall. Tonight she would go easy. There must be no more black holes.

Molly answered on the third ring. 'Yes?' she said peremptorily.

For an instant Anna felt like slamming the receiver down, hiding in silence. The prospect was too lonely. 'It's just me,' she said, sounding unnecessarily cheerful.

'How are you feeling?' Molly asked and Anna knew she would not be allowed to pretend last night had never happened.

'Better than I was,' she admitted.

'A little hair of the dog?'

'No,' Anna lied. 'Anyway, that's not what I called to talk about.'

'Better me now than the entire staff at Hazeldon in a couple of years. You've got a problem, Anna.'

Anna took a long sip of the Chardonnay in a lame gesture of rebellion. 'No. I've got a solution.'

There was a sucking silence then Molly mumbling: 'Ten, fifteen, twenty, twenty-five . . .'

'What're you doing?'

'Trying to count up how many times in my umpteen years practice I've heard that one. It's no go, Anna. Normal people – at least people over the age of seventeen – don't drink until they black out.'

'I didn't black out.' Second lie in as many minutes. Anna was beginning to worry herself.

'What did we talk about the third time you called me?' Molly demanded.

'Oh shit.' Anna vaguely remembered the one call. 'Okay. I blacked out.'

'Hah.'

' "Hah"? Is that substance abuse parlance? One black-out does not an alcoholic make.'

'What's the magic number? Three? Ten?'

Anna chose not to answer.

'Okay, talk about Stacy Meyers.'

'Maybe I don't want to.' Anna felt peevish.

'That's not the idea I got during call number three at four-ten this morning.'

Anna sighed, fortified herself with another draught of wine. 'How many times did I call?'

'I don't have the foggiest. After number three I unplugged my phone.'

Depression settled like coal dust across Anna's mind. 'Tough love? Or are you just in a very bad mood?'

'I want you to take this seriously, not to weasel, charm or rationalize your way out of it.'

'It won't happen again,' Anna snapped.

'It happened.'

'A friend of mine was murdered.'

'Stacy Meyers.'

The conversation had come full circle. Anna told Molly about Stacy, his wit and intense brown eyes, his undeserving wife and high ideals.

When she had finished, Molly said: 'You kept calling him Zach last night.'

'Caught the girl in the Freudian slip?' Anna teased.

'Freud was a deeply troubled man,' Molly returned.

'In vino veritas, then?'

'Hardly. Maybe in mucho vino mega confusion. You had the two men mixed up in your mind last night. There was a physical resemblance?'

'Slight.'

'A similar intensity?'

Anna said nothing.

'Confusion, Anna. That's what I heard. Lots of it. Psychological wounds are like soft tissue injuries. You get hurt in the same place twice and they may never heal. You need clarity right now, not oblivion. The time for that, if there ever was one, is long past. No sense playing that scene out again. This time you might not survive and boy would I be pissed.

'Gotta go,' Molly finished. 'Stay alert.'

'What's a "lert"?' Anna whispered the childhood joke into a dead phone line.

She finished the glass of wine but didn't pour herself a second. Clarity: she thought about that for a while. There were times reality didn't have all that much to recommend it. 'Like now,' she said to the face in the mirror, then, thinking of Bella, was shamed out of her self pity. 'Clarity,' she repeated aloud and slipped on her moccasins. At least she could do what she was good at: aggravating people into telling her more than they wanted to.

Down on Chapin it was significantly warmer. The difference between summer and fall, shorts and long pants.

Anna slowed the Rambler to an idle and crept past the houses trying to organize her thoughts. Day's end; it was warm and the light would last till nine o'clock or later. People were out walking dogs, sitting at picnic tables gossiping while dinners cooked on outdoor grills. Several members of the helitack crew sat on the steps of the fire dorm drinking beer. Drew waved her over, pointing at the can of Colt 45 in his hand.

'The devil is at mine elbow,' Anna muttered. She pulled the Rambler in and parked in front of the dorm. Drew, Jimmy and Paul sat on the steps looking for all the world like fraternity boys on a Saturday afternoon.

'How goes the hunt?' Drew asked.

'An arrest is imminent,' Anna said and declined another offer of a beer.

'It won't help Bella,' Drew said. 'She's breaking my heart, poor little kid. Who'd've thought she'd take it so hard? Stacy wasn't even her real dad. With all that threat of cutting her legs up, I'd've thought she might be relieved. She hid it pretty good, but it scared her a lot.

What a waste.' Drew sucked down half a Colt at one gulp and crushed the can into a wad of tinfoil.

'Sure you won't have a brewski?' Jimmy asked as he popped another for Drew and one for himself. Anna wasn't at all sure she wouldn't so she took her leave.

By the time she parked under the tree in front of the Meyers' bungalow, her plan still hadn't taken on any real form. She toyed with the idea of returning to Far View but the need to keep busy forced her out of the car.

The door was open. She peered through the screen. The front room was a mess of magazines and newspapers. The couch, desk, and much of the floor were littered with them. No toys, she noted. A television, a T.V. guide open on top of it, stared with a blank eye from a small table in the corner. Familiar sounds of an evening game show came from elsewhere in the house.

A T.V. in the kitchen or bedroom, Anna guessed. 'Hello, anybody home?' She rapped lightly on the door-frame.

Clattering from the kitchen answered her query. A moment later Rose Meyers appeared on the other side of the screen. 'Yes?' she said when she saw Anna on the doorstep.

'In the neighborhood,' Anna said. 'Just thought I'd drop by.'

'No one is here. Hattie and Bella went for a walk.'

'That's okay.'

Rose looked nonplussed. Several seconds ticked by during which she evidently remembered her manners. 'Would you like to come in for a minute?' she offered.

'Thanks. That would be nice.'

Rose stood aside, holding the door, while Anna slunk by. 'I hope I'm not interrupting anything . . .' Anna began and waited for the usual reassurances but none were offered.

Shoving aside several days worth of coupons in the midst of the clipping and sorting process, Anna settled on the couch. 'I've always liked these little houses,' she said, looking around the room with its wooden floor and wood-burning stove. She'd seen the homes redone for permanent employees. They had wall to wall carpeting and more recent paint jobs – more comfortable but less picturesque.

'It's cramped,' Rose said.

'After dorm living, a dog house would look like a mansion to me if I had it all to myself.'

Rose gave up her post at the door and went so far as to perch on the edge of a chair but she didn't get comfortable. That this was not to be a long visit was made abundantly clear.

'I can't stay long,' Anna said to put her at her ease. 'Only an hour or two,' she added just for the fun of watching Rose flinch.

Mrs Meyers looked as if she were ill and Anna, remembering widowhood, softened. 'How are you doing?' she asked. 'That's really all I came by for. This is a hard time.'

'Yes.' The rigid cast of Rose's features trembled and for a moment it looked as if her control might crack but she recovered herself. 'Hard.'

'Was Stacy depressed over anything?' Anna ventured. 'Poor health, family problems, finances – anything like that?'

Rose's head jerked up, her face so full of anger Anna was half surprised her hair didn't catch on fire. 'Stacy was in perfect health,' Rose said coldly. 'And, not that it's any of your business, but, no, there were no "family problems" as you put it. If you're implying my husband killed himself, you can put a stop to that line of thinking right now. This minute. Stacy wouldn't do that to me.'

Anna waited a minute, letting Rose cool off. She searched her mind for a way of connecting with the woman, breaking through the wall of fury. 'My husband was killed,' Anna told her. 'I had a real bad time for a while.' Still have, she thought, but didn't say it.

'How was he killed?' Rose asked without interest.

Anna hated this part. More than once she wished Zach had had the good taste to die rescuing a child from a burning building, or skiing in avalanche country. 'Crossing Ninth Avenue against the light, he was hit by a cab.'

Another silence began. Anna watched Rose's drawn face and downcast eyes. Her need for information seemed petty in the face of this grief and she made up her mind to quit badgering. 'Are you going to be all right?' she asked impulsively.

'All right?' Rose laughed. 'Now that's relative, isn't it? I have no job, no income, a child with special needs. All right?' Rose's voice was becoming shrill. The dam was breaking and Anna wasn't altogether sure she wanted to be there when it gave way. 'No, I'm not going to be all right. Maybe if the Park Service would stop piddling around and find out who did this, I could be all right. You can bet your cozy little government job I'm going to sue for everything I have coming to me. No health insurance, no retirement, no death benefits. Like Stacy was a migrant worker, no better than a strawberry picker. Temporary appointment!' she spat out the words. 'We can't even stay here much longer. Not that that's a big loss but it is a roof over our heads.

'Oh, yes,' she continued, as if Anna had argued. 'I'm going to sue all right. Tell that to Mr Hills Dutton. And tell him to stop writing parking tickets and talk to Ted Greeley.'

'Ted Greeley?' Anna probed.

'Money can buy anything, anybody,' Rose said then snapped her mouth shut so hard her jowls quivered. Anna doubted she would get another word out of Rose with anything short of a crowbar.

'Well . . .' She levered herself up out of the nest of papers. 'I'll sure tell him. We can use any help you can give us. Let me know if you need anything.' With that and other platitudes, Anna paved her way to the front door and escaped down the walk.

She'd gotten what she wanted, a flood of unedited words. Out of which, 'Ted Greeley' and 'Money can buy anything, anybody' merited consideration. Rose seemed to be suggesting Greeley had bought off Hills, paid him to steer the investigation away from him or his. If he had, Greeley was a fool. Hills wasn't the head of this incident, the Federal Bureau of Investigation was. Their man was due in in the morning.

That left the possibility that Rose believed the contractor had something to do with her husband's murder. Coupling Rose's finger-pointing with Bella's admission that the fight on the phone between her mom and Stacy was over some man made for interesting hypotheses. Was 'some man' Greeley? Was Greeley jealous of Stacy, in love with his wife?

Anna made a mental note to mention this interview when she met with the Federal Investigator.

She dropped the Rambler in gear and pulled around Rose's Oldsmobile. Her mind flashed back to the day she and Stacy had confronted Tom Silva about the fore-skin note. Greeley had said something that chilled or angered Stacy. Anna remembered: 'How's my little Bella.'

Could Greeley be Rose's rich first husband? No, Anna remembered, Number One was a lawyer. Greeley as Rose's lover? Worth pondering. Uncharitable as it was, Anna thought it unlikely any man would kill for the pleasure of Mrs Meyers' company but she knew that was pure prejudice on her part. On like occasions her father used to say: 'Perhaps she has talents we are not privy to.' The human heart, though often predictable, remained unfathomable. People loved who they loved and killed who they killed. Rhyme and reason, when they entered in, were often so skewed as to be meaningless to an outside observer.

Anna shoved these new ingredients to the back burner of her mind to stew a while.

Killing time, she drove down to the museum loop and through the picnic grounds. Snuggled down in the evergreens, the picnic area seemed common, if charming, but a few steps carried one to the lip of Spruce Canyon. There the mesa fell away in staggered steps of fawn-colored sandstone, before a sheer drop to the wooded ground below. Like many canyons cut into the mesa,

Spruce was small. For Anna there was always a sense of Shangri La about these hidden places. Each had its own dwellings, long since abandoned by their owners and bleached back to the color of the earth.

Since Mesa Verde's cliffs had first been inhabited the Anasazi, the Utes, the Navajo, cowboys, hunters and tourists had all tramped the trails. Yet there remained a tremendous sense of discovery. In that lay much of the park's allure.

Anna parked the Rambler and walked out toward the canyon rim. The sun was just setting, casting golden light that made the trees greener and the sandstone seem to glow from within. Blue- and black-winged butterflies settled on the milkweed as if trapped in the amber light.

Since there was no camping on the mesa top, the picnic grounds were gloriously deserted in the evenings. Anna breathed in the solitude.

Not wanting to break the peace, she made her way through the band of junipers between the picnic area and the canyon with great care, placing each moccasined foot on bare ground to avoid snapping needles and twigs.

Such stealth had paid off several times since she'd moved to Colorado. Once she had seen a mother lion with two speckled cubs behind Coyote Village and once a bull elk looking fat and fine and full of himself at Park Point.

This evening she crept up on a much stranger game.

Out on the canyon's lip the sandstone had been worn into a shallow trough sixty feet wide. Over the centuries summer rains had scoured it smooth. In the middle of the pour-over a stone block the size of a sofa and relatively the same shape had come to rest. Lying on the

rock, dyed red by the setting sun, was the body of Bella
Meyers. Her hands were crossed on her breast in the
classic pose of the deceased. Aunt Hattie, her hair a frizz
of sun-drenched brown, bent over the child. The woman's
small, perfect hands were doubled under her chin. She
was murmuring or singing.

Anna stopped at the edge of the trees. The little scene
played on; the child motionless, Hattie moving occasionally as if exclaiming or weaving spells. After a time,
Anna ventured out into the dying light, her footfalls
soundless on the stone.

When she was eight or ten feet away she heard Hattie
asking in her high pleasant voice: 'Shall I kiss you awake
now?' and was relieved to see a small shake of Bella's
head. The child had not been slaughtered in some arcane
ritual.

'Oh my, but she was such a beautiful girl, beloved of
all in the kingdom,' Hattie sighed over the little body.

Hattie glanced up then and saw Anna. 'Some one else
has come to pay their last respects to the lovely Bella,'
she said in her storybook voice. To Anna she whispered:
'We're playing Dead Princess.'

Anna cocked an eyebrow.

'It's a game Bella made up when she was little,' Hattie
explained in a whisper, careful not to break the spell.
'The princess lies in state and is admired by all and
sundry until she is awakened by the magic kiss.'

'Sounds like my kind of game,' Anna returned.

'The princess has been dead a very long time today,'
Hattie said sadly. 'She doesn't seem to want to be kissed
back to life.'

'Aunt Hattie!' came a remonstrance from the side of

Bella's mouth. Her eyes were still squeezed shut.

'Yes, Royal One?'

'Okay. Now.'

Hattie leaned down and placed a gentle kiss in the middle of the child's forehead. Slowly Bella opened one eye then the other and looked around as if she were in a strange place.

'Welcome back, little one,' Hattie said. 'The crowds are cheering your return to the world of the living. You have been sorely missed.'

Bella smiled a little. 'Okay. I'm done.' She sat up abruptly and swung her short legs over the side of the boulder.

Hattie sat beside her and both of them looked at Anna. 'We're done,' the aunt said.

Anna squatted on her heels. The sun threw their shadows a dozen feet, shading her eyes. 'I didn't mean to interrupt your game,' she apologized.

'That's all right,' Bella assured her. 'I was about to come to life anyway. My behind was getting tired of the rock. Being dead isn't as easy as it looks.'

'I guess not.'

'Do you want to play?' Bella offered. 'My behind's waking up some.'

'I don't know how,' Anna told her and Bella looked disappointed. 'Maybe your Aunt Hattie could teach me,' Anna relented and won one of Bella's smiles.

'It's a good game,' Bella promised as she laid back down and folded her hands over her chest.

Anna stood and looked down at the little girl with her angel's face and stunted legs, so peaceful in her pretended and admired state of suspended animation. Anna was glad Hattie had come. Everybody needed someone to kiss her back to life.

'Does the kiss always work?' Anna teased the other woman.

'It does if you do it right.'

Chapter Twelve

First thing the following morning, Anna received a second-hand message by way of Jennifer Short that she was to meet Hills at the CRO. Unable to sleep, she came down early and sat on the bench opposite the office door, enjoying the freshness of the day. Soon buses and cars would begin puffing the park full of carbon monoxide and noise. The first hours after sunrise were new made, hinting of wilderness, of what the world was once and, in dreams, might be again.

Across the walkway, amid the knife-point leaves of the agave, a yellow and black bull snake uncoiled himself into the warmth of the sun. The snake lived in a hole in the stonework of the superintendent's porch. At least that's where Anna'd seen him flee other mornings when the first foot traffic of the day began.

She stretched her shirt against her shoulder-blades and took primal pleasure in the sun's rays. 'I think I'm an exotherm,' she said. The snake didn't even blink.

An unnatural sound, high heels clacking on paved ground, got a better response. Anna looked in the direction of the racket and when she turned back her narrow fellow had gone.

'You scared away my snake,' she complained as Patsy Silva came down the walk.

'Good. Nasty things.' Patsy was dressed in a colorful Mexican skirt with a turquoise blouse and sandals. She looked chipper. But she always looked chipper so Anna deduced nothing from that.

'You look chipper,' she said to see if it were so.

'Found my keys.' Patsy dangled a ring with a neon pink rabbit's foot on it. 'Good omen.'

''Bout time. What with chindis and—' she almost said 'dead guys' but realized to those not in law enforcement it might seem unnecessarily cavalier '—what not,' she finished safely. 'Find them in the last place you looked?'

Patsy laughed. 'Usually. Not this time. They were in my purse all along. They'd fallen down among the used kleenex and dead lipsticks – the bottom-feeders.'

'Speaking of: how goes it with Tom? Since I haven't heard I've assumed no news is good news.'

'I suppose so.' Patsy sat down beside Anna, deciding to take time for a proper chat. 'He's not around. I mean he's here and I see him and the girls see him, but it's like he's sneaking. Lurking sort of.'

'Spying?'

'Not spying, I don't think. I'd have reported that for sure. No, it's sort of like a storm cloud always on the horizon. Not really threatening you, but you know it's raining on somebody somewhere.'

Anna shook her head. 'I'm still not getting the picture. Does he come over and moon at you or leave notes or what?'

'No. I'd've called you for that too, I think. He's just

around, in our peripheral vision sort of. Like the girls'll be waiting for the bus and he'll drive by at a time he should be working. Or I'll come home after dark from somewhere and he'll just be walking by my house. Mindy and Missy and I came out of the movies in Cortez and he was across the street having coffee at that little lunch place.'

'Following you?'

'Maybe – but from a big distance.'

'Does it scare you or the girls?'

Patsy laughed again. 'I suppose it should but it doesn't. It's sort of comforting, like that old song "Someone to Watch Over Me".'

Tom's behavior struck Anna more in the stalker than the guardian angel mode. 'He doesn't talk to you or the girls, he just sort of skulks?'

'Doesn't talk. In fact he seems to be avoiding us. A couple of times we've responded, you know – like friends – and Tom acted like he wanted to get away.'

'Well, holler if he starts scaring you,' Anna said because she could think of nothing else to say. She looked at her watch: seven-fifty-seven.

Adept at taking hints of dismissal, Patsy stood and arranged her purse on her shoulder. 'Waiting for Hills,' Anna explained. 'I've been summoned for God knows what.'

'Oh.' Patsy brightened. 'I bet it's to go to Durango. The F.B.I. man is arriving on the ten-eleven from Albuquerque. The superintendent had me book it.'

'That's it then. Pigeon's taxi service.'

Patsy picked up on her annoyance. 'Hills thought you'd

want to go. It turns out the investigator is an old friend of yours, a Frederick Stanton.'

'You're kidding! Frederick the Fed? I'll be damned.'

'He's not an old friend?' Patsy had such a practiced look of concern Anna would've pegged her as a mom even if she hadn't known of the girls.

'We worked together once,' Anna said. 'We're more like old acquaintances.'

Hills strode up looking lean and marvelously ranger-like with his blond bulk and tight pants. Her assignment was, indeed, to fetch Frederick Stanton from the Durango airport ninety miles to the east.

The drive between the park and Durango wound down off the mesa and through the Mancos Valley nestled between the snow-topped La Plata mountains to the north and the red mesas to the south. Fields were carpeted with dandelions and blue irises lined the streams. Several hundred sheep, herded by men and boys on horseback, stopped traffic for twenty minutes, making Anna late to the airport. Fortunately, the flight was even later.

Abandoning the terminal for the out of doors, she sat on the concrete with her back against the warm brick of the building and passed the time remembering Frederick the Fed.

Isle Royale had been a while ago but she still remembered the gory details. The F.B.I. agent was a tall gangling man with well-cut features a size too large for his face. Anna estimated his age at thirty-five. Dark hair, cut in the inimitable style of a third grader, class of '58, flopped over his forehead; skin showed white around the ears where the clippers had cut too close.

Stanton had a vague and bumbling manner but was usually a step or two ahead at the end of every heat. Too much Columbo, too much Lord Peter Wimsey, Anna thought. Or, perhaps, 'Revenge of the Nerds' and 'Saturday Night Live'. Stanton didn't fit the mold. It made him hard to type and impossible to predict. Which was, Anna guessed, exactly why he did it.

He used people. He'd used Anna and he'd done it effortlessly; that was the part that rankled.

A twin-engine prop plane, the commuter out of Albuquerque, roared in from the taxiway and came to a stop on the ramp beyond the chain-link fence.

Anna eased herself up, ankles and knees cracking in protest.

The fourth passenger off was Stanton. Anna laughed at how like himself he looked. Same haircut, even the same clothes. He wore a short sleeved madras shirt he must have unearthed from a vintage clothing store, rumpled khaki shorts, white socks and brown lace-up shoes. As he came down the metal steps that folded out from the fuselage, he kept looking behind him, swatting at his posterior.

Absorbed in this activity, he ambled across the ramp. When he reached the fence he looked up. If he was surprised to see Anna, he didn't show it. 'I think I sat in something ooky,' he said, wrinkling his long nose. 'Anything there?' He turned to give her an unobscured view of his backside.

There was perhaps a speck of something on his right hip pocket but Anna wasn't in the mood to enter into a discussion of it. 'Looks fine to me.'

Stanton craned his neck and looked down over his shoulder. 'Okay then,' he said. 'I'll have to trust you on this one. Sure felt sticky for a minute.'

'Luggage?' Anna said to get things moving.

'Got it.' He shook the strap of an oversized leather shoulder bag he carried.

'You must be planning on wrapping this one up in record time.'

'I heard you were on the case so I only brought one change of underdrawers.'

There wasn't much to say to that so Anna merely nodded.

With what seemed a maximum of fuss and fiddling around she got the federal agent buckled into the passenger seat of the patrol car and started the trip back to the park.

As they drove to the main highway Stanton waved graciously at passing traffic. 'Boy, I love riding in cars with lights and sirens,' he said. 'Everybody waves back. They think they did something and you're not stopping them for it. Kind of makes you pals.'

Anna laughed. 'I wondered what it was.'

Stanton made idle conversation, the kind she'd grown used to working with him on the island. During the weeks of that investigation she'd come to look upon it as his personal music, the kind designed to sooth the savage beasts; charming in its whimsy, disarmingly inane. When one became complacent, convinced he was a complete boob, he'd pounce.

'Okay,' he said as she pulled out into highway 160. 'Tell me the good parts version.'

Anna switched off the radio and pulled her thoughts together. As succinctly as possible, she recounted the disappearance, the discovery of the body, the widow's whereabouts the night of the murder and Rose's casting blame in the general direction of the pipeline contractor.

Stanton sat for a while humming 'I Heard It Through the Grapevine' under his breath. The patrol car crawled up the long slope out of Durango. Anna unfettered her mind and let it wander over the now green ski slopes of Hesperus and the fresh new-leaved poplar trees skirting the mountain ravines. The sky was an impossible blue, a blue seen only on hot midwestern summer days and high in the mountains. Cornflower blue – the phrase flickered through her mind though she'd never seen a cornflower.

'That's no fun,' Frederick said finally. He twisted around in his seat till the shoulder strap pushed his collar up under his right ear and his bony knees pointed in Anna's direction. 'Tell me the gossip, innuendo, lies, suppositions, weird happenstance. Dead guys are pretty dull without some good dirt. Do dish me.'

'The dead guy was a friend of mine,' Anna replied irritably.

'Oops.' Stanton looked genuinely contrite and she was sorry for such a cheap shot. She'd thought of Stacy as the Dead Guy not three hours earlier. She'd almost made up her mind to apologize when Stanton spoke again.

'Callous, that's me all over. How about this: Deceased individuals, however meritorious in life, lack the essential spontaneity to generate interest. So those left living must keep their spirits alive through the practice of the oral tradition.'

Anna snorted. 'Callous is right. The dirt.' Out of spite

– or self defense – she told Stanton everything she could think of that occurred in the park, or in anyone's imagination in the park, around the time of the murder: Jamie's chindi, the pipeline, medicals, evacuations, the Superintendent's secretary's marital problems, the monkey wrenching, the dorm, Piedmont's foster home, Bella's dwarfism. She got bored before he did, running out of words as they passed through the tiny town of Mancos.

'And the meritorious deceased?' Stanton pushed.

Anna was torn between a desire to snub the fed for his flippancy and a need to talk of Stacy. The need to talk won. She'd used that need a dozen times to pull information from people. Mildly, she cursed herself for giving in to it now. To retain some vestige of self respect, she culled all emotion from her tone. Dispassionately, she recounted Stacy's sensitivity, love of the parks, his attachment to Bella and addiction to Rose.

At the word 'addiction', Anna realized she was being catty. Hoping it had slipped by Stanton, she made a mental note to talk to Molly about it.

'Rats,' he summed up when she'd done. 'Sounds messy and domestic. Widows and orphans and who's divorced and who's dead. Any drug dealings, you think?'

He sounded so hopeful Anna laughed as she shook her head. 'Doesn't seem like it.'

'Too bad.' Stanton screwed himself around in the seat, draping one long arm over the back and looking down into the valley as the car climbed the winding road cut in the side of the mesa. 'Drug dealers make such satisfying bad buys. Not so good as Nazis or Hells Angels, but then who is? Hate doing the widows, especially when they're all fresh and weepy.'

Hills Dutton was waiting for them in the CRO. In the past Anna had often found rangers loath to turn an investigation over to an outside agency. Some hated surrendering the power, others suffered a natural discomfort at letting anyone not a member of the family paw through the dirty laundry. Lord knew what they might choose to air.

Dutton was the exception; he couldn't wait to dump this one in somebody else's lap. Statements, paperwork, the photographs, and the autopsy – unopened and dated two days previously, Anna noted – had been stuffed into a manila envelope. Hills thrust it into Stanton's hands the instant the introductions were over. Lest the abdication appear incomplete, he added: 'This is our busy season and I've got a park to run so I'm giving you Anna for whatever while you're here.'

'My very own ranger,' Stanton gloated as he and Anna walked back to her patrol car. 'Just what I always wanted . . . well, next to a pony.'

Anna grumbled because it was expected of her but she was pleased with the assignment. Parking tickets and medical evacuations had begun to pall, replaced by an undoubtedly unhealthy obsession with Stacy Meyers, living and now dead.

She took Stanton, the envelope still clamped under his arm, to Cliff Palace and played tour guide as she led him down the steep path into the alcove where the village was built. During the descent a metamorphosis took place.

By the time they stood before the ruin, Stanton had lost his puppyish ways. Even his physical appearance was altered. The angles of his bones had sharpened, his stride was no longer gangling but purposeful, and his step had softened till the leather soles fell with scarcely a sound. Anna was put in mind of the time they had sat on a rock overlooking Lake Richie on Isle Royale waiting for a murder suspect; the sense she'd gotten then of the wolf shedding its sheep's clothing.

The ruin was packed with tourists moving through the ancient pueblo in a sluggish stream. At the base of the tower where Anna and Stacy had found the asthmatic child, people were backed up twenty deep waiting to stick their heads through the window to see the paintings.

'Like the Matterhorn at Disneyland,' a voice from above and behind Anna sneered.

Jamie Burke was seated high on a boulder in the shade. A silver counter rested in her right hand and she clicked off tourists as they came by. The usual questions: when? who? how? and where did they go? were all answered in the same way: 'It's in the brochure.'

Anna was not impressed. Unlike the wilderness parks which she staunchly believed were for the animals and plants dwelling therein, Mesa Verde was for the visitors. Humans paying tribute with curiosity and awe to human ancestry. On Isle Royale and in Guadalupe, law enforcement was there to protect and preserve. The main function of rangers on the mesa was to keep the flow of traffic orderly so the interpreters could bring this history to life.

'Hi, Jamie,' Anna said neutrally.

Ignoring her, Jamie slid down from the rock to land on legs strong as shock absorbers. 'Are you the F.B.I. guy?' she demanded of Stanton.

The agent stuck out his hand. The unhinged, bumbling look had returned, donned like a disguise. 'Yes indeedy.'

Jamie didn't shake his hand. Putting fists on hips, she squinted up at the walls filling niches high above the dwelling. 'You're too late. Too bad Stacy had to die. He was my closest friend,' Jamie said. 'Maybe he'd still be alive if you'd listened to me.'

'You' was generic, as in 'they', and Anna didn't bother to challenge it.

'How so?' Stanton asked politely.

'Al said this strip-mining was killing the sacred land. They've got to be given their home, their peace. Are you going up into the ruin?' she asked suddenly.

'That's what us F.B.I. guys do.'

'It's a sacred place. Fragile. People aren't allowed to go stomping around up there and for good reason.'

Annoyance was nibbling away at Anna's already strained patience. She drew breath to speak. Stanton heard and shot her a look that shut her up.

'What's the good reason?' he asked.

'Death.'

He didn't react to the melodrama. 'Wow,' he said with seeming sincerity. 'Whose?'

'Stacy was not the first. You want him to be the last, then stop intruding.'

Stanton looked mystified. Jamie was enjoying her part in this home-made theatrical and would play it out as long as she could.

Anna jumped in with the punch line. 'Old ones, Anasazi, chindi, ghosts, spirits,' she told Stanton. 'Jamie believes—'

'Along with a lot of other people,' the interpreter stuck in.

'—that the ghosts or spirits of the original inhabitants of the mesa are popping up out of the underworld now and then showing their displeasure at the modern tourism industry by striking down a select handful of the hundreds of thousands of people who pass through here every year.'

'Not exactly!' Jamie snapped.

'Girls, girls,' Frederick chided and Anna quelled an impulse to bite him.

'We'd best get moving,' she said, glancing at her watch as if time was of the essence.

Jamie puffed out an exaggerated sigh. 'I'd better go with you. That's an easily impacted area.'

'Stay,' Anna ordered.

Jamie bristled but stayed. Anna didn't add 'Sit!' but she thought about it.

'Will you be here for a while?' Stanton asked the interpreter. 'I'd like to talk with somebody who really has a feel for this place.'

Jamie's bristles laid back down. She tossed her braid over her shoulder and almost smiled. 'I'll be here.'

'More flies with honey, Anna. Got to get them flies,' Stanton said as they walked down the path.

The kiva had not been disturbed since the body was carried out. Yellow tape marked POLICE LINE DO NOT CROSS and held down with stones was placed in an 'X' over the top of the kiva. Once Stanton had examined the scene the tape would be removed and the floor raked smooth.

The F.B.I. agent sat down on the edge where the roof had once been and dangled his legs over the side. 'Other folks find bodies in dumpsters, storm drains, vacant lots. Yours turn up in bizarre places. Your karma must be very strange,' he said to Anna.

'Out in the sticks you've got to take what you can get.' She sat down next to him.

He took the envelope he'd been carrying under his arm for the last forty minutes and pulled out the photographs of the crime scene. Pictures of the body had been blown up into 8×10 color prints.

Looking at the photos, Anna knew memories of Stacy in life would be hard to come by. This was how she would remember him: a banquet for flies. She'd never viewed Zach's body really, just the barest of glimpses to ID it. Studying pictures of Stacy, the value of open casket funerals, the laying out of the body, night watches – rituals that cut across religious and cultural lines – became clear. To let the living see the dead were most certainly dead and so to let them go. Ghosts were not the spirits of the dead returning but the memories of the living not yet laid to rest.

'The man is dead,' Frederick startled her with an echo of her thoughts. 'He's curled himself up—'

'Or been curled up by somebody.'

'In a what . . . a fire pit?'

'Yes.'

'Gun on, radio on, no marks of violence, no tracks but

his, the ground all raked neatly and his little hat tidy on that wall thing.'

'And his shoes off. See.' Anna pointed to the cordovan shoes tucked up near the brown-stockinged feet.

'You know what I like? I like big old bullet holes and somebody standing a few feet away with a smoking gun screaming, "My God I killed him! I killed him!" '

'That happen often?'

'All the time. How do you think we catch as many as we do?'

Anna stared down at the trampled kiva floor. 'At least this gives us job security.'

Stanton laughed and she realized how rare that occurrence was. Too bad, it was a good wholesome sound.

He put the photographs back and took out the autopsy report. 'The envelope please,' he said as he ripped it open. 'And the winners are . . .' his voice trailed off as he looked over the three single-spaced typed pages.

Anna couldn't read the small type without all but sitting in his lap so she possessed her soul in patience, passing the time by imagining how the village would have looked with cook fires burning, people hauling water, weaving cloth, children playing on the kiva roofs.

'Time of death.'

Her attention snapped back to the twentieth century.

'Somewhere between eight p.m. and three a.m. Monday night the twenty-first of June. Had rice and chicken for dinner and red licorice for dessert. Cause of death, heart failure.'

'Can't be!'

'Right there.' Stanton pointed a big-knuckled finger at

the bottom of the second page.

Anna took the report and read the offending sentence. 'Natural causes?' she ventured then read on. 'Doesn't say.'

'Could be a lot of things. Did he have a history of heart disease?'

'His wife said he was in perfect health. Perfect. And that's a quote.'

Stanton pondered the underground room. 'Shock, fear, drug overdose, respiratory failure, what causes the heart muscle to stop?'

'Electrical current, lightning, blunt trauma.' Anna couldn't think of anything else.

'I opt for one of those,' Stanton said. 'Even if he had a bad heart, I can't see a guy with chest pain, nausea, having trouble breathing, climbing up, crawling down, kicking his shoes off and the bucket.'

'Callous,'

'Sorry.'

'Neither can I.'

'Read me that third paragraph on page two – after all the chemical breakdown gobbledygook,' Stanton said.

'There was no sign of drugs or alcohol in the blood or muscle tissue.'

'There goes drug overdose,' Stanton said sadly.

'No bruising of the soft tissue.'

'There goes blunt trauma.'

'No sign of ingested poison. No entrance or exit wounds. No occluded arteries or symptoms of arteriosclerosis.'

'Damn. So much for natural causes. That pretty much

leaves us with your Miss Burke's spirits. Fear and shock. Guy lays down for a nap in the fire place, up pops a sipapu and WHAM! scares him to death. Case closed.'

'A sipapu's a place, not a thing.' Anna pointed to the crockery-lined hole. 'Your bogey man had to come out of there. Pretty tight squeeze for a truly terrifying critter.'

'Bad things come in small packages.'

Anna went back to the autopsy report. 'Oval burn marks approximately one inch by an inch and a half, first degree, on the right arm between the elbow and the shoulder. Similar mark on the left upper arm two inches above the antecubital space.

'I saw that. That mark. I thought it was a bruise. I get bruises there sometimes from the butt of my gun banging my arm.'

Stanton pulled a pair of half glasses out of the breast pocket of his madras shirt and shoved them up onto his nose. They were the kind with heavy black frames sold by drugstores. A children's show host Anna had watched as a child wore those same glasses. Uncle Happy, she remembered.

The agent held the photo they'd been discussing under his chin and stared down at it through the magnifying lenses. 'Oval burn marks. That smells clue-y to me. What did they look like?'

Anna took her eyes from the picture, rested them on the stone of the kiva floor and let Stacy's corpse rematerialize. 'I didn't inspect them closely at the time. Like I said, maybe bruises from the gun or being grabbed too hard. Thinking back, they were brownish – no purples, greens, blues, or yellows you might find with a healing bruise. And scaly. I touched one and it felt the way sunburned skin does when it's just beginning to peel.'

Stanton whistled 'An Actor's Life For Me' from Pinocchio. Lost in thought, he waggled his feet over the open air. 'Leaning against something hot,' he suggested. 'Like a motorcycle manifold.'

'Both arms and both on the inside? Odd.'

'True. He'd have to be hugging the Harley. Pretty silly he'd look too, if you ask me. Sorry,' he apologized automatically.

They thought a while longer. 'Something dripped?' Anna ventured. 'Hot wax. He was reaching up to take a candle off the mantle of something.'

'Could be. Kinky sex stuff? I've seen wax used in S & M movies – strictly Bureau research of course.'

'Of course. Stacy didn't seem the type.'

'Still waters?'

'Maybe.' But Anna didn't think so.

They fell into silence again. The steady hum of the tourists below provided white noise, the occasional call of a canyon bird a pleasing counterpoint.

Grating sounds cut through and Anna pulled her thoughts up out of Stacy's grave. Jamie Burke marched toward them along the wall that accessed the kiva where they sat, her heavy tread designed more to garner attention than to protect an 'easily impacted area'. Claude Beavens was behind her. There was no tow rope visible but he moved with the reluctant hitching motion of a vehicle not under its own power.

'That's him.' Jamie pointed an accusatory finger at

Frederick Stanton. 'The F.B.I. guy.'

Stanton scrambled to his feet and stuck out his hand. 'How do you do?' he asked formally.

Beavens looked around for someplace else to be. Not finding one, he took the proffered hand and mumbled, 'Please to meet you,' the way children are taught to in grade school.

'Look,' Beavens began. 'This isn't my idea. I just—'

'Tell him,' Jamie insisted.

Looking annoyed but beaten, he shrugged. Beavens had been so anxious to be a part of the murder investigation the day the body had been found, Anna wondered what held him back now.

'Claude was here the night Stacy died,' Jamie said for him and Anna understood. Few people wanted to participate quite that intimately in the investigative process.

'Not *here* here,' Beavens defended himself.

'But here,' Jamie said. 'Tell him.'

Frederick folded himself back down onto the lip of the kiva and stared expectantly up at the interpreter.

'I was out on the loop Monday night – that's when Jamie says Stacy was ... was here. That's all. No big deal.'

Stanton seemed less interested in Beavens than in Jamie. She stood with her profile to them, her long black hair trailing down her back. Her arms were crossed and her feet were planted wide apart in what, for good taste's sake, Anna hoped was an unconscious parody of Hiawatha.

'Monday night. You hit it right on the nose, Ms.

Burke.' Stanton flapped the papers from the autopsy. 'The coroner says that's the date.'

Not willing to break the pose, Jamie shot him a scornful look from the sides of her eyes. 'Summer solstice.'

Stanton waited. Beavens fidgeted and Anna watched. Claude was clearly uncomfortable about something but there was no way of telling what sort of ants were inhabiting his mental trousers. Guilt, embarrassment at being dragged into Jamie's little drama, nervousness at being questioned by the F.B.I. – all were possible as were a dozen things that didn't come readily to mind.

Jamie was basking in the limelight, dragging the interview out with cryptic sentences and pregnant pauses.

Anna was sorely tempted to spoil the show, but Stanton was satisfied to let the scene play out.

'It's when things tend to happen,' Jamie said after a moment. 'Some people have a feel for these things. A kinship. I felt it. Ask Anna. Something was coming down on the twenty-first.'

'Or up,' Anna said pointing at the sipapu.

'Go ahead. Investigate me, Mr. F.B.I.' If one could judge by the glint in Jamie's pale eyes, the prospect wasn't unwelcome. 'You'll have to look in your paranormal files for this one,' she finished.

'The X Files,' Stanton said gravely.

Jamie liked that. She turned on Beavens, now with hands deep in pockets poking at a dung beetle with the toe of his shoe. 'Tell him,' she ordered.

'Better tell me,' Stanton said. 'Just the facts, like Joe Friday says. Nobody'll interrupt you.' He didn't glance at Jamie when he said it. Somehow he didn't need to.

'Doggone it, Jamie!' Beavens exploded then took a deep breath. 'It really is no big deal. I was out here that night – Monday. I didn't go to Balcony House with everybody. That New Age stuff – crystals and mantra-ing at the moon – is crud.' His hand went to his throat and he nervously fingered a tiny gold cross Anna hadn't noticed before. 'I just rode my bike out here. Sat on the rocks over the canyon till the moon was up. Later I guess, two or two-thirty, maybe. Then I rode home. No big deal. I didn't see Stacy or anything.' He stopped, waited for a moment, then shrugged. 'That's it. No biggie.'

'God, I hate invertebrates masquerading as men,' Jamie sighed. Turning her back on Claude, she said to Stanton: 'Claude saw.'

Anna remembered the phrase; the words she had used the morning the body was discovered. She'd hissed it as Anna squeezed through the gate above Cliff Palace.

'Just spit it out,' Anna growled.

Stanton dead-panned in her direction. 'You're such a people-person, Anna.'

'Claude saw what?' she pressed.

'Where they come through, the veil,' Jamie said triumphantly. 'He told me Tuesday morning, before anybody'd even thought to look for Stacy. He said he'd seen the shimmer in the light of the solstice moon as if the spirits were passing through.'

'Not exactly,' Claude complained.

'Exactly,' Jamie countered.

'Exactly in your own words,' Stanton stopped the argument.

'What's the time?' Beavens asked.

All three of them glanced at their watches. 'One-ten,' Anna said before anyone else could.

'Gotta go. Balcony House tour in twenty minutes.'

'The veil?' Anna asked again.

Beavens pulled his hands out of his pockets. Again the shrug Anna was beginning to think was a nervous habit. 'I was just kidding around. Jamie's always on about this spirit garbage. I was kidding. Ask the other interps. I heard some of them leaving the loop in their truck later than I did.'

They watched Beavens trot off, sure footed, down the balcony to disappear into the ancient alleyway.

'He is a lying little weasel,' Jamie stated.

It was the first thing she'd said all day that had the ring of truth.

Chapter Thirteen

Anna and Stanton followed Jamie out of the closed part of the ruin and left her at the entrance clicking visitor statistics into the metal counter.

Rather than go against the flow of traffic, they climbed the four ladders at the western end of the alcove and regained the mesa top. The climb always winded Anna but she forced herself to breathe silently through her nose, enjoying the sound of Stanton's puffing. 'Want to rest?' she asked solicitously as they walked back toward the parking lot.

'Yes, please,' he said humbly and threw himself down on half a log-round smoothed to make a bench. Gratefully, Anna sat beside him and refilled her hungry lungs with the thin air. Her childishness made her laugh.

'I hope you're duly impressed,' she said. 'It's damn hard to hold your breath after that climb.'

'Tell me about it. I do it to impress the young agents. Nearly did myself in last training session. Gets harder every year.'

They sat for a while just breathing and feeling the sun on their faces. Anna made small talk with the visitors who came panting up from the ruin. The uniform made it mandatory and it was a part of the job she took pleasure in. Sharing beauty with total strangers made the world seem a friendlier place. In a culture dominated, if not by violence, then certainly by the overheated reports of it dished out by a ratings-starved news media, it reassured her that the love of peace and natural order were still extant in the human soul.

'Let's do lists,' Stanton suggested after a while. 'Pretend we're organized.'

Anna reached in her hip pocket and fished out the yellow notebook. She'd already written 'Life Insurance', 'Enemies', 'Where Else Should We Have Looked', and 'Greed/Rose'. 'Life Insurance' was crossed out since she'd overheard Rose telling Hattie that Stacy had left her and Bella with nothing.

'I'll be the secretary.' Stanton lifted the notebook from Anna's hand and the government-issue ballpoint from her shirt pocket.

'No life insurance?' he asked.

'Apparently not.'

He wrote 'CHECK' beside the crossed out words. 'Greed, always good. Was there an inheritance? That's a good one for Greed.'

'No. Stacy wasn't rich.'

'Where Else Should We Have Looked?'

'It's my guess we were meant to find the body and be mystified by it. Too coy, too precious, to be an accident. The only reasons not to hide the corpse are to prove death to get insurance or something or to stop people from looking for it in embarrassing places.'

'Good point.' Frederick underlined it. Beneath he wrote, speaking the words aloud as he did so, 'C. Beavens on scene. Interpreters in truck. J. Burke knew date. Spirit Veil. Anything else?'

'Put down Greeley. The widow wants us to talk to him. It's worth finding out why.'

Dutifully he wrote the name at the bottom of the list, then tapped the pen against his teeth. The top row was white and even but his bottom teeth were crowded, one pushed forward. As he tapped he hummed a tune Anna didn't recognize.

'So,' he said finally. 'We've got the wife because – who knows? Because there's always a good reason to kill your husband. Beavens because he was in the neighborhood. Burke because she knew the time of death and hates the white man's depredation of sacred grounds. Stacy was a white guy?'

Anna nodded.

'I remember.' Stanton shook the autopsy envelope. 'Said so. And we've got Greeley because the wife says he might know something. What else?'

'There's always us,' Anna stated the obvious. 'A ranger. We've all got what it takes.'

'Oooh.' Stanton looked impressed. Anna chose not to be amused.

'Keys to the ruin, to the Four-Way, knowledge of the upper kiva. Stacy would trust one of us. We could get him up here. All we'd have to say is we'd found some archaeological crime – graffiti, digging, theft, whatever.'

'Any ranger got a motive?'

Other than her own story of unrequited bullshit, Anna

couldn't think of any. She shook her head. 'He was a temporary employee so he wasn't a threat to anybody promotion or job-wise. He should have been – he was one of the best rangers we had. But without permanent status he couldn't get promoted. He wasn't even eligible for pay raises and I don't think he had anything worth stealing. Unless you count his wife and I'd question that one. Sorry,' she apologized for the nasty remark. 'Personal taste. Count her. Nobody seemed to hate him and if he was blackmailing anyone or selling drugs he was good at it. No rumors.'

'Somebody offed a nice, poor, unthreatening park ranger. Not promising.'

'Nope.'

Stanton closed the notebook and pocketed it along with Anna's pen. 'Let's do Greeley first since nothing else makes a whole lot of sense.

'Want to have lunch first?' he asked as they drove past the Navajo taco stand.

'Not hungry.'

Stanton looked pitiful but Anna didn't notice.

Ted Greeley was sitting at the break table in the maintenance shop along with Tom Silva and several other construction workers. Tom and two of the others were smoking. Ashtrays, already full, and soda pop cans cluttered the scarred formica.

Greeley's feet, crossed at the ankles, were propped up amid the debris. Even in heavy Red Wing boots his feet looked small. His white curls were stuck to his forehead with sweat and he sucked on a Diet 7-Up.

'Hey, Ted,' Anna announced herself. 'Don't you guys have to work for a living?'

'Not much longer if *Ms* Stinson has her way. We can sit right here in the shade drinking sodie pops and whistle for our paychecks. The old witch – spelled with a "b" – is trying to get the pipeline shut down till they dig up some beads and bones. A shit-load of money to keep a handful of eggheads employed, if you ask me.'

'Ain't nobody ever asks you, Ted,' one of the men said.

'Boy, you got that right.'

Anna would have expected the smart remark to come from Tom Silva but he sat a little apart from the others quietly smoking his Marlboros. He showed no interest in the banter. To Anna he looked thinner than when she'd last seen him, and paler – not as if he'd been out of the sun for a while – it wasn't so much a lack of color as a lack of energy, vividness. Somehow he'd turned in on himself, faded.

She remembered Patsy talking of his haunting her and the girls and hoped he wasn't winding up to a psychotic break of some kind.

'Howdy fellas, Tom,' Anna said to check his social reflexes. There were none. The others nodded or grunted, said 'hi' or cracked jokes. Absorbed in his own thoughts, Silva gave no sign he'd even heard her.

'What's with him?' she asked Greeley.

'Time of month.'

The men laughed and Anna knew there was no use pursuing that line of questioning.

'This is Special Agent Stanton of the F.B.I. Agent Stanton's here to investigate the death of Stacy Meyers. I'd appreciate it if you could give him all the help you can.' Her little speech given, Anna was happy to step out of the spotlight. As Stanton shook hands all around, she slipped back to the refrigerator, put a dollar in the coffee can and took out two Cokes. One she put in front of Stanton, the other she kept. Not only was she thirsty, but the role of waitress rendered her comfortably invisible.

The construction workers, with the exception of Silva, were taken by the romance of the F.B.I. They clustered as happily as scouts in a den.

Opening her Coke, Anna leaned back against the tool bench and watched.

For a few minutes they chatted about the shutting down of work on the pipeline. Ted held forth on the financial burdens of running a construction company. Stanton got an unedited earful about Al Stinson. The nicest thing she was called was a fruitcake. Occasionally, when the language grew rough, one of the men would remember Anna and mumble 'excuse my French, but it's true' or 'I'm no sexist, but . . .' and then, conscience salved, dive back into the conversational fray.

Stanton listened, made all the right noises and looked as solemnly interested as a priest taking confession. Once the political landscape had been colorfully painted, he moved the talk around to the investigation.

To Anna's surprise, the construction workers didn't hold her high opinion of Stacy. 'Full of himself', 'A little light in his loafers', were some of their comments.

Greeley summed it up. 'Meyers was a nineties kind of guy. Sensitive, caring, proud of his feminine side.'

'Yeah, what's that cologne he used?' a man still wearing his hard hat asked.

'Jasmine Dick,' a short block of muscle replied and spat tobacco juice in an empty Pepsi can.

By the practiced laughter, Anna knew it was an old joke and had no doubt what they called Stacy behind his back.

Buoyed along on the Old Boy laughter, Stanton managed to get the whereabouts at the time of the murder of everybody but Greeley and Tom before they caught on.

'Alibis?' Ted asked finally and raised his eyebrows. 'Hey, we're suspects!' This amused them nearly as much as Jasmine Dick. Still, the men who'd cleared themselves looked relieved. 'How 'bout it, Tom,' Greeley took over for Frederick. 'Where were you the night Stacy was tagged?'

'Nowhere,' Silva snapped.

'I guess that lets Tom off the hook,' Greeley laughed. 'Me too. At least nowhere I can say and keep in the lady's good graces.'

'Better to keep in mine,' Stanton said with a half-smile that sobered Ted instantly.

'When I gotta say, I'll say. Not till then,' Ted returned sharply. 'Break's over.' Greeley fixed Anna with a cold look. 'You want to make yourself useful? Catch the s.o.b. who's been screwing with my equipment.' The men gathered up their cigarettes and left Anna and Frederick in possession of the battered lunch table.

'Well, that was certainly productive,' Stanton said. 'All non-suspects were in jail with seven nuns at the time of the murder; the two suspects were "nowhere" and "nowhere with a lady".'

'Is Silva a suspect? I don't think he even knew Stacy to say hello to.'

'It may end up being a choice between Silva and the chindi,' Stanton cautioned.

'Now that you mention it, Silva looked guilty as hell,' Anna said.

'If you ever quit rangering you might try the F.B.I. I think you've got a flair for this sort of work.'

Anna glanced at her watch. 'It's three-thirty. Do you want to drop by the Widow Meyers before we quit for the day?'

'Is she all sad-eyed and teary?'

'Nope.'

'Looks guilty as hell?'

'I don't think she was in the park that night.'

'Too bad.'

'She could have made it,' Anna said hopefully. 'There's a phone call placing her in Farmington at seven p.m. That's only two hours from here. She could have driven up and back in one night easily.'

'Well, that is good news,' Stanton mocked her amiably.

'Beats chindi.'

'Could we have something to eat first?' he asked plaintively. 'I'm faint.'

'Sorry. I forget.'

'Probably how you keep your boyish figure.'

Rose was at home. When not shopping in Durango or Farmington, Rose was usually at home. Nature apparently held little allure. The front windows of the bungalow were closed and the shades drawn to shut it firmly out of doors. All the interior lights were ablaze. Rose was on the sofa opposite the woodstove. Magazines – *Self, Money, House Beautiful* – littered the floor. The remains of an iced tea and a plate covered in crumbs held down a pile of like literature on the coffee table.

A single bed, the kind on wheels that folds in half to be rolled into storage, was made up in one corner beneath the window. It was the brightest spot in the room. A cotton coverlet in rich red, green and blue paisley covered the mattress. Throw pillows in similar colors – some prints, some solids – were tumbled in organized chaos giving the bed the look of a gay and welcoming nest.

The window above was the only one in the room open, the shade up. Hattie sat cross-legged amid the kaleidoscope of color, holding a sketch pad. Bella had a pad of newsprint propped up against her aunt's thigh. She lay on her belly with her legs bent at the knee, little bare feet in the air. They stopped their work long enough to be introduced to Frederick Stanton.

Rose fussed with the magazines, moving them from one place to another without creating any real order. She was more on edge than Anna had seen her in the past week or so. Though the death was tragic, Anna would have thought the wait would have been worse on the nerves and the conclusion harder on the heart. Short controlled movements as she stabbed at the clutter and tight muscles around her mouth spoke of something more than anxiety or irritation. Rose was furious.

There was bound to be some anger at Stacy for having had the bad judgement to die – if Rose had not profited by the death – but it was more specific than that. It was directed at Anna.

Frederick was offered a chair and a glass of tea. Anna was snubbed. She was not even invited to sit. Indeed there was no place left to do so. But for Hattie's bed and the couch, Stanton had been given the only chair in the room, an office swivel tucked in the kneehole of a old wooden desk.

Sensing this production of 'good cop bad cop' had already been cast, Anna left the federal agent to question Rose and wandered over to the sunlit bed.

Obligingly, Bella scooted over and Anna sat down, happy in the cheerful disarray. 'What are you guys drawing?' she asked to make conversation.

'We're doing landscapes,' Bella told her. 'Here.' She tore off a sheet of newsprint and handed it to Anna. 'You can do it too. Put a coloring book under it so you can write on it. You can share my pens.'

Obediently, Anna put the paper on the hard cardboard cover of a *Birds of the Southwest* coloring book and selected a pink felt-tip pen from the pile. 'Aren't we supposed to have a landscape to draw from? Or are we just drawing the living room?'

'We're doing *inner* landscapes,' Bella said importantly. 'Tell her, Aunt Hattie.' The little girl dropped the black pen she was drawing with, picked up a dark purple one and promptly forgot them in her concentration.

Anna looked expectantly at Hattie. The woman stopped sketching and thought for a second. Her hair was pulled up in a knot, curled wisps escaping in all directions from where she'd stored and plucked colored pencils. Seven or eight still resided in her bun, poking out like the spines of a rainbow porcupine.

'We-ell,' Hattie said, dragging the word out. 'You close your eyes.'

Anna waited.

Hattie waited.

Anna realized this was for real and closed her eyes.

'You go down your esophagus.'

'That's your throat,' Bella volunteered helpfully.

'Turn left at your breastbone.'

Anna snuck a peek. Hattie's face was serious.

'Go into your heart.'

'Cree-aa-eek,' Bella provided the sound of a heavy door opening on rusted hinges.

Maybe because I haven't opened it in a while, Anna thought, caught up in the game.

'Look around you,' Hattie continued. 'What do you see? Don't tell it, draw it.'

Anna wasn't about to tell it. Or draw it. In her mind's heart she'd seen a lot of furniture covered with drop cloths. Molly would have a field day with that one.

To keep her credit good, she drew a picture that was supposed to be of Piedmont. A great orange blob with four legs and a tail. The eyes she made emerald green because Bella didn't have a bronze pen.

Hattie stopped drawing, a frown creasing her otherwise smooth brow. She was looking down at Bella's picture.

The child had made black and purple concentric circles filling the page. It looked like the top view of a tornado or giant whirlpool. In comparison, shrouded furniture seemed perfectly okay for decorating a heart.

'What is that, Bella?' Hattie asked easily but the worry was still on her face.

'Just colors,' Bella replied. 'Like in a flower.'

More like a bruise, Anna thought.

Stanton and Rose emerged from the kitchen where they'd vanished a while before. Stanton was just finishing a tall iced drink and Anna realized with some annoyance how thirsty she was. After her time on a damp island in Lake Superior, she had forgotten how the arid climate of the southwest could suck the moisture from the human body.

Stanton looked at her lumpy pumpkin-colored drawing. 'Are you done?' he asked politely.

'All done.'

'Can I see?' Bella asked.

Anna showed the child. 'You forgot his whiskers,' Bella told her. 'If you don't draw him whiskers, he'll run into things. That's how cats know how big the world is. They feel it with their whiskers.'

Anna picked up a black pen and began to fill in the missing items. 'I'm making them extra long,' she said. 'In case Piedmont wants to explore the galaxy.'

'Good idea,' Bella agreed.

'Honey, come here,' Rose said to her daughter as Anna and Frederick let themselves out. 'Momma needs to talk to you.'

The sun was still high but the angle had changed. Light streamed between the trees in long fingers filled with golden dust. The cicadas had hushed and the bulk of tourists gone from the mesa top.

Loath to confine themselves inside the patrol car after the claustrophobia of Rose Meyers' living room, Anna and Frederick leaned against the Ford, their backs to the bungalow. In front of them a fringe of trees separated the houses and Spruce Canyon. From where they stood the piñon-juniper forest, not a hundred yards wide, seemed to stretch on forever.

'I had fun,' Anna said.

'Bully for you. I didn't. The good news is I did get some iced tea.'

'Rub it in.'

'What's she got against you?' Stanton asked. 'The claws were definitely unsheathed whenever your name came up.'

'Beats me. Today's hostility is a new development.'

'The bad news is we're back to Silva and chindi as far as suspects go – unless Burke or Beavens show some spunk.'

'How so?'

'Rose was in Farmington with Ted Greeley.'

Anna thought about that for a moment. It fit none of her preconceived notions. 'I thought Rose hated Greeley.'

'She does. Not only did she say she'd had no intercourse – her word, not mine – with that "little, little man" since Farmington, but she alibied him through clenched teeth. I got the feeling she'd've rather put him in the gas chamber than admit she'd been with him in Farmington. But she swore to it.'

'All night?'

'Most of it.'

'Go figure.' Anna shook her head, remembering Bella saying the argument her mom had on the phone with Stacy that Monday night had been over some man. 'Maybe we're back to suicide, maybe Stacy couldn't hack another wife cheating on him.'

'It's been known to happen.' Stanton didn't sound convinced. 'No gunshot wound, no knife cuts, no pills, no poison – "it is a good day to die"? Meyers just lay down and willed his life away?'

'Not likely.' After Zach died Anna'd tried it enough times to know it didn't work.

'Frederick!' Rose was calling from the front steps. 'Do you have Stacy's things? Hills said Anna had taken them.'

She made it sound like petty theft. It took Anna a minute to realize what she was referring to.

'His shoes and hat,' she said. 'I'd forgotten. They're in the trunk,' she hollered to Rose as she walked around to the rear of the Ford.

They were still where she'd tossed them the day of the body recovery. The hat was a little the worse for wear, crushed by the tool box. Anna pushed the dent out. She had to dig under traffic cones, shotgun, and shovel for the shoes.

'Got 'em,' she called and pulled them out. As the clear afternoon light hit them, she sucked in her breath. 'Hey, Frederick, come here for a minute.'

Reacting to something in her voice, the F.B.I. agent was beside her in seconds.

'Look familiar?' Anna showed him the low-cut cordo-van shoes. On the heel of the right and the instep of the left shoe were the same oval burn marks the coroner had described on Stacy's arms.

Sipping the Beaujolais, Anna was careful not to let the wine glass clink against the telephone receiver. She was in no mood for another lecture from her sister on the evils of worshipping Bacchus.

She'd just finished an acerbic account of the interview with Mrs Meyers. 'The Green Eyed Monster,' she said. 'One of us is acting like a jealous woman.'

'Gee, yah think?' Molly returned sarcastically. 'Obviously you had a proprietary interest in her husband, for whatever reasons. Maybe because he had some of the same characteristics as Zach?'

'Maybe because he had a brain. Rare in these back woods.'

Molly laughed. 'Your jealousy is obviously rooted deep in childhood trauma and will require umpteen thousand dollars worth of therapy to root out. What's more interesting is why she's jealous of you – if the anger was inspired by jealousy.'

'I sure don't know. Maybe Stacy said something.'

'It started before the murder?'

Anna thought about that. 'No. After. Way after. I mean she was never My Friend Flicka but the outright hatred is new.'

'Something since? She could have found a torrid entry in his diary or an unmailed love letter.'

The idea thrilled Anna in a morbid sort of a way. She

sighed deeply and sucked down some of the red wine.

'Somebody telling tales out of school?' Molly suggested.

'Stacy and I were never together except professionally,' Anna said. 'It could be all in her head, a way to justify a less than ideal marriage. Looking at it from the outside, it didn't seem to be based on the principles of wellness. More mutual need than mutual respect and admiration, if you know what I mean.'

Molly chortled her evil-sounding chortle. 'Why do you think I never married? Nothing like an internship in Family Counseling to put the fear of matrimony in one's soul.'

'I hate feeling jealous!' Anna said with sudden vehemence. She pulled in another draught of wine and felt comforted. 'It makes me feel like such a *girl*.'

'Ah, yes. Such helpless, emotional creatures. Given to anorexia and fainting fits. Run like a girl, throw like a girl, whistle like a girl.'

'My point exactly.'

'Stacy's gone on two counts,' Molly reasoned. 'He's dead and he wasn't yours. I'd recommend you grieve like a girl. Let it run its course. It's not cancer or frostbite, it's just pain.'

'Like the phantom pain in an amputated limb?'

'Very like. Not much you can do with a feeling till you give in and feel the damn thing. As long as you mask emotions, anesthetize yourself, the confusion will only get worse.'

Anna had the irritating sense that Molly wasn't talking only about jealousy.

'You know, Anna, you don't have to do everything alone. Even out there in the back of beyond there are bound to be support groups.' Molly cut the inevitable argument short: 'Just think about it. It works. Lord knows why. It's not profitable to us honest shrinks. If there weren't plenty of nuts around to keep me in pin money, I'd keep mum about it.'

After that Molly let Anna change the subject and they talked on for a while but it failed to eradicate the hollow feeling behind Anna's breastbone.

When she'd hung up, she sat a while on her twin bed playing with the fringe of the Mexican blanket that served as a spread.

To the lamp, she said: 'I could sure use a good game of Dead Princess long about now.'

Chapter Fourteen

Winter was never far from the high country and Anna woke into a day cold and dreary enough to remind her how fragile the warmth of summer could be.

Thunderheads pressed low on the mesa but didn't obscure the view. Beneath the lowering gray, black piles of cumulonimbus rolled like billiard balls from the mountains of Arizona to the Colorado buttes. Through the thin walls of the dormitory, Anna heard the grind of thunder.

Helitack crew would be delighted; good fire weather. Lightning could bury itself deep in a juniper and smolder for days. When the weather let up and the fuels dried there might be hazard pay all around.

Throwing back the covers, Anna leaped out of bed. In the lowlands around Lake Superior weather fronts, with their attendant changes in pressure, gave her headaches. Not so the mountain storms. Cracking thunder and flashing lightning filled the air with ozone till it tingled in the lungs, rejuvenating body and spirit much the same as the air at the seaside or near waterfalls.

Having braided her hair off her face, she jammed herself into uniform and, cat-like to avoid getting wet, ran from the dorm to her patrol car. Thunderstorms made for good thinking weather: the tourists were chased safely indoors and the brass wouldn't venture out and so catch one cogitating.

Anna drove the short distance to the Far View cafeteria parking lot and pointed the nose of the Ford toward the panorama of northern New Mexico. Many-tined forks of lightning in the grand tradition of Frankenstein movies shattered a slate sky. Virga fell in curtains, now obscuring, now lifting to reveal a distant butte or valley. Colors were muted, the greens almost black, the reds of the earth somber.

The car radio was tuned to National Public Radio and something vaguely high-toned was being played on a harpsichord. The ordered gentility of the music and the wild vagaries of the weather suited Anna and she rolled down the window to better enjoy the concert.

Special Agent Stanton had taken Stacy's shoes with their odd marks to Durango so they could be sent to the lab in Hobbs, New Mexico for analysis. Since she'd been assigned to him for the duration, she wasn't on Hills' schedule. The day was pretty much hers to do with as she pleased.

She took the lid off her plastic coffee mug and took a sip. Once she'd had a severe coffee habit but luxury had cured it. After she'd begun fresh-grinding beans and using heavy whipping cream, the brew with non-dairy powders found in most offices didn't tempt her in the least. However, two cups of the good stuff each morning was a ritual she never missed.

Anna unbuckled her seat belt, rearranged the .357 and cuffs, and settled in for some serious thinking. Humanity, thus examined, struck her as sordid. Rose and Ted Greeley having their affair – or whatever it was they were having – in a motel in Farmington with little Bella ... where? Left in the car? Packed off to a movie? Anger and disrespect – at least from Rose's side – the hallmark of the encounter.

Drew's love of Bella seemed a bright spot in this dreary landscape but it too was tinged with anger. For reasons of his own he was tilting at what Anna hoped was a windmill: the abuse of that lovely child. To Anna's way of thinking the operations might cause less pain in the long run than fighting the good fight against prejudice.

Tom and Patsy Silva held together even after divorce by greed on Patsy's side and some as yet inexplicable obsession on Tom's. A fixation that had gone from an alarming but active harassment phase to an even more alarming but passive stalker phase.

Jamie and her posthumous affair with Stacy – in the past two days it had gone from 'dear friend' to 'dearest friend'. A bizarre form of psychological necrophilia, rare but, according to Anna's sister, not unheard of. Molly lamented the loss of the melodrama that had been such a part of American life before the turn of the century. A time when people took themselves more seriously, were less bored, less sophisticated. A time when widows wore black veils, the occasional duel was fought, and, though there were no documented incidents of it, people were believed to die of shame and of love.

The human animal needed their dramas, the psychiatrist believed. Denied, they sought them in unhealthy ways. Like imagined romances with dead married men. This last thought struck too close to home. Made physically uncomfortable by the parallel between her and Burke, Anna literally squirmed in her seat.

An affair with a dead married man. 'That's got to be it,' she exclaimed. Taken back to her non-existent romance with Stacy, she flashed on their one rendezvous: the curtailed cocktail hour at Far View Lounge. Ted Greeley had been there. Anna remembered him making a mock toast as she grabbed Stacy's arm, remembered the leer he was passing off as a smile.

That's why Rose was so hostile. In the last couple of days Greeley must have told her, or led her to believe, Anna had been having an affair with her husband.

'Damn!' Anna struck the steering wheel with an open palm. Everything seemed so sordid. Everything.

Lightning struck through the looping black clouds, the wide fork straddling the valley between Chapin and Park Mesas. Automatically Anna began to count, 'One Mississippi, two—' Thunder drowned out the thought. The strike had been less than a mile away.

She took another sip of excellent coffee and leaned back, letting past conversations with and about Rose drift through her mind. Why hadn't Rose said right off the bat that she was with Greeley in Farmington? It certainly got her off the hook more effectively than one seventeen-minute phone call several hours before the murder. Embarrassment over being caught in a compromising position? Possibly, but had she been up front about it, no one need have known. It was the nineties. No one believed dinner – even a late dinner – with a member of the opposite sex doomed a woman to wear the scarlet 'A'.

Earlier in the investigation Rose had been pointing the finger at Greeley. A lover's quarrel now patched up? Love me or go to the gas chamber? Anna shook her head. The facts, if such a hodge-podge of information and instincts could be labeled that, didn't support the theory. Stanton said Rose was loath to let the contractor off the hook, said she hadn't seen or spoken to 'that little, little man' since Farmington.

Rain came down more heavily, blowing in sheets against the windshield and Anna was forced to roll up her window or drown.

Rose's hostility had sprung full blown less than an hour after Stanton had questioned Greeley in the maintenance shop. Ergo, whatever had turned Rose against Anna had occurred recently, within the last couple of days. If Anna was right, and Rose's ire stemmed from jealousy, and that jealousy was ignited by Greeley, then Rose had lied. She had 'had intercourse' with that 'little, little man' since Farmington.

Did Greeley invent Stacy's infidelity so Rose would be less reluctant to expose hers, thus giving them both an alibi?

Surely Greeley was aware it also gave them both a motive.

Sharp rapping at the window startled Anna out of her reverie. She yelped in a decidedly unranger-like fashion and slopped coffee on her knee. Adding insult to injury, a kindly-looking elderly woman under an enormous black and white umbrella said, 'Sorry to wake you up,' as Anna rolled the window down. 'Could you tell me how far it is to the cliff dwellings?'

After the information was disseminated, Anna opted to move her brown study to a less accessible locale. More because it was secluded than for its ghoulish ambience, she chose the closed section of Cliff Palace. In her exalted capacity as the F.B.I. guy's chauffeur, the ruin was still open to her.

Weather had driven the tourists from the lesser-known sites but Cliff was doing a booming, if soggy, business. It was one of the most famous cliff dwellings in the world. Visitors, some on the mesa for only a day, had traveled from as far away as Japan, Germany, Australia. Come hell or high water, they would see Cliff Palace.

Tucked up in the ruin, out of sight lest she stir envy in lesser beings, Anna felt her privilege. Deep within the alcove she was completely dry and out of the wind, yet privy to the wondrous perfume the rain struck from a desert land. One hundred feet below the mesa top, Cliff Palace was still several hundred feet above the bottom of Cliff Canyon. Anna had a lovely view out past ruined walls and turrets. Along the canyon rims rain water had begun to pour over the sandstone, cascading down in thin ribbons of silver.

Near Jug House, a closed ruin on Wetherill Mesa, there was a stone reservoir built at the bottom of such a pour-over. The archaeologists surmised it could have been a tank to save the water. Anna was surprised there wasn't one at every ruin, but then the Anasazi were such accomplished potters, perhaps they had caught and stored rainwater in earthenware vessels.

Impromptu waterfalls delighted the tourists as much as they did Anna. From her hiding place she could hear the occasional squeal of pleasure. Leaning back on her hands, Anna let the sounds wash over her. She couldn't identify with Jamie's need to invent supernatural phenomena. As far as Anna was concerned these were the spirit veils. Common miracles that never lost their power to stir the human soul.

Just for the hell of it, she said a vague, non-denominational prayer for the spirit of Stacy Meyers.

Feet dangling into the abandoned kiva, the white noise of running water and muted voices to still her mind, she let the world settle around her. Details came sharply into focus: a small hand-print in black on the alcove overhead, the stark clash of a vulture's feather fallen in the center of an ancient building block, concentric circles marking the butt of a centuries-dead juniper hacked down by stone axes.

Half an hour melted away. No earth-shaking realizations came to her, no revelations as to why Greeley might have told Rose she and Stacy were having an affair. No guesses as to why Rose lied about having communicated with Greeley after the night of the murder; whether Beavens lied to Jamie when he said he saw the veil or lied to Anna when he said he didn't.

Hunger and cold overcame pastoral beauty and her thoughts began to turn materialistic. She stood and slapped some life into her rear end, then surreptitiously made her way back to the populated areas of the ruin.

A tall gray-haired interpreter, a retired philosophy professor from San Francisco State, was talking to a group of people near the tower. His long arms, encased in NPS green, semaphored information and enthusiasm.

Claude Beavens held down the post at the mouth of the alcove. Not only was he not speaking to the visitors but didn't seem interested in them even as statistics. Anna could see the silver counter dangling from an elastic band around his wrist. Binoculars obscured the upper half of his face. Because of the rain, birds were roosting, deer tucked up somewhere dry and Anna wondered what he stared at so intently. She followed the direction of his gaze down Cliff Canyon toward Ute reservation lands. Without the assistance of field glasses, she couldn't see anything out of the ordinary.

'What've you got?' she asked. Beavens jumped as if she'd goosed him with a cattle prod.

'Nothing!' he snapped, pulling the binoculars from around his neck as if they could testify against him.

'No law against looking,' Anna reassured him.

A visitor stopped beside them and asked what the Anasazi used for bathrooms. Beavens escaped into an earnest discussion of waste disposal in thirteen-hundred A.D.

Anna stepped up to the rock where he'd been holding his vigil and looked down the canyon. All seemed to be as it always was. Then it came to her. 'Somewhere out there Jamie's spirit veil does its elusive thing, doesn't it?' she asked as the visitor moved on.

'Who knows?' he said with his signature shrug. Whatever it was, it had ceased to interest him and, so, to be of much interest to Anna.

She was not sorry to reach her patrol car. Not only was it warm, dry and upholstered, but a moving vehicle was one of the few places in the modern world a person had some semblance of privacy. Cellular phones were an abomination. Along with bullet-proof vests and panty hose, it was a piece of equipment she'd never submit to. The radio was intrusion enough.

Driving back to the Chief Ranger's Office, she went as slowly as the traffic would allow. There was something about rain that opened the doors to dreaming. The steady beat, a softening of the edges of things, promoted a meditative state that unraveled the threads of linear thought. The drift was restful and Anna found herself glad to be freed from Stanton's sharp mind for the day.

Through the CRO's windows she saw enough gray and green to color a medium-sized swamp. The office was clogged with rangers holing up till the rain stopped. Not quite ready to rejoin the real world, she ducked around the building to the balcony in back. Set as it was into the side of Spruce Canyon, the front of the Chief's office was only one story high, its door opening directly onto the walk to the museum. The rear of the building was comprised of two stories. A heavy wooden balcony framed in the blocky saw-cut gingerbread of the south-west provided a picture-perfect view down into the canyon. On the far rim three silvery ribbons fell from pour-overs smoothed into troughs edging the cliff top. Through a screen of huge pine trees, black now with turkey vultures sitting out the storm, was Spruce Tree House; one hundred and fourteen rooms and eight kivas tucked neatly into a natural alcove.

The timbers framing the balcony were dark with water.

A sand-filled standing ashtray and a bench built in the same massive style as the framing were the only furnishings.

To Anna's relief there was only one visitor seeking sanctuary there. A woman in an ankle-length cranberry slicker and a canary yellow nor'easter hat stood near the far corner looking at the sky where the storm was darkest. Clouds hung down in bruised mammalia. Lightning was generated not only between heaven and earth but from cloud to cloud, as if the gods fought among themselves.

The woman turned slightly and bent her head. Anna amended her earlier census: there were two seekers of sanctuary. A child sat on the wide railing, enfolded securely in an ample cranberry embrace.

It was Hattie and Bella. Somehow they didn't qualify as destroyers of solitude and Anna was surprised to find she was glad to see them. Lest she be the one to shatter the peace, she slipped quietly onto the bench and watched the lightning play against the curtains of rain.

Thunder's grumbling was foreshadowed and echoed by faint feral sounds closer to home. Soon Anna lost interest in the meteorological show and watched Bella and her aunt with rapt attention.

They were growling.

Because of the innocence that blessed both faces, the sight was not frightening but it was disturbing. Bella Meyers' perfect little mouth was pulled back into a square exposing small white teeth. Her cheeks pushed up till they made slits of her eyes, and her hands – at least the one Anna could see clutching the sleeve of

Hattie's rain coat – was curled into a caricature of a claw.

The growls, nearly soft as purrs, were not amusing. There was too much anger for that. Bella snarled and clawed at something very real – at least to her. What kept the scene from being alarming or, worse, pathetic, was the power. A definite force, even in so small a girl, commanded respect. It was not the desperate anger of helplessness. It had focus. And, too, the child was safe in the loving arms of her aunt.

Growling at the universe isn't half scary when you know you're loved, Anna thought.

Hattie was snapping and snarling too, but her fury was diluted. Maturity and understanding had undermined the purity of her attack. Hers was more of a supportive growl, giving Bella's anger confirmation.

The minutes passed. The storm moved to the south. Bella's growls and snarls grew less ferocious. Hattie rested her chin on top of the child's head and hugged her tightly. Finally the last little 'grrr' was squeezed out and they stood still as statues. The rain stopped.

'Well. I guess that's that,' Hattie said.

'Sure is,' Bella returned with satisfaction. Using her bottom as a fulcrum and her aunt's arms as a brace, the little girl levered her legs over the rail and slid to the balcony floor.

'Hi, Anna,' she said, apparently unsurprised. 'Aunt Hattie and me were making it storm. But mostly me because I'm the maddest.'

'You sure cooked up a doozy,' Anna said. 'I practically got drowned.'

'Everybody did,' Bella said, unrepentant. 'Even the vultures.'

'How did you make it storm?'

Bella pulled herself up on the bench beside Anna and patted the seat, inviting her aunt to join them. 'Aunt Hattie taught me. First you have to really, really, *really* mad. Then you screw it all up into a ball and put it right here.' She reached up and tapped the middle of Anna's brow where the Hindus often drew the mystical third eye. 'Then you just point it at some clouds and order them to do it.'

'Ah,' Anna said.

'It helps if they're the black piley-up ones.'

The three of them were quiet for a minute, just sitting in a row listening to the pine needles drip. 'Do you say something like "rain rain, don't go away, come and stay today"?' Anna asked after a while.

'No.' Bella sounded as if that was an exceedingly stupid question and Anna felt as if she'd asked Willard Scott what he meant by partly cloudy. 'You talk cloud language,' Bella explained and growled for Anna – but not too loudly lest it unleash another deluge.

'You must have been really, really, *really* mad,' Anna said. 'That was one of the best storms I've ever seen.'

'I was pretty mad,' Bella conceded.

'What were you mad at?'

Bella looked at her aunt.

'You can be mad at anybody you want to, honey. It's okay. Sometimes I even get mad at your uncle Edwin.'

'Really, *really* mad?'

'Yup. Sometimes I get really mad at God.'

Bella looked impressed.

'She doesn't mind one bit,' Hattie said. 'She probably gets mad at the angels sometimes.'

'When would anybody get mad at an angel?' Bella asked skeptically.

'Maybe when they're molting,' Anna offered. 'Dropping feathers all over heaven.'

That seemed to make sense. 'Okay.' Bella dropped her voice to a whisper. 'I'm really, really mad at Momma.' She waited. No stray lightning bolt struck. With greater confidence, she added: 'Rose is a thorny, thorny, morny, dorny, thorny old Rose.'

Anna laughed and Bella was offended. 'What're you mad at your mom about,' Anna asked to win the child back but it was too late.

'Can't tell you,' Bella said and jumped down from the bench.

'Why not?' Now Anna was offended.

'Because Momma said blood's slicker than water.'

'I can't argue with that.'

'Nope.'

The sun was beginning to peek through. Hattie and Bella left. Anna waited a few more minutes to allow the newly clement weather time to lure the crowd out of the office, then walked around to the front door. Jennifer Short sat on the table behind the counter swinging her legs and eating candy out of a jar Frieda kept stocked. Her hair was squashed flat against her head from crown to ears, then stuck out at right angles.

'Isn't it awful,' she was complaining to Frieda. 'Ah feel

like something out of a horror flick. The one that goes crazy and hacks everybody up at the slumber party.'

'Terminal Hat Head,' Frieda contributed. 'Occupational hazard.' The dispatcher sat behind her desk, her computer for once dark, the radio mike near her right hand.

'Hey,' Jennifer greeted Anna.

'Howdy.' Anna leaned her elbows on the counter. Beneath the sheet of glass that topped it were maps of the park and surrounding areas. 'Talked to Patsy lately?' she asked Frieda when it became obvious she'd killed the conversation in progress.

'Matter of fact.' Frieda laughed her delicious laugh. 'She's doing okay but Tom's got her and the girls all a-twitter.'

'She'd better be careful,' Anna said. 'Stalking is stalking, not flattery. This guardian angel in a Chevy truck routine strikes me as a bubble or two off plumb. I think Tom is one weird guy.'

'I think Tom Silva's cute,' Jennifer said. 'Kee-ee-yoot.'

'Better watch out,' Anna kidded her. 'Remember what happened to the last guy you thought was cute.'

'Serves Stacy right for bein' married,' Jennifer retorted. 'All the good ones are married.'

'All the good ones are dead,' Anna said before she thought.

She was rewarded with an awkward silence and averted eyes.

'Guess I better look like I'm doing something constructive.' Jennifer smashed her hat down over the ruined hairdo and swaggered toward the door. It wasn't braggadocio, Anna knew from experience. For a short woman there was no place left for the arms once the gun-belt was strapped in place.

'I should too,' Anna said. Grabbing a handful of Frieda's butterscotch candies, she made her way back to the eight-by-six foot cubby hole that served as an office for Hills, the Fire Management Officer, Anna, half a dozen seasonals and the xerox machine.

Her desk was nearly as bad a rat's nest as Hills' and most of the rubble wasn't of her making. Space shared – shared with Homo sapiens who'd not yet attained their thirtieth birthdays – was reduced to chaos. Anna preferred order and knew herself to have entered upon that stage of the game Molly dubbed the Pre-Curmudgeon Warmups.

Everything that wasn't hers she scraped into an accordion envelope, marked it 'The Poltergeist File,' and stowed it in the kneehole under Hills' desk. Before anyone dared to dig that deep the stuff would be transmogrified into Historical Artifacts by the sheer passage of time.

To impose some semblance of organization, she unearthed all the 10–343 Case Incident and 10–344 Criminal Incident reports that had been turned in since the beginning of the tourist season in April. Thanks to Frieda, they had all been neatly filed in chronological order. Hills hadn't yet found the time to stir them into his ongoing stew of papers.

Anna separated out all the incidents that had occurred in or around Cliff Palace and ordered them again according to date. The last was the report she had written on the discovery and evacuation of Stacy Meyers' body.

Reading through it, the day was recreated in her mind but no new details or connections were generated.

Slouching down in the chair, she put her feet up. More blood to the brain. Again she read the report. Words on a page: no leaps of logic, no sparks of genius.

Putting the 344 aside, she picked up the sheaf of 343s and thumbed through them. Most were medicals: broken wrist, respiratory failure, anxiety attack, tachycaradia w/ confusion, asthma, fractured C-spine from a kiva diver – the local parlance for tourists who tumbled into the underground rooms.

Anna selected out all the evacuations. But for the wrist and the C-spine, each carry-out was in some way, shape or form, a heart, brain or breathing difficulty. Not unusual at seven-thousand feet with a high percentage of elderly visitors. She set the two fractures aside and looked through the remaining reports.

Pretty standard stuff; the only thing peculiar was the number of them. Anna carried the file into an ex-coat closet now pressed into service as a computer room and called up all the 343s for six summers past. Even accounting for the steady increase in tourism, medical evacuations had quadrupled at Cliff Palace this season. She checked reports for Balcony House and Spruce Tree House. They had remained more or less constant.

'Frieda, are you busy?' she hollered.

'Always.'

'Too busy?'

'What do you want?'

'Computer nerd stuff.'

'Come here then, I can't leave the front desk.'

With Anna breathing down her neck, Frieda used D-Base to cross reference all the evacuations by the patients' point of origin, age, sex, color, and primary complaint. 'Looks like a normal group,' Frieda said. 'Old people and sick people. You were expecting somebody else?'

'I don't know what I was expecting.' Anna sat down on Frieda's desk and looked through the reports again: ten-thirty, eleven o'clock, eleven-eighteen, April twelfth, twenty-sixth, May third, twenty-fourth and thirty-first, June seventh, June fourteenth. 'Try by time.'

Frieda complied. 'All but two were in the morning.'

That was something. The usual time for rescue excitement was mid-afternoon when the day's heat was setting in. 'Try by date.'

'Hey Ho.' Frieda clicked the keys. 'Well lookie there!'

'What?' Anna demanded.

'All but two – the afternoon ones – fell on Tuesday. And I thought Mondays were tough ... Coincidence?'

'Got to be,' Anna said. 'Thanks, Frieda.'

Back at her own desk Anna fanned out the reports now reduced by two, the two neither in the morning nor on a Tuesday. 'What do I know now?' she whispered to herself.

'What?' Frieda called.

'Nothing,' Anna answered both her own question and the dispatcher's. She pored over the paltry bits of information she had gathered. Rose lied about when and where she'd seen Greeley both the night of the murder and since.

Greeley was still grousing about the sugar in his D-14 cat's fuel tank. The murder had so overshadowed it there'd been no further investigation to speak of.

'Hey, Frieda,' Anna interrupted herself. 'Do private vendors like Greeley have to show proof of insurance before they're hired?'

'Yes. Too much liability otherwise. Why?'

'Just wondering.' Even if Stacy had been the sugar-slinging chain swinger, his ecotage had been aborted. Had he succeeded, all Greeley would have suffered was a fat check from the insurance company – not even much in the way of inconvenience or delay. Greeley killing Meyers to avenge the caterpillar was absurd.

Tom Silva was sullen and scared or angry – Anna couldn't tell which. Beavens was lying to somebody, either her or Jamie about his veil sighting. His report of leaving before the other interpreters had yet to be checked out. Jamie was claiming a closer kinship with the deceased than Anna believed existed and riding the revenge of the Anasazi theory pretty hard. She had even filed a backcountry permit to hold a vigil all night in the fatal kiva. The request had been denied.

How any of that tied in with seven evacuations from Cliff, all cardiopulmonary or central nervous system problems, all early in the day on a Tuesday, Anna couldn't fathom.

An unpleasant thought wandered through her tired mind. 'No,' she breathed as she dragged a calendar from the middle of a pile. On it she marked all the days of the evacuations with a tiny, faint 'X' in pencil. Forgetting her gun and radio, she took the calendar over to the museum.

Jamie Burke was working the front desk. Several visitors clustered around a single brochure arguing over the drawing of Mesa Verde's road system. Jamie stood behind the counter, her elbows resting on the glass, reading Louis Lamour's *Haunted Mesa*.

'Got a minute?' Anna asked.

Jamie raised her head with a practiced look of long-suffering patience. When she saw it was Anna, she relaxed. 'I'm stuck here till five-thirty.'

Anna pushed the calendar over the glass. 'Could you mark the veil sightings for me if you remember when they were?'

Jamie studied the calendar for a minute, then borrowed Anna's pen. 'April the eleventh, May twenty-third, the thirteenth of June, and, no matter what he says now, Claude saw one on the twenty-first.' As she counted each day she made a big black check mark on the page.

'Thanks.' Anna gathered up the calendar without looking at it and tucked her pen back in her shirt pocket.

'Aren't you going to tell me what this is all about?' Jamie asked.

'When it gels,' Anna lied easily.

Back at her desk in the CRO, she took out the calendar and studied it. All alleged veil sightings were on Monday nights before the Tuesday morning medical evacuations.

'Damn.'

'What?' Frieda hollered.

'I said I'm calling it a day, giving up the ghost, so to speak.'

Chindi.

'Pshaw!' Anna used her sister's word for 'expletive deleted.'

Chapter Fifteen

'You show me yours, I'll show you mine,' Stanton said.

'No dice. Yours first.'

Stanton hummed the first few bars of 'Getting To Know You' from the *King and I* and Anna laughed. There'd been too many times on Isle Royale when he'd gotten her to share more than she intended, then failed to return the favor.

'I got the marks on the shoes analyzed,' he said. 'You know what amazed me the most?'

Anna waited.

'That the NPS actually makes you wear them. They're symptomatic of a severe fashion disorder.'

'The marks . . .' Anna prompted.

'Yes. The marks. They were spaced right for finger-prints.' She and Stanton were sitting on the ledge above the Cliff Palace Ruin, a wide chunk of sandstone tucked up in the shadows under the trees. In front of them stone fanned out in an apron to the cliff's edge then there was darkness; the gulf of Cliff Canyon. Beyond the black was another pale ribbon where the far side of the canyon cut down through reservation lands. Even without a moon the sandstone picked up illumination from the night sky, reflecting back the dim glow of starlight. The soft down-canyon wind brought on by cooling air settling had died and the air was absolutely still.

Stanton scrunched his legs up more tightly, hugging his knees to his chest, and sucked air through an architecturally generous nose.

'Sitting on a cold rock in the dark is so much more fun than crawling into bed after a long day. Wish I'd thought of this years ago.'

'You were showing me yours.'

'You've no romance in your soul, Anna. Too many years hobnobbing with Mother Nature. Too pragmatic a lady for my money. In south Chicago we know what moonlight's all about.'

'Moon's not up.'

'In Chicago we have glorious street lights and we can turn them on whenever we want. But have it your way. Showing you mine.' He dropped a long arm down and snatched off his shoe without untying it. The white sock was pulled partway off and dangled trunk-like over the rock. 'The marks were here, here and here on the right shoe.' He placed his thumb and two fingers so the thumb was on the inside of the shoe and the index and middle fingers on the outside, his palm cupping the heel as if the shoe walked on his hand.

'They weren't smudges so much as burns. Something reacted with the leather and caused the discolorations.'

'Funny I never noticed them till the other day,' Anna said.

'They may not have shown up right away.'

'Any idea what made them?'

'Acid – what kind he didn't know.' Stanton studied the shoe. 'But looky.' He held it up at eye level, still grasping it with his palm beneath the heel. 'We can figure Meyers didn't pull it off himself. It wouldn't be impossible to take your own shoe off with your hand in this position, but highly unlikely.'

'So something with caustic digits removed his shoes after he was dead?' Anna teased.

'That seems to about sum it up.'

'That fits hand in glove with what I've come up with.'

'Goody.' He stretched his legs out in front of him and waggled his feet. His bare shins gleamed in the starlight. 'Now do I get to find out why I'm sitting on a rock in the middle of the night instead of curled snug in my little bed?'

'We're on chindi patrol.'

Stanton groaned.

'I'm getting overtime,' Anna added helpfully.

'I'm exempt.'

'Too bad. This promises to be a long one.' Anna told him her story of carry-outs and spirit veil sightings, Monday nights and Tuesday mornings, and left him to flounder with cause and effect.

He continued wagging his feet as if transfixed by the metronomic motion. 'Ms Burke lying?' he suggested after a minute or two. 'Putting her paranormal next to the normal to lend it credence?'

'I wouldn't put it past her, but I didn't tell her when the medicals were or why I wanted the sighting dates.'

'Could she have gotten the dates of the medicals out of the files?'

'I suppose. She doesn't have a key to the CRO and it

would cause comment if she came in and looked through the files. They're no guarded secret or anything, interps just never look at them; it'd be something to gossip about when who's sleeping with whom grew thin.'

'Could she get into the office at night, when no gossips were about?'

'Sure. Somebody'd probably let her in if she asked. Security – except for the administration building – is pretty lax. It seems a stretch though. Why bother? She never bothers to substantiate any of her other stories. Anyway, at least one Monday night I heard her talking about the veil and then the next day we had that medical. There's no way she could've planned to have all the cardio pulmonary and central nervous system problems occur on Tuesday mornings.'

'Was she on duty each time there was a carry-out?'

Anna thought about it. Near as she could remember, she was. 'I'll check on it.'

'Jamie Burke, Medicine Woman.' Stanton bounced his eyebrows suggestively. Light and shadow dappled his fair skin, and Anna realized the moon had risen.

'Wouldn't Jamie love that,' she said. 'She's an opportunistic actor. Takes every chance to dash out on stage. But I doubt she has the tenacity to write the script to that extent.'

'If she didn't set it up and she's not lying, then we really are out here waiting for the dead to walk?'

'When you've ruled out the impossible, whatever's left . . .'

They sat a while without speaking. Anna was enjoying herself. A smear of lights over Farmington, fifty miles distant, was the only flaw in a perfect sky. Deep in the canyon an owl called and was answered.

'So write me your autobiography and we'll get this life-long friendship rolling,' Stanton dropped into the stillness.

Anna would have laughed but, remembering how sound carried in these natural ampitheatres, settled for a smile.

'Aw, come on,' Stanton pleaded. 'Since we can't have cheeseburgers and coffee out of styrofoam cups that's the next best thing for making this feel like a real stakeout.'

If an expectant stare indicated anything, he was serious. Suddenly Anna felt shy.

'Just start any old where,' he encouraged.

'Well, I was born naked—'

'Not the ishy parts! I don't want to know you that well.'

'I thought you should know the worst if we're to be life-long friends.'

'Okay then. Ever married?'

'You consider that the worst?'

'My ex wives did.'

It was Anna's turn for raised eyebrows, metaphorically if not literally. '*Wives?*'

'Two.'

'Children?'

'Several.'

'Ages?'

'Oooh, that's a toughie. Thirteen going on fourteen – second marriage. Nineteen and twenty-three – introductory marriage. Girl, girl, boy, respectively.'

Anna revised her estimate of Stanton's age from late thirties to mid-forties. She didn't ask what had happened. Once or twice in the past, when she was feeling excessively polite or nosey, she'd asked that question. Nothing new happened under the sun and certainly not before the altar.

'You ever married?' Stanton asked again.

'Yes.'

'Died?'

'How'd you guess?'

'A lady who finds corpses on sunken ships and in kivas wouldn't be so bourgeois as to be divorced. No glamour, no drama.'

A pang of embarrassment let Anna know he was right. Like other widows, especially young widows, she was prone to wearing her weeds like a badge of honor. Widowhood conferred a mystery and status divorce lacked. The difference between returning WWII and Vietnam veterans. Both had been through a war, but a judgmental public conferred glory only on those who had been victimized in a socially acceptable manner. In divorce, as in a police action, nobody truly won and everybody got wounded.

'You know the only reason Romeo and Juliet didn't get a divorce is because they died first,' Stanton said.

A rustling stirred the pine needles behind them. 'Are there snakes?' he demanded abruptly.

'Snakes don't tend to be nocturnal. They're too cold-blooded.'

'Most of the cold-blooded creatures in Chicago are exclusively nocturnal.'

'Our tarantulas come out at night,' Anna offered.

'Stop that!' He pulled his legs up again. 'Don't tell me that. You're such a bully.

'So tell me about the dead guy,' he said after he'd gotten himself rearranged in a defensive posture.

'I already told you all I know and then some.'

'Not the kiva dead guy, the dead guy you're married to.'

Anna noticed he didn't use the past tense and wondered if he'd tapped into her idiosyncracies. 'Neurosis,' she heard her sister's voice in her mind. 'Spade for spade.' All at once she felt terribly tired. A middle-aged lady up past her bedtime sitting on a rock in the dark.

Stanton was still looking at her, his face open and interested. Briefly, Anna thought of what she might tell him, wondered if it would have the cathartic effect of confession. Or if she'd merely paint the old pattern of the perfect marriage. Romeo and Juliet Go To New York.

'Nothing's perfect,' she said finally. 'It was a long time ago.'

Stanton laid a hand on her arm. At first she resented his pity, then realized that wasn't inherent in the gesture. He was shutting her up, pointing to the west where a quarter mile distant the walls of an ancient ruin appeared in a flicker of light then vanished again into darkness. The effect was unsettling, as if, like Brigadoon, the pueblo had appeared momentarily in the twentieth century.

'Headlights,' Anna shattered the illusion. 'That's Sun Temple. It's on another part of the mesa but your headlights rake across it when you come around the bend before the Cliff Palace parking lot.'

'The last ranger sweeping out left-over tourists?' Stanton ventured.

Anna shook her head. 'Too late. Jennifer went out of service at midnight.' She squeezed the tiny button on the left side of her watch and squinted at the barely illuminated numbers. 'It's after one. Probably interps. Maybe Jennifer gave them the key. They may be out for the same reason we are.' Levering herself up, she stomped some blood back into her feet. 'Might as well go after them. We're legal; they're not: in a closed area without a permit.'

'A firing offense?'

'Definitely a calling-on-the-carpet offense.'

The roar of an engine followed after the lights. 'Sounds like a truck.' Following the deer trail they'd taken to the mesa's edge, Anna began threading her way quickly through the junipers.

'You must have eyes like a cat,' Stanton complained.

She stopped, took the mag light of her duty belt and shined it back down the trail for him. He wasn't far behind. When he chose he could move quietly.

The sound of an engine being gunned stopped them both. 'Saw the patrol car,' Anna said. She began to run and heard Stanton follow. In less than three minutes they reached the parking lot but the truck was gone. 'Rats.'

'No lights and sirens?' he asked as she backed the patrol car out.

'They have no place to go,' Anna reminded him. 'We'll catch them at the gate unless they left it open.' Still, she drove as fast as the winding road permitted. Partly to catch the offending vehicle and partly for the sheer fun of it.

'Whee!' Stanton said and pulled his lap belt tighter.

'Three-one-two, three-zero-one.' The radio commanded their attention.

'That's you,' Stanton said. 'Boy you've got an exciting job. Wish I were a Park Ranger.'

'Stick with me. You may get to see a dog off leash.' Anna picked up the mike and responded with her call number. 301 was Freida's personal number.

'Are you still on duty, Anna?'

'Yes. I'm on Cliff Palace loop with Agent Stanton. We've a vehicle in a closed area.'

'You may want to leave it. There's a disturbance at Patsy Silva's residence. It sounds serious. Al called. She said she's heard shouting and what she thinks might be gun shots.'

'I'm headed that direction. See if you can't get somebody else out of bed to lend me moral support.'

'Ten-four. Three-zero-one, zero-one-thirty-four.'

Anna made an educated guess that the instigator of this particular melee was Tom Silva and refreshed Stanton on the Silvas' post-matrimonial relationship.

'Bet you're glad I'm along,' he said smugly.

'And why would that be?'

'You'll need somebody to calm the hysterical wife while you're disarming and subduing the enraged husband.'

Anna laughed. 'You've got the more dangerous of the two jobs.'

'I wish you were kidding.'

She took the turn at the Three-Way too fast and scared herself into taking her foot out of the carburetor. By the time they reached the Four-Way intersection she'd slowed to a safer speed.

The gate was closed and the chain in place.

'We couldn't have been far behind. Where's the truck?' Stanton demanded.

'They hid out somewhere along the way. Looped back around or ducked up a fire road. We won't catch them tonight.'

In the headlights she could see the padlock's arm was through the chain links but not clicked closed. 'The gate is false-locked,' she told Stanton. 'Get it for me, would you?'

Stanton complied, relocking the chain behind him. 'Maybe we'll get lucky, lock 'em in.'

Anna's thoughts had moved ahead to the upcoming festivities. Shortly before reaching the tower house, she told Frieda she had arrived on scene, then opened the car window and turned off the headlights. Moonlight was enough to see by.

'Stealth ranger?' Stanton whispered as the car crept up the short drive.

'The dark is my friend,' Anna quoted a self-defense instructor from the Federal Law Enforcement Training Center in Georgia.

The Silva's residence was dark and, at the moment, quiet. Anna unclipped her flashlight from the recharger and pushed open the car door. Stanton folded himself out his side. 'This is the creepy part,' he whispered.

For a moment they stood in silence not softened even by the hum of night insects or the rustling of predators and prey. Just when they'd come to count on it, the stillness was destroyed by the sound of shattering glass and shouting. 'God damn you, Pats! Let me in. Jesus, Mary an' Joseph, listen to me for Chrissake!' Fierce pounding followed.

'Ahh. Better,' Stanton said. 'Now we know where he is and his church of choice.'

'It's Tom.' Quietly, Anna led the way up the flagstone walk curling around the building. Behind the jut of the square kitchen, set into the curved wall of the tower, was the front and only door. It and the small porch protecting it, were wooden. The rest of the dwelling was stone.

'You're a dead woman if you don't let me in!' came a cry so slurred it hardly sounded like Silva.

Anna switched on the flashlight. In her peripheral vision she saw Stanton melt out of the moonlight into the shadows as the beam spotlighted the man on the door step.

Looking like a refugee from the movie set of 'Bus Stop', Tom Silva, in Levis, boots, an open white shirt and battered straw cowboy hat, leaned on the front door. Both arms were raised, fists balled, propping him up. He rested his forehead against the wood. The hat was pushed to the back of his head.

'Tom,' Anna said softly.

'Gun,' Stanton said just as quietly, his voice penetrating from the shadows.

Almost swallowed up in Silva's right fist was a derringer. Anna took her .357 from its holster and trained it on him.

'Tom,' she said again. 'Put the gun down. It's Anna.'

Silva turned. The act unbalanced him and he stumbled backwards, his shoulders crashing into the planks. The derringer sparked in the light as his arm swung up. Anna's stomach lurched and her finger tensed on the trigger but he was only shading his eyes with the weapon, squinting to see past the glare.

'Fucking idiot.' Shaken by the anger adrenaline leaves behind, Anna said: 'You just nearly scared me into shooting you, you know that? Put that gun down. Slow! Don't you dare scare me like that again.'

'Anna?' Tom staggered half a step forward then fell back once more against the support of the door. '*Ranger* Anna? No shit?'

'The gun,' Anna reminded him. 'Put it down.'

Tom brought the derringer in front of his face and studied it. Anna's breath caught at the movement. She was becoming uncomfortably aware of the strain of holding the revolver at arm's length in one hand and the six-cell flashlight in the other.

'This is my door-knocker,' Tom said. It looked a match to the one he'd given Patsy.

'Drop the damn thing,' Anna snapped.

'Jeeze-Louise,' he mumbled. 'Keep your pants on.'

'Now,' Anna ordered, trying to cut the alcohol shrouding his mind.

'I'm not dropping it,' he said petulantly. 'It's got a pearl handle. How 'bout I set it down real nice like? Okay?'

'Okay. Just do it.'

Silva bent down to lay the little pistol on the cement, lost equilibrium and fell against a post supporting the porch roof. The derringer clattered to the concrete. 'Fuck,' Silva growled. 'If you've busted it . . .' He reached for the pistol but a hand shot out of the shadows and snatched it away.

'I'll go ahead and take care of this for you, Mr Silva,' Anna heard Stanton saying politely.

Flashing blue lights and a screaming siren made Anna jump. She squeaked as well but fortunately the clamor drowned her out. Silva screamed outright. 'Sheesh!' He collapsed on the welcome mat, his back to the door, and hid his face in his hands. 'Pats is a dead woman. Missy and Mindy: dead. Fuck.' In slow motion, he rolled to his side and vomited into the petunias.

Anna holstered her weapon and took a deep breath to steady her nerves. Stanton materialized out of the shadows and began patting the incapacitated Silva down for weapons. 'Now you've done it, Anna,' Stanton said.

'Don't I know it. I took "it" out.' Anna said, refering to her revolver.

'Gonna be paperwork to atone for that.'

Loud bootfalls on the flagstone announced Jennifer Short's arrival. 'The pitter patter of little feet,' Anna muttered unkindly. 'Hey ya, Jennifer,' she said as the other woman came up beside her. 'You might want to call "in service" when you go out and "on scene" when you arrive. It's okay to spoil the surprise.'

'Sorry. Damnation. I'm always forgettin' that.'

The porch light came on, giving Stanton light to work by, and Anna switched off her flashlight.

Jennifer's face was flushed and her eyes bright. Clearly she was scared, but excited too. Maybe she'd arrived a bit like Wyatt Earp into Dodge but she'd made a quick response from Far View and she hadn't hung back. 'Good to see you. Come to join the fun?' Anna asked.

'Looks like it's all been had. Ol' Tom the only perpetrator?' Jennifer asked, disappointed. 'Frieda made it sound like a riot.'

'He had a gun,' Anna tried to sweeten the pot. Jennifer perked up a little. 'Why don't you go work with Special Agent Stanton,' Anna suggested. 'I need to check on Patsy and the girls.'

Tom Silva was still retching, Agent Stanton standing beside him looking mildly ill. Jennifer strode up, jammed her hat more tightly down on her head then fumbled out her handcuffs. 'You have the right . . . Oh shit.' She pulled her stetson off and tugged a bit of paper from inside the hat band. 'Hold this.' She handed the hat unceremoniously to Stanton and finished reading Tom his rights from the paper. When she'd done, she turned to Anna. 'What now? Cuff him?'

Anna nodded. 'There's a belt in the trunk of my car. A leather one with some metal rings on it. Put it around his waist and cuff his hands in front of him and to the belt. Frederick will assist. You're looking good.'

'It's my first,' Jennifer said and grinned. 'Y'all be gentle with me,' she said to Silva. He threw up again.

Anna waited till Jennifer and Stanton had helped Tom to his feet and led him away, then she knocked on the tower house door. 'Patsy, it's me, Anna. Tom's gone. Are you okay?' There was a scraping sound from within as if something heavy was being dragged away then the door opened a crack. Looking terribly young with her short hair and pink pajamas, Patsy stuck her head out and looked around to discern the truth of Anna's statement.

'Are you all right?' Anna repeated her question.

'I guess. Mindy! Missy!' The girls came up from the living area and stood on the landing looking wide awake and confused. 'Yes, we're okay,' Patsy said, comforted by having her girls around her. 'He never got in or anything.'

'He wouldn't have hurt us,' Mindy complained. At thirteen or fourteen, she was the younger of the two daughters. 'You don't have to take him anywhere. He was drunk,' she added as if this exonerated him.

'Maybe you could make me a cup of coffee,' Anna said to Patsy. 'Instant would be fine.'

The girls settled in the little booth in the kitchen. The domesticity of Mother putting the kettle on seemed to soothe all of them. Patsy poured the water over the coffee crystals when it was barely warm and handed Anna skim milk from the refrigerator.

Anna leaned against the counter and forced down a swallow. 'What happened?' she asked now that a semblance of normalcy had been restored.

'It was Tom,' Patsy said unnecessarily. 'He came over earlier. I could tell he'd been drinking and I wouldn't see him. He went away again but came back about half an hour ago. He was pretty drunk.'

'Blotto,' Missy said.

'Not blotto,' Mindy contradicted her.

'Blotto.'

The girls were so close in age and so alike in blond

good looks, Anna often got them confused, which didn't endear her to either one of them. Both wore their hair long and straight, framing round scrubbed faces marked with a scattering of pimples. Mindy wore a nightshirt with Bart Simpson's likeness on it and Missy an oversized T-shirt and boxer shorts, both the worse for wear.

'Go on,' Anna said to their mother.'

'That's about it. He was drunk. Blotto,' she added, giving Mindy a yes-he-was-too look. 'He tried to get in. That's when I locked the door.'

'What did he want?'

'I don't know.' Patsy started to cry.

'He kept yelling he was going to kill us,' Missy said.

'He did not!' Mindy punched her sister in the arm.

'He did too, you little creep.'

'Girls, that's enough!' Patsy slapped the table top with the flat of her hand and the girls were quiet.

'He didn't say he was going to kill us,' Patsy said. 'He just said things like "you're dead if you don't listen to me" and "you're a dead woman, Pats." Things like that. He did not threaten to kill us, Missy. Don't you go saying things like that.'

'Like that's not a threat.' Missy tossed her hair and started french braiding it back off her face.

The comments struck Anna as threatening as well, but Patsy and her daughters, even Missy, didn't seem particularly terrified by the incident, so maybe they weren't. Maybe it was a fairly standard family inter-action. 'Is that all you can remember?' she asked Patsy.

'That's about it. I think he maybe shot that little gun off once or twice. He was mad that I gave it back to him. I left it in his pickup the other day. With the girls, I didn't want it around the house.'

Anna waited a moment but no more information was forthcoming. 'Okay. We're going to arrest him and take him down to Cortez. What do you want to charge him with?'

'Arrest him?' Patsy looked alarmed. 'You don't have to do that. Can't you just take him somewhere till he sobers up? You don't have to arrest him.'

'I already did.'

Now she looked aggrieved. 'I won't press charges.'

'I will.' Anna rinsed her cup and put it in the sink. 'Drunk and disorderly, Disturbing the Peace, Unlawful Possession of a Firearm In a National Park, Refusing to Obey a Lawful Order, Obstructing a Federal Officer in the Execution of Her Duty, Public Intoxication, D.U.I if he drove here, Noise After Quiet Hours, and Brain Off Leash. If I were you, I'd think it over before I let him off the hook. His behavior is unacceptable, illegal and unsafe. You let me know if you change your mind.'

Anna left the three of them sitting at the table giving her and each other dirty looks.

Tom was cuffed and belted into the back of the patrol car. Jennifer and Frederick stood by the open door waiting without talking. As Anna walked up, Frederick stepped away from the vehicle and addressed her in hushed tones. 'Can you and Ranger Short take Mr Silva in by yourselves?'

'I think we can manage that,' Anna said dryly.

'Oh whew. You don't have to give me a ride home even. I can walk back to my quarters from here easy.'

'Tired of my company?' Anna asked as he turned to go.

Stanton looked over his shoulder. 'He's going to throw up in your car. All the way down the hill. Ish.'

'Coward.'

'Hypersensitive gag reflex,' he called back cheerily.

Blue lights still blazing, Jennifer had parked the 4×4 truck behind the patrol car. She was leaning against the fender, apparently enjoying the evening.

'Agent Stanton opted out,' Anna told her. 'Follow me to maintenance. You can leave your vehicle there and ride down to Cortez with me.'

'Guess I gotta turn out the overheads,' Jennifer sighed. 'Too bad. They're kinda pretty.'

As Anna pulled into maintenance, the patrol car's headlights shone on the gate to the locked yard where the pipeline contractor kept his equipment. In the beams Anna could see the red water truck and the ubiquitous yellow of heavy machinery. A man in dark clothes, welding gloves stuck in his hip pocket, was fiddling with the lock to the enclosed area. Anna flipped on her high beams and drove up to him. Shielding his eyes, he turned. It was Ted Greeley. She glanced at the dashboard clock: two-nineteen. Greeley didn't stay on the mesa top nights; he rented a place in Mancos.

''Morning, Ted.' She stepped from her vehicle and stood behind the open door. 'You're up early.'

'So're you. But I knew that. Running my little buddy out of town?'

'Something like that. What're you doing up here at this

hour?' It was late, and she was too tired for prolonged pleasantries.

'Why Anna, I didn't know you cared. As it happens, I was visiting a sick friend. I heard on the radio that my boy Thomas was on the rampage and I got to wondering if he'd borrowed a cup of sugar from any of the neighbor ladies. That boy's one butt short of a pack and he's got a key to the yard. His kind of help I don't need.'

'I didn't know you had a radio.'

'I don't.' Greeley winked and said goodnight.

For a moment Anna was nonplussed. Then she remembered: neither she nor Hills had gotten Stacy's personal protective gear from the widow. Rose still had his revolver and his radio. But a lot of people had radios: Drew, Jimmy, Paul, Jennifer, Al, Frieda. Though most of the seasonal interpreters didn't carry them, they all had access to those kept in the museum for use in the ruins.

Anna let the thought go. Something else had been triggered by Greeley but she was at a loss as to what it was. She let her brain empty and the thought floated up: Tom Silva had a key to the equipment yard. Had his sudden increase in cash flow that washed Patsy's new watch into the picture come from pilfering parts? Tools?

Stanton was right, of course. Silva vomited half a dozen times on the way down. Jennifer, riding beside him in the back seat, swore every time he threw up. 'These're my Class "A"s, damn you,' she snarled at one point. Anna rolled down her window and turned the air-conditioning on to clear the air. By the time they reached the Cortez Sheriff's Office Silva was nearly comatose. During the car trip he'd been too far gone to question;

now it would have to wait till morning.

Anna turned him over to the booking officer who wrote him up for Drunk and Disorderly and Illegal Possession of a Firearm, knowing without Patsy's corroboration not much else would stick.

She and Jennifer took the car over to an all-night Shell station on Main Street and swamped out the back seat.

It was after four AM when they started the long drive back up to Far View. Anna'd never been comfortable in the cold predawn hours, that waiting time from after midnight till sunrise. As a child she could remember standing shivering watching her parents load suitcases in the trunk of the old Thunderbird. On their rare vacations, the importance of getting an early start was paramount. Upon reaching adulthood she'd expanded the concept of 'vacation' to include sleeping in and seldom booked a flight before noon if she could help it.

Now those unholy hours were allocated for pacing the floor on bad nights.

At Anna's request, Jennifer was driving. The late hour and the abandoned road had awakened the Indy 500 driver lurking just under the surface of every American and Short was taking the curves with expert and nauseating speed. The two swallows of instant coffee Anna'd choked down in Patsy's kitchen felt like they'd lodged behind her breastbone and were trying to burn their way out.

'Slow down,' she griped, 'or we'll be mopping out the front seat.'

'Sorry.' Jennifer didn't sound it.

Events of the night had pushed the truck Anna and

Stanton had heard on the loop out of her mind. In her irritation it resurfaced.

'You had late shift?' she asked knowing the answer.

'I got two lates now Stacy's kaput.'

'What time did you lock Cliff Palace loop?'

Jennifer thought a moment. 'Maybe ten or thereabouts.'

'Did you have to go back out later? Get a call or anything?'

'No. Why?' Jennifer's voice changed slightly, that touch of wariness that signaled the end of conversation and the beginning of interrogation.

'Around one-thirty a truck of some sort drove through the Cliff Palace parking lot,' Anna told her. 'About then I got the call to come rescue Patsy. We were right behind the truck – not close enough to see it, but we had to be close. Somehow they hid out. Nobody was at the Four-Way when we got there. The gate was false-locked so whoever was in there had access to a key. I wondered if Jamie'd talked you out of yours so she could go play with her little dead friends.'

'That's against the rules,' Jennifer said piously.

'Everybody bends the rules once in a while,' Anna tempted confession.

'Not everybody,' Jennifer put her in her place.

'Did anybody have a backcountry permit for tonight?'

'No. I checked. I always check.'

'Who of the interps owns a good-sized truck?'

Jennifer was more comfortable with this line of questioning. It didn't cast aspersions on her merits as a ranger. 'Nobody I know of,' she said after a minute.

'Interps have subcompact minds – you know; no extra irreplaceable fossil fuels and shit.'

Claude Beavens had said the 'interp's truck' left after he did the night of the murder. Offhand Anna couldn't remember if he'd seen or only heard it. She made a mental note to ask.

'Jimmy Russell's got a truck,' Jennifer volunteered. 'He'd've took 'em. Jimmy's always looking to get his horns clipped or at least a couple of free beers. If it was a party, he'd have been there.'

'Have you been locking the Four-Way funny? Like Stacy used to, all twisted and tight and hard to undo?' Anna asked abruptly.

Jennifer hooted. 'Ranger Pigeon, what is the matter with you? You're as fussy as a cat with new kittens. You on the rag?'

'Past my bedtime,' Anna grumbled. 'Have you?'

'My locks aren't twisty and tight,' Jennifer said primly and turned on the radio to drown out any further assaults on her character.

Anna didn't push it, but promised herself she would do some serious checking of stories when the world opened for business: Jamie, Beavens, Jennifer, Russell. She had a feeling if rangers were puppets, the mesa would have more long noses than trees.

Chapter Sixteen

'I'm not looking forward to this.' Anna switched off the ignition. She and Frederick sat in the patrol car under the shade tree in Rose Meyer's front yard. 'What I'm looking forward to is a nap.' By the time she and Jennifer had returned to the mesa it had been close to five. She'd had less than two hours sleep before she went on duty at seven a.m.

'Getting old?' Stanton teased.

'I'm too tired even to yawn.'

'Want me to do it?'

For a second Anna thought he was offering to yawn for her. Then she focussed on the task at hand. 'It's bound to be tedious, personal and unpleasant. Of course I want you to do it.'

'Generous to a fault.'

Anna twisted in her seat till the bones in her lower back popped. 'I'll do it, but you'd better come with me in your capacity as Hysterical Wife Sedative.'

Hattie answered the door in her nightgown, a knee-length poet's shirt in burgundy with the sheen of satin and the wrinkle-free texture of good polyester. Graying hair was wild around her face. She looked the embodiment of an elemental force. Whether of earth or sky, for good or evil, Anna couldn't hazard a guess. Greek mythology had never been big in Catholic school.

'You're just in time for a cup of tea,' Hattie said. Much of her usual spark was banked beneath fatigue or worry, still she sounded genuinely welcoming. 'C'mon in, Anna. Agent Stanton.'

'Fred,' Stanton said and Anna shot him a startled look. In the years she'd been acquainted with him 'Frederick' was the only accepted form of address. She looked back at Hattie. The elemental force: the quintessential Aunt with all the rights and privileges conferred therein. One's aunt would scarcely call one 'Frederick' unless some formal trouble were in the air.

'Fred,' Hattie said warmly. 'I've never known a weak or dishonest Fred.'

'Or a pretty one, I bet,' Stanton said.

Hattie laughed as she opened the screen and waved them in. 'Maybe to a Frederica.'

'The only one who finds a papa moose handsome is a momma moose.'

The banter carried them indoors where they pooled in front of the archway leading to a small built-in eating nook that separated the living area from the kitchen. Rose and her daughter sat in their nightgowns over breakfast. Rose had two plastic curlers clipped on the crown of her head, just enough to give her coif that rounded pouf short hairdos seemed to require. A definite chill radiated from the woman as she looked at Anna.

Bella, in a sleeveless white nightie covered with little

blue sailboats, huddled on the bench opposite her mother. Knees tucked up and arms pulled inside the armholes, she hid her face in the open neck of the gown; a personal fallout shelter.

Anna guessed discussion over this morning's bananas and Grape-Nuts had been somewhat strained.

'Yes?' Rose said in lieu of a greeting. She opened her hands to encompass the food-littered table. 'As you can see, it is a bit early for receiving callers.'

It was after ten o'clock. Anna resisted the urge to glance at her watch. In true coward's fashion, she stepped aside and drew Stanton into the line of fire.

'Agent Stanton and I are just tying up a few loose ends,' she said. 'Did Hills happen to collect Stacy's duty belt?'

Rose looked blank but she knew exactly what was referred to, Anna would have laid money on it.

'C'mon Punkin,' Hattie said. 'Let's get dressed and go for a walk.'

Eyes full of alarm, Bella glanced at Stanton.

'We'll change in your mom's room,' Hattie assured her.

Modesty met, Bella climbed from the bench.

'Hiya, Bella,' Anna said.

'Hello.' Bella was merely being polite, she didn't meet Anna's eyes.

While Bella slid to the floor, Rose had managed to pluck the rollers from her hair and secrete them away somewhere. 'Would you care for a cup of coffee?' She was talking to Stanton.

'No thanks,' Anna replied just as he said: 'That'd really hit the spot.'

257

Accordingly, Rose went to the kitchen and returned with a mug of coffee for the F.B.I. agent. Anna wondered if she would have gotten one even if she'd said yes.

'Any progress finding Stacy's murderer?' Rose asked as she regained her seat.

Stanton sat down across from her. 'Not as much as we'd like. But Ranger Pigeon and I are still chipping away at it.'

Rose didn't look up at Anna leaning coffeeless in the archway.

Amid the breakfast debris on the table were papers that had an official fill-in-the-boxes look to them. 'Looks like we've caught you at a bad time,' Stanton said apologetically.

'Yes, rather.' This time Rose did look at Anna.

Disrespect, verbal and sometimes physical abuse was often directed at the uniform, the badge. Anna'd become practiced at not letting it get under her skin. But this was personal and it felt personal. She found herself becoming irked and began to count to ten in Spanish.

'Death and taxes?' Stanton asked solicitously.

'Medical forms for Bella,' Rose said.

Anna'd just gotten to 'cinco, seis.' She quit counting. The conversation was getting interesting. 'Is Bella sick?' she asked.

Rose ignored her. 'Bella's getting an operation,' she told Stanton. Excitement was clear in her voice. 'It's been something I've been wanting for a long time. She can't have it yet, but in a few years. They think they can fix her legs, make her normal.'

'That's wonderful,' Stanton said.

Anna was undecided. 'We're the variety that adds spice,' she remembered Drew saying.

'Stacy's insurance left us with enough money to cover medical expenses.' Rose volunteered the information and Anna wondered why.

'Stacy had a life insurance policy?' she asked.

Rose took a second to respond. In that second the silence shouted 'not that it's any of your business but—' 'Yes, he did Miss Pigeon. Stacy was a good husband.'

Good was emphasized and, logically or not, Anna found herself wanting to defend Zach for dying broke and unprepared. She chose not to rise to the bait – real or imagined.

'You're welcome to see the policy if you want, Miss Pigeon.'

'Sure, why not.'

Rose rolled her eyes for Stanton's benefit and left the table to get the form.

There was a murmured exchange in the bedroom then Hattie and Bella emerged and slipped out the back door with exaggerated sneakiness. Anna suspected some Hattie-led game was afoot.

Rose returned. Her hair was combed and Anna's female eye detected a discreet layer of blusher brushed on the high cheek bones.

'Miss Pigeon?' Rose held out the insurance policy then, dismissing Anna with a look, sat again. 'All that's of no interest to the Federal Bureau of Investigation, I imagine,' she said sweetly to Stanton. 'Is there anything I can help you with this morning, Agent Stanton?'

'Coffee's all I need,' he said. 'Anna?'

She laid the two-hundred-thousand dollar life insurance policy on the table. 'Just Stacy's duty belt – gun, radio, leather gear.'

'I have no idea where I put it,' Rose said disinterestedly. 'I'll drop it by the CRO later this afternoon if it turns up.'

In a house the size of a postage stamp, inhabited by a six-year-old child, it was unlikely she'd mislaid her recently deceased spouse's gunbelt. Whether she lied to hide something or just for spite, Anna hadn't a clue. Admitting defeat she said: 'Thanks, Mrs Meyers. That'd be a big help. We won't take up any more of your time.'

'Thanks for the coffee,' Stanton chimed in.

'Anytime, Fred. It was so sweet of you to come by.' Rose blessed him with a Pepsodent-perfect smile.

'Watch out,' Anna said ungraciously as they climbed into the patrol car. 'You've got Husband Number Three written all over you.

'First there's insurance, then there isn't, then there is. There's chindi, then they're gone, then they're back. Gates are locked, unlocked, locked. Silva's a thug, a guardian angel, then presto chango, a thug,' she ranted.

Stanton rolled up the windows of the car and cranked up the air conditioner.

'Everybody's got a radio, then there's not a radio to be found. Interps have trucks, then they have subcompacts. The truth is getting to be such a variable. New realities to be announced as needed.' Anna turned the air conditioner off and rolled down her window. 'What now? You're choreographing this show.'

'Gee, thanks.' The radio cut off anything further. Jamie

Burke at Cliff Palace was reporting a medical. Unceremoniously, Anna shushed Stanton and turned up the radio. A boy, fourteen, was complaining of faintness and shortness of breath. He insisted he could walk out, his parents demanded he have medical attention.

'Do you need to go?' Stanton asked.

Anna shook her head. 'Hills and Jennifer are both on today. They can do it.' For a second she stared at the radio thinking. 'Damn,' she said finally. 'Let's go anyway. I've got some questions to ask.'

Cliff Palace parking lot was full and a line of cars extending a hundred yards back up the one-way road followed those creeping slowly through the lot looking for non-existent parking places. Anna turned on her blue lights and, driving on the shoulder, nudged past the sluggish stream. She parked with two wheels in the dirt and two in the 'motorcycles only' zone.

The sun burned through the thin atmosphere touching the skin ungently. Anna loved its rough kiss and had the wrinkles and age spots to prove it. Red faced tourists queued up at the drinking fountains.

Down in the Palace the heat and the crowding would be exacerbated. To keep from adding to the congestion, Anna and Stanton stayed on the mesa top monitoring events over the radio.

In the fifteen minutes it had taken them to get to Cliff, the boy's condition had deteriorated sufficiently and Burke's voice had gone from self-important to mildly panicky. Hills had called in on scene. From the two patrol vehicles parked in the lot, Anna guessed in all the excitement Jennifer had forgotten yet again.

Stanton found a bench in the shade at the trail head. Two German women, both in their seventies or early eighties, wearing print dresses and straw hats, moved over to make room for him.

Anna leaned on the split-rail fence behind the bench and tilted her head back to catch the sun on her face. The heat drew wind up the canyons and she revelled in its touch.

'Some questions to ask, you said. Let me in on your secret?' Stanton asked.

'I wish I had a secret. It'd make me feel superior. This doesn't even qualify as a hunch.' Since she didn't choose to add to that, Stanton made small talk with his bench companions in German and Anna was duly impressed. She would have been more so had the ladies not laughed so much as they tried to puzzle out what he was saying.

The ambulance arrived, Drew driving, Jimmy riding shot-gun. They came to wait with Anna.

'They're walking him out,' Drew said. 'A kid again. Asthma, up at seven thousand feet. His parents ought to be shot.'

Hill's voice, phlegmatic as ever, came into the conversation via the airwaves. 'Seven hundred, three-eleven. We're going to need some help. Fella's collapsed on us. If the stokes isn't already up top don't wait on it. We're to the metal stairs. Send me some big boys 'n' we'll hand carry the kid out.'

'Lifting heavy objects, that's you, Drew,' Anna said. The helitack foreman and Agent Stanton followed her toward the overlook at a trot.

Looking disgustingly heroic, Hills was halfway up the

metal stairs, in his arms a pale young man in khaki shorts
and a blue T-shirt. Oversized unlaced sneakers – the
fashion that summer – made the boy's legs look even
skinnier than they were.

Walking beside and behind, Jennifer carried an oxygen
bottle, the mask affixed to the patients' face, plastic
tubing connecting him to the cylinder. Following so
closely they trod on Short's heels were the boy's parents.

A panting woman with permed reddish hair and an
overheated complexion held onto one of her son's feet
to comfort him or herself. The father was lost in testos-
terone hysterics. Fear masquerading as anger, he berated
the stolid Dutton even as Hills carried his boy. Behind
them walked an older couple, grandparents, Anna
guessed.

Drew came alongside Hills. They propped the young
man, still conscious but barely so, against Anna and
interlaced their arms. The boy's breathing was labored,
the wheezing audible without a stethoscope. His lips
pursed with effort and he sipped at the air, sucking it
into his lungs a bit at a time, working to push it through
shrunken bronchial tubes. Anna eased him into the chair
the men had made of their arms. 'You're almost there,'
she said encouragingly. He nodded and made a valiant
attempt to smile.

Her part in the drama acted out, Anna stepped back,
letting Hills and Drew carry their patient to the waiting
ambulance. She fell into step with the elderly couple.
They seemed the sanest of the group. Both wore wide-
brimmed hats, baggy shorts and the comfortable walking
shoes of experienced tourists.

'Grandson?' Anna asked.

'Our first,' the woman said.

'And probably last,' the man snarled. Obviously this was an old bone of contention in the family.

'Not now, Harold. He has had asthma ever since he was a baby,' the grandmother told Anna.

'It's usually not bad,' Harold argued. 'I told Daryl not to bring him up this high.'

'Okay, Harold. I don't think its the altitude,' she whispered conspiratorially though her husband could easily hear. 'Dane has been up to seven thousand feet half a dozen times and been just fine. It's radon. Like in caves. Last time Dane was taken this bad it was something like that.'

'Irma! Leave the lady alone. It wasn't radon. He was sniffing that glue like the kids all got crazy about.'

'Nonsense.'

The party reached the parking lot and the grandparents were lost in an organizational shuffle.

As the ambulance drove away, Stanton came to stand by Anna.

'All your questions answered?' he asked.

'Oh, yeah. The pattern's crystal clear. I have no idea what it's of, but it's clear.' She twisted the watch band around on her wrist and showed the face to Frederick. 'Tuesday, eleven-twenty-eight a.m. Another collapse, another carry out, right on schedule.'

'Whose?' Stanton asked.

'You tell me.'

Chapter Seventeen

A pretty little mouse with ears Disneyesque in their cuteness and whiskers Gus-Gus would have been proud of poked her nose out of the kitchen and contemplated crossing the risky expanse of carpet in the living room.

'You're getting fat,' Anna warned. 'One day you won't be able to squeeze under the door.'

The mouse looked up at the sound of her voice but was otherwise unmoved. When Anna had first arrived at Far View there'd been no mice. With the largesse left on counter tops and on dirty dishes by her roommates, the little creatures had come to stay. This one was so plump Anna was put in mind of an ink drawing in her childhood copy of *Charlotte's Web*; a very round Templeton the Rat lying on his back at the county fair saying: 'What a gorge!'

Early on Jennifer and Jamie had set out D-Con. Dying mice had staggered out with such regularity the living room began to resemble the stage after the final act of *Hamlet*. Disgusted, Anna'd thrown the poison out. 'Not cricket,' she told her housemates. 'You can feed them or kill them. Not both.'

Since then they'd all come to terms with one another and the dorm no longer had pests but, as Jennifer had dubbed them, politically correct pets.

Anna's wristwatch beeped. The mouse squeaked on the same frequency and ran behind the refrigerator. Three a.m. on the nose: Anna tried a combination of invisible-to-the-naked-eye buttons on the watch to turn off the hourly alarm. The beeping stopped but she had no idea whether it was of natural causes or if she'd won. 'Man against Nature: Woman against Technology,' she mumbled.

Half a glass of burgundy sat before her on the table. Her third, but since the first two were downed six hours earlier, she figured they didn't count. Hopefully, this one would help her to sleep and without the usual cost: waking with the jitters just before dawn.

Jack of diamonds: she put it on a black queen in the solitaire game she'd been playing since one-thirty. A space was freed up and two more moves revealed a second ace. She enjoyed a vague sense of triumph. Her mind wasn't on the game, merely in freefall, unloosed by solitaire's mantra of boredom. This game had many of the earmarks of the one she and Stanton had spent the day pursuing. One by one they'd peeled away lies in hopes of uncovering a truth they could play, one that would start the game moving again.

Another of Frederick the Fed's infernal lists cluttered up her notebook. While Jennifer and Hills attended to the medical at Cliff Palace, the two of them had divided up all the stories in need of checking. 'The lie detector part,' Stanton had called it. A line cut down the middle of the yellow note paper. On Anna's side was 'Policy, Truck. Rose/Radio,' and 'Beavens/Veil.' In her own handwriting was added 'Stephanie/Dane.' On Stanton's side was 'Silva/Gun/Threats.'

Stanton's day had been a complete washout. Before he could question him, Silva had been let out on bail, paid not by Patsy but by Ted Greeley. Neither Greeley nor Silva could be found.

Anna's half of the investigation had gone well. One phone call proved Rose Meyers a member of the liars' club. The two hundred thousand dollar life insurance policy she'd shown Anna had been canceled six months previously for lack of payment.

Knowing the truth without knowing the rationale behind it was fairly useless. Maybe Rose was not yet aware the policy had been canceled – or knew but wasn't ready to admit it to herself or anyone else. Maybe she'd been trying to impress Stanton. An underpaid public servant might find a lady a wee bit more enticing if she had two hundred grand. Money was a proven aphrodisiac.

Whatever the reason, Mutual Casualty and Life told Anna there was no policy, no payoff. Rose had said Stacy'd left them with nothing, then changed her tune when the truth was nothing.

Red seven on black eight; nothing revealed. She turned over another three cards.

It seemed unlikely Rose would be lying to Bella and Hattie about the operation. That would be cruel and, despite her dislike of the woman, Anna believed that in her own way Rose loved her daughter. Therefore logic would suggest Rose did have money. Fact indicated it did not come from where she'd claimed.

Anna was too old to believe that people always lied for a reason. Mostly they lied because it was easy, felt good, or was habit. However this particular lie was complex, suggesting a more focussed motive. If Rose wanted to hide the source of the money it was probably illegal or embarrassing.

Greeley as a potential new step-daddy might have that kind of capital. Would Rose want to admit she and Ted were that intimate? Sharing a bed meant nothing but sharing a checkbook was a real commitment. And money was a stronger motive for murder than love.

Anna put a red four on a red five, woke up to her game and took it back. Things just weren't adding up: murdering one's spouse was *passé*. Stacy had no inheritance, no insurance and, though in a divorce he might sue for custody of Bella, he had the proverbial snowball's chance in hell of winning. Rose could be intimate with whomever's checkbook she pleased without much in the way of adverse consequences.

If there was a good reason for Rose to kill her husband Anna was missing it. A woman scorned crossed her mind but she dismissed it. Her own presumed affair with Stacy might possibly foment a woman miffed, but hardly scorned.

Twenty-four carat motive or not, Rose had a lot of money and was lying about where she'd gotten it. That qualified her as a suspect.

'Truck,' the next item on Stanton's hit list, referred to the elusive truck Beavens reported hearing and Anna and Stanton had chased. A tour of the housing areas revealed the whereabouts of thirteen trucks. Trucks were in vogue even for suburbanities. In parks they were *de rigueur*. Without exception they were teensy little Toyotas, Ford Rangers – toy trucks. Only Tom Silva owned a good old-fashioned bubba truck complete with shovel and gun rack. But even Silva's Chevy couldn't grind out the kind of racket that had pulled Anna and Stanton from their chindi vigil.

The thought of Silva jogged something in the back of Anna's tired mind. She set down the playing cards and stared into her wine as if waiting for a vision. Trucks and Tom and noise and trucks and Tom . . . It was coming to her. Back in June, before all the fuss, Tom had complained a 'big goddam truck' almost ran him off the road. Anna remembered following up on his complaint just to prove she was fair minded and finding nothing. She'd even written a case incident report to keep her credit good. Later Silva'd said he was just 'jerking her chain.'

Tom drove a real pickup and wore cowboy shirts with the sleeves ripped out. What would he consider big? Surely not a snubby-nosed little Mitsubishi. To a construction worker 'big truck' would mean a Kenmore, a Peterbilt, a Mack.

First a truck, then no truck, now a truck. Another lie. Anna swallowed the medium through which the oracle had revealed this truth.

Next on the list was Rose/Radio. That had been a worthless line of inquiry. Rose had returned belt, gun and radio to the CRO around two o'clock. When Anna'd dared ask if she'd lent or used the radio, Rose had climbed into an uncommunicative huff and departed.

Feeling spiteful, Anna had taken the radio out of its leather holster and dusted the hard plastic case for fingerprints. There wasn't a print on it. Either Rose was an anal-retentive housekeeper or it had been wiped clean so the last user could go undetected.

Beavens/Veil had proved a bit easier. At least Beavens was still speaking to Anna, that was a start. She'd found him down in Spruce Tree House just as he was being relieved for a meal break. He'd brought a bag lunch and they sat together in the cool of the alcove at the rear of the ancient pueblo amid the prosaic needs of a modern day Park Service: oxygen bottle, backboard, first aid kit and white helium-filled balloons. The last interpreter out of the ruin in the evening affixed these to the upper ramparts. Al Stinson's brain child, the balloons kept the vultures from roosting and whitewashing the national historic treasure with bird droppings.

Beavens had been his usual self: shrugging, replying to everything with 'no big deal'. Halfway through his bag of Doritos – that and a ruin-temperature Dr Pepper constituted lunch – Anna noticed he was nervously fingering a gold chain around his neck. At an earlier meeting she remembered him holding on to a small gold cross suspended from it as Stanton had questioned him about the veil.

On a hunch, she turned the conversation along more spiritual lines. After a moment's silence, she said, 'One thing I don't like about living in the park is it's so far to church.'

Beavens' face, pasty despite the best efforts of the high desert sun, lit up for the first time in Anna's short acquaintance with him. Animation lent him youth and even a certain charm. 'Have you accepted Jesus as your personal savior?' he asked.

Such was the hope in his voice, Anna might have felt guilty had she not been fairly sure she'd stumbled on the key that would unlock his confidence. 'Washed in the blood of the lamb a year ago next month,' she said.

A boyish smile curved up the corners of his mouth and transformed his face. 'You!' he exclaimed. 'I never would have guessed.'

'The Lord works in mysterious ways.'

'Amen. Which church to you go to?' He was leaning forward, defenses down. Anna didn't want to lose him with a wrong answer.

'I've only been here a couple of months. So far I haven't found anything that really works for me,' she equivocated.

Beavens nodded sympathetically. 'I can't find anything either. This New Age stuff is like a cancer. It's eaten away a lot of real belief. Maybe we could get together a bible study group up on the mesa?'

Anna had a sinking feeling she was going to pay dearly for this particular deception. 'The park is kind of a magnet for the New Agers,' she said. 'What with crystals and the American Indian thing that's caught on.'

Beavens' face continued to look receptive, so she pressed on. 'All this sitting around in Kivas waiting for spirits, I don't know . . .' she trailed off hoping he would fill in with his own ideas. She wasn't disappointed.

'It's just an invitation to satan, that's all it amounts to,' he said eagerly. 'The Bible warns us that there'll be stumbling blocks on the road to heaven. These people are just providing the devil with tools – or maybe I should say fools – to do his work. It's like holding seances or messing with ouija boards. You can't go calling up this kind of stuff. You've got to turn away from it, turn to the Bible.'

'Prayer,' Anna said.

'Yes!' Beavens looked relieved beyond measure; someone understood him.

Anna ignored a mild pang of remorse. 'What with all that's been happening, I kind of think the demons have been called up already.'

In the middle of a sip of Dr Pepper, Beavens nodded his agreement and nearly choked himself to death. When he'd recovered somewhat, he managed to squeak out: 'Burke, the spirit veil.'

Now Anna leaned forward. 'Summer solstice – the night you saw the interp's truck—'

'Heard it.'

'Heard it then. Did you really see the veil?' she asked as one conspirator might ask another.

'I saw something,' Beavens replied in the same tone. 'But we can't give it credence, can't spread the bad word. I say get thee behind me satan!' He laughed, but Anna could see he was serious, nervous and serious. He was fiddling with the cross again.

An instinct to pounce welled up strongly. Forcing it down, she leaned back and crossed her ankles. 'That kind of thing spreads like wildfire,' she agreed. 'People want to believe in signs and portents.'

'Original sin,' Beavens said.

Anna didn't know where that fit in or exactly what it was. Sister Mary Judette had explained it in religion class but that was close to thirty years before. To say something, she threw in a cliché from her own formative years and hoped it was general enough to fit any conversational requirement: 'If you're not part of the solution, you're part of the problem.'

'Exactly.'

'What was it like, the something you saw?'

'Weird,' Beavens confided. ' "Spirit veil" is a pretty good description. It's Jamie Burke, she'd better cut it out, too. She's got no idea who she's messing with.'

Anna looked interested.

'She's got half the interps in the park watching and thinking and waiting. So it shows up. You call up the devil, he comes.'

Anna nodded sagely. 'Was it like a kind of curtain?' she brought the conversation back to where she wanted it.

'Kind of. An iridescent shimmer. Maybe a hundred feet long. It was really neat looking,' he said, then, thinking better of it added, 'But then it would be, wouldn't it?'

Another interpreter, a frosted blond art teacher from Oklahoma, came into the shade of the alcove. 'They're all yours, Claude,' she said as she took a Flintstones lunch box out of the first aid cabinet and sat down cross-legged on the smooth stone floor.

Anna walked Beavens out into the sunlight. 'You

didn't want to admit seeing the veil because it'd just give the devil his due? Recruiting for him, sort of?'

'No sense being Lucifer's patsy.'

As Anna turned to go he followed her a couple of steps. 'Let's do that Bible study, okay?'

'Anytime.' Anna escaped into a knot of visitors.

So there had been something – a spirit veil or the devil's shirttail – but definitely something.

Anna stared at the cards on the table. Nothing left to play. Miss Mouse was back, poking her little gray nose around the door frame from the direction of the kitchen. 'I've got a cat,' Anna threatened. The mouse twitched her whiskers but didn't run away.

Eyes down at the table top with its scattered playing cards, Anna rested her head in her hands. Three choices: finish her wine and try to get some sleep, deal another hand of solitaire, or cheat. Cheating seemed the most profitable course.

Shuffling the remaining cards into what she hoped would prove a more cooperative order, she eyed the last item on the list, the one she had written, Stephanie/ Dane.

Hills would have a few choice words to say about the phone bill she'd run up tracking them down. Stephanie McFarland was the asthmatic girl she and Stacy had carried out of Cliff Palace. The child who had died. Dane was the boy Helitack had evacuated earlier in the day. Both were young and, other than asthma, in good condition. Both sets of parents had insisted the children had been up at seven thousand feet before without ill effects.

Fourteen long-distance calls had gathered the information Anna'd been looking for. Both the children had had previous attacks of like severity. Stephanie's had been triggered by fumes when as a child she'd locked herself in a broom closet and shattered a bottle of cleaning solution in her attempts to dislodge the door. By the time her mother had found her she was suffering statis asthmaticus and very nearly lost her life.

After a bit of cajoling, the ER nurse at Southwest Memorial in Cortez told Anna Dane's parents, Eli and Dina Bjornson, were staying at the Aneth Lodge. Immediate danger to their son past, they'd been fairly communicative. Dane had one serious attack before, brought on not by radon or sniffing glue but by exposure to chemical mace some boys at his junior high school had been playing with.

One solution to the Cliff Palace incidents was that the ruin was exhaling poisonous vapors, perhaps the dying breath of the fabled underworld blowing through the sipapus. Stacy had been reaching toward the entrance to that world with his last dying gasp. Or so the corpse had appeared. Anna put no credence in the underworld as a mythical entity but there had been cases of poisonous gas, naturally generated, escaping to the detriment of humankind. Could that be the real reason for the sudden and complete departure of the Old Ones? A reason that for some geological reason was just now reasserting itself?

Another solution was coincidence. Two asthmatic kids with similar medical histories collapse within a few weeks of one another on a Tuesday morning. Not really much of a coincidence. It wouldn't have raised an eyebrow with

Anna had it not been for Stacy and the rest of the Tuesday Morning Club.

Anna was stuck with the facts: something or someone was causing people to collapse in Cliff Palace on Tuesday mornings. Not random, not coincidental, not paranormal, but cause and effect. Anna figured the culprit or culprits were individuals with greater material desires than your average ghost.

She turned her mind back to her solitaire game. Reshuffling hadn't broken a single space loose. She gathered up the playing cards and reboxed them. Miss Mouse had gone to bed. Anna would follow suit.

She'd just swallowed the last of the dry red sleeping draught when the phone rang. In the dead of night it was always a sickening sound, though at Mesa Verde nine times out of ten it was a false alarm from the concessions facility. Their new motion detectors were so sensitive the least vibration set them off, sometimes two or three times in a night. Anna often wondered how much money the hapless tax payers had forked out in overtime so fully armed rangers could shoo mice out of the Hostess Twinkies. With the monies concessions pulled in they could easily afford Pinkertons.

Again the phone rang. Anna threw herself on it as if it were a hand grenade. Half the night she'd been up, and if there was any overtime to be had she was damned if she'd let anyone else get it.

'Mesa Verde.'

A short silence followed, punctuated by a sharp intake of breath. 'What?' came a faltering voice.

'Mesa Verde National Park,' Anna elaborated. 'You've

reached our emergency number.'

'This is an emergency?' the voice said uncertainly. It was either a very timid woman or a small child.

'What can I help you with?'

'A car's gone off the road down here. I think somebody's still inside.'

Anna felt her stomach tighten and her mind clear. 'Where are you calling from?'

'A phone by the road.'

There were only two, one at Delta Cut and one at Bravo Cut, two places where the road to the mesa top sliced through the side of a hill. 'Are you closer to the bottom of the mesa or the top?'

'The top, I think.'

'Are you hurt?'

'I don't think so, I mean, I'm not. We ... I was out on the point looking at the lights when we ... I saw the headlights go over. They're way down. Somebody drove off. That's all I know.' There was a click and the interview was over. Whoever had called had been out frolicking under the stars, Anna guessed, with an inappropriate 'we' and, now that the altruism brought on by shock had worn thin, had thought better of involvement.

Delta Cut was sheer on one side, a dirt and stone bank rising vertically from the road bed. The other side dropped off precipitously in a jungle of service berry and oakbush. Unless traveling at impossible speeds, a passenger car wouldn't have the clout to break through the iron and concrete. A vehicle over the edge would've had to run past the railing on one end or the other.

Anna changed phones and put in a call to Frieda from the bedroom as she pulled on her uniform trousers. Frieda would wake up someone to bring the ambulance and call out helitack in case a low angle rescue was needed.

The call completed, Anna banged on Jennifer Short's bedroom door. No one grunted. Jennifer slept like the dead. Anna pushed open the door but the room was empty. Either Jennifer was partying late or had gotten lucky and found a more entertaining bed for the night.

Stars hung close to the mesa, not dulled by moisture or atmosphere. A half moon spilled enough light to see by. Garbage was strewn over the walk and, as she walked to the car, Anna saw a big brown rump vanishing into the underbush. When she returned she'd clean up the mess and not mention the marauder to the brass. At Mesa Verde the solution to problem bears might be to shoot first and justify later.

As she backed the patrol car out of the lot and started down the main road the three miles to Delta Cut she ran through her EMS checklist. Rehearsing emergency medical procedures and inventorying available equipment calmed and centred her.

With no traffic to slow her, she reached Delta Cut before she'd played out more than a few possible scenarios. Not surprisingly, no car waited at the pull-out. The phone box hung open as if deserted in haste. Anna pulled the Ford into the left lane, switched on her alley light and cruised slowly along the guardrail.

Service berry grew thickly down the bank, camouflaging drops and ravines. Late blooms glowed white.

Beyond, the thickets were impenetrable in their darkness. Anna rolled down the car's windows and listened but nothing was audible over the hum of the engine.

A crank call? It hadn't sounded it. Crank calls were usually accompanied by a background of party animal noises. A trap? The thought made the little hairs on the back of her neck crawl. Could someone have lured her out in the dead of night for sinister purposes? Highly unlikely, she soothed herself. For one thing, there was no guarantee she'd be the one to answer the '69 line, for another, who could've guessed she'd come alone other than Jennifer and whomever she was with? The only reason for making her a target was the Meyers investigation and she hadn't exactly been burning up the turf in that department.

Reassured by her own sense of inadequacy, she left the patrol car to walk the same ground. Free from the distraction of machinery, she found what she was looking for. Eighty or a hundred feet down the bank, almost hidden by the thick foliage, was the yellow glow of automobile headlights. To the left of the lights she could just make out the pale shape of a vehicle's body and adjusted her thoughts: not a car, a pick-up truck, white or yellow in color.

Having radioed in the exact location of the wreck, she collected the jump kit and a flashlight, backtracked to the end of the barricade and shined the light into the brush. A barely discernable trail of broken branches and scarred earth showed where the truck had left the pavement. There were no skid marks, no deep cuts in the sod indicating the brakes had been applied.

Hunching up like a woman in a windstorm, she forced her way through the brush, following the broken trail. Four or five yards down the steep bank the ground fell away. A cliff, maybe thirty feet high, was cut into the hillside where the undergrowth had let go of unstable soil during the previous winter's snows. Dirt and scree dropped down to a rubble of boulders scattered on a shoulder of land. Past that was a sheer drop to the valley floor where the lights of Cortez twinkled invitingly.

The pickup had cut through the brush at the point where she stood, then hurtled over the embankment. Boulders stopped its fall. The nose of the truck was crushed, the windshield and both side windows smashed. Either time was of the essence or all the time in the world would not be enough. Whoever was inside would be lucky to be alive.

Anna'd been carrying the orange jump kit in front of her like a shield. Now she strapped it on her back. Eroded soil made the bank soft enough she could work her way down crab-like, heels and butt breaking the descent. Prickly pear sank disinterested fangs into the palm of her right hand and she swore softly. Tomorrow, without adrenaline for an anesthetic, the barbs would itch and burn.

From above, she heard the whooping cry of the ambulance approaching and was glad of the company.

At the bottom of the broken bank, the ground leveled out in a litter of rocks from fist- to house-size. Anna leaped from one to another, her balance made uncertain by the moving flashlight beam.

The truck was wedged between two rocks. One

beneath the front axle, the other crumpling back the hood and holding the vehicle at an angle almost on its right side. Both rear wheels and the front left tire were free of the ground. The front tire still turned slowly. The crash had been recent and Anna felt a spark of hope that she was not too late.

'Anna!' It was Hills on her radio.

'Down here,' she responded flashing her light up to the road till she got an answering flash.

'What've we got?' Hills asked.

'Stand by.'

Between her and the cab were two boulders roughly the size of Volkswagens and woven together by a tangle of oakbrush. For lack of a better place, Anna shoved the flashlight down the front of her shirt then, hands free, scrambled to the top of the first boulder and jumped the crevice to the second.

The tilted cab was on a level with the rock, the driver's door parallel with the top of the stone where she stood. Heat radiated from beneath the hood; the engine was still running. Anna rescued her flash and surveyed the scene. Broken and hanging in fragments, the safety glass of the side window fell in ragged sheets. Isolated pieces sparkled in the beam. From the interior came strains of country western music. A faint green glow emanated from the dashboard lights. All else was lost in a darkness fractured by moonlight through fragmented glass.

Anna unstrapped the jump kit. Cursing her slick-soled Wellington boots, she inched down the boulder where it sloped to within eighteen inches of the truck. Spinning gently, the pickup's front tire, along with the broken angles of metal and stone, gave her an unsettling sense of vertigo, as if she might topple into the window as into a bottomless well.

At the boulder's edge she stopped, recovered her equilibrium, and peered inside. From her new vantage point, the cab and a small slice of the passenger door were visible. On the far window, where it had been forced inward, drops of ruby mixed with the glittering diamonds of glass.

Fresh blood was startlingly red – too red for paintings or movies. Comic book red; believable only in fantasy and real life.

Gingerly, Anna pushed at the truck's exposed undercarriage with a foot. It held steady. Apparently the truck was wedged firmly between the rocks. How firmly, she was about to find out.

Getting down on her knees, she restored the flashlight to its bruising hammock between buttons and breasts and crawled her hands out onto the door. Bit by bit she transferred her weight from the rock. The truck remained stable. Emboldened, she brought one knee onto the door, catching hold of the handle to keep herself steady.

Moonlight reflected off the white paint. Details, overwhelmed by the hard light of day, were surrealistically clear: a pencil thin scratch beneath the side mirror, a square patch where a sticker had been inexpertly removed, fading black stenciled lettering, once showy flourishes almost obliterated by time, spelling the initials T.S.

Tom Silva, Anna realized. It was his truck. Better a stranger; no psychological buttons pushed interfering with efficiency.

Pulling herself up to her knees on the slanting metal, she braced butt on heels and took the flashlight from inside her shirt. Silva was crushed down on the far side of the cab, his back to her. One leg trailed behind him, still wedged beneath the driver's pedals. His left arm, the palm turned up, rested on the hump between the seats. She couldn't see his face. 'Tom,' she called clearly. 'Can you hear me?' No response.

Having wrested the King from her duty belt she made her assessment out loud, sharing it with Hills. 'One individual, white male,' she began, avoiding Silva's name lest Patsy or the girls should hear in such a manner. 'About thirty-five. Unconscious, no seat belt. He's half on the floor at the far side of the cab nearest the ground. He submarined,' she added, taking note of where the operator's pedals had bent and the floor mat ripped when Silva's unrestrained body was hurled beneath the steering wheel. 'His right leg's broken. The foot caught beneath the clutch and twisted a hundred and eighty degrees from anatomical position. I can't see his face but there's a lot of blood on the dash and windows.'

In the minute the climb and assessment had taken the rubies had pooled into a puddle of crimson. As she spoke it spread, a bright beautiful stream dripping from dash to windshield. 'Bring the stokes, backboard, oxygen and jaws of life. I'm off radio now, I'm going to try and get to him.' She heard the ubiquitous 'Ten-four' as she doffed her gunbelt and tossed it back onto the boulder. The radio she kept, using its heavy leather case to knock the remaining glass from the window frame.

'Sorry about that,' she muttered as fragments rained down on Silva's back, caught shining in his hair.

One hand on either side of the window, she lowered her legs into the cab until she straddled the body of the man inside. Her left foot was on top of the passenger door above the shattered glass. Her right foot she wedged in the angle made by the windshield and the dash inches from where Silva's head rested.

Hanging on tightly to the outside door handle lest her precarious perch give way, she stretched down and switched off the ignition. Blessedly, the tinny sounds of country pop were silenced and the bizarre party feeling quenched. A click of the headlight button turned on the interior light and she freed up the hand she used to hold the flashlight.

Edging down till her knee rested along the upper edge of the passenger door, she slipped two fingers between Silva's jaw and shoulder, seeking by touch his carotid artery. Blood, warm and slippery, reminded her she'd forgotten to put on rubber gloves. Rangers with emergency response duties were required to be given Hepatitis B vaccinations, but at a hundred and fifty bucks for each ranger, Hills couldn't bring himself to comply. Aids, there was no shot for.

'You better be clean, Tom,' Anna said as she pressed down. No pulse. Holding onto the rearview mirror for support, she crouched lower and repositioned her fingers in the hollow of Silva's neck beside his trachea.

'Bingo,' she breathed as she felt the faint and thrilling thread of life, Given the mechanism of injury – a headlong flight off a cliff – and the absence of a seat belt, there was a good chance Silva had suffered damage to his spine and she was loath to move him without at least a short backboard. 'Hills,' she barked into the radio. 'Where are you guys?'

'Just starting down.'

'Jesus,' she whispered. Since she'd dropped into the truck it seemed as if half an hour must have passed but she knew in reality it had been minutes. 'It's bad,' she said. 'Bring a short spineboard. He's all crunched down on the passenger side and the truck's tipped. We'll have to haul him straight up through the driver's door.'

Hills undoubtedly responded but Anna'd quit listening. Silva had made a sound. She crouched as low as she could, the man's dark head between her knees. Cupping his chin in her left hand, she supported his head and neck in the position she'd found it. 'Tom. Tom, it's Anna.'

A gurgle, half felt through her fingers, half heard, came from the injured man. Liquid trickled over her fingers where they curled around his chin. 'Hang in there Tom, help's here. Stay with me. We'll get you out.'

'No,' came out with more blood. 'Killed Pats.'

The adrenaline rush in Anna turned to cold horror. With her free hand she fumbled the radio from where it rested on the drunken tilt of the dash and held it to her mouth. Her right leg had begun to shake uncontrollably. 'Hills, send somebody to check on Patsy Silva.'

He asked something but Anna'd dropped her radio. The fragile beat of life beneath her fingers had stopped. 'Fuck.'

Silva was wearing a denim jacket, the collar turned up. Grasping collar and shoulder seams in her fists, she pulled the dead weight upwards, straightening her legs to take some of the strain off her back. Silva's head fell against her forearm. In the uncompromising light of the dome she could see the gash in his forehead. White bone gleamed through the torn flesh.

Grunting with the effort, she pulled him chest high and wedged her right knee under his rump. Locking him in her arms, she looked up at the driver's window a couple of inches above her head. Impossibly far. Silva was a slight man, not more than one hundred and thirty-five or -forty pounds, but she doubted she could push that much weight over her head.

'Come on Tom, don't wimp out on me, damn you, come on,' she murmured in his ear. Blood dripped onto her neck. 'On three, ready, Tom. Jesus!' Anna coiled the strength she had into her legs and back. 'One, two, three!' With all the power she could muster she pushed Tom up toward the night sky. Her back creaked in protest and she felt the muscles burn and grow watery in her shoulders.

Eyes squeezed shut she tried to force him beyond her strength, but the soft weight of him was slipping from her.

Then, miraculously, he went, his body light as air. Anna's eyes sprang open and the air exploded from her lungs. Her hands fell away and still Silva rose like Christ on Easter. As his feet drew level with her face, Anna heard voices. For an instant, Drew's face was visible in the glare of someone's light. He held Silva by the shirt front, supporting him with one arm.

'Get him flat,' Anna shouted. With shaking arms, she tried to lever herself out of the cab. Drew grabbed her wrists, lifted her clear of the truck and set her on the rock near Tom. 'Get me an airway,' Anna said. 'he had breath and pulse not a minute ago.'

Crawling, she positioned herself over Silva's chest, placed two fingers on his carotid and her ear an inch from his mouth. 'Damn.'

'Nothing?' Drew asked.

'Nothing. Airway,' she snapped. Behind her she could hear Hills pawing through the jump kit. She tilted Silva's jaw, pinched his nose and blew two slow breaths into his lungs. 'Compressions, Drew.'

The big man leaned over Silva and, elbows locked, depressed the man's chest for five counts, forcing blood through the now quiet heart and into the dying organs. Anna breathed for Silva. Five more compressions and another breath.

Sour vomit from Silva's stomach filled Anna's mouth and she spat it out, refusing to let her own bile rise in its wake. 'Airway,' she barked as Drew compressed the chest.

A curved plastic oropharyngeal airway was pressed into her palm and she took a second to work the plastic into Silva's throat to keep his airway patent.

Drew compressed and Anna performed rescue breathing while the backboard was moved into place. The time for delicacy was past. Emergency personnel often referred to the Golden Hour, those first sixty minutes where quick transport to a medical facility can still save a life. Time for Silva was running out, if, indeed, not already gone.

Unceremoniously, Silva was slid onto the board and strapped in the stokes. Paul Summers took one end, Hills the other and lifted. Anna breathed, Drew compressed.

'Can't do it,' Paul cried, shame and anger hot in his voice. The downward pressure of the compressions were too strong for him to support.

'Switch,' Anna called.

Drew moved to the head of the stokes and Paul took over compressions. 'Breath,' she said and blew into Silva's lungs.

'And one and two . . .' Paul counted off as they crabbed awkwardly along the two boulders.

'Stop,' Drew ordered when they reached the edge of the second rock. Anna and Paul stepped back. Drew set the litter down, Hills knelt still holding his end. The helitack foreman jumped from the rock then took up the stokes again.

Hills scrambled down and they moved with startling speed over the river of boulders. Paul and Anna ran after. The big men, the litter, the moonlight, the rocking and rocky passage, gave the scene a jerky, keystone cops look and Anna felt inappropriate laughter pushing up in her throat.

It came out in gasps as they reached the foot of the steep incline.

'Now,' Drew said.

Anna felt for pulse, listened for breathing. Nothing. Again she gave two slow rescue breaths, then Paul began compressions. Bones broke – Silva's ribs – another rescue breath, five compressions.

Jimmy appeared from somewhere with ropes. Stanton's voice behind Anna said, 'Can I spell you?' Anna blew oxygen into Silva's lungs then shook her head. Five more compressions, more ribs snapping.

'Stop,' Drew commanded.

Gratefully, Anna stepped back and wiped her mouth on the back of her hand. The stokes was roped up. Jimmy and Stanton had regained the top of the dirt slope and on a three count began to haul Silva upwards.

CPR couldn't be interrupted for more than a minute. Without bothering to catch her breath, Anna began to claw her way up the incline. On the other side of the stokes, she could see Paul bounding up the hill and envied him his youth.

The stokes bumped to a halt on the cliff top. Anna was there waiting. 'Now,' Drew ordered. No breath, no pulse: Anna blew into the lungs. Paul did compressions. Bile spewed up, the acid burning Anna's lips. She spat it out and heard gagging. For a second she thought it was Silva breathing on his own, but it was Stanton.

The agent pushed ahead, trying to keep the oakbrush from scraping the rescuers away from their patient. Branches scratched Anna's face and hands but she was only aware of them peripherally, she didn't feel the sting or cut.

Finally they broke free of the brush. In minutes, the stokes was loaded in the ambulance. 'Jimmy drives. Me, Drew, Paul, here in back. You guys see if you can figure out what happened. Hills slammed the door on the last of his words and the ambulance drove off leaving Anna and Frederick standing in the middle of the road.

Darkness and stillness returned. The moon, temporarily eclipsed by the ambulance lights, reasserted its dominion. Shadows softened. Night creatures began timid explorations. Anna noticed she was cold and her back hurt like the dickens.

Pressing her hands into the small of her sacrum she stretched in an attempt to ease it. 'I've lost my strength of ten men,' she said to Stanton.

The F.B.I. agent was looking at her oddly and pawing at the side of his mouth. Moonlight gave his face a ghoulish cast. Primitive fear of the dark pricked Anna's sensitized nerves.

'What?' she demanded. 'What is it?'

'You've ... um ... got something ...' Tentatively he reached toward her but pulled back short of actually touching her. 'It's ... ah ... vomit.'

Anna wiped her mouth. Sour smelling chunks came off in her hand. 'I hate CPR. They're dead. If they don't sit up and take notice in the first sixty seconds, they're going to stay dead. But we've got to pound and poke and blow just like it made sense. Got a hankie?'

Stanton fished an enormous white handkerchief from his hip pocket and handed it to her. She scrubbed her mouth and cheeks then pocketed it out of deference to his hypersensitive gag reflex.

'So, what happened?' Stanton turned and looked down the hill. Oakbrush and service berry had closed ranks creating a wall impervious to the moonlight. Beyond. down the sharp slope, the pickup's carcass showed as a paler boulder in the boulder field.

'Drunk, I would guess. The cab reeked of alcohol among other things.' Anna, too, stared down the slope. The excitement over, fatigue weighed heavily and the thought of climbing back down the hill wasn't pleasant.

'Got a flashlight?' Stanton asked.

'It's down there. You?'

'Not me. Got a spare in your car?'

'Of course. Doesn't work though.' The dark grew darker. Prickly pear spines lodged in Anna's hand were making themselves felt.

'The blind leading the blind?' Stanton asked.

'I'll go first.'

'Good. Snakes and things, you know.'

'First person just wakes them up and makes them mad. They always bite the second person. That's a proven statistic.'

'Where'd you read it?' Stanton demanded as he hurried after her into the arms of the oakbrush.

'U.S. News and World Report.' Anna gave him the standard comeback of the 1968 Mercy High School debate team.

Without lights, music and Silva, the wreck looked old, all life gone, metal bleached like bones. Anna appreciated its peacefulness. Lowering herself back down into the cab she felt a kinship with Tom. It had less to do with ghosts than with the now all-pervasive odor of alcohol.

'Here but for the grace of God' crossed her mind like a prayer as she remembered the night she'd lost to booze and self pity.

By the dome light, she retrieved her flashlight from where it had fallen down next to the door and passed it up to Agent Stanton.

Searching the cab was a job for a contortionist. Anna squatted over the broken passenger window and poked through the debris that had been shaken from under the seat and floor mats. A pack of Marlboros, two cigarettes remaining that would go unsmoked, five empty cans of Budweiser and one full, still cold to the touch, a McDonald's bag, the contents so old they no longer smelled, bits of paper, maps and registration from the glove box, a pencil with a chewed eraser and broken lead and a golf ball completed the inventory. But for the golf ball, it was more or less what she had expected to find. Silva didn't strike her as a golf sort of guy. A bowling ball or squirrel rifle would have been more in keeping with the image she had of him.

Hoisting herself out of the cab, she sat on the door with her feet still inside. The effort cost her a wrenching pain in her lower back, muscles protesting the lifting of one hundred and forty pounds.

'Ooof!' Stanton dragged himself up on the boulder nearby. 'Find anything?'

'Just what you'd expect, beer, cigarettes, fast food. The detritus of a misspent youth.'

'I didn't find anything revelatory outside the truck,' Stanton said. 'We ought to come back by the light of day but it looks like what it is: DUI with fatality. Back on the hill the truck left the ground and was airborne till it struck here. What I want to know is where Silva was between getting bailed out of jail and getting killed.'

'Killed. Patsy!' Anna remembered with a fresh sense of horror. 'Tom said he'd killed her.'

Chapter Eighteen

Patsy was fine, at least until they told her about Tom. 'Seriously injured' was how Anna put it. One of the great contributions of cardiopulmonary resuscitation was that nobody ever died on a carry-out, or in an ambulance for that matter. Through the vomit and the cracking bones and the blood, the body was kept pumped up with oxygen, the organs pantomiming life till a doctor pronounced it officially dead.

Patsy wept like a shattered bride. Regardless of divorce, this had apparently been a till-death-do-you-part kind of relationship. 'There's always hope, Mom,' Missy said, holding her mother's shoulders in an odd moment of role reversal.

Anna had ambivalent feelings about hope. Just because artists depicting the last refugee from Pandora's box always dressed the horrid little bugger like Tinkerbell, people tended to think hope was a good thing. Often it was the worst of the evil let loose to plague human kind.

'Is there hope?' Patsy pleaded.

'It was pretty bad,' Anna told her. 'He was still talking when I got to him. He said your name.'

Patsy cried harder but it was different and Anna was glad she'd kept the context of Tom's remark to herself.

The sun was rising when she and Agent Stanton left the tower house. Too tired to sleep, Anna sat for a moment behind the wheel of the patrol car, staring stupidly in front of her. 'My back is killing me,' she said to no one in particular though Frederick was in the seat next to her.

'Want me to drive?'

The offer sounded so half-hearted, Anna realized she'd never seen Stanton behind the wheel of a car. 'Have you got a licence?' she asked abruptly.

He laughed, a sound that soothed her frayed nerves. 'Almost like new, only use it on Sundays.'

'Don't like to drive?'

'I'd rather look out the window.'

'It's not far.' Anna referred to the tent frame Frederick was bivouacked in. 'I'll drive.'

'Goody. I'll give you a back rub. My first wife – or was it my second? Anyway, I come highly recommended in the back rub department.'

Leaving the tower house, Anna turned right and drove three hundred yards the wrong way on the one-way to the tent colony where VIPs and stabilization crew were housed.

Like the other service areas in Mesa Verde, this was on a loop. Communal showers, toilets, washer/dryer, and pay phone occupied the island created by the gravel drive.

Some of the dwellings were charming. Of native stone, they were built in the round style of Navajo hogans, but the majority were single-room plywood shacks called tent frames. Sixteen by sixteen feet square, they had just room for a bed, stove and refrigerator. There was no running water. At one time they'd been wooden platforms with canvas forming the walls and roof. When housing became short, they'd been walled in and wood burning stoves added to give them a longer season of use.

Though cramped and primitive, Anna saw in them blessed privacy and a home for Piedmont. When Stanton left, she would lean on Hills to give her his tent frame till permanent housing became available.

She pulled the Ford into the graveled spot in front of number seventeen. A picnic table under the junipers provided a platform for two scrub jays squabbling over a bit of orange peel. A fire pit with grill was near the table. 'I could live here,' Anna said.

'Come in. I'll give you the fifty cent tour. Make some decaf.'

Not ready yet to go home, Anna accepted. The tour consisted of 'Honey, I'm home,' called to imaginary scorpions. Anna sat on the single bed. It was made up so neatly it worried her. What kind of man made his bed when called out on a motor vehicle accident at three a.m.?

Apparently reading her mind, Stanton said: 'Not anal retentive.' He pointed to the long wooden table that occupied the wall between the woodstove and the foot of the bed. It was covered with papers and sketches, some in tidy piles, some scattered about where he'd been working into the wee hours.

Anna got up and looked to keep herself occupied

while Stanton busied himself with coffee, drawing the water from a five gallon plastic container with a spigot.

Photos of Stacy in the kiva, of the shoes with burn marks were laid out neatly. Drawings of the kiva, of Cliff Palace – quite good drawings – with entrance and exits marked in, were placed like maps above the autopsy and 10–344 report. Lists were everywhere: lists of clues and suspects, lists of things done and things left to do, lists of lists.

'Not anal retentive, you say?'

'Well, not about housework anyway. Although my second ex-wife – or was it my first – thought I should be.'

'You don't think much of marriage, I take it?'

'Are you kidding? It's my favourite hobby. Spend every spare penny on it. I'm completely in favor of it, wish both ladies would remarry today.'

Anna laughed. 'No doubt about it, widowhood has its upside.' She took the coffee he offered and sat in the straight-backed wooden chair. There being no others, Stanton perched on the foot of his bed.

'Come up with any bright ideas?' Anna indicated the desk. The hasty report she'd written on her previous day's findings was lying above a legal pad where yet another list was forming. A pair of half glasses served as a paper weight.

'Nothing brilliant. I'm getting slow,' he said. 'Can't solve them in record time any more. I used to do it with one victim. "One corpse Stanton" they called me. Now it takes two or three before I catch on.'

He was poking fun at himself but Anna understood.

There was no solving a crime till it happened. By then the damage was done. What kept the chase worth the effort was the hope a second could be prevented.

'Pushing forty-five,' Stanton said. 'Headed over the proverbial hill.'

'Over the hill,' Anna echoed.

'You aren't supposed to agree with me,' he complained. 'For a park ranger you sure don't know anything about fishing.'

'No,' Anna said absently. She put down her coffee and took the golf ball from her shirt pocket. 'This was in Silva's truck.'

'And?' Stanton looked at the little ball with interest. His instant attention was gratifying. He trusted Anna not to waste his time.

'Over the hill,' Anna repeated. 'In a conversation once Tom said he couldn't play golf because he wasn't over the hill yet.'

'Not his ball.'

'What do you figure would happen if you wedged a golf ball in the linkage over a gas pedal?'

'When the car crashed the ball would roll out.'

'When the pick-up crashed.' Anna swiveled in her seat to set the ball down amidst Stanton's case work. Twisting tore the damaged muscles and she groaned.

'Ready for that back-rub?' Stanton asked.

'No thanks.' Anna had been given a goodly number of back rubs over the years. They'd been anything but relaxing and healthful. Most had degenerated fairly quickly into wrestling matches. She was too tired to defend her virtue.

'You'll like it. It'll be good for you. Really.' Stanton was bustling: setting down coffee, grabbing up pillows and blankets. 'I've been to school. I'm certified and everything.' He carried the bedding out through the screen door.

He was shaking an army blanket out on the picnic table. The jays had fled to the branches of a nearby juniper and watched with interest. 'Soft is no good,' he was saying as Anna came up behind him. 'You can't really do much with soft. Padded is best but this'll do.' He plumped a pillow down on one end of the table. 'Climb on up,' he said. 'Office hours have commenced.'

More out of curiosity than anything else, Anna complied, laying belly-down on the table top.

'I'm a rolfer,' Stanton said, climbing up and straddling her. 'A proponent and practitioner of the art of rolfing.' With that he pushed his knuckles into her back.

What followed was the least sexual and most healing experience Anna had ever had. His strong fingers seemed to knead and pry the pain from between her muscles and realign her much maligned vertebrae.

When he'd finished, she lay quiet for another minute or so, enjoying the heat radiating through her back. 'That's the first honest-to-God back rub I've ever had,' she said truthfully.

By mutual agreement she and Stanton put the investigation on hold till they'd rested. Anna suffered from the pleasant but frustrating sense that things were just about to come clear, words on the tip of the tongue, connections about to be made. She doubted she'd be able to sleep but natural fatigue and the continuing warmth

Stanton's fingers had worked into her back conspired to shut down her brain and she slept without dreaming.

Around two-thirty that afternoon she awoke. Even that late in the day she was doomed to a cold shower. 'Sorry,' Jennifer said when she stalked into the kitchen to make coffee. 'I didn't figure anybody else'd be showering so late. I was steaming me out a hangover. A doozy. Alcohol poisoning of the worst kind. Have some of my coffee as a peace offerin' whilst yours does its thing.'

Anna accepted a mugful and dressed it with a dollop of heavy whipping cream.

'How do you stay so skinny?' Jennifer demanded. 'I get fat on Nutrasweet and water.'

'Are you on late today?' Anna asked.

'Yes ma'am. Till forever. I can't wait till you stop messin' with that F.B.I. guy. With both you'n Stacy off the schedule seems all I do is work night shifts.'

Anna tried to look sympathetic out of gratitude for the coffee. 'Where'd you get your hangover?'

Jennifer laughed then clutched her head. 'Jamie and I did Durango. She's still in bed. You should've seen her. She got to arm wrestling boys for drinks. She's just too strong for her own good. We like to drownded.'

'Sounds like fun,' Anna fed the conversation. Not yet through her first cup of coffee and already prying suspiciously into other people's lives; she'd be glad when the investigation was over and she could resume the life of a disinterested third party. 'Who drove you home?'

'The bartender at Flannigan's took Jamie's car keys. We had to crash in her stationwagon till he opened up around ten this morning.'

Jennifer buckled on her gun and left Anna to finish the coffee.

By four-thirty Stanton still hadn't called. Anna left word with dispatch to radio her if he checked in, and drove down to the CRO. The events of the previous night were settling in her mind and she needed to sort them out. Laying facts out in the no-nonsense format demanded by government form 10–343 seemed to help. As senior person on the scene, Hills should have written the report but Anna had no worries that he'd beaten her to the punch. Like a lot of district rangers, Hills had joined the NPS because of a love of hiking, canoeing, shooting, backpacking, climbing – challenging himself physically. When he climbed up into management he was forced to confront his worst fear: paperwork. Brawling drunks he could handle. The sight of a computer lit up the yellow streak down his broad back.

As she banged into the CRO, she asked Frieda, 'Has Stanton called?'

'Not yet.'

'Silva?'

'D.O.A. Massive cerebral hemorrhage.'

'Too bad.'

'Yes indeedy. You, Hills and the guys are scheduled to do a fatality debriefing with Dr. Whitcombe Friday morning. Write it down.'

Successfully resisting the urge to unload the night's pressures on Frieda, Anna slipped around the partition to her desk. As usual it was piled with clutter not of her making. Evidently Hills had dumped Stacy's personal defensive equipment there after inventorying it. Anna scooped it up to dump back on the district ranger's desk. The radio's leather case tumbled out of her clutches. 'Whoa!'

'What?' Frieda called over the room divider.

'Nothing.' Anna dropped the gun belt back where she'd found it and pinched up the radio case between thumb and forefinger. Burnt into the leather were two prints, etched marks such as had manifested on Stacy's shoes. The prints on the case hadn't been there when Rose had returned it. Anna was sure of that. In her fingerprinting frenzy she would have noticed.

The prints on Stacy's shoes had taken between one and three days to appear. Lost as they'd been in her trunk, Anna couldn't be more precise.

If these marks came from the same hand, and it was hard to imagine they hadn't, they'd been made not more than one to three days previously, considerably after Stacy had died and before Rose had returned the radio.

Anna closed her eyes and ears and marshaled her thoughts. Whoever removed Stacy's shoes had used the radio. Whoever used the radio had access to Rose's house. Did Stacy's murder have anything to do with Silva's death? Probably. Two murders in one sleepy park was highly unlikely. Rose might have killed Stacy for some matrimonial crime as yet unpublished, but why Tom? Greeley killing Silva for pilfering, monkey wrenching? Overkill to say the least. Strangers on a train? You kill mine, I'll kill yours?

There weren't enough players for a really good game of detection, Anna thought. Drew was in and out of the picture. Clearly he felt Stacy and Rose were making the wrong choices for Bella. Did his protectiveness over children extend to Silva's? Did he believe Tom was abusing Missy and Mindy in some way? Anna thought back to the wreck. Drew's efforts to salvage Silva's life seemed genuine enough.

Rousing herself, Anna called over the wall. 'Frieda, Stanton call yet?'

'You're sitting on the phone back there. Did it ring?'

'I guess not,' Anna conceded. Taking the radio case, she again gave Frieda the message to let her know when Stanton woke up. Frieda rolled her eyes but Anna was wrapped up in her own thoughts and missed it.

There was one last thing to check, then she would go stir Stanton up whether he was rested or not.

The maintenance yard was empty when she drove in. Maintenance and construction worked seven a.m. to three-thirty Monday through Friday. By three-thirty-one there was never any sign of them.

As she'd expected, the chainlink gate to the fenced off area where Ted Greeley kept his heavy equipment was locked, the chain and padlock as she had thought they would be.

Frieda called then and Anna abandoned her train of thought. Stanton was awake. She found him sitting on the picnic table with his feet on the bench nursing a cup of coffee.

'Good morning.' She sat down beside him, adjusting her gun so the butt wouldn't pry against her ribs. 'Get a good nap?'

'Yes indeed. Is it still Monday?'

'All day.'

Anna told Stanton about chains and locks and their connection with Stacy Meyers, Monday nights, and the Cliff Palace loop. 'What I can't figure out is why and how. Without those, "who" is pretty worthless.'

Stanton took another sip of coffee. Anna wished he'd offer her some. Not because it looked particularly good, but because it was something to do with her hands. In lieu of the coffee, she picked up a twig and began methodically snapping it in small pieces.

They sat in silence for a time. The sun was low in the sky and bathed them in amber light. To the west, Anna could just see the tops of thunderheads. It was probably raining in Dove Creek. A small doe wandered out from behind the tent frame. The air was so still they could hear the tearing sound as she cropped the grass.

Stanton seemed transfixed by the nearness of the graceful animal.

'Missing Chicago?' Anna ribbed him.

'In Chicago we have rats bigger than that.'

'Her.'

'How can you tell?'

'No antlers.'

'I thought they fell off.'

'They grow back.'

'No kidding!'

Anna felt her leg being gently pulled and laughed. 'You're such a rube, Frederick.'

The doe's head came up at the sound of laughter but the deer was looking not at them but down the foot path leading along the canyon's edge to the housing loop.

Frederick and Anna watched with her. Moments later Bella and her aunt came into view. Bella was in the lead. In her arms she carried a basket woven of pastel strips, a relic of a previous Easter. If the care she took not to let the basket bump or tip was any indication of contents, Anna would've guessed nitroglycerin or at least goldfish. Hattie followed with a plastic spatula, the kind cooks use to scrape the last of the cake batter from the bowl.

'Howdy, Bella, Hattie,' Frederick called.

'Fred and Anna!' To Bella, Hattie said: 'I told you this was going to be a good walk. So far we've seen three deer, a chipmunk, a park ranger and an F.B.I. agent.'

'An' a Abert squirrel,' Bella added, clearly more impressed with the long-eared rodent than the last two sightings on her aunt's list.

Hattie left the footpath and forged through the high grass toward the picnic table. Rye grass was beginning to plume and bright yellow mustard flowers dipped gracefully in her wake. Bella followed a few steps then stopped, hanging back.

'There's no snakes,' Frederick assured her. 'I made Ranger Pigeon check.'

'Only babies are afraid of snakes,' Bella returned. Anna forebore comment but bumped Stanton's knee with her own. 'I don't want to get any stuff on you.' Bella held the party-colored basket up like a dangerous offering.

'Is it full of nitroglycerin?' Anna asked.

'I don't know,' Bella replied. 'But probably not.'

'Nitro's a liquid but it explodes like dynamite,' Anna told her.

Clearly Bella didn't believe a word. 'That'd be silly.'

'You're right,' Anna conceded.

'Battery acid,' Frederick guessed.

'This is a basket,' Bella said with a touch of impatience. 'It'd leak out.'

'Spiders,' Anna tried.

Bella looked like that wasn't a bad idea but she shook her head. 'It's sad thoughts. *Really* sad thoughts. Me an Aunt Hattie thought up all the saddest thoughts and we put them in the basket and we're going to dump 'em in the canyon when the winds go down.'

'The winds aren't up,' Anna remarked, noting the stillness of the evening.

'They are. Drew said. The winds go up in the morning and down at night.'

Anna grabbed Frederick's arm. 'Bella's right. You're right,' she said to the child.

Slightly mollified, 'Up at day, down at night,' Bella reiterated. 'We gotta go,' she told her aunt.

'Gotta go,' Hattie echoed and, 'take care.'

'Out of the mouths of babes,' Anna said to Frederick as they watched the woman and girl pass out of sight behind a stand of piñons. 'Firefighters always watch the winds. When the sun warms the air in the mornings it begins to rise and a wind blows up canyon. In the evening, as the cool air settles, the wind shifts, blows down canyon. In the still of night it settles in the low areas. That's pounded into your head with a pulaski in every fire class.

'You dump the sad thoughts at night, they blow down canyon, away, out to the wide valleys and are dispersed.

You dump them in the morning, when the sun rises, they blow up canyon, into the alcoves, settle into the ruins.'

'Holy smoke,' Stanton said. 'A blinding flash of the obvious.'

Chapter Nineteen

Cliff Palace loop was closed; the gate at the Four-Way closed the road and the starless night closed down the world. Clouds obscured a fledgling moon. Trees, crowding close to the road, seemed impervious even to headlights. Shadows were sudden, long, and unnatural.

'This whole place is one big graveyard. Doesn't that give you the willies?' Stanton asked.

'Only when I think about it.' The Ford's beams were on low. If Anna'd had her druthers she'd've driven without lights but the night was too dark for that.

When the road widened into Cliff Palace parking lot, she switched them off.

'Yikes! What have we here?'

From the dim glow of the dashboard Anna could see where Stanton pointed. Along the split-rail fence separating the parking area from the trees were dozens of tiny glowing eyes, as if a herd of rats or other small night predators waited for the unwary.

'Glow worms,' she told him. 'Want to catch one?'

'No thanks. Wow. As in "glow little glow worm glow"? I'm disappointed. Not a "glimmer glimmer" in the lot.'

'Poetic licence.'

Again the road was enclosed by darkness. Anna slowed but didn't switch the headlights back on. From here to the Ute reservation the road ran along the canyon's rim. Though in most places there was a fringe of trees between the road and the canyon, any stray light could give them away.

At the Navajo taco stand on the tiny piece of reservation land accidentally surveyed into the park, Anna pulled off.

Around the souvenir and taco stand the land had been leveled and graveled in. Beyond, a dirt road led back into the brush and trees. There'd once been a barrier across it to keep out adventuresome tourists but it had long since fallen into disrepair. For several years no one had been caught camping back there so there had been no impetus to get it fixed. Brush made a quick and dirty barrier, a solution often employed to make a track or trail less desirable.

Anna loosed her flashlight from beneath the dash and climbed out of the car. Hands deep in pockets, Stanton followed. 'The mesa runs out there in a big finger of land with cliffs on all sides.

'You can see where the brush has been dragged back and forth.' Anna shined the light on the bottom of the makeshift barricade. Twigs were snapped and dusty. 'Not much in the way of tracks but we've not had rain for a while. Dry, this soil's like concrete.'

'Here.' Stanton had walked around the pile and poked a toe into the spill of her light. 'Truck track. Old but still pretty clear.'

Together they moved the brush aside. It took only a

minute; the barricade had been culled down to three good-sized bitterbrush bushes so dry they weighed next to nothing.

'A real deterrent,' Anna said drily. 'I'm surprised we haven't had wild packs of Bluebirds and Brownies rampaging around back here.'

She drove the patrol car through, then they carefully replaced the brush the way they had found it.

The one-lane dirt road was rutted and, though she drove at a foot-pace, the car jounced from side to side. Without headlights, the trip put Anna in mind of Mr Toad's Wild Ride in Disneyland. Three-quarters of a mile and it ended in a wide turn-around where dirt and rock had been scraped away to help build roads in the park. On the far side of the tree-shrouded clearing was a pile of slash fifteen or twenty feet high.

Anna eased the Ford around behind it, forcing the car over the rubble of limbs. 'I feel like a cat hiding behind a blade of grass, like there's bits of me sticking out,' she said as she turned off the ignition.

Stanton laughed. He was at the same time more relaxed and more alive than she'd ever seen him. 'You love this, don't you,' she said.

'So do you, Anna, admit it. Cops and robbers.'

Anna wasn't admitting anything.

Stanton tapped the long-lensed camera on the seat between them. 'The Colorado Highway Patrol is on stand-by. We watch, we take pictures for the judge. We call Frieda. Frieda alerts the Highway Patrol. They nab our perpetrator at the entrance station. We're heroes. What's not to like?'

Anna thought of Stacy with his warm brown eyes and

passionate love of the natural world. 'I'd rather beat a confession out with a rubber hose,' she said.

'You may get your chance. Odds are our sniffing around has set the alarm off and we won't get a thing. So far our evidence is pretty thin.'

'It's Monday. For whatever reasons the veil was always on Mondays,' she insisted. 'If it was worth killing for twice, it'll be worth a last run or two. My guess is this particular chindi doesn't scare off easily.' She turned off both her belt and the car radios. 'It's got to happen because basically we've got zip.'

'We know zip but we can't prove zip,' Stanton corrected. 'I hate these last-minute assignations.'

'It's Monday night,' Anna defended herself. Maybe the last Monday night load. Clicking free of her seat belt, she let herself out of the car taking the flashlight with her. A yellow circle of light joined hers as Stanton walked around the back of the vehicle. Familiarizing themselves with the area, they played their lights over the slash heap and around the car. The slash pile was comprised of the limbs and rounds of trees cleared from near the buildings by the hazardous fuel removal crew. The idea was that, should a wildfire break out on the mesa – a common occurrence during the thunderstorm season – there wouldn't be enough dead and down wood to carry it to any of the historic structures, a theory not yet tested and not inspiring of much faith among fire fighters. But it kept the stoves supplied all winter and a crew of high school and college students busy all summer.

Anna walked one way and Stanton the other till they'd circumnavigated the pile and satisfied themselves that the settled weave of pine and juniper branches was dense enough to hide the patrol car. Then Anna turned her attention to the clearing. Red soil, garish in the flashlight beam, was torn up by the tracks of heavy equipment. Most were run over so many times the tread was indecipherable.

'There's enough for some good casts,' Stanton said. He was down on hands and knees examining the dried mud.

'I'll take your word for it.'

'Flunked plaster casts?'

'I don't remember being taught that. I thought it was a Sherlock Holmes kind of thing.'

'*Au contraire*. We still do it. It's getting to be a lost art, though. Crime has come out of the closet. They do it right out in the open, then we just arrest 'em. Don't have to finesse much these days. Or else they do it all with computers and mirrors and we never know what hit us until we read about it in the *Tribune*.'

Anna traced the mish-mash of tracks toward the mesa's edge. They formed a broken fan narrowing to a drop-off point where an opening about forty feet wide made the canyon accessible. To either side trees and sandstone slabs closed in.

Careful not to walk on any salvageable tracks, she made her way to the cliff. Blackness swallowed the feeble beam of her six-cell. Instead of vertigo, it gave her a false sense of security, as if the drop wasn't there at all, as if it were solid and soft: black velvet.

'Don't stand so near the edge.' Stanton's voice at her elbow made her flinch.

'Don't creep,' she retorted.

'Don't shout.'

'Don't snap.'

'Nerves shot?'

'Yours too?'

He laughed easily. 'A little moonlight would help. Stars, Streetlights. Neon signs. Anything. It is way too dark out here.'

'The dark is my friend.' Anna flipped off her light. 'The invisible woman.'

Stanton turned his off as well and they stood in the darkness and the silence. As her eyes adjusted, Anna began to see the faint light that lives in all but deep caves: a blush of peach on the underside of the clouds to the south over the town of Shiprock, a trailing edge of silver where a thunderhead thinned near the moon, a barely discernable difference in the quality of dark between earth and sky, cliff and treeline.

A cold breath of air, just enough to tickle the hair on her arms, was inhaled into the depths of the canyon; air settling as it cooled. Anna closed her eyes and breathed deeply.

'Almonds,' she said.

Stanton sniffed, seeming to taste the air in nasal sips. 'Could be.' He turned on his flash and, in contrast, the night became impossibly dark again. The finger of light stirred in the dirt at their feet. Here the soil was more black than red and the truck tracks amorphous, as if made in soft mud. 'Whatever it is, we're standing in it.' With the light, he traced the discolored soil to where the canyon claimed it. 'Whatever is being dumped goes over right here.'

Anna took a plastic evidence bag from her hip pocket and scraped a sample of the dirt into it with the blade of her pocket knife. Not anxious to get a snootful of anything unfriendly, she sniffed it delicately then offered it to Stanton. 'Almonds,' he confirmed.

Having rolled the dirt into a package reminiscent of a lid of marijuana, Anna stowed it in her shirt pocket. 'Tomorrow we'll get down into the canyon bottom. Cliff Palace is up there at the head of the canyon. From the top of it this spot's clearly visible. If every veil sighting was in reality a Monday night drop that'd be at least four dumps – at least – on a night like this nobody would see a thing.'

'Up-canyon winds when the sun begins to warm and whatever gasses this muck gives off drift to the Palace and pool in the alcove. Them what's got weak hearts and lungs fall by the wayside,' Stanton said. 'If the stuff's heavy it'd settle in the lowest spot. Maybe it filled the kiva Stacy was in, overcame him. That'd account for the single set of tracks.'

'Burning prints from the flaming digits on Stacy's arms,' Anna reminded him. 'Marks like we found on his shoes and appeared on the radio case. I doubt Stacy's murder was quite so second degree.'

For a minute longer they stood on the lip of the canyon, Anna feeling there was something more she ought to be doing but uncertain of just what.

'All we're going to do tonight is mess up what evidence there is,' Stanton said finally. 'Let's find a front row seat and wait for the curtain to go up.'

On the eastern edge of the clearing, they found a flat

slab of sandstone partially screened by a thicket of juniper. Their rock was several yards above where the dirt road entered the clearing. Headlights of approaching vehicles wouldn't find them.

For a while Frederick tried to keep the conversation afloat. When he'd exhausted stories about his kids, Anna's pets, and ascertained that she had seen none of the recent movies, he fell silent.

Anna enjoyed the quiet. In complete darkness there was no awkwardness. Alone but not lonely; Stanton was there but invisible and, now, inaudible. Small stirrings as he shifted position, the crack of a joint as he straightened a knee, were comfortable, comforting. Sounds a man made in the bed as he slept beside you, Anna realized. It had been a while since those living human sounds had been there to lull her back to sleep when the nightmares woke her.

Within a couple of hours the meager heat the stone had collected during the day was gone. Beside her, Frederick's deep even breathing suggested he'd fallen asleep. She didn't begrudge him a nap. Could she have slept, she would've had no qualms about waking him to watch while she caught forty winks.

Cold was settling into the low places and Anna's spirits settled with it. In the wee small hours of the morning, as the song went, was when she missed him most of all. The long and most thoroughly dead Zachary, the husband of her heart – or as Molly caustically put it when Anna waxed maudlin – the husband of her youth, back when all things were possible, all dreams unfolding.

Stacy's haunting brown eyes had a ghost of Zachary's

intensity, a shadow of his remembered wit. Unfortunate as Meyers' death was, Anna knew it saved her from making a complete ass of herself. Had the affair become full blown, her life would have disintegrated into that morass of guilt, deceit and recrimination even the most carefully orchestrated adultery engenders.

Despite Stacy's avowals of dedication to Rose, Anna had little doubt that the affair would have blossomed. Lust leveraged by memory was a powerful force. Ultimately it must have disappointed them both. The Hindus preached that there were three-thousand-six-hundred gates into heaven. Anna doubted adultery was one of them. Like alcohol, it was just a short vacation from life-as-we-know-it.

Stanton's long fingers closed around her knee and Anna was startled into thinking a short vacation might be just what the doctor ordered.

'Listen,' he whispered.

She strained her ears but heard nothing. 'Sorry, too much loud rock and roll music in my youth.'

'Shhh. Listen.'

An engine growled in the distance. 'I hear it now.' They fell quiet again, tracking the sound. Anna frisked herself, loosened the baton in its holster, unclipped her keys from her belt and put them in her shirt pocket where they wouldn't jingle when she moved.

'If the tracks are any indication, the truck will pull in, headlights on the slash pile, turn perpendicular to the canyon, headlights pointed somewhere south of us, then back as close to the rim as possible to make the dump.' Stanton went over ground they'd covered in earlier discussions. 'I'll stay here. Maybe work my way further around where I can get some clear pictures of the truck, the license plate, and, if we're lucky, the driver actually unstoppering the tank.'

'Nothing like a smoking gun,' Anna said. Then, because it was safer than assuming, she spoke her part: 'I go behind the car, get the shotgun, stay put, shut up, and hope your career as a photographer is long and uneventful.'

'Let's do it.'

Anna felt Stanton squeeze her knee then he was gone without a sound, like the mythical Indian scouts in children's books. Moving as quietly as she could, Anna was still aware of the crack and scuffle of her footfalls. She comforted herself with the thought that it was like chewing carrots, more audible to the doer of the deed than any accidental audience members.

In less than two minutes, she'd popped the trunk, unsheathed the shotgun and was in place by the left rear fender of the car trying to regain the night vision the trunk light had robbed her of. 'Damn,' she cursed herself. It was those details that got one killed. If the flash of light from the trunk had been seen, they'd either be in for a fight or the truck would simply keep going taking all the good, hard courtroom proof of malfeasance with it.

Prying her mind from this treadmill of extraneous thought, Anna slowed her breathing and opened her senses. A feeling of clean emptiness filled her, body and mind receptive to the physical world: the earth firm beneath her feet, the smooth wood of the shotgun stock against her palms, the breeze on her right cheek, the weight of her duty belt, the smell of pine, the sounds of the night and the engine.

Fragments of light began filtering through the trees. She closed her eyes and turned her head away as the truck grew close. Spots of orange danced across her eyelids. The drone became a roar and she felt a moment's panic that she would be run down.

Lights moved, the roar grew louder. She opened her eyes. Headlights stabbed into the woods on the east side of the clearing. Confident the din would cover any sound, she moved to the end of the slash pile and took a stand behind a dead pine branch.

Racket and exhaust filled the clearing, then the sound of clanging as a big red water truck backed toward the canyon. When it was less than a yard from the cliff edge, the roar settled to an idle and the clanging stopped. Placing her feet as much from memory as sight, Anna moved to the rim of the canyon. Twin sandstone blocks, each the size of a small room, were at her back. To the left, between her and the cliff, were three stunted piñon trees. They were scarcely taller than she but, on this harsh mesa, could've been a hundred years old or more. A bitterbrush bush eight or ten feet tall screened her from the water truck with spiny brown arms.

Headlights were switched off. The night drew close. Far to the west heat lightning flickered from cloud to cloud. If there was distant thunder the truck drowned it out. Engine noise filled all available space, creating confusion where stillness and clarity had reigned.

Tingling in her fingers let Anna know she'd tensed, her grip was too tight. Again she opened her mind, rocked on the balls of her feet and moved her hands slightly on the shotgun. Over the idle of the engine she heard the slamming of the door. In her mind she heard the click of the camera shutter as Stanton captured the driver on film, the door, the truck, the license plate.

A shadow came around the back of the water truck, bent down and began pulling or pushing at something. Envying Stanton his infrared scope, she strained her eyes, opening them so wide tears started, but there was no more ambient light to be gathered and she could see nothing more.

Metal clanked on metal and a liquid hiss followed as something cascaded onto the packed earth. Anna smelled almonds. Memories from old movies and Agatha Christie novels flooded sickeningly through her mind. Cyanide gas was said to smell of almonds. She stopped breathing – a temporary solution at best and one not conducive to clear thinking. Shrinking back toward the slash pile, she hoped the down-canyon winds would carry the fumes in the opposite direction. From all reports these night dumps lasted only minutes.

Sudden light flooded the clearing. The figure was spotlighted and Anna sucked in a lungful of almond scent. Not a man, but a creature with a human body, the head of an insect, and one, long, clawed arm hunkered there.

In an instant her mind recoiled from appearance to reality: a human wearing the self-contained breathing apparatus found on fire trucks stood in the spill of light brandishing a pipe wrench. Liquid, rainbow bright in the headlights, gushed from a line of sprinklers on the rear of the water truck in a fine even rain. It would take only a beam of moonlight to turn it into a spirit veil.

Like an afterthought, blue overheads and the ululating wail of a siren added to the confusion. Someone shouted. A door banged.

'God dammit!' Anna whispered as Jennifer Short, fumbling her .357 from its holster, ran into the light. Once again the woman had neglected to call into service or Frieda would have headed her off.

'Freeze! Freeze!' Short was shouting like a cop in a TV movie. The insect head turned slowly, the pipe wrench fell from sight, hidden behind a trousered leg.

Anna stepped clear of the sheltering brush and chambered a round of double-ought buck. The unmistakable sound cut through the low grade rumble of the engine and the siren's whine. Insect eyes swivelled toward her. She shouldered the gun. 'Drop the wrench,' she shouted. 'Drop the wrench.'

The pipe wrench was moved away, held out to the side, the blank eye plates of the mask black, unreadable.

'Drop it.' Anna leaned forward flexing her knee, ready to take the recoil if she had to pull the trigger. A cold vibrating in her stomach and the feel of the butt of the shotgun against her shoulder were all she was aware of. The world had shrunk, her vision tunneled till all that existed was the creature with the pipe wrench, clear and contained as a figure viewed through the wrong end of binoculars.

Movement pried open her field of vision. Jennifer, her pistol worked free of the holster, circled to the west, putting the insect directly between herself and Anna's shotgun.

'Jennifer, stop!' Anna cried. Either deaf from noise or adrenaline, Short ran the last yard, completing the line. Now she and Anna stood less than forty feet apart, guns pointing at one another.

The insect realized it as Anna did. Glittering eyes turned from her to Jennifer. The wrench disappeared behind a leg. Slowly, mesmerizing with the gauntleted hands and inhuman head, it walked toward Short. Jennifer was shifting her weight, her feet dancing in the dirt. Even from a distance Anna could see her hands shaking. 'Stop where you are,' Anna shouted. Nausea churned in her stomach and she wondered if it was nerves or whatever she was breathing.

Aware that if she pulled the trigger, when the smoke cleared, Jennifer might be dead as well, the insect ignored her.

To Anna's left was the canyon. If she shifted right the water truck would block her target. 'Jennifer, move!' she yelled. 'Move, damn you.'

'Stop. Stop now. Don't come any closer,' Jennifer was shouting. Shrieking like a banshee, the masked figure dodged right and charged. Anna saw the flash from the barrel of Short's .357 and hurled herself to the ground. High-pitched and ringing, a bullet struck stone. Sparks flew and Anna felt the sting of rock splinters hitting the back of her leg. Two more wild shots rang out, then a scream. Anna looked up to see Jennifer clubbed to the ground by the pipe wrench. The monster-headed figure leaped from sight behind the far side of the truck.

Head and torso beneath the right rear wheel, Short lay without moving.

Another fracture of sound and a muzzle flash came from the boulder beyond where Jennifer lay. Stanton. Like Anna, he'd ended up their fool's chorus line.

Flickering blue lights lent his body the fast-forward movement of early films as he ran.

Anna was on her feet running, the shotgun clutched to her chest. Siren and engine roar clouded her brain, clogged her thoughts. Cacophony or cyanide was eroding her synapses. A car door slammed. The ground was uneven and becoming slippery. A stabbing pain, muscles outraged by sudden movement, nearly tripped her.

Stanton was shouting. Then a loud regular clanging cut through the engine's throb. The water truck had been thrown into reverse, the warning bell ringing the intention to back up. Through the shimmering curtain of toxic waste, Anna saw the rear wheels begin to tear free of the mud, crush the strip of ground between themselves and Jennifer Short.

No time to think. Anna threw the shotgun from her, guaranteeing the canyon would be the first to claim it, and hurled herself backwards, clear of the moving vehicle.

The tire, silhouetted by garish blue, filled her field of vision. A couple of feet away, in its path, Short lay on her side, an arm thrown above her head reaching toward Anna. A glistening line of blood ran down her temple, over her closed eyelid and onto the bridge of her nose.

In a heartbeat the water truck would roll over her, cut her in two. Scrambling till her butt was on the ground and her feet splayed to either side of the unconscious ranger, Anna grasped Short under the arms and dragged her back, pulling her up like a blanket. Digging heels into the ground Anna shoved the both of them back. Something gouged deep into her side, raking the flesh from her ribs: a stick from the slash pile. Ignoring the pain, Anna pushed hard with her feet. The staub had caught where the butt of her .357 hooked up and back and, push as she might, she could go no further.

The gap between the tire and Jennifer's legs was gone. No time: Anna unsnapped the leather keeper that held her gun in the holster. Again she dug heels into earth and shoved back with all the strength in her legs. A tearing at her hip slowed her, then the gun broke free of the break-front holster and with it the staub. Loosed like an arrow from a bow, Anna shot back several feet, dragging Jennifer with her.

Light was eclipsed, noise crushed down. The truck with its burden of poison rolled toward the cliff's edge. Trees snapped like gun shots as the rear axle crashed over the lip of sandstone. Blue light scratched across Anna's vision. She was seeing them from beneath the chassis of the truck. Tons of metal levered into the air, headlights stabbing wildly into the sky to rake the bottom of the low clouds.

Screeching wrenched the night and the underbelly of the truck scraped down, pulled backward by the weight of the load. A moment of shocked silence followed, broken only by the oddly peaceful sound of small rocks pattering after. Then a rending crash and stillness so absolute the faint oscillating whine of the patrol car's overheards was clearly audible.

Jennifer's head was on Anna's shoulder, her weight

pinning her to the ground. 'Hope I got your feet out in time,' Anna whispered into the stiff web of sprayed hair that fell over her mouth and nose. She worked her right arm from beneath Jennifer's and found the seasonal's throat with her fingers. A pulse beat reassuringly in the hollow of the woman's neck.

'Hallelujia.' Anna's voice rang loud in the new-made quiet and she wished she'd not spoken. As gently as possible, she eased herself from under Short and pushed up to her knees.

'Anna!' Stanton's voice.

'Here.'

'Anna!'

Stanton was beginning to annoy her. 'What the fuck . . .'

'Behind you!'

Anna dropped and rolled as a metal bar crashed into the ground where she'd been kneeling. White light flashed off the sightless eyes of the insect head. A heavily gloved hand raised again, the pipe wrench swung in a deadly arc.

Anna scuttled backward, fell to her left shoulder and rolled again, grappling for her revolver.

The staub had torn it free of the holster. It lay somewhere in the dirt between her and her attacker.

Crouched, pipe wrench on shoulder like a ball player at bat, the insect ran toward her. Bent low and pressed close to the slash heap, the gamble was Stanton wouldn't shoot for fear of hitting one of the women.

Apparently it was going to pay off. 'Shoot,' Anna screamed and kept rolling. Iron glanced off her upper arm followed by numbing pain, then smashed into the ground with such force she felt it through the torn earth.

Then Anna's collapsible baton was in her hands. In one desperate motion she rolled to her feet and whipped the weighted rod out to its full length.

The pipe wrench struck her shoulder. For a sickening instant she felt her fingers loosen on the baton but no bones had been broken and strength flooded back.

'Shoot!' she yelled as she lunged at her attacker swinging the baton. It connected somewhere between the gauntleted elbow and shoulder with a bone-cracking jar that pleased Anna to her toes.

The insect grunted but didn't fall down or back. The wrench was tossed from right to left hand and slashed at Anna's face.

Jerking the baton up, she braced the tip across her left palm and blocked the blow. The force shot angry pains down her wrists and left her hands tingling. Before her attacker recovered balance she kicked out, hoping to connect with a knee cap. Her boot cut along the inside of her assailant's ankle.

A scream was ripped loose. The wrench chopped down.

Again Anna blocked it but this time her baton was forced to within an inch of her face. Her assailant was stronger and more heavily armed.

'Shoot,' she screamed.

'Get out of the way!'

'Jesus.' Anna jerked the baton back. Overbalancing, the insect stumbled forward a step. She stepped into the opening and rammed the tip of the baton into the exposed gut with all her strength and weight.

Her attacker bent double. Both hands on the baton, she swung the butt down toward the back of the canvas-covered neck. The pipe wrench caught her across the shins. Her blow fell wild, glancing off the breathing apparatus.

A shoulder slammed into her chest and she fell back. Mud softened the landing but breath was knocked from her and her head snapped back, splashing muck into her hair and face. Curling up like a spring, Anna held the baton perpendicular to her body to ward blows from her face and upper body. With her feet she kicked out, keeping the pipe wrench at a distance.

'Shoot, goddamn it!'

The wrench arced up. Anna kicked but the cloying mud hampered her, adding to the nightmare feeling. Bracing her arms to absorb another strike, she yelled 'Look out!' in the slim hope of unsettling her assailant.

The insect should have heeded her unwitting advice. A gun's report hit Anna's ears at the same time the bullet struck. The force of the shot pushed her attacker upright.

For a bizarre moment the insect head hung over her, the wrench half way down its arc, as if deciding whether to complete the strike or not. A second shot rang out and the fingers gripped so tightly around the wrench sprang open. The wrench fell, cracking Anna's knuckles against the baton, then slithered heavily into the mud at her side.

The masked figure stepped back stiff-legged then crumpled, muscles and ligaments no longer receiving orders from the central nervous system; the strings that moved the puppet had been cut.

Anna felt as if the second shot had cut her strings as well. Her head dropped into the sludge, the baton fell from her hands, her legs were rubbery, useless. Confusion clouded her mind, her heart pounded and she felt as if she were going to vomit.

Sirens and sucking sounds took over but she had little interest. A face formed over hers and she yelled.

'Take it easy,' Stanton said. 'Are you all right?' Taking her hand, he pulled her to her feet. Disoriented, nauseated, Anna shook her head to clear it. Nothing cleared. She tried to remember if she'd taken a blow to the head and couldn't. Cyanide gas: she remembered the almond smell.

Sirens closed in and the clearing was filled with chaos. 'I called the cavalry,' Stanton said.

Anna dragged her hand across her eyes trying to gather her wits. Her eyes began to burn viciously. Tears blinded her and she couldn't force her eyes open. Wherever the sludge had come in contact, her skin burned.

'My eyes,' Anna said. 'My eyes . . .'

'Holy smoke,' Stanton said softly as she reached blindly for him. 'Let's get you out of here.'

Anna held tight to his arm and stumbled over the uneven ground. 'Did you kill him?' she shouted over the sound of the sirens.

'I'm afraid so.'

'Was it Greeley?'

'Yes.'

'Good. What a son of a bitch.'
'You're going to be all right,' Stanton said.

Chapter Twenty

'Does it have to be so fucking cold?' Anna barked.

' "Flush with copious amounts of cool water",' Stanton quoted sententiously.

'Cool, damn it, not cold.'

Anna heard the protest of antique plumbing as Frederick turned the shower knob. 'That better?'

'No.'

'Well, think about something else, like July in Georgia.'

'Shit. My eyes!' Water cascading down from her hair washed more acid into her eyes. The burning made her whimper. It felt as if the jelly of her eye were being eaten away.

'Keep flushing,' Stanton said. 'Tilt your head back.' Anna felt his hand on the back of her head and tried to do as he said. 'Try and open your eyes so clean water gets into them.'

'Can't. Hurts.' Anna heard the whine in her voice and shut up. She was shivering and not only with the cold. Blindness: now there was a bogey man to put the fear of God into one. Blindness, paralysis and small closed spaces.

'You'll see. We got it in time,' Frederick reassured her. 'I drove like the wind. You would've been proud. A regular Parnelli Andretti. Open now. Come on. A teensy, weensy little peek,' he coaxed, and Anna was able to laugh away a bit of her terror.

His fingers were plucking at the buttons of her uniform shirt, peeling it off her back as gently as if he feared he might peel the skin off with it. His very care scared her and she tried to help, jerking blindly at her shirttail.

He pulled it free for her. 'Yowch! You've got an ugly gouge down your ribs. Greeley get you with the wrench?'

For a moment Anna couldn't remember. Her brain was fogged and that, too, scared her. The answer came in flashback. 'Stick took my gun,' she said. 'Scraped me.'

'You're burnt,' Stanton said.

'What does it look like?' Anna strove for a conversational tone but missed.

'Not bad. Not bad at all. Looks like a sunburn but not blistering or anything. Here.'

Cold water was deflected to stream down her back. Keeping her face tilted so the dirty water would run away from her eyes Anna gathered her hair and held it out from her body.

'Let me get your shoes off,' Stanton said. 'We don't want this pooling in 'em and dissolving your toes.'

'That's a soothing picture,' Anna mumbled. She kicked off one shoe and felt him pull the other off as she lifted her foot.

'I'm going to cut your trousers off, okay?'

'Cut. And warm up the water. I'm getting hypothermic.'

'Just a tad.' The aged metal creaked in protest and the edge went off the cold.

Anna pushed her face into the stream and pried her eyes open with her fingers. She must have cried out because Stanton was asking what was the matter and she could feel the warmth of his hand on her bare shoulder.

'Don't touch me,' she said. 'You'll get this shit on you.'

'Right. Are you okay?'

Anna shook her head. She couldn't hold her eyelids open for even a second. The fact that she could see light beyond her eyelids seemed a good sign, but the flourescent light over the stall in the women's communal shower at the tent frames where Stanton had brought her was so bright even a blind woman could see it. The thought sent another stab of fear into her and Anna tried harder to get fresh water under her lids.

Stanton slit her pantlegs and Anna gasped with the cold and the relief. Her skin burned and itched where the acid-drenched mud had soaked through. As he cut away her underpants he said, 'Oooh. Black lace. A collector's item. I shall have them stuffed.'

Anna was grateful for the banter. Pain and panic had destroyed any vestige of modesty but she appreciated the thought. 'As I recall, you never wanted to know me this well.'

He didn't reply.

'How much more time have I got?'

'Thirteen minutes. "Flush with copious amounts for twenty minutes," the doctor said. You've done seven.'

During the wild and, for Anna, sightless ride from the cliff's edge, Stanton had radioed Frieda to call the emergency room in Cortez. The doctor on call had given instructions for treatment. Stanton was carrying them out with kindness and precision. For the first time in more years than she cared to count, Anna felt taken care of. It made her weak and she was afraid she would cry.

Hoping Stanton would attribute the gesture to modesty, she turned her back on him. 'Distract me,' she said when she could trust her voice. 'What do you figure? What happened?'

'The obvious: Greeley had the water truck rigged to smuggle toxic waste into the park to dump it. It shouldn't be too hard to trace where the stuff was from.'

'Cyanide gas,' Anna said. 'Almonds, remember? And acid. Some kind of acid wash used in industrial manufacturing maybe. Stacy stumbles onto the scheme. Greely kills Stacy.'

'Maybe.'

The doubt in his voice irritated her. She ignored it. At present the topic held little interest for her, but it was the only thing she could think of besides her eyes and she didn't care to think about that. 'Greeley must've made Stacy breathe the fumes,' she went on. Fleeting sadness darkened her mind. 'The prints on his arms and shoes were etched with whatever it is I've been rolling in.'

'Think Greeley dumped him in the kiva just to be mysterious?' Stanton asked.

'We'll never know, but probably. Jamie'd been babbling on to everybody about the solstice and angry spirits. He might have been taking advantage of Jamie's ghostly brouhaha.'

'So he carries him into the kiva, folds him up in the fire pit, rakes it all smooth, puts on Meyers' shoes, backs out, and tosses the shoes back where he got 'em.'

'Mysteries are like magic,' Anna said. 'Once you know how the trick is done, it's obvious to the point of stupidity. I'll bet dollars to doughnuts Silva was blackmailing Greeley,' Anna said, suddenly remembering the short-lived spate of expensive gifts he'd poured into Patsy's lap. 'He reported seeing a truck at night once. He was out at all hours harassing Patsy. Maybe he saw something else. Put two and two together.' Anna pressed her face near the shower head, hoping the water pressure would force it beneath her lids.

'Tom must have gotten greedy,' Stanton said. 'Ted probably started threatening the wife and kids to shut him up.'

So Tom had been guardian angel and not stalker after all, looking after his girls the only way he knew how. 'Killed Pats' wasn't firsthand homicide but guilt at putting her in danger. 'Threats against his family would shut him up all right,' Anna said. 'Tom was obsessed with his ex.'

'But you can't trust a drunk.'

'Nope. And nothing easier than getting a drunk to take a drink. Point the truck in the right direction and wedge a gold ball in the linkage. Greeley was a golfer. Tom mentioned it one day.'

Silence. 'Are you still there?' she demanded. Panic rose in her chest and a sour taste poured into the back of her throat.

Something heavy slammed into the tile near her head.

Covering her face and neck, Anna collapsed to the floor of the shower. 'I can't see, goddamn it! I can't see!' she was screaming.

'Sorry, sorry, sorry, I'm so sorry. It was me, Frederick the idiot,' Stanton's voice was in her ear, his hands on her shoulders. 'A spider. A black widow. No kidding. As big as a ping-pong ball. Huge. It looked ready to pounce. I hit it with your shoe. Sorry.'

'Fuck you. Fuck you.' Anna began to cry. Stanton crouched down in the shower and held her. The slick fabric of his windbreaker stuck to her cheek and his arms were warm around her. Water dripped from his hair to her face. He held her as she would hold a frightened kitten, tightly, carefully so it wouldn't hurt and couldn't fall.

When she could finally stop, he helped her to her feet.

'Four more minutes,' he said.

'Thanks,' was all she could manage.

When she had only a minute left to go Frieda took over. She and Frederick discussed Anna's disposal in hushed tones till she couldn't stand it anymore and shouted at them.

Frieda shut the shower off and wrapped a shivering Anna in clean towels. 'Can you see?' she asked.

Anna forced her eyes open a slit. 'I guess. No. Sort of.' The pain was there but not so intense and she could make out shapes, light and dark.

'Keep your eyes shut,' Frederick said and Anna felt him winding soft gauze around her head. 'I'm going to bandage them both closed. You know the routine. Don't want you looking hither and yon scratching things about.'

The bandaging done, he kissed her on top of the head and left to return to the crime scene.

As Frieda wrapped Anna's hair in dry terry cloth, she said: 'I'm going to drive you to Cortez. Hills is out at the scene. Paul and Drew took Jennifer down soon as they got there. She'd come around. She got a hell of a wallop on the head, but it looks like a concussion and a good story's all she's going to come away with. Short's lucky.'

'If I weren't so glad she weren't dead, I'd kill her.'

'C'mon, you were young once,' Frieda chided.

'No I wasn't.' With her aching muscles and acid-etched body, Anna felt as if it were true.

Dr Dooley kept Anna overnight for observation but released her the next morning with eye salve and a cheap pair of sun-glasses. The world was still a little fuzzy around the edges but it looked good to Anna.

She pulled on a pair of mechanic's overalls and rubber shower thongs Frieda'd dug out of her trunk and left for her. Her own clothes were ruined. Hopefully the duty nurse hadn't thrown them away. They were evidence.

On the way out, she stopped by Jennifer Short's room. Jennifer's head was swathed in bandages and both her eyes were swollen shut. She was so contrite Anna's anger, never heartfelt, evaporated entirely. It had taken a good deal of courage to go up against Greeley all alone in the dead of night. Tombstone courage that needed leavening with common sense, but courage all the same, and Anna respected that.

To her surprise, Short was determined to keep on

being a ranger. 'I'm going to get on permanent,' the woman lisped through swollen lips. 'Get me some trainin' and get damn good.'

'I'll hire you,' Anna said and was pretty sure she meant it.

Hills was waiting near the emergency room desk when Anna walked out. 'Where's Frederick?' she asked.

'Glad to see you too,' he returned. 'Get your stuff. We're gonna have paperwork up the wazoo over this thing.'

'I'm wearing my stuff. And I'm on sick leave for a week. Doctor's orders.'

'Doggone it. You gotta be more careful.'

'You're glad I'm all right, admit it.'

Hills grunted. Anna took it for an affirmative. The depths of his feeling were revealed on the drive back up to the mesa top. He'd found Patsy and the girls lodging. The tower house was hers.

'When?' The question was so abrupt, Anna laughed at herself.

'If you was a tomcat I do believe you'd be up there peein' in every corner,' Hills retorted. 'It's yours today, I guess, if you want. Patsy had the movers there this morning. I'd think you'd want to let the sheets cool off before you went hopping in.'

'Nope.'

'Need help?'

'Nope. Thanks though,' Anna added belatedly. What she had was in storage in Cortez. Her estate consisted of little more than a futon and frame, a rocking chair and a few good Indian rugs.

The movers were late and, as it turned out, Anna had to spend one more night in the dormitory. A little after eight the next morning she had her belongings stuffed in boxes and paper sacks and piled into the rambler.

Zach's ashes were last to be loaded. As she carried the tin out through the living room she took a last look around.

'Find anything to miss?' Jamie asked.

'Not much. The company,' Anna lied.

'Hah!' Jamie was unoffended. 'You forgot your wine cellar.'

Anna paused for a second in the kitchen and looked at the five bottles lined up on the counter beneath the shelves she'd claimed as her own. 'Share it with Jennifer,' Anna said. 'Sort of a goodbye toast.'

'My, my.' Jamie clucked her tongue. 'And they told me it was Jennifer who got hit on the head.'

On her way down to Chapin, Anna stopped by Frieda's and gathered Piedmont into the canvas satchel that served as his travel carrier.

By two o'clock she'd brought all of her worldly goods up from storage. Her boombox had pride of place on the mantle and Louis Armstrong poured out 'It's a Wonderful World' like honey-laced bourbon. Anna amused herself dragging rugs and pictures from place to place, then standing back to discuss the effect with a disinterested cat.

The only furniture she'd arranged so far was a rocking chair and, beside it, a small marble-topped table where the phone sat in solitary splendour. Soon she'd call her sister. Anna'd been promising herself that for three hours but had yet to drum up the nerve. There were things needing to be said, confessions to be made.

Rapping at the front door interrupted both her nesting and her dithering. With less than good humor, she went to the door.

Stanton waved at her through the screen. Despite a flash of awkwardness engendered by their unscheduled intimacy in the shower, Anna was glad to see him. Because it seemed less stilted than leaving him on the doorstep, she invited him into the kitchen and sat down in the booth. The little vinyl benches and polished tongue of formica were too small to accommodate his lanky frame.

'Kitchens are made for girls,' he complained, turning sideways to stretch his legs. 'Just to reach the sink without bending double I've got to stand with my feet so far apart I'm almost doing the splits.'

'Sounds like an excuse to get out of doing dishes to me.'

'How're you doing?' he asked when he'd gotten himself arranged.

'Fine. Can't offer you anything. The cupboard is bare.' Without the case to lean on, Anna was finding conversation difficult.

'I've been tying up loose ends,' he said. 'Rose is willing to turn state's evidence in return for clemency.'

'For the false alibi?'

Stanton nodded. Anna shoved three carpet tacks the movers had managed to leave on the kitchen table into a pinwheel shape. 'The woman's husband gives his life to stop the dumping, Greeley kills him, and Rose is still willing to alibi him. Go figure.'

Stanton looked uncomfortable – miserable, in fact. He looked like Anna's dad when he had bad news about Fluffy or Bootsie or Pinky-winky – whichever of their multitude of pets had succumbed to the inevitable.

Anna waited. Everyone she knew was safe. Still, there was a hollow place in her belly.

'Stacy was on the take,' Frederick said apologetically. 'Greeley paid him to unlock the Four-Way and make sure the coast was clear. That's why Greeley did it Monday nights; Stacy was on the late shift. After he was killed Rose gave Greeley Stacy's radio so he could keep tabs on the rangers. Without Stacy's keys, Rose says she doesn't know how he unlocked the Four-Way. Presumably at some point Stacy made him a copy.'

Anna looked at the table, her mind playing with something as her fingers played with the tacks. Patsy'd said the night Tom broke in and left the derringer, she'd been awakened twice. The next day she mentioned she'd 'lost' her keys. 'Greeley stole Patsy Silva's keys, copied them then put them back,' Anna said. 'I can't prove it, but that's what happened.'

Stanton nodded. 'Rose said Stacy'd decided to turn Greeley and himself in after a little girl died after being carried out of Cliff Palace.'

'Stephanie McFarland.'

'He and Rose argued about it over the phone the night she was in Farmington, the night Stacy was killed. Up till then he was in collaboration with Greeley to dump the toxic waste.' The F.B.I agent seemed to be repeating the news in case Anna hadn't quite been able to grasp it first time around.

Anna had understood just fine. The devil buys on the

installment plan. People are always shocked when he shows up to collect his merchandise.

'Everybody's got their price,' Frederick said.

'Stacy's wasn't money.'

'But money could buy it.'

'And money bought Rose's alibi.'

Stanton took his head. 'Matrimony. She hated Ted but he said he'd marry her and put Bella on his health insurance plan. Strictly business.'

Anna pushed the carpet tacks around till they formed a jagged line, like a bolt of lightening, and she remembered the storm Bella had made with Hattie because her mad was so big. Rose had made her lie, say Greeley was in Farmington. At six telling a lie is still a great burden.

'What was Greeley dumping?' Anna changed the subject.

'There's electroplating plants in the area. One in Cortez, one near Shiprock, and a couple around Farmington. They use an acid for the wash and cyanide in the brass plating process. Greeley was contracted to dump it. I haven't got the particulars yet but evidently Greeley Construction was in financial trouble. Greeley couldn't finish the pipeline, he'd already spent the money. By dumping illegally he hoped to fix his cash flow problems long enough to avoid the penalties.'

'Worth killing for?'

'One hundred thousand dollars a day for every day over schedule. Greeley didn't do his homework – or didn't care. He dumped the acid and the cyanide in the same place. Mixed, it creates cyanide gas. Sometimes it mixed sometimes it missed. But the gas was what was drifting up the canyon. Nausea, palpitations, confusion, tachycardia, hyperventilation, hypoxia.'

'A smorgasbord of ills.'

'Unless it was suspected for some reason, no doctor would even think to test for it.'

For several minutes they sat without speaking. Piedmont, alerted by the silence, came and jumped onto the table between them. 'Remember the monkey wrenching I told you about? Brown boots, insurance, key to the yard: my bet is it was Greeley. A little self-sabotage to claim the insurance money, keep himself afloat a while longer.'

Stanton nodded.

'Case closed?' Anna asked.

'Fun part's over. The lawyer part will drag on till neither one of us can remember who did it.' Stanton tweaked up Piedmont's long yellow tail and absently tickled his cheek with the tip of it. Murder might make for strange bedfellows but that wasn't always such a bad thing.

'We're not co-workers anymore, Anna. Want to go out to dinner? Maybe a movie?'

'A date?' Anna sounded appalled and Stanton laughed.

'A date. I come pick you up at the door at seven sharp. You wear lipstick, can't touch the check and have to call the women's toilet the "powder room". How about it?'

'I have to make a phone call,' Anna hedged.

Stanton glanced at his watch. 'Okay, you've got just under five hours. Then the date.'

'I guess. Sure.'

Anna would have felt awkward but he didn't give her

time. With startling grace he sprang from the cramped booth. 'Got to figure out what to wear,' he said, and: 'Seven.'

He was gone, the screen door banging behind him.

Anna stood up. Then sat down. All at once she didn't know what to do with herself. Scooping up Piedmont for support, she went into the living room and to the phone.

It was Wednesday. Maybe her sister wouldn't be at the office.

Molly picked up on the fourth ring. 'Doctor Pigeon,' she snapped.

'Hi,' Anna said. 'My name's Anna and I'm an alcoholic.'

'Hi, Anna,' Molly droned in parody of the group response, but her voice was warmer than Anna'd heard it in a while.

More Compelling Fiction from Headline

Martina Cole

DANGEROUS LADY

SHE'S GOT LONDON'S BIGGEST VILLAINS IN THE PALM OF
HER HAND . . .

Ducking and diving is a way of life down Lancaster Road: all
the Ryans are at it. But Michael, the eldest, has ambitions way
beyond petty crime. His little sister, Maura, turns a blind eye to
her beloved brother's misdeeds – until they cost her the only
man she's ever cared about. And then Maura decides to forget
love and romance and join the family 'firm'.

No one thinks a seventeen-year-old blonde can take on the
hard men of London's gangland, but it's a mistake to
underestimate Maura Ryan: she's tough, clever and beautiful –
and she's determined not to be hurt again. Which makes her
one very dangerous lady.

Together, she and Michael are unbeatable: the Queen and
King of organised crime, they run the pubs and clubs, the
prostitutes and pimps of the West End. With Maura
masterminding it, they pull off an audacious gold bullion
robbery and have much of the Establishment in their pockets.

But notoriety has its price. The police are determined to put
away Maura once and for all – and not everyone in the family
thinks that's such a bad idea. When it comes to the crunch,
Maura has to face the pain of lost love in her past – and the
dangerous lady discovers her heart is not made entirely of
stone.

'A £150,000 success story . . . her tale of gang warfare and
romance centred on an Irish immigrant family in 1950s
London' *Daily Mail*

FICTION / GENERAL 0 7472 3932 0

More Crime Fiction from Headline

BLOOD STOCK

JOHN FRANCOME & JAMES MACGREGOR

'Dick Francis's nearest rival in the pen and quill
stakes' *Daily Mail*

As a racehorse, Moondancer had been a champion; but as a
stallion he was a total failure. So when he is found dead in
his box at the Drumgarrick stud one morning, his owners
feel more relieved than sorry, and promptly make a massive
five million pound insurance claim.

But then Drumgarrick's owner disappears and his son
Fergus is left facing financial ruin . . . and a corpse. A
brilliant amateur jockey, Fergus has a vested interest in
seeing the claim is met in full. But Jack Hendred, the
insurance investigator, is sure that it is fraudulent, and
determined to prove it . . .

The lush countryside of Ireland forms the background to this
gripping tale of intrigue and greed in the bloodstock
business. An attempted betting coup at Leopardstown, hair-
raising National Hunt racing scenes, two grisly murders and
a dramatic Dublin trial are the ingredients of this new high-
voltage thriller from the winning team of Francome and
MacGregor.

'The racing feel is authentic and it's a pacy, entertaining
read' *The Times*

'Rattling good storytellers' *Horse and Hound*

'Gets off to a galloping start . . . with a surprise twist in the
final straight' *Evening Standard*

'The local characters are well drawn, the suspects
gratifyingly violent, equally motivated and suspicious'
Books Magazine

'A captivating read . . . goes at a cracking pace all the way'
Woman and Home

FICTION / CRIME 0 7472 3416 7

More Crime Fiction from Headline

A TAPESTRY OF MURDERS

P. C. Doherty

Chaucer's pilgrims, quarrelling amongst themselves, are now in open countryside enjoying the fresh spring weather as they progress slowly towards Canterbury. A motley collection of travellers, they each have their dark secrets, hidden passions and complex lives. As they shelter in a tavern from a sudden April shower they choose the Man of Law to narrate the next tale of fear and sinister dealings.

In August 1358, the Dowager Queen Isabella, mother of King Edward III, the 'She Wolf of France', who betrayed and destroyed her husband because of her adulterous infatuation for Roger Mortimer, lies dying of the pestilence in the sombre fortress of Castle Rising, where her 'loving' son has kept her incarcerated. According to the Man of Law, Isabella dies and her body is taken along the Mile End Road and laid to rest in Greyfriars next to the mangled remains of her lover, who has paid dearly for his presumption in loving a queen. Nevertheless, as in life so in death Isabella causes intrigue, violence and murder. Nicholas Chirke, an honest young lawyer, is brought in to investigate the strange events following her death – and quickly finds himself at his wits' end trying to resolve the mysteries before a great scandal unfolds.

FICTION / CRIME 0 7472 4588 6

A selection of bestsellers from Headline

OXFORD EXIT	Veronica Stallwood	£4.99	☐
BOOTLEGGER'S DAUGHTER	Margaret Maron	£4.99	☐
DEATH AT THE TABLE	Janet Laurence	£4.99	☐
KINDRED GAMES	Janet Dawson	£4.99	☐
MURDER OF A DEAD MAN	Katherine John	£4.99	☐
A SUPERIOR DEATH	Nevada Barr	£4.99	☐
A TAPESTRY OF MURDERS	P C Doherty	£4.99	☐
BRAVO FOR THE BRIDE	Elizabeth Eyre	£4.99	☐
NO FIXED ABODE	Frances Ferguson	£4.99	☐
MURDER IN THE SMOKEHOUSE	Amy Myers	£4.99	☐
THE HOLY INNOCENTS	Kate Sedley	£4.99	☐
GOODBYE, NANNY GRAY	Staynes & Storey	£4.99	☐
SINS OF THE WOLF	Anne Perry	£5.99	☐
WRITTEN IN BLOOD	Caroline Graham	£5.99	☐

All Headline books are available at your local bookshop or newsagent, or can be ordered direct from the publisher. Just tick the titles you want and fill in the form below. Prices and availability subject to change without notice.

Headline Book Publishing, Cash Sales Department, Bookpoint, 39 Milton Park, Abingdon, OXON, OX14 4TD, UK. If you have a credit card you may order by telephone – 01235 400400.

Please enclose a cheque or postal order made payable to Bookpoint Ltd to the value of the cover price and allow the following for postage and packing:

UK & BFPO: £1.00 for the first book, 50p for the second book and 30p for each additional book ordered up to a maximum charge of £3.00.

OVERSEAS & EIRE: £2.00 for the first book, £1.00 for the second book and 50p for each additional book.

Name ....

Address ....

....

....

If you would prefer to pay by credit card, please complete:
Please debit my Visa/Access/Diner's Card/American Express (delete as applicable) card no:

Signature .... Expiry Date...............